DIVIDED

WE

FALL

Carl Berryman

Author ReputationPress ®
Creativity & Branding

Author Reputation Press LLC
45 Dan Road Suite 36
Canton MA 02021
www.authorreputationpress.com
Hotline: 1(800) 220-7660
Fax: 1(855) 752-6001

Ordering Information:
Quantity Sales. Special discounts are available on quantity purchases by corporations, associations, and others. For details, contact the publisher at the address above.

Printed in the United States of America.
Library of Congress Control Number
ISBN-13   Softcover   978-1-951020-27-9
               eBook   978-1-951020-28-6

FOREWORD

History and experience dictate that seminal events occur not singly, but simultaneously or in sequence. Demographers inform us that if current immigration trends are not checked or reversed, North America will virtually be one hundred percent Hispanic by the end of the twenty-first century. Authorities on Islam predict that Europe will be one hundred percent Islamic by the end of this century. The world population will increase by fifty percent by 2050, from six billion to nine billion. In the next decade or two, India will equal or surpass China in population. China is currently expanding its influence on a global scale through its concept of soft power while very quietly developing a massive technological military capability. The Chinese naval capability is expected to surpass that of the United States Navy by the year 2020. China is concentrating on air independent propulsion submarines to counter the U.S. Navy's carrier battle groups. It is reasonable to expect regional wars over arable land, potable water, all forms of energy and the last of the earth's natural resources. The government of the United States has continued to expand at the expense of individual liberty; the march toward the complete social welfare police state continues as politicians ever enact more legislation that concentrates power in their hands and in the bureaucracies they create. The Tenth Amendment of the Bill of Rights has become meaningless. United States citizens have little recourse against the bureaucracies of government, especially as the government grants itself immunity from prosecution. Most U.S. citizens are ignorant of, or do not appreciate, nor are they willing to defend the Constitution and the Bill of Rights. These factors combined with political correctness offer the spectrum of regionalization of the United States along regional, racial and economic lines.

Some of the characters in this novel are borrowed from a previously published novel, _2013: World War III_ that addresses some of these issues on a global scale.

In this novel is the hope that the myth of freedom of the individual still exists in the upper Rocky Mountains and Great Plains and that the citizens of these regions are willing to forcefully resist the tyranny of government. It remains to be seen if this myth still exists and if this scenario is an alternative to the social welfare police state.

CHARACTERS

Adams, Samuel, MD, Director of FDA under President Walsh, Newkirk's predecessor.

Allen, Robert, 2LT, Computer guru

Andretti, Edward, Chief of Homeland Security under President Newkirk's Administration

Aspins, Ronald, Colonel, Commander, USA Medical Research Institute of Infectious Diseases

Bartlett, Elizabeth, mother of Martha, wife of Nelson Bartlett

Bartlett, Martha, wife of Ethan Bradley, mother of Samuel and Joshua

Bartlett, Nelson father of Martha; rich lawyer from Baltimore

Brady, Jack, Sheriff, Washakie County, Wyoming

Bradley, Ethan, Major, USMC, major protagonist

Bradley, Robert, retired Army Veterinary Corps Officer and Ethan's father

Bradley, Joshua, "Josh", Ethan and Martha's second son

Bradley, Samuel, Ethan and Martha's first son.

Bridger, Governor of Wyoming

Campbell, Naomi, Secretary of Defense in Richard Newkirk's administration

Cantor, Norma, Vice President under Richard Newkirk

Carlson, Texas Ranger, Head of Texas Department of Public Safety

Carlton, David, Speaker of the House

Cartagena, Juan, Mexican provocateur and labor organizer

Charbonneau, Jacques, European Union Trade Representative

Darnell, Paula Jean, High class call girl from Las Vegas

Darlington, Janice, President Newkirk's secretary

Chang, Mao Lin, General, Chinese Peoples Liberation Army-Navy 20 years earlier

Chang, Wi Lang, General, PLAN, son of Mao Lin

Chu, Soo Li, Ph.D., Chinese virologist and humanitarian

Ferguson, Jim, Captain, Wyoming NG, Stryker Co. Commander. Worland, WY

Fulbright, John, Corporal in Congolese Provisional Army and rebel leader

Gates, Ronald, Captain, WY NG, Medical Co. Commander, Cody, WY

Gilbert, Robert, CIA Officer

Harrison, Jared. Washakie County, WY commissioner, Chairman

Hassan, Mohammad, Palestinian Virologist

Hemmings, Alvin, Reverend, aka Mohammad bin Abram bin Selim

Hoskins, George, Ph.D. Virologist at Genetics Engineering, Inc., Seattle, WA

Johnson, Deon, Baltimore gang member

Johnston, Jared, Governor of MT and interim President, Nation of Missouri

Kennely, U.S. Senator from Massachusetts

Killian, Michael, Regimental Sergeant Major for Colonel Ethan Bradley

Laroutte, John, U.S. Congressman from Maryland, Martha's first lover

Li, Lin Pao, MD, Ph.D. Chinese virologist

Lippsitz, Jacob, Senate Majority Leader from NY during Richard Newkirk's administration

Livingston, William, Captain, Wyoming NG, Engineer Co. Commander, Powell, WY

Longley, Dale, Master Sergeant, (Company 1st Sergeant), WY NG, Basin, WY

Malik, Fatima Palestinian spy in USA; engineer, wife of Youssef

Malik, Youssef, ibn, Virologist at USAMRIID,

McCortle, Peter, Captain, Company Commander, Basin, WY NG, Basin, WY

McIntire, John, MG, Wyoming National Guard Adjutant General

McDougle, Douglas, Commander, USN, PhD Virologist at USAMRIID

Mitchell, Floyd, HHS Secretary under President Newkirk

Neville, Jim, Patriot and garage owner

Neville, Jan, Big Horn Café owner and patriot

Newkirk, Richard, President of U.S.A.

Perkins, Peter, U.S. Attorney General under Richard Newkirk

Perroud, Gypsy Lee, physicist, waitress; Ethan Bradley's lover

Rockland, Chris, U.S. Senator from Wyoming

Rosenberg, David, Surgeon General, U.S. Public Health Service,

Sedgley, Frank, General, US Army, Chief of Staff

Singleton, Dewey, General, USAF, Chairman, Joint Chiefs of Staff

Stokes, Frank, Secretary of State under Richard Newkirk

Strother, Harry, Director of National Intelligence

Thompson, Frank, Staff Sergeant, Company C, Worland, Wyoming National Guard

Thorsen, Ronald 1LT, Maintenance Company Commander, WY NG, Basin, WY

Tomlinson, Mark Chief Operating Office, Seattle Branch, Engineering Genetics

Toussaint, Jean, Gang leader in the Baltimore Ghetto

Walker, Robert, Undersheriff, Washakie Co, WY

Walsh, Donald, President of USA prior to Newkirk

Wheaton, Gordon, LTG, Commander, Army of the Nation of Missouri

Whitehorse, Roger, Captain, 105 Howitzer Battery Commander, Thermopolis, WY NG

Wilkerson, Bridgette, wife of Wyoming rancher Fred Wilkerson

Wilkerson, Fred, Wyoming rancher, north of Cody

Winston, Leonard, Brigadier General, Commander, Cheyenne (3rd) Bde, Nation of Missouri

Wu, Ho Li, Chinese Ambassador to USA

CHAPTER 1

HE HAD BUILT THE SNOW CAVE TWELVE HOURS EARLIER. The blizzard had almost blown itself out. The man was ravenously hungry. It had been almost twenty-four hours since he had eaten. He couldn't build a fire in the blizzard without adequate shelter for it; there was no opportunity to gather wood for fuel. He had been running for two days when the blizzard struck. He sensed, rather than observed, that he was being hunted. The snow cave was small, but he had removed his boots and outer off-white snow parka shell and snuggled into his sleeping bag, clothes and all. He had built the cave on the leeward side of a large fir tree with drooping branches. He dug it out to be seven feet long, three feet high and four feet wide. It provided the barest of wiggle room. He felt the one man backpack tent he carried would be too easily seen. He felt confident the blizzard had eradicated any tracks he had made. The snow cave should provide some protection against infra-red telescopic sights of the Regular Army, not that the National Guard would have such equipment in the first place. Most of the Wyoming National Guard was on the same side of the fence as he, but only a few had participated in active resistance. If anyone came after him, it would either be the Regulars, probably from the 10th Mountain Division out of Fort Drum, New York, or perhaps National Guard troops from the Columbia Autonomous Region, out of Fort Lewis, Washington. Columbia had worked its way through the most difficult part, but there were some who were still in the throes of decision.

He had maintained a small opening through the snow, about a foot in diameter, to provide fresh air and a peep hole for observation. He was looking directly across the Clark Fork River, at a bend. A small clearing one hundred meters ahead occupied most of his attention. It was difficult to see between or though the trees around and on the other side of the clearing, particularly with the snow still falling and blowing. Now, he dozed back to sleep, thinking only of food. All that he had in his backpack was frozen solid. It would require a fire to thaw and cook. In his dream, he remembered his wife and two sons. She had taken them and fled to her parents.

Ethan awoke with a start. He didn't initially move, but then slowly looked for his peep hole. It was covered with snow. He poked a hand through it, to discover it was rather bright, although snow was still blowing or falling. Some sixth sense warned him to remain immobile. He watched for a few minutes. Something moved across the river, close to the edge of the bank. He pulled on his sunglasses and waited. He detected movement again. A white parka clad figure emerged across the river. *"How in God's name did they get across the river?"* he thought to himself. The river in front of him was flowing fast enough that it never froze, and it was twenty meters wide. He watched the figure move very slowly, in a semi-crouched position, rifle at port arms. *"The SOB is a professional,"* thought Ethan. *"No run of the mill National Guardsman would be out in this blizzard. I can't believe the Department of Natural Resources officers would be hunting me. Hell, it's been ten days since I shot that mule deer doe for food. By now a cougar should have found and devoured the remains. They are the best trackers in this weather but they aren't professional killers. They must want me awfully bad, more than I realized."* The figure looked in his direction, hesitated for a minute, and then slowly moved eastward, down the river, but staying back in the trees. *"Where there is one, there are a dozen, he must be part of a patrol. Thank God he didn't have an infra-red scope on that rifle, or if he did, he didn't use it,"* thought Ethan. He slowly slid his grandfather's .30-06 up from his side, taking care not to disturb his snow cave. He opened the Velcro closure over the butt, and slid the rifle out of its waterproof Cordura nylon case. He always kept a round in the chamber, safety on, so he would not have to work the bolt and therefore make unnecessary noise. He looked at his watch, and waited for an hour before enlarging the entrance to his cave in small handfuls of snow. He was cold, very cold.

"How could it have come to this," Ethan thought has he crawled forward through the opening he just enlarged. He removed a small pair of binoculars and scanned the area immediately in front of him, then, crawling a foot forward, the area to the left, then to the right. He saw neither movement nor anything unnatural. He replaced the binoculars in the case, and pushed his rifle in front of him. He had wrapped white sheeting around it as camouflage. Only the action and the weatherproof scope covers were left uncovered. He completely slid out of his snow cave into a sitting position, and scanned the area behind him. He detected no movement. Quickly he pulled his sleeping bag and boots out, put on his boots and parka shell, stuffed the sleeping bag in its stuff sack, and tied it to the bottom of his packer frame. *"Thank God for Schnee brand boots,"* Ethan thought to himself as he pulled them on. Ethan packed snow onto the entrance of his snow cave to hide it. He put his rifle case on the top of his pack, shouldered the pack and carried his rifle in the port arms position. He moved back into the trees and headed downriver. He had to eat and soon, and he realized. He was beginning to shiver uncontrollably. He began to move away from the river bank and then turned to follow its general course. He had to avoid hypothermia and dehydration or he would die and he knew it. He had been in the woods for fourteen straight days. He knew that he must soon return to civilization in some form. He was running out of beans rice, salt, and energy.

Thirty minutes later he stopped and began to gather wood. He hoped the sound of the wind would cover the noise of his breaking smaller branches. He pulled a folding wood saw out of his pack for everything over two inches in diameter. He built a small fire, hidden behind a downfall in the middle of a spruce grove. He hoped that way the fire would not be seen and the smoke would be dissipated by the trees. He cautiously crept to the river and filled the small coffee pot and a one liter aluminum pot. He placed both on the small griddle which was over half of the fire. In the small pot he put a handful of rice and a hand full of oatmeal. He unrolled an oiled canvas and added two strips of dried deer jerky to the pot. In the coffee pot he put a tea bag. He fed the fire until both were boiling. He wished he had a can of tuna fish to add to the rice and oatmeal rather than the jerky. The oil would do wonders calorically speaking not to mention the protein, the Vitamin E and the taste he loved. The ocean fisheries were in deep distress, and only the rich could afford tuna fish any more. Hell, he would have been happy with a can of sardines, but sardines were almost as much in demand and depleted as tuna. *"Oh well,"* he thought, *"at least the venison will provide good protein. I just wish I had some seasoning to put on it."* He spent two days cutting the mule deer doe meat into thin strips and drying it over the fire. He worked about sixteen hours a day just gathering wood to smoke and dry the meat. Most of the wood was dried pine or fir or spruce, which imparted a lousy taste to the meat, but he knew he would need it regardless of how it tasted. After he had eaten the oatmeal, rice and jerky concoction, he drank the hot broth. Then he drank all of the tea. He scrubbed the pot out with snow and repacked everything in his pack. It was getting dark again. He unrolled his one man survival tent under a low hanging spruce, crawled in and went to sleep. He asked himself again, *"how did all this happen?"* His second thought was *"I wonder if this is as rough as Dad had it in the second Korean War?"* As he drifted to sleep, he mentally rehashed the events of the last twelve years of his life.

Ethan Bradley was the son of an Army Veterinary Corps officer. While Colonel Robert Bradley liked the military way of life, he didn't care for clinical veterinary medicine, and discouraged Ethan from entertaining thoughts of veterinary medicine as a career, although he did not try to influence Ethan or any of their other children on any particular career path. Ethan never seriously considered the field anyway. His extroverted personality and athletic abilities steered him in other directions. He too, decided upon the military way of life. Ethan simply became imbued with the military. He considered the Army, but determined the Marine Corps was more to his liking. He elected to be a Marine. The Marines go first and fight the most. That is what he wanted to do.

The Arab-Israeli War of 2022 was limited to conventional weapons and had settled nothing, other than eliminating a good deal of the population of both protagonists. The Palestinians, backed by several Arab and African states, thought they could take advantage of the geopolitical situation of the United State's response to the Chinese invasion of India, Pakistan and Afghanistan in 2022. That was not the case. The new President of the United States pulled out all the stops. The United States had provided Israel with the intelligence and state of the art smart weapons to insure Israel's victory. It did not take the Palestinians long to realize how severe was their disadvantage. They called for a truce at the end of ten days of conflict. Now, the world waited and watched in fear once more as the Middle East threatened to explode. The Chinese began to mobilize their forces in their bases in the former states of Pakistan and Afghanistan. Speculation was rife that the Chinese were supporting the Palestinians, and would use it as a distraction while they invaded Iran. The Democratic President elected in 2020 re-enrolled the United States in the United Nations, with a promise to pay back dues and would send a delegation to the UN Headquarters in Geneva.

Shortly after the war, the Palestinians acquired mortar rounds filled with nerve gas from Iran and began lobbing them into Israeli settlements both from Gaza and the West Bank area. Israel retaliated with conventional artillery fires that were directed by radar that were usually, although not always, successful. The Palestinians increased their use of mosques, school yards and hospital courtyards from which to launch their attacks, so that the Israeli return fire would kill innocent civilians and garner more worldwide sympathy.

It didn't take long before the Palestinians were on the verge of starvation as a result of Israel's retaliatory economic and physical strangulation. Their population had continued to expand over the decades. Families averaged six children. Almost all received little or no education other than makeshift Madrassas, the schools of the fundamentalist versions of the Islamic religion. Their literacy and formal education was roughly equivalent to the fifth grade level of the United States. The Palestinian population was terribly skewed toward the uneducated, frustrated youth in their teens and twenties. Over sixty percent of their population now was twenty-five years of age or less. They had no economy independent of Israel. Their fellow Muslims from neighboring Arab states had refused to provide capitol or business acumen or any form of support other than weapons for use against Israel. Leadership and technical skills were increasingly provided by more educated Muslims from other countries, particularly Iran and Syria. The Palestinian attacks against Israel grew worse with every year, and more sophisticated.

Palestinians then began to kill foreign Christians touring the Holy Land. They particularly targeted buses and larger tour groups to kill as many in a single stroke as possible. In retaliation for perceived support for Israel from the United States, suicide bombers in the last decade had struck in a number of American cities. The consequences resulted in severe FBI monitoring of Muslim citizens of the U.S. That in return, diminished the flow of money and support into their coffers. As their next strategy, the Palestinians began to recruit native born American Muslims as assassins. They were trained in isolated terrorist camps, mostly in remote parts of Appalachia, but also in isolated parts of the southwest, where the Palestinian Authority or front groups for them had purchased large tracts of land in the mountains and desert. Several camps were established in Mexico, with the acquiescence of Mexican authorities, to whom they paid large bribes. These native born American Muslims then began to assassinate prominent Jewish Americans. They were controlled by a shadowy network; the cell leader received a coded message whereupon an assigned assassination was carried out. In this way no pattern was established so that the killings appeared to be random. Physicians, bankers, lawyers, accountants, brokers, businessmen and their families were murdered without remorse in numerous cities throughout the United States.

The Palestinians began to dynamite sections of the wall separating Israel from both Gaza and the West Bank. The Israelis would immediately respond, sometimes with small arms fires, sometimes with mortars. The Palestinians would tunnel under the wall, lay explosive charges with timers and beat a hasty retreat. They began to use coordinated attacks to simultaneously breach the walls in numerous places. Consequently, the Israelis couldn't cover all of the breaches. The Palestinians would then move a few raiders through the breaches. Israel then planted mines and seismic equipment all along the walls to detect tunneling efforts. To counter that, the Palestinians then began to use lightweight artillery pieces and rocket propelled grenades filled with the highest order of explosives to provide direct fires to breach the walls. Israeli unmanned aerial vehicles, as both surveillance and attack vehicles, backed up by helicopter attacks soon eliminated that threat.

That year, due to the tremendous national debt, the United States decided to reduce the billions of dollars paid each year to Israel and to Egypt to maintain the peace. Both the Egyptian and the Israeli economies plunged, Egypt's far worse than Israel's. Egypt had food riots. The large, unemployed, poorly educated, disenfranchised young men in their teens, twenties and thirties, rioted in the streets against the United States and Israel. They demanded war to eliminate Israel, once and for all.

Israel, faced with the possibility of war on two fronts, and increasingly frustrated with the constant attacks, made the strategic decision to close the Gaza Strip. Israel began by attempting to deport Palestinians from Gaza to the West Bank. Israel suffered several thousand casualties, both military and civilian, before abandoning that strategy. In its place, came one of full military weight. They attacked Gaza with infantry and armor along its entire length, forcing all of the residents towards the sea. Caught completely off guard, the residents of Gaza could not fight back without heavy weapons. They were given the choice of fleeing west towards the sea and then south into Egypt or being killed where they stood. Israel dynamited all the settlements, buildings, or anything that might be of future use to the Palestinian Authority. Israel stopped one kilometer from the Mediterranean to provide a corridor for those Palestinians still alive to flee into Egypt. Hundreds of thousands of Palestinians poured into Egypt which only increased the severity of Egypt's crisis. Egypt couldn't feed its own people, let alone such a flood of refugees. Egypt made public cries of despair and threatened to immediately attack Israel. Egypt ordered complete and immediate mobilization.

Anticipating such a response, Israel announced its own complete mobilization. Hezbollah, Hamas and the Egyptian Brotherhood vowed to destroy Israel at all costs. Syria ordered full mobilization, as did Iraq, Jordan, and Iran. Lebanon, a captive of Syria, followed suit. Saudi Arabia, in the throes of internal disorder, and on a knife's edge of civil war and revolution, didn't know which way to jump. Riots of Saudi youth demanded the destruction of Israel and expulsion of the United States troops guarding their oil fields. They ignored the threat that China once actively provided, and still did so on a more sophisticated and surreptitious plane.

Volunteers poured into Egypt from the world of Islam; they came from Indonesia, the Philippines, Yemen, Algeria, Sudan, Turkey, and even from the United States. Egypt assumed strategic leadership to coordinate all of their efforts. Israel was threatened from all sides. Only the seaward side of Israel was deemed safe because it was controlled by the Israeli Navy.

Syria, Jordan, Lebanon and battalions of Turkish volunteers massed in the Bakaa Valley. At the appropriate hour, 03:00 on a fine March morning, the walls surrounding Israel were smashed in dozens of places by direct fires from tanks and artillery pieces of the Syrian army. Light infantry, really Palestinian irregulars, backed up by Syrian troops, poured through the breaches. The massed troops of the Bakaa Valley began to move. At 04:00, Israel placed small yield tactical nuclear warheads delivered by long range artillery on the Bakaa Valley. There were no survivors that lived more than forty eight hours. A three kiloton bomb destroyed two Syrian Divisions half way between the Golan Heights and Damascus. At 06:00 the Dome of the Rock disappeared under a tremendous barrage of artillery fire.

Every Israeli citizen twelve years of age and up had been issued a rifle and a 9 millimeter handgun. Adults were also issued two hand grenades. Starting in the year 2013, Israeli school children learned to shoot small bore rifles, .22 caliber, in the sixth grade as part of their regular curriculum. In the ninth grade they graduated to military small arms. Palestinian platoons and companies that poured through the holes in the walls were assigned specific neighborhoods or targets for the complete destruction of Israeli citizens. Now, as the Palestinians poured through the breaches with orders to kill every Israeli regardless of sex or age, they were met with an armed civilian force of overwhelming desire to survive as individuals and a nation. Vicious house to house fighting lasted until noon, by which time most of the Palestinian attackers were killed. That same morning, Iran invaded Iraq through the Khoramshahr-Basra Gate under the guise of marching to destroy Israel. Israel informed Cairo that if further hostile armies marched towards its borders, Cairo itself would disappear under a series of mushroom clouds. At 13:00 that day, Egypt sent a message to all Muslim combatants to cease hostilities and return to their native borders. Israel, in the meantime, began to hunt down and kill every Palestinian man, woman and child they could catch within their borders.

John Fulbright was one of the first recruits of the Congolese Security Force. Educated in a local Jesuit School, he had a high school level education before joining the Executive Outcomes brigade, which came to be known as the Congolese Provisional Army. Being educated by the Jesuits, he had a distinctly socialist philosophy. He quickly learned to hide his true feelings and beliefs in the goal of gaining as much education as possible. Highly intelligent, egocentric, a member of the Hutu tribe, he secretly maintained his belief in animism, never accepting the Jesuit concept of Christianity. He thought that if Jesus Christ could rise from the dead and return to earth before departing for heaven, if the Holy Ghost could be a Spirit in mankind, then why wouldn't the same concept also apply to other spirits? He was slowly co-opted by the Russians who fed his ego as a warrior and constantly sang praises of his tribe. The philosophy they espoused to him was essentially a variety of fascism, based on irrationality, a love of his homeland and allegiance to his tribe. The individual's allegiance to his tribe takes precedence over the state. They encouraged his animalistic beliefs by attacking Christianity as a tool of the western powers who would exploit his tribe and his homeland.

One year after Executive Securities was selected by the Congolese government, Ethan Bradley graduated as a Second Lieutenant, United States Marine Corps, from the United States Naval Academy at Annapolis, at the ripe old age of twenty-three. Ethan majored in engineering with a minor in physics, but elected the infantry as his basic branch. He was on the varsity soccer, judo, and swimming teams. He ran in intramural track, and played intramural handball. Because of emphasizing his athletic activities rather than scholastics, he graduated at the twenty-fifth percentile of his class. He exercised the Marine Corps option as a freshman and accordingly was commissioned a Second Lieutenant in the USMC. He loved it. His father tried to persuade him to take a Navy Reserve Officers Training Corps scholarship rather than attend the Academy, but Ethan would have none of it. He saw the prejudice of flag rank Army officers against those who took R.O.T.C. commissions on all of the army bases where he grew up. Informally, it was known as the WPPA, the West Point Protective Association. Participating in summer programs with Marine Corps R.O.T.C. cadets, he recognized that many of his classmates, actually the majority of them, and most of the Marine academy graduates as second rate compared to many of the Marine officer cadets who took the R.O.T.C. scholarship route or received their commissions through the Marine Bulldog program.

Immediately on graduation from the Academy he requested and received temporary additional duty to attend the Army's Airborne School at Fort Bragg, North Carolina, for parachute training and then Air Assault School at Fort Campbell, Kentucky, again courtesy of the U.S. Army. He loved it. He considered applying for Delta Force or the Navy Seal program, but decided to attend the Marine Reconnaisance Course first. He graduated first in the course, which was mostly composed of enlisted Marines in their mid twenties with a scattering of company grade officers.

Martha, now a college senior and lovelier than ever, was courted by every rich man's son at Johns Hopkins University. By invitation, Martha and her parents attended Ethan's graduation from the United States Naval Academy at Annapolis, Maryland. She suddenly realized she was seriously attracted to this handsome, aggressive, athletic young Marine. His first permanent assignment was to Camp LeJune, North Carolina. At every opportunity, he drove north to Washington,

D.C. where Martha and her roommate had their own apartment. Martha's parents did not exactly approve of the courtship. As senior partner in one of Baltimore's most prestigious law firms, Nelson Bartlett had other plans for his daughter. There were a dozen bright and promising young men less than thirty years of age from prominent families with appropriate business and legal foundations, social position, and correct political views that he would have preferred as a son-in-law to a Marine grunt. When Nelson and Bridgette walked in on Martha and Ethan in her apartment while they were in the middle of a wild sex episode in the middle of the floor, Nelson knew he was defeated.

June was a tremendous month for Martha and Ethan. In June, Ethan was promoted to First Lieutenant and Martha completed her first year of law school at Georgetown University.

As he curled to sleep in his sleeping bag, Ethan remembered when he planted their first backyard garden, just after he and Martha were married in June, just a few days after he was promoted. They bought a small house outside Jacksonville, North Carolina, next to Camp LeJune. They had worked in it together many evenings and weekends, watching for the ever threatening weed and insect pests. They raised tomatoes, sweet corn, carrots and bush green beans. They planted two apple trees and two peach trees. Martha used to say it was because of the garden that she got pregnant so quickly. In October of that year, he received orders for the Congo with a reporting date of 1 November. Thirteen months after they were married, in July, Martha delivered their first son. She named him Samuel. Ethan had been in the Congo for seven months.

Three years after graduation from the Naval Academy, First Lieutenant Ethan Bradley found himself as a Marine reconnaissance platoon commander in Africa. He was sent there under the guise of being a trainer, but really to augment the Congolese Provisional Army. It was realistically to provide additional security at the request of Executive Securities, Inc. Executive Securities had been hired by the Congolese government to train an army to modern standards and was doing an excellent job of it, but they failed in a basic premise. That premise was political indoctrination. Executive Securities was now growing ever more wary of the loyalty of the Congolese Provisional Army that it trained as the army grew in size and competence. Indications of an opposition political organization based on a cult were growing within the Congolese Provisional Army and several Congolese provinces.

Among the vaccinations he received for tropical diseases prior to deployment was an experimental vaccine against a genetically engineered strain of Influenza A virus, although the recipients did not know it. They were told it was a booster immunization for a new amebic dysentery vaccine under investigation. Participation was not voluntary. The President ordered it under the Project Bioshield Act of 2022.

New oil fields were discovered in the eastern provinces of the Republic of the Congo. A pipeline was built from the fields in the Kivu Province to Bujumbura. Oil barges took the crude oil down Lake Tanganyika. A second pipeline carried the oil to Lake Malawi (Lake Nyasa), down the River Shire, around the Kholombozo Falls and down to the mouth of the Zambezi River. There, refineries were built to transport fuels to North America and Europe. It was cheaper to refine petroleum there and transport finished fuels rather than crude oil through the Suez Canal. It also assuaged environmental concerns about new refineries in the United States. It became almost mandatory for the United States to secure the new fields in order to assure continued imports as oil fields in the U.S. were quickly depleted by hydraulic fracking. Methane gas fields, commonly called natural gas, were discovered that increased the estimate from thirteen percent of the world capacity to almost twenty percent. Hydroelectric resources came into play as more hydroelectric dams were built, particularly along the Congo River. Most were built by European consortiums, particularly the Dutch with their vast experience in reclaiming land from the sea. Thermal power plants also expanded bringing power especially to the mining and refining industries. Fifty percent of the world's cobalt and a third of the world's industrial diamonds came from the region. Hydroelectricity transmission lines were being laid all through Central and East Africa. Along with the oil, mineral ores also were transported over the same route by trucks and ore carriers on the lakes. The Secretary of Defense (SECDEF) introduced the use of private military companies as a cost cutting measure to provide security for the oil fields. He argued this allowed greater flexibility for the Department of Defense to conduct its concerns with a more business oriented mindset, what he called "efficiencies." It was never stated that it eliminated the expense of military retirement and medical benefits for military retirees. Many former service members from many countries were hired by such contracting firms. DOD provided heavy weapons support and maintenance was performed by the private contractors. What they lacked was strategic intelligence capabilities. The Marines were to assist Executive Securities in securing and protecting this field in the face of possible civil revolt while Executive Securities continued to train a national army. Executive Securities finally began an intelligence effort, attempting to determine whom they could trust among native informants within the ranks. First Lieutenant Ethan Bradley and his platoon were responsible for long range reconnaissance patrols to guard against rebel infiltrators intent on sabotaging the oil fields and pipelines being constructed. They would be in the field for a week, then in their base for three or four days to rest and recoup before taking to the field again.

After the Chinese seized much of the Caspian Sea Basin oil in the early years of the third decade of the twenty-first century, and with a combination of bribery and blackmail, persuaded Iran into supplying them with most of their oil output below market prices, the remainder of the world economies had to scramble for known petroleum reserves. The United States was invited by the constitutional monarchy of Saudi Arabia to develop permanent bases there, which the U.S. Army immediately did. With the sudden end of the last Arab-Israeli war, and under considerable diplomatic pressure, Iran had little choice but to return within its own borders. Iraq invited the European Union to supplement their forces as a coalition partner, which they did, primarily under the banner of the French. Iraq was afraid of both Iran and China.

In order to reduce the consumption of oil, a world wide major push was made to utilize coal and nuclear fuel, and ownership of more than one vehicle per family became prohibitively expensive in both Europe and America. In the United States, taxes of 200% were imposed upon all second family vehicles that provided less than fifty miles per gallon. Consequently, motorcycles increased in popularity. Only one motorcycle per family was allowed tax exempt. Motorcycles were mostly used by heads of households for commuting to work because of their fuel economy. Seventy and eighty miles to the gallon were the norm for most models. Both the European and American economies more or less crashed, at least became seriously constrained, but the European economy all the more so. The American military had first priority on fuels; airline traffic was reduced to less than fifty percent; traveling vacations became the thing of dreams, past and future. France had led the way with nuclear power plants and Germany with mass transportation systems. Railroads in the United States regained a national priority not seen since the nineteenth century. Efficient diesel engines continued to support the trucking industry, but those which belched smoke and wasted fuel were seized on sight by state and local police agencies. The fines for an untuned eighteen wheeled tractor trailer were enormous, in some cases, exceeding the value of the cargo in the trailers they pulled. Food distribution had the highest priority, followed by fuels. Backyard and rooftop gardens suddenly appeared everywhere.

Lieutenant Bradley and his platoon sergeant studied everything they could about the Congo. They trained relentlessly the first two months in-country, learning everything they could about the peoples, cultures and environment. He studied French for three years at the Naval Academy. French was the official language in that part of the world. Since he had a penchant for languages Bradley quickly learned much of Lingala and Kikango, the most two widely spoken native languages, essentially immersing in Lingala. They both had a sufficient working knowledge of Kikango to know whether or not their interpreter was accurately translating. Then they initiated patrolling. Unusually lenient with his new platoon commander Lieutenant Bradley, the battalion commander gave him essentially carte blanch in training and arming his platoon. His company commander, a disheartened Captain, didn't care. The battalion commander, disgusted with the company commander, vacillated between micromanaging his company for him and relieving him. He didn't relieve him because the Captain's father was a U.S. Congressman, he didn't have a suitable replacement and he didn't want to put Bradley in the position because of professional jealousy.

Their African environment was mixed jungle interspersed with large areas of grasslands several miles square. Fingers of one projected into the other as the forest retreated from the lack of water and increasing temperatures due to global warming. Lieutenant Bradley gave his men their choice of weapons. Some chose twelve gauge riot shotguns with buckshot, some chose 7.62mm x 39 mm assault rifles with grenade launchers and select fire capability, essentially modified AK-47s, while some chose heavier 7.62mm x 51mm. semi-automatic battle rifles, known in America as the old M14 rifle and in civilian guise as the .308 Winchester cartridge. Each man was responsible for drawing and carrying his own ammunition supply. Such a variety of ammunition requirements did not support the concept of sharing ammunition on the battlefield, but Bradley was willing to trade that for the morale factor of confidence in their weapon for his men. The battalion logistics shop didn't like having to manage a variety of ammunition types, but Bradley didn't much care what the captain who was the battalion S-4 logistics officer thought.

Eleven months in the African bush took its toll and Bradley and his platoon. His platoon was down by a third of the original members, mostly due to disease, booby traps and mines. The remainder had all suffered various tropical diseases, dysenteries nobody ever heard of, and a plethora of minor wounds, just none bad enough to require evacuation from the theater. On a moonless fourth night in the jungle during a long range patrol, one of his men hit a trip wire. It blew the man's left leg off just below the knee. A sharp piece of shrapnel buried itself in Bradley's tibia, resulting in multiple bone fragments. The patrol evacuated the two wounded to a clearing two kilometers away, where a Medical Evacuation (MEDEVAC) helicopter picked them up. The remainder of the patrol continued on its mission under the leadership of the Staff Sergeant. The field surgeon did an excellent job on the traumatic amputation of the corporal, and both were evacuated to Bethesda Naval Medical Center on different days. Bradley was flown to the states on a stretcher, with a red hot osteomyelitis that could not be controlled after eight days in the 121st Evacuation Hospital. The 121st Evacuation Hospital laboratory could not identify the infectious agent; whatever it was it demonstrated resistance to all the standard antibiotics in their inventory. It was touch and go for amputation, but the latest generation of intravenous macrolide antibiotics just approved by the FDA finally conquered the infection. After twelve weeks in traction, a sufficient bone callous developed that he could walk with a cane. He was given 120 days convalescent leave from Bethesda Naval Medical Center and sent home to rest and recuperate. That's when Martha became pregnant for the second time. It was in the fall of the year and Martha was in her junior year of Georgetown law school via Interactive television.

Three weeks into convalescent leave, Ethan began walking without a cane, then jogging by the eighth week, and then running by the tenth. A month later he was again running five miles. In sixteen weeks he was doing five miles in forty minutes, the requirement for the Army Ranger School. He was back up to one hundred push-ups and a hundred sit-ups by the time his convalescent leave was over. He reported back to Bethesda Naval Medical Center for evaluation for fitness for duty.

Martha came home from her eighth week obstetrical examination imbued with enthusiasm. Ethan knew that she would broach whatever when she felt the time was right. After a bout of wonderful sex, they were laying entwined in each other's arms when she brought up the subject. "Darling, while you were in Africa, a new law was passed allowing limited experimentation in human engineering. They have done it for years on a wide variety of nonhuman primates, and it has had exceptional results. I think we should consider doing it for this baby. Dr. Lassiter is really excited about it. She believes it will be the wave of the future. Children born without the manipulation won't stand a chance in any future world in her opinion. It won't cost anything, as it is still classified as experimental, and the biological company pays for everything. What do you think?"

Ethan sensed how much she wanted to intercede in this second pregnancy with the newly licensed for experimentation genetic engineering of fetuses. Ethan sensed that Sam had bonded more with himself during his leave than with his mother. He didn't know why this should be a problem, or if his perception was even accurate. Perhaps she wanted more of this second child for herself, the thought. The procedure itself is relatively simple. The challenge was identifying which genes controlled what, which alleles were the most productive, could be activated while other alleles were depressed, and could most easily be incorporated into the chromosome if not naturally present. On a limited trial basis, by special license, selected mothers-to-be were permitted to apply to genetic engineering of their fetuses during the eighteenth week of pregnancy. Only certain genes were authorized for modification. They included the controlling genes for certain hormones; erythropoietin for red blood cell production, somatotrophin for body size, and a newly recognized neurotrophin that increased synapses in the central nervous system by an estimated twenty-five percent. The genes that resulted in the production of these hormones themselves were not altered. Rather, it is the controller genes that act like switches that turn the genes off and on to produce the hormones. That way, the responsible hormone genes just produce more than their normal amounts or for longer times. In experimental Rhesus monkeys, in the genus commonly called macaques, of several species, in baboons, and four lowland gorillas, the neurotrophin increased their intelligence ten fold. Some researchers somewhat cynically claimed that the monkeys were smarter than a lot of dumb humans, lacking only efficient vocalization and language to challenge mankind. Male macaques that weighed fifteen pounds on maturity reached twenty-five pounds from the increased somatotrophin and could kill an adult human male without difficulty. Ethan feared such genetic tampering. Martha wanted it.

When he returned to duty, he was dismayed to find that he would be wearing the blue helmet of the United Nations. Being promoted in October, he was now Captain Bradley and the commander of a company of light infantry Marines. His battalion was assigned to peace keeping duties along the Golan Heights as part of a United Nations peace keeping effort.

The United Nations demanded that the United States Marine Corps and all of its assets be turned over to the United

Nations to act as its International Police Force. It was to be their peacekeeping force. The United Nations promised to augment it with troops volunteered by other nations. In a rare act of courage the Congress of the United States refused to comply with the President's determination to honor the UN's request.

Three days after Ethan left for duty on the Golan Heights, Martha checked into the GenSciences outpatient clinic for insertion of modified controller genes into her eighteen week old fetus. The Y chromosome had been identified at the eighth week examination. It will be a boy. Permission by the father of the fetus was no longer required. The mother alone could make the decision for genetic modification.

Martha Bartlett was an only child, and a very bright one. Born and raised in Baltimore, she was cum laude through the pre-law program at John Hopkins. She and Ethan met at a social arranged between the Naval Academy and her dormitory. She preferred to live in the dormitory her freshman year rather than home, for the experience. After her freshman year however, she and a friend shared an apartment for the next three years. Martha loved the city. She didn't really understand why all the fuss Ethan, who grew up in Wyoming, made about owning guns. "What's the big deal," she used to say. "Why do you need guns anyway? Do you just want to kill those poor helpless animals out there? You shouldn't be allowed to do that unless they are causing you some harm or damage?" Ethan took her shooting a few times, but he could never get her to go hunting. Ethan loved to go hunting with his father and grandfather in the summer and fall in Wyoming. They shot ground squirrels in the summer at the request of local ranchers, early season deer, and once, Ethan missed the first two weeks of his senior high school year to go elk hunting with his grandfather and father. He was rewarded with a very nice six by six bull, six points on each side of the antlers. His grandfather proudly had the head mounted for him, and promised him it was his whenever he had a house to hang it in.

Martha developed into a sophisticated young lady who tended to look upon those of rural upbringing as somewhat backward folks, whose ideas of political science were somewhat outmoded, antiquated, she would say. Martha blossomed when she was sixteen. She became an extremely attractive young woman. She swam for exercise and recreation, and regularly jogged. These sports gave her an extremely attractive figure. She was the most popular girl in her high school. With her Bachelor's degree in pre-law, a mixture of business administration, political science, journalism, drama, history, English, Spanish, psychology and sociology, she was accepted on her first application into Georgetown University Law School. Her father, being the senior partner of the famous law firm of Bartlett, Brown, and Goldstein didn't hurt either. She felt that Georgetown would offer a greater diversity of curriculum and expertise in international law. She and Ethan married two weeks after she graduated with her Bachelor's degree. Her father liked Ethan, but didn't exactly approve of his career choice. He felt that it was too risky for his daughter to marry someone who wanted a military combat career. Nelson Bartlett secretly hoped he could persuade Ethan to resign his commission as soon as he was eligible. He was sure he could find a position of significance for him somewhere among his business contacts. He realized however, that there was no reasoning with his hopelessly in love daughter. So when they were married at the Chapel in the United States Naval Academy, a procession of over one hundred cars then proceeded to the Baltimore Hilton for the reception. It was the most lavish reception of the season. Martha absolutely glowed, and Sam was the envy of every man who saw her but did not know her.

Martha enrolled in graduate international law and relations courses while Ethan was on the Golan Heights. Joshua was born in May, to Ethan and Martha. Once again, Ethan missed the birth of his son because he was overseas. After a year on the Golan Heights, Bradley reported back to Camp Lejune, NC, on 1 October. Ethan considered this tour there the best time of their married life even though he sensed a deep change had come over her in his absence. It wasn't anything that he could define, but a vague ill feeling began to creep into him regarding her value system. Their second son, Joshua, seemed remarkable in every way. Josh, as Ethan called him, seemed stronger and smarter than any kid he had ever seen among the children of his fellow officers. Josh began reading the newspaper at age three. By age four, Ethan, Sam and Josh spent a good deal of backyard time playing soccer together. A few years later, Josh dominated the soccer field in his soccer league. Ethan was selected for the year long Marine Officer's Advanced Course, the Amphibious Warfare School, or AWS as it was commonly called at Quantico, Virginia. So, the rented out their house in Jacksonville and rented one outside of Quantico.

The Secretary General of the United Nations again placed a resolution before the General Assembly demanding the authority and right to tax individual citizens of the world. That was widely interpreted as a proposed mandate to tax the more wealthy individual citizens of the United States and some of the European nations. In spite of the western European nations and the U.S. lobbying against it, it passed the General Assembly by a vote of 145 to 25. President Walsh of the United States directed the U.S. Ambassador to the UN to inform the UN that the United States had not made a decision whether or not to comply, regardless of what the General Assembly voted. That decision would be made after the guidelines regarding how the tax would be levied were written.

Africa continued to sink into chaos and another quagmire. Two thirds of the Provisional Congolese Army mutinied and followed John Fulbright into the Kivu Province where he established a provisional government. In their withdrawal in to the bush, they killed as many of their former comrades in arms that remained loyal to the central government as they could. The mutiny occurred at midnight one quiet evening without warning. Most of those soldiers who were loyal to the government were bayoneted in their bunks or decapitated with razor sharp machetes. A few managed to escape. Fulbright's troops slaughtered civilians from all other tribes wherever they encountered them in their withdrawal into the Lualaba River drainage. From several bases there Fulbright launched a series of attacks against the elected government and seized the oil fields. Many of the Executive Securities trainers were caught unawares. Fulbright declined to attack the capitol city at this time in order to allow foreigners to escape. He did not wish to invoke the wrath of the United States or involved European nations out of concern that a rain of cruise missiles would descend upon his bases. Consequently an orderly evacuation of all foreign personnel was conducted by the 26th Marine Expeditionary Unit, Special Operations Capable, standing by off the coast. Bradley watched the events unfold every night on television news and just shook his head in total disgust. Fulbright then initiated negotiations with the international oil consortiums working the basin oil fields. Oil prices on the international market began to rise again.

Bradley served in several jobs during this tour at Camp Lejune, as Battalion S-3, Plans and Operations; as Battalion S-4, logistics; and finally, company commander again, only this time of a reconnaissance company of 150 gung-ho Marines. He trained his company very, very hard. They went through the Jungle Warfare Training Center in Colombia, then through Arctic Warfare and Survival School in Alaska. Martha received her Master of Jurisprudence, specializing in international and treaty law.

Race riots erupted in Houston Texas, between black Americans and Hispanics. They were initially limited to specific neighborhoods where the two communities, black and Hispanic, were mixed, or bordered one another. Nobody seemed to know which Hispanics were American citizens, which were legal immigrants and which were illegal aliens. The situation was exacerbated by illegal aliens from the Caribbean Basin, especially Jamaica, Colombia and Venezuela. Following the population distribution of San Antonio, the population of Houston shifted towards Hispanics being the majority. Except for the very high paying white collar executives and scientists, the white population of Houston began to migrate north. Simultaneously, black Americans were migrating into the southern states from the more northerly ones. There were initially a few small riots in San Antonio, but limited to areas of a few blocks square. Order was quickly restored in San Antonio.

In the Presidential election, Senator Newkirk ran on the platform of internationalism. The United States would provide the leadership for the United Nations and the world. He promised greater trade would provide more jobs for Americans. He pledged that the social security account, in very severe arrears, would not go bankrupt, and that the unemployed would have benefits sufficient to maintain their lifestyle. He claimed the states mismanaged the federal funds returned to the states for welfare programs. Unfunded mandates were ignored. He promised greater training programs for the unemployed, in technical schools, and on the job training in foreign owned factories. International corporations that agreed to build their plants in the United States also provided top management without regard to the nationality of the Chief Executive Officer. He pledged to work towards a greener environment worldwide. He was elected by the popular vote of 65%. Yet, the only states he carried in the Electoral College were on the Pacific, Atlantic and Gulf coasts and the Great Lakes states.

When the promotion list for majors, Officer Grade 0-4, was released, Bradley was selected below the zone with a promotion date of 1 January. Given his choice to attend the next higher level of military education, he elected to attend the Army's Command and General Staff College at Fort

Leavenworth, Kansas. He loved the area, enjoyed the year long course, and thought about staying for the Advanced Military Studies course, a year long course of studying military history and trends for the future. He took his son Sam, now old enough for a hunting license, hunting and fishing at every opportunity. They bought out of state deer licenses for Missouri and hunted white tail deer on both sides of the Missouri River. They hunted turkeys in the spring, and fished in the spring, summer and fall. At six years of age in spite of his size, Martha refused to let Ethan take Joshua on their "sporting expeditions," as she called them. Martha hated the area. She thought the local population was mostly ignorant, uncultured hicks. In spite of her personal philosophy, she played the perfect military wife, knowing its influence on her husband's career. She threw lavish parties, danced with most of his classmates, and all of his instructors. She played the game to the hilt. A month before graduation, Ethan received orders to return to the Golan Heights, wearing the blue helmet of the United Nations, but as a brigade staff officer. This time, Martha informed him she was not waiting for his return. He remembered very clearly her words on his departure, "Who is your wife, me or the Marine Corps?"

That Christmas Martha took the boys and moved to Baltimore rather than remain in the Fort Leavenworth area. Her parents purchased her a house in their immediate neighborhood. The deed carried only her name. It was a gated community, complete with its own security force. The least expensive house in the community was Martha's, which sold for two and half million dollars. Nelson Bartlett felt he stole it at that price. D'Arcy Estates was laid out in a four leaf clover pattern. The main gate was at the base of the stem. Each leaf was a cul-de-sac containing six widely separated houses, thereby providing a sense of isolation and privacy. The community had its own power substation just inside the gate. Each house came with at least five acres of land. All of the homes were at least two stories, some had four. In the center of the clover leaf was a large grassy park where the stables were maintained. The riding field had two arenas for the owners to work their mounts. Adjacent to D'Arcy Estates and connected by a single road was the local country club and golf course. An Olympic sized swimming pool and elegant club house containing half a dozen private two room apartments adorned the grounds. This single road also had a gated entrance. Brick walls with iron bars ten feet high extended twenty meters on each side of both gates. Beyond the walls hardwood trees became the norm except where some of the homes had individual privacy fences.

Elizabeth Bartlett was delighted to have her daughter and grandsons close by. Her father had some misgivings about his daughter's emotional state, but kept his concerns to himself. Nelson Bartlett found her a job with a subsidiary firm to avoid blaring nepotism. She soon proved her worth however, as she began to deal with the international business community. She proved to be as shrewd and decisive as her father. The boys did very well in their private school; both were academic leaders in their class. Josh was taller, heavier, stronger, and quicker, physically and mentally, than any other boy his age in the school.

In spite of having two children, and now in her late twenties, Martha was lovelier than ever. When men first met her, their first thought was inevitably, *"how can I get this woman in bed."*? As Martha moved in the legal circles, she shrewdly observed her colleagues, the young men in her father's firm and younger business associates. The only thing she missed about Ethan was his passionate love making. She longed for a warm, passionate body next to hers more than she cared to admit to herself. She began to make the social scene once again. She accompanied her parents to the parties, the art exhibits, the symphonies, and the theater. It wasn't long before interested men began to inquire of her marital status. She always informed them with a smile that "I'm separated from my husband." She never defined that she meant a geographical separation, an emotional separation, or a legal one. She left men guessing as to her true status to determine who was bold enough to court her. It didn't take long for a number of men, including several married ones, to emerge from the woodwork.

Martha's firm was hired to negotiate trade in agricultural commodities with several European consortiums. Since The European Union represented one of the world's major markets, with over 500 million people, a recovering currency in the Euro that was successfully challenging, indeed, replacing the dollar as the international currency, European Union regulations required compliance. As a negotiator, Martha had few peers. She quickly realized that if she very subtly flashed the outline of her body, particularly her long, lean legs, men had a way of becoming eager to negotiate. She studied diligently to learn everything she could about the agricultural products that the Europeans wanted to sell here, and the U.S. products they were interested in purchasing. There weren't that many U.S. agricultural products the Europeans wanted to buy other than non-modified cereal grains and beef raised without growth promoting hormones. President Newkirk as a campaign pledge to address the high cost of food had said "to hell with Brussels and the European Union standards on barring genetically modified foods. We will subsidize American farmers and meat producers who raise genetically modified plants and use hormone implants as growth factors in beef cattle for their exclusive consumption here in the USA. Those farmers who wish to meet the European Union's requirements and world markets can do so, but without any subsidies. Americans will eat cheaper and well, better foods in quality and quantity. Those Europeans and those who adhere to the EU's standards can pay a lot more and get lesser quality for their Euros."

He made good his promise. His newly appointed Secretary of Agriculture encouraged genetically modified rice, wheat and corn crops for overseas sales as well as non-GMO crops for domestic consumption. He pointed out that the Chinese were carrying on such genetic experiments in the open, without concern about such implanted genes being spread to non-modified crops by the wind carrying pollen, by insects, or other means. He also made a major thrust towards pond raised fish to supplement the rigid controls on the oceans' fisheries. Rigid rules concerning the catch of ocean fisheries bankrupted many fishermen, as attempts to allow the ocean species to recover from over fishing. Martha found it difficult to persuade the EU to change its policies.

The European Union did everything it could to subtly support Europe's small farmers with concealed subsidies, tax breaks, trade regulations and labor requirements while using the same arguments against American products, claiming unfair American trade and tax practices. Their practices made Martha's negotiations all that more difficult.

One of the men attracted to Martha was a newly elected U.S. Congressman from Baltimore, in his mid thirties, who was married and had a daughter of his own. He was handsome, courteous, extremely suave and debonair. Martha decided that this individual posed minimal risk as a lover. He had much to lose should any extramarital affairs ever come to light. Martha didn't care about his family, only that she might be named in a scandal that could make national news. John Laroutte was a member of the House Committee on agricultural commodities trade. Late one Friday afternoon, after conferring with the committee dealing European Union regulations on grain sales, he invited her for drinks at an upscale bar. She declined because both of them were too well known by the patrons of that establishment, but hinted that a more secluded environment would be acceptable.

Two weeks later Martha accepted an invitation from Jacques Charbonneau to attend a ball at the French embassy. Monsieur Charbonneau was a Frenchman, a diplomat assigned to the European Union office in Washington, D.C. Monsieur Charbonneau was a very engaging man. He was a geographical bachelor, having left his family in Europe. His specialty was European agricultural commodities, but he particularly represented the European wine and spirits industry. European wines had lost a considerable portion of the U.S. market for a decade, but were now making a comeback with increased sales on the east coast of the United States. European cheeses were his second area of expertise. Congressman Laroutte attended the same function with his wife. Laroutte did everything he could to hide his displeasure, his jealousy, at seeing Martha dance with the Frenchman. Martha played the subtle coquette to the extreme, smiling at Laroutte at every opportunity. The two men knew each other of course, which made it all the more interesting. The Congressman's wife noticed the interplay between the three, her husband, the Frenchman, and Martha, with interest.

The following weekend, Martha and Charbonneau met early on Friday afternoon. They drove north from Washington in his car, to the Pocono Mountains of Pennsylvania for a lost weekend. Martha felt she had suffered sufficient sex deprivation, and was absolutely wild in bed with her new lover. Charbonneau became completely overwhelmed with her beauty, wit and wild sexual abandon. In short, he fell passionately head over heels for Martha. Over the course of the next several months, they had a number of such lost weekends. Martha always left the boys with her parents, with no explanation other than having a working weekend out of town. Neither Nelson nor Elizabeth Bartlett questioned their daughter regarding her whereabouts or activities. In fact, they both hoped she was forming a sufficiently strong relationship that she would divorce Ethan and marry someone on her own social, intellectual and financial scale. On the social circuit, Charbonneau could not conceal his infatuation with Martha. It was obvious to everyone but him. Most of all, it stung Congressman Laroutte, himself of French ancestry, although dating back to the nineteenth century when a great-great-great grandfather came over during the American Revolutionary War. Laroutte's lust grew stronger every time he saw Martha. Realizing an opportunity to play the men off one against the other to the benefit of her company, Martha let Laroutte invite her to a motel one Saturday night. Sex with Martha only whetted Laroutte's appetite for her. He couldn't get enough of her. Now the two men entered into personal competition as well as economic and political. Laroutte grew more and more bellicose towards the European Union's regulations. No one on the agricultural commodities committee realized that Laroutte's recalcitrance was really aimed at the EU's representative Charbonneau. Committee Chairman Rosener counseled Laroutte several times behind closed doors not to be so aggressive, to no avail. Martha realized during one meeting just how serious the situation had become. She left word at his office to call her before close of business that day. When he called, she arranged what was to appear as a casual meeting in an upscale bar. Over two drinks, Martha informed Laroutte that he was out of control that she had no particular interest in either him or Charbonneau, and they would not have another tryst. Without hesitation or thinking, Laroutte abruptly stood up from his chair which knocked it over backwards, leaned over the table, doubled his fist and drew back to punch Martha. He suddenly caught himself, severely blushed, picked up his chair and walked out without saying a word. The scene was observed by a gossip columnist from the Washington Post who was a regular patron of the bar. Her column the next day questioned why the Congressman was so angry at the beautiful lady lawyer. Was it business, or something more personal? To avoid drawing more attention to himself, Congressman Laroutte was more restrained and obsequious to committee chairman Congressman Rosener. At the end of negotiations, the European Union gained a large advantage to sell its wine and cheeses to the United States, and Martha's firm received several million dollars in fees.

That fall, representatives of the states of Washington, Oregon, and the Canadian Province of British Columbia met and drafted a constitution to form an autonomous unit they called Columbia. It was presented the United States Congress. With the withdrawal of Quebec from Canada, the remaining provinces felt free to pursue what they believed to be in their own best interests. The Maritime Provinces of Canada were discussing forming a separate state behind closed doors.

Within the United States, the positions of complete secession and as an autonomous unit within the union were fervently discussed and cussed among state governors. In the southwest, representatives of the governments of Arizona, New Mexico, and leaders of several lesser political parties in those states, met in a secret congress. Politicians from west Texas and southern California were invited and accepted the invitations. Participants masked their travel and absence as vacations, visits to relatives and friends, or personal business trips.

Western energy companies, both American and European, had competitively squeezed China out of oil and gas resources and pipeline contracts in the Middle East and Caspian Basin late in the twentieth century and early in the twenty-first. China came to the negotiating table a little too late. Consequently, early in the twenty-first century, China courted the other major sources of oil left to it, most notably Iran and Russia. Russia has deteriorated to a tyrannical state, governed harshly in the face of internal unrest by the educated middle class. Because the cheapest way to ship oil to China was by supertanker, China invested in the expansion and development of ports and oil terminals on Iran's southern coast on the Arabian Sea. China assumed control of the pipelines running northeast from Iran across Turkmenistan, Uzbekistan and Kazakhstan, diverting the oil by new pipelines from Qaraghandy, Kazakhstan, into western China. China explored the costs of new pipelines through the mountains of Afghanistan and Tajikistan, geologically unstable and prone to earthquakes, and decided they were too enormous. The Chinese began shipping oil out of what were Karachi, Pakistan as well as Bandar-Abbas, Iran. They extended the gas pipeline from Almaty eastward into central China. The Peoples Liberation Army Navy known as PLAN, expanded their blue water naval capabilities correspondingly to protect their sea lanes of communication.

China became a major purchaser of the corn and wheat and rice crops of the United States for human consumption. They invested heavily in major agricultural companies. The corn crop increased in value as the competition for it between foreign markets, between ethanol production for fuel and domestic animal feeds increased. Meat prices began a slow but inexorable rise, reducing meat consumption in the American diet. More and more poultry was consumed, less and less beef and pork; rice and beans together make a complete protein, and this with the occasional addition of pond raised fish pressed into comminuted cakes constituted much of the lower class American diet.

"Mr. Prime Minister, Lu Wa He Sin, your visit is most timely. Welcome to Tehran. Please, sit, and we will discuss our concerns." The Iranian Prime Minister turned to his Secretary and clapped his hands, "Sari, tea for our guest, please." Turning back to his Chinese counterpart, he spoke, "Just last week our Supreme Islamic Council has instructed me to negotiate with your government for increased prices for our oil and natural gas. The increased prices we are to negotiate reflect the fact that the costs of the fast breeder reactors you are building for us are exceeding their estimated and budgeted costs."

"Mr. Prime Minister, Mohammad ibn Saleh, our economic situation is very precarious. I am sure you understand. Thanks to your government and the uninterrupted flow of oil and natural gas, all is smoothly flowing for the moment. Your oil and natural gas fuel our economy. In exchange, our weapons

keep you safe; our submarines patrolling the Strait of Hormuz
and the Indian Ocean challenge the U.S. Navy or the remains
of it, for supremacy in the region, keeping them far from your
shores. Japan is quiet, even though they are building tactical
nuclear weapons. Your Great Satan is in internal turmoil and
probably won't survive as a nation. Smaller nations are easier
to deal with. You will be able to expand westward. Your
ancient Sunni enemy of Iraq is vulnerable and is yours for the
taking. We have promised the west we will never militarily
interfere with Saudi Arabia and Kuwait, South and Central
America. We have every reason to believe the west will
peacefully accept our word. Really, they have little choice and
it is obvious to all.

Our nuclear plants will continue to replace our older coal
fired generating plants over the next twenty years. The fast
breeder reactors we are building for you will further lessen
your need for oil and gas plants to generate electricity. No, our
current problem is an economic one. We respectfully request
to renegotiate our contracts for oil. We need more fuel for our
engines and we need it at lower rates. Both gasoline and diesel
fuel are required for our transportation systems. Our railroads
and trucking systems are in constant chronic supply. We are
offering to trade chemicals, and water piped from our Afghan
Provinces, to your eastern provinces to increase your irrigated
agricultural production, and increased small arms shipments."

"Mr. Prime Minister, we want higher prices, you want
lower prices. Your point of the PLAN protecting our southern
flanks is not lost on us. Yet it serves you equally, guarding
your sea lanes of communication. We have become a major
market for your goods, so our trade is truly a two way
market."

"What then, shall be our best course of action? Shall we
let our negotiators meet in two weeks, each with their
proposals? I leave the choice of a meeting place to you."

When Bradley returned from the Golan Heights after a one year tour of duty that was extended into the winter, he really no longer had a wife. Disappointed that she had moved from Leavenworth to Baltimore, he nevertheless accepted it without complaint. When he returned from the Heights he was re-assigned to Camp LeJune. When he went to what was supposed to be their home in Baltimore enroute to Camp LeJune, he found their divergent political views had grown ever wider over the years, until she could no longer share their bed. That she no longer loved him was blatantly obvious. He loved her very much, and his sons even more, if that were possible. He was crushed. His greatest fear was that their sons would share their mother's political philosophy. Martha had become a rabid internationalist. She had become a fanatical supporter of the United Nations and one world government. Her chosen specialty of international law and regulations led her to believe that world peace and world trade could only be facilitated and accomplished by one world government. There was no room for a martial United States in her view of the world.

Ethan Bradley had tried to inculcate into Sam the meaning of the Constitution of the United States, and the Bill of Rights on their "sporting expeditions." Joshua was a little young to comprehend political concepts and what they meant, but Bradley hoped it would dawn on them both when they began to be able to better reason for themselves. His wife regarded them as outmoded documents, anachronisms from another age and no longer valid. Now she especially despised the Second Amendment, which Ethan held most dearly.

Ethan regarded the Second Amendment as the first among equals, the Amendment that put the teeth into all the others. Now, it no longer existed. It was the first Constitutional Change the Democratic Party attempted to initiate when they controlled the White House and both houses of Congress. It was backed by many Republicans, even those who hypocritically called themselves conservatives. The proponents all claimed there would be less violence, less race riots, and less crime. When it was not immediately ratified by two thirds of the states, the Democrats simply outlawed possession of all unlicensed firearms. When it took effect one year later, the effect was far more devastating that anyone expected. Citizens in Appalachia and most of the western states initially took to shooting federal officers wherever they were encountered or attempted to enforce the law through confiscation. Neighborhood and community groups banded together. It took platoon sized units of the Bureau of Alcohol, Tobacco, Firearms and Explosives to subdue individual rural residents who refused to surrender their firearms and battalions to subdue the small towns, with much bloodshed. Many buried their firearms or hid them to use them later on that rare occasion when a local law enforcement officer would make the fatal mistake of allowing his position of supporting no privately owned firearms to be known. The FBI and the BATFE then began to bring in portable ground penetrating radar units to uncover buried firearms. Local law enforcement officers very quickly learned that supporting the federal government would cost them their standing in some of their rural communities through utter ostracism, if not their lives. The coastal cities on both coasts on the other hand, welcomed the destruction of the Second Amendment. It was the Civil War all over again, only it was urban versus rural with severe regionalization.

Somebody at the National Rifle Association Headquarters was smart enough to have a very powerful electromagnet in place. When the BATFE raided the place for all of the records for members, especially competitive shooters, all they found were erased disks. The only records the feds had then were those of the Olympians and what they could gather by raiding local gun clubs and the homes of their officers for knowledge of the local members. Some of them burned their paper records and disks. The national media kept quiet about the raids on the NRA, but word went out over the Internet over the next couple of days. That's when the local clubs started destroying their records.

Texas, New Mexico, Arizona and the southern halves of Colorado and California were now openly discussing some form of autonomous unit, similar to Columbia. Texas however, couldn't make up its mind as a state. It couldn't decide whether or not to split east and west, or north and south. Political forces were pulling it into quarters. Colorado had similar concerns as to where to draw a line. From a practical, political perspective, the thirty-seventh parallel seemed a logical demarcation. Riots in southern California and the cities of Texas were growing more numerous and more severe.

Governors of the Midwestern states, Ohio, Indiana, Illinois, Missouri, Iowa, Kansas, Kentucky, and Tennessee began to discuss what the possibility of autonomy for Columbia and the southwest would mean for their states.

The U.S. Treasury issued a report, classified as Critical, "for the eyes only" of the President and a few selected members of Congress. It predicted bankruptcy of the United States unless immediate solutions to curtail entitlements were found. Elimination of discretionary spending could no longer satisfy payment of the national debt. There was simply no other way to pay off mature federally issued bonds and treasury bills. The purchase of U.S. financial instruments by foreign powers, particularly China and Japan, declining for several years, continued to dwindle to almost none. It was their purchase that financed continued deficit spending and borrowing. Now, that source was gone.

In late November, thirty days after his return from the Middle East, Ethan received orders to report to the United Nations for an undisclosed assignment. Major Bradley made an appointment with the Marine Corps Personnel Office at the Pentagon. He appeared at the appointed hour and met with the Marine Corps Infantry Branch controller. The controller refused to inform Major Bradley as to the nature and location of the assignment. The handler informed Bradley that several negative reports outside normal personnel channels regarding his political activities had been received and placed in his file. Surprised, Bradley demanded to see the letters of reprimand which had been placed in his personnel file without his knowledge. The handler refused, stating that his career was already somewhat compromised.

"Like hell I have engaged in political activity. I haven't publicly supported any political candidate at any time, or either party at any time in my military career. Any such letters of reprimand are not only false, but are illegal as I have never been counseled, nothing has ever been said, and I have no idea to what you are referring."

The handler merely grinned and replied, "You supported 'the Constitution as it was written' that's a quote, in this document from a former battalion commander of yours. Another report says you strong armed members of your company to write their congressmen regarding support for the Second Amendment. Now that's considered political activity in this five sided wastebasket." He was advised to accept the mysterious assignment without question. Bradley was given the choice of accept the assignment or resign. He submitted his resignation on the spot and drove to Wyoming.

CHAPTER 2

"WELL ETHAN, I'M GLAD YOU'RE HERE. I've been kind of anxious about you. I wouldn't be at all surprised if you were arrested and charged with political crimes. It was bad enough that you got a surreptitious bad efficiency report for preaching adherence to the Constitution that caused you to resign your commission. I understand that they have jailed some officers for that. Of course, that is what your oath called for, to 'Uphold and Defend the Constitution, against all enemies, foreign and domestic," before the SOB in the White House had it changed to 'Uphold and Defend the Office of the President." It's kind of bad when the domestic ones turn out to be politicians the people elected. I don't know how much you heard, read, or saw on television about what is politically going on over here while you were safeguarding Israel, or how slanted it was."

"Dad, our service members have been brainwashed through the educational system. They don't understand the Constitution or the Bill of Rights. Quite a number of them have told me that in their high school civics classes, that they were taught these were outmoded documents, whose concept was really only applicable from colonial times until the close of the nineteenth century. That is, in those who had a civics course in their high school curriculum in the first place. Most of these kids never had inkling really, of their opportunities. Quite a lot of them were pushed by the system toward technical or trade crafts in middle school. By the end of their freshman year of high school all that federal testing more or less determined whether or not they were college material. It is awfully hard for a late bloomer, somebody in their twenties who sees the light, to get into college. Then again, the much of the Armed Forces are now made up of foreigners, especially Hispanics, mostly Mexicans, and Asians that are either foreign born or first generation. My last company command was twenty-five percent black and forty percent Mexican or Hispanic and twenty percent Asian and fifteen percent Anglo Americans. At the Academy, discussion of the Constitution was assiduously avoided. We didn't even read the Bill of Rights. Instead, we had the United Nations Charter and its precepts taught. I understand a little bit about how this all came about, but certainly don't understand all of it."

"Ethan, the politicians are making promises they can't keep, have been for decades. Promises of economic recovery and middle class lifestyle for everybody through state run control of all aspects of the society and economy; agriculture, business, medical, the media, everything. Today's young people never realized that democracy is meaningless of itself. It depends entirely on the government the people allow. If the people elect charlatans, tyrants or murderers, who in turn put their cronies and supporters in power in the bureaucracies, they get the tyranny they deserve. Remember, Hitler did not break a single constitutional law on his rise to be Chancellor and Der Fuhrer. Stalin purged and killed so many Soviet citizens that some historians believe he killed more than died in World War II from the Japanese invasion of Manchuria in 1931 until the end of the war in August, 1945. That's what is happening now. We are putting in power those who believe that only they, as an elitist oligarchy, are fit to rule over the rest of us; only time will tell just how far they will go. They are already using state organs, the FBI, the BATFE, INS, and so on, as legal, personal police forces to imprison political opposition. They will probably make most of the Bill of Rights meaningless. That's why they devastated the Second Amendment as a first step is so critical to them.

Now that Martha has taken the boys and gone to her parents, have you any ideas what you want to do? Jobs around here are pretty scarce, unemployment here is running between fifteen and twenty percent, but we ought to be able to find something for you, even if it is just driving a truck. I have a few friends still around who could use some help."

"Thanks, Dad, but I think I'll just load up my truck with beans and gas and fishing equipment and go camping and backpacking by myself for a week or so, while I think things out. I have no idea right now what to do about Martha and the boys or with myself. I know I don't stand a chance in the divorce court because of being overseas so much, my radical conservative views and her family's money. At any rate, she had too many lovers in my absence. She apparently bonded with a couple of them, according to rumors even playing one off against the other. I'll just go up towards Beartooth Pass and meander around for a while. I have my wrist Phone/GPS/ watch, but I'll dig out our old topographical maps and compass anyway, I'll just float for a while, see how many trout I can catch. I'm still a resident of North Carolina, so I'll get a nonresident's fishing license and just hang out."

"The wildlife situation has changed since you were a teenager, son. The elk or deer herds are rebuilding and doing well, but there isn't much hunting left right now. The anti-hunting eco-terrorists came up here, the People for the Ethical Treatment of Animals and others, bussed lots of them in from California, the tree huggers and leftist loonies tried to pack all the hearings, and it got pretty violent. They initially lost their battles over the environment to the energy companies, times when you were in school and service. The oil and gas companies came in here and drilled over 30,000 oil and gas wells. They are still digging up coal in various locations around the state. Over the twenty years that they extracted all the oil and gas they really destroyed the environment while they claimed to protect it. After the oil and gas played out, the energy folks didn't give a damn about restoring it for the wildlife. The environmentalists then got the upper hand because nobody else cared. Everybody thought it was too late. You know, they never showed any of that on the national news though. All you ever saw was where the anti-hunting groups were winning and most of that was staged. This political fight isn't over by a long shot but it is playing second fiddle now to the politics of the country. The environmentalists, the Greens if you like, were politically successful in trying to get much of it restored to what they think was pristine, before the coming of the white man. I don't know where they got the money for all that political influence. The wolves and grizzly bears and mountain lions and even the wolverines have returned in limited numbers and they get the lion's share of deer and elk. Hunting seasons are quite short now. The environmentalists and anti-hunting movements coalesced and rather wrecked the hunting and backcountry packing and outfitting industry. Still, given another fifty years it will probably be closer to a more natural ecological system that existed before the white man arrived. You better take a rifle if you have one. A lot of the irrigation has ceased because of the demand for water by the cities downstream, so we don't have the hayfields we used to. Much of the land has gone to grazing for cattle, but the cattle herds are way down. It takes eighty acres to feed one cow on summer range now here in this desert. People can't get enough hay to feed a lot of cattle through the winter so the ranching industry is way down. Even when the ranchers had irrigation water, they could only manage to raise seven percent of the national cattle herd on all the federal land through grazing rights. Most of the beef is now produced in the Midwest where they have enough rain to grow forage without irrigation. A bunch of the stock growers associations bribed the politicians to allow overgrazing after the energy companies pulled out. They just almost totally destroyed the land. What used to be called drought is now the standard shortage of water. The desertification process just grew and grew."

Ethan said "the Bureau of Alcohol, Tobacco, Firearms and Explosives gave me the choice of selling my guns for peanuts or outright confiscation with disposal by a judge. I sold the unregistered ones to the underground. Martha was happy to get them out of the house. The BATFE paid a paltry sum for them, a token payment, really. Actually, I am convinced that the judge took most, if not all of them. It seems all of the politicos suddenly acquired a taste for fine firearms and quickly acquired substantial collections."

"That's a shame. You had a great collection. They collected a lot from around here, too! Quite a number of BATFE agents got shot in the process though. They would try to descend on isolated homes and ranches and overwhelm them in the middle of the night, just like the Nazis of a hundred years ago. Those BATFE agents would bust in without knocking, wearing Ninja suits and bullet proof body armor and Kevlar helmets. Then some of the neighbors got together in the towns and started ambushing them when they conducted their raids. Wasn't much folks could do about the isolated ranches, though. The ranchers started hiding their firearms in the hills and woods or burying all their guns but one or two which they kept around the house. The anti-hunting bunny huggers, eco-terrorists and BATFE have formed quite a cabal. A lot of those tree hugger folks that moved here from the east and west coasts, Sierra Club types, fingered folks out here that had guns. Some of them were politely but very strongly, asked to leave. Most did. Some didn't. Of those that stayed, most will never leave as a result of being regarded as traitors. A lot of them met with one kind of an accident or another. Now the shoe is on the other foot; those few that are still alive are being very closely watched by their neighbors. They are kind of regarded as Quislings. It must have been something like this in the Revolutionary War, when the Redcoats tried to disarm the colonists. I'll bet you never about heard any of this on the network news channels.

The feds in combination with many of the state police departments started throwing up roadblocks and searching every vehicle for guns and drugs. Anybody with a gun went to jail. Part of the anti-drug program they said. Of course, that's a whole different ball game. Drug money reaches to the highest levels of government. They don't want to end the drug trade. It is too profitable for the politicians. If they wanted to end it they would put their money on the demand side, not the supply side. They could address it two ways to simply take the money and crime out of it. First, they could eliminate all the anti-drug laws. If people want to become addicts and kill themselves that would be their choice. Alternatively, the government could provide treatment for addicts, give them two chances for staying off the drugs, and then put them on a chain gang for a few years if they didn't. That way we would not have poured billions and billions of dollars into failed programs in failed South American states. Hell, they were even searching buses and trains, stopping buses on the highways and trains in the stations. All you had to do was bad mouth somebody you didn't like. Tell the state and federal folks you thought somebody had illegal guns or drugs. Search warrants are no longer required. Hearsay was enough for the police to act. Police would come in dressed in ninja suits in the middle of the night. Many of the big city police agencies went to armored cars, old military armored personnel carriers, heavy weapons and tactics used against ordinary citizens.

A couple of vanloads of BATFE and FBI agents showed up one day. They went to some homes where they knew the owners kept firearms. They roughed up some of the people, even a couple of wives and kids. They did shoot one home owner in the leg when he resisted. He still limps from it. It didn't take long for the word to get out. On the way back to Denver, they had a bad accident in the canyon. Seems like a landslide hit just at the wrong time. A couple of the vans tumbled into the river and most of the agents in them drowned. Several of them died as a result of blunt trauma when the landslide hit the vehicles. A couple had broken necks. One of the agents talked for a while before the ambulances and wreckers arrived. He was busted up pretty bad. From what he said, the FBI has been illegally keeping records of all firearms sales since the Brady Law was passed in 1998. The law said they were supposed to destroy all of the records of purchases, but they never did. FBI director after director broke the law and nobody in any administration or Congress made them adhere to it. The politicians knew it and were glad about it. Therefore the FBI had decades of records of firearms purchases at the NICS, the National Instant Criminal Background Check System in Clarksburg, West Virginia. They knew who firearms enthusiasts were and who weren't through multiple purchases. They went after the hunters and shooters who were collectors, the so called gun nuts at first, one at a time. Anyway, most of the firearms were recovered and returned to their owners. An investigation supported the theory that the landslide was initiated by an explosion, but the investigation came to naught. Nothing more was ever said about it.

I'm sure you have heard, Wyoming, Montana, Idaho, the Dakotas are threatening now to form an autonomous unit the way Columbia did, or maybe even secede and form a separate country. Alberta and Saskatchewan might even join, although there are a number of issues to be resolved for them to do so.

Colorado was invited to join the potential coalition, but the consortium that controls that state, Denver, Colorado Springs, Greeley, Boulder, and Fort Collins all got together and more or less made the whole state a park where hunting is almost banned; even restoring grizzlies to the Colorado Rockies. The bears are driving the few remaining ranchers nuts. Wolves moved down from Yellowstone thirty years ago and a dozen packs are now established as far south as Pueblo, Colorado. Now they are compensating the ranchers for livestock losses to bear and wolves-if you can prove wolves or bears killed them first and the carcasses were not just fed on by the bears and wolves. They claim in a lot of these cases the cow died of other causes. Another part of that equation is that many people can't afford to eat beef the way they used to twenty or thirty years ago. Now America's main diet is beans and rice and poultry and a little pork. Let's go outside and enjoy a cigar, Son."

Father and son donned heavy coats and cowboy hats and went out to the gazebo in the backyard. The gazebo wasn't quite level. The old man pointed at it and said "They even moved the gazebo to see if I had any guns buried under it. The BATFE came in with ground penetrating radar and went over the whole damned yard. When they set the gazebo back they didn't get it quite right, but they didn't care. They even dug up and pumped out the old septic tank that is buried here in the yard. That was before we got on the city sewer system. Somebody told me that the septic tank was the first place they looked in country dwellings. Of course they didn't find anything. You can't trust your neighbors anymore. The word I have is that about twenty-five percent of our fellow American citizens are rats informing on the other seventy-five percent, just like the old East Germany, with their Stazi, or secret police. That's in the cities and suburbs of course. It isn't like that out here anymore since we drove the loony liberals back to the coasts and their cities where they belong. Of course, the Stazi was before your time, before the old Soviet Union collapsed and broke apart and that all came to light when Germany re-united. Now I understand Europe is almost back to the way it was in those days, too. By that I mean they are at the point where all the power is in the hands of a tightly controlled European Union bureaucracy and the politicians. The bureaucracy's primary purpose is to sustain itself. The people have little choice anymore; every aspect of their lives is very tightly regulated. The politicians passed a law against criticizing any politician in office. Some folks spent a year or two in jail for speaking out. Internal Revenue Service claims take priority over the Bill of Rights. It only has to be based on an IRS audit. The courts wouldn't recognize independent audits. When I signed a petition to do away with the IRS and go to a flat rate tax at the retail level so citizens would know what their government really costs them, the IRS agents came and threatened to take everything I have; bank accounts, coin collection, land, house, everything. A lot of private property was seized in this manner without ever going to court. Most of it ended up in the hands of local politicians, sheriffs, county commissioners, judges and the like. They don't have much room for the individual. Anybody who questions the bureaucracy or government is in trouble, big trouble. The Supreme Court ruled decades ago that the police had no responsibility to protect the individual, but only the community as a whole. If that isn't hog manure I don't know what is. Then that Supreme Court in 2014 ruled that private property could be seized and turned over to private corporations for the economic good of the community; not for the government but to line the pockets of private companies who undoubtedly bribed the local zoning and building commissions. The right of Eminent Domain went out the window.

In reading history, I realized that the Founding Fathers realized that once the legislative ball to increase government power started rolling, it would be very difficult if not impossible to stop. That was the driving force behind the Bill of Rights. Well, the ball has continued to roll, to grow exponentially until it flattened and disintegrated the Bill of Rights in to oblivion under one excuse or another. It is so bad that more than ten percent of all American males go to prison today. It is fifty percent of all black American males. Of course, most of them being in jail are the result of drug charges.

It is just as bad in Europe, so we can't expect anything from those countries. Part of Europe's problem as I understand it is that they have become so Islamic. Bernard Lewis, the most imminent western authority on Islam in the early days of this century said Europe would be one hundred percent Muslim by the end of this century. Well, France and Spain have been leading the way for fifty years. Now the mullahs are exerting a powerful influence in the name of Allah and are expending the drive towards police states throughout Europe."

The father handed a cigar to his son, and stripped the wrapper off his own. He lit their cigars with a butane cigar lighter and walked to the edge of the hill overlooking the Big Horn River. He pointed to a small body of water at the foot of the steep bluff. "They even drained our little holding pond we use to pump water up for the sprinkler system for the yard. They found nothing. I told them I sold all my guns for cash only at guns shows years ago. I don't think they believed a word of it, but they couldn't prove otherwise. I suspect our telephone is an open microphone these days, along with many other folks' telephones. That's why we're out here, smoking these cigars. If you're going into the mountains, especially the west side of the basin, you better take a big rifle. I can give you a .30-06 or a .338, and my old Ruger single action .44 magnum. Which would you prefer?"

Ethan smiled and said, "The .30-06. Thanks, Dad. I expect it has an old fashioned scope on it?"

"Matter of fact, it is still wearing the 1.75-5X Burris Signature Safari variable your Grandad put on it back in 2000. It has stood in mighty good stead. It's the old Winchester Model 70 Classic stainless synthetic. Better take plenty of ammo, however much you're comfortable in carrying, just in case. I suggest at least 50 rounds of each. I'll have them for you tomorrow morning.

"How did you manage to hide Grandad's guns from the Feds anyway?"

"As soon as I got the call from the Highway Patrol that Mom and Dad were killed in that head-on collision by that drunken Indian in the Wind River Canyon, I dashed over to their house and scooped them all up. Of course I had a key to their house. I threw them in the truck and brought them back here until I could figure out where and how to hide them. The state police came to their house a couple of hours later and put padlocks on their doors. I didn't know where some of their officers stand on the issue. I thought some of them are with us, but I didn't know which ones at the time. I ultimately did figure out where and how to hide them, but I won't tell you, so as not to involve anybody else.

Why don't you take my old pickup truck with four wheel drive and leave yours here? No great loss if it gets dinged, and this time of year you might have heavy snows. It could come at any time and stay till spring. I'll give you some of my gas ration coupons."

"Thanks, Dad, I will. Dad, where did I go wrong with Martha? You and Mom were the happiest couple for fifty years. I know you miss her terribly, these last few years."

The old man thought for a moment, sighed and puffed on his cigar. "Well, I think it's partially our fault. After your little sister died in infancy, and your brother was killed in an auto accident as a teenager, as an only child, you were spoiled rotten. You really didn't have any discipline until you got to the Academy. There you learned discipline enough to do well. You are gifted athletically and intellectually which helped your ego. But I've always felt that you never developed the character, the quality of character, that deep down value system of sacrifice, delayed gratification, putting other things, like institutions and concepts and some people ahead of yourself, until you were about thirty. Then you discovered Sam, but by then it was too late. Martha too was an only child, a spoiled rotten rich girl, kind of like you only without us being rich. She is a product of the eastern liberal establishment. She was even more spoiled than you were. The difference was, you outgrew it. She never did. She couldn't take having a husband with an opposite political philosophy and a love of country. Her view had to predominate; she had to have her way in everything. When she couldn't control you, your politic and your career, it was too much, so she left. " Ethan didn't say any more. They just stood there in silence, smoking their cigars until the darkness overtook them at 16:45.

At breakfast the next morning the venerable .30-06 was standing in the corner adjacent to the kitchen table. The Ruger Vaquero .44 magnum rested in a cross draw flapped belt holster.A thick two and three-quarter inch leather belt was threaded through the holster's belt loop but also held a leather rifle cartridge box, a Cordura nylon pouch containing an ammo wallet with twelve round of .44 magnum ammunition in it, a heavy survival knife with a seven inch blade, and a Marble's hunting knife with a four inch upswept blade. Also present were a pair of small binoculars, a backpacking rifle cleaning kit, a folding camp saw, five plastic ammunition boxes with twenty rounds of .30-06 with 180 grain bullets in each, and a plastic ammunition box of fifty rounds of .44 magnum loaded with 280 grain wide flat nosed LBT bullets. A freighter pack frame, a Quallofill sleeping bag rated to thirty below zero, a backpacker's closed cell foam mattress, topographical maps of Park County, and a Cordura nylon waterproof rifle case were stacked along side the rifle.

Robert Bradley served the two of them a breakfast of bacon, pancakes with eggs on top, plenty of syrup, butter, coffee with half and half, milk and orange juice. Ethan devoured two plate sized pancakes with eggs on top drowned in syrup. The coffee was the best he ever had, heavily laced with the half and half. It was all he could do to finish it. Robert Bradley laid a key ring with two truck keys on it on the table.

"Thanks for the great breakfast, Dad. I'll pick up enough food for a week and head up towards the North Fork of the Shoshone. Even though they are closed for the season, I'll stay at one of the campgrounds outside the Park that has a flowing stream through it so heavy snow won't keep me bottled up in some small valley. I'll see you in a week or so."

The father nodded towards the pile of equipment in the corner. "Whatever else you might need you'll find the camper's box, that old footlocker in the bed of my truck. There's a cot there too, so you can sleep in the bed under the topper shell if the weather really gets nasty. Take my Quallofill parka too, just in case we get a really cold snap, and that pullover white parka shell I used when I went coyote hunting in the snow. They are all in the utility room closet. Help yourself to whatever else you think you might need. You have plenty of room in the pickup, and better to have and not need, than vice versa. The fishing tackle is all in the garage. Take the big yellow tool box that I use for a tackle box. It has plenty of everything in it for both spinning and fly fishing."

Ethan stopped at the all night grocery store on the way out of town. He bought granola bars, two dozen eggs, powdered milk, pancake mix, bacon, a small canned ham, dried fruit, a combination salt and pepper shaker, syrup, several cans of spam, stew, and ravioli. He threw the eggs, bacon and milk in the cooler in the back of the pickup and headed north. Two hours after he left his father's house, a team of two federal agents knocked on his father's door. They presented their identification; one was an FBI agent, the other from the Bureau of Alcohol, Tobacco, Firearms, and Explosives.

As soon as the two federal agents left, Robert Bradley phoned the county sheriff and informed him that a team of two federal agents, one FBI and one BATFE, just left his home five miles outside of town. They were looking for Ethan, but produced no warrant. They were driving a late model Ford in a plain brown wrapper with three antennas protruding from it, and a U.S. Government license plate. The sheriff alerted his deputies and the city police on their combined radio net. A deputy parked on Big Horn Avenue observed them parking in front of the Big Horn Café which they entered.

A few minutes later the sheriff, Jack Brady, entered the café followed by a youthful looking deputy. Both wore their standard grey uniform shirt and pants and blue clip-on necktie underneath heavy down filled parkas. The sheriff approached their booth and said "Morning boys, mind if I join you?" Without waiting for an answer, he took off his parka and put it in an adjacent booth, removed his baton from his belt and took a seat adjacent to one of the agents. "What brings you fellas into our quiet town?"

The two agents looked at one another, and the FBI spoke while the BATFE agent just sipped his coffee. "Strictly federal business, sheriff, nothing to get excited about." The waitress and owner, Jan Neville, approached the sheriff, and spoke, "Morning, Jack, want some coffee?" She had a pot of hot black coffee in one hand and two cups and saucers in the other, with half a dozen little vials of half and half girdling the top saucer, just the way the sheriff liked it. He smiled, and said, "Absolutely, Jan. It would be nice while these gentlemen and I chat." She smiled and poured his coffee and left. She gave the other cup and saucer to the deputy sitting two tables away, who just smiled is thanks as he listened to the conversation.

"I hear you have an interest in one of our locals, Ethan Bradley. What has he done to bring federal investigation into our little town? Whatever happened to professional courtesy to coordinate with us locals?"

The BATFE agent frowned and said "We want to question him, that's all."

"Do you have a warrant for his arrest?" asked the sheriff. The two federal agents looked at one another, and the FBI pulled a folded piece of paper from his breast coat pocket. The sheriff unfolded the warrant and read it, then folded it and handed it back to the agent.

"It says he is wanted for sedition. What does that mean? What did he do that was seditious?"

The BATFE agents put down his coffee, and looked at the sheriff. "While he was on active duty, he agitated to retain the Second Amendment. He advocated retaining all privately owned firearms and not registering anything. It is illegal for anyone in uniform to be politically active. He continued to agitate even after the Supreme Court ruled that the possession of any firearms is by special permit only issued by the BATFE and confiscation of all handguns was legal. Additionally, why did he resign a field grade commission in these times of high unemployment? We believe he is planning to form some kind of anti-government group or join one already in existence. He has significant military skills that he acquired at the expense of Uncle Sugar, and we feel he should not be using those skills except in the service of his government. Additionally, while his father-in-law is rich, he still has the legal responsibility to support his wife and kids regardless of how much money she makes or her daddy has. He might be in violation of federal family support laws. He can't support them when he doesn't have a job, and he can't have one because he resigned his commission."

"I remember when child support was a state concern. Now it requires the federal government. Doesn't the Tenth Amendment mean anything these days?" asked the sheriff.

"Not much," said the FBI agent admittedly. "There aren't many areas that are not of federal concern these days."

"Just what groups of seditious citizens do you think our Ethan Bradley might join? We don't have anything like that around here."

The two agents looked at each other again, and again the FBI agent took the lead. "There are several organizations, still rather loosely bound, of citizens of your county that are holding meetings and discussing the possibility of supporting secession of this state. Additionally, there is a National Guard Mechanized Infantry Company, a Stryker Company, located in this county."

"So now the National Guard constitutes a treasonous group?"

"If they support withdrawal from the Union, then yes, they do. Since they are under the command of the Governor until or if, they are federalized by the President, we can't let allow them to support such a position."

"What federal offices are you boys, from, I mean, where are your offices located?"

"Billings", said the FBI agent.

"Well, I hear rumors that Billings just might be the capitol of a new union of mountain and prairie states if they decide to secede and band together. It is interesting that you come down here to Wyoming when it appears that so much might be going on in Billings. By the way, what's your take on the Mexicans trying to break Arizona, New Mexico, Texas, and half of Colorado out of the Union? LaReconquesta and the Barrio Warriors have put together quite a coalition with the politicians and have formed an irregular army, I understand. I see on the television news that they appear pretty well armed with assault rifles, the ubiquitous AK-47. Why aren't you down there disarming them? I hear tell they might even try to take the southern half of California if they think they can get away with it. What about the Deep South? I saw riots in Atlanta by the black folks down there, agitating, as you say, for their right to form a separate black United States if they don't get their welfare checks. We sure don't have any riots like they are in L.A. or San Antonio or Atlanta. Seems to me you boys should be down there, not here." Neither agent spoke; they just looked at one another and then back to the sheriff.

"Well, you boys enjoy your coffee. This is a good place to eat lunch, too. It is a long drive back to Billings, and I wouldn't want you to get hungry along the way. By the way, don't ever come back into this county again. You aren't welcome here. You just cause trouble that we don't need." The sheriff got up and replaced his baton in its holder on his belt. He looked at the two, and then said, "You boys have a nice, safe drive out of Wyoming. We'll just stay here and keep you company until you finish your meal; we wouldn't want anyone to harass you." As Sheriff Brady walked to a nearby table, the FBI officer facing the street saw through the window two city police cars parked out in front with two uniformed officers in each of them. He knew that had trouble erupted they would be seriously outnumbered, and probably would have been shot for their troubles. It had happened to several other federal officers in western states. Their report would mention the sheriff's threat and that Washakie County's citizens would probably support secession. After the agents left, Sheriff Brady signaled Jan to join them.

"Did you pick up any of their conversation Jan?" he asked.

"Sure did, Jack. The one in the brown sport coat said that Ethan was too dangerous just to try and question let alone try and take into custody. They should shoot him on sight, and if he wasn't armed, put a throw away gun on him and claim self defense in the line of duty. They argued about shooting his dad, too. The blue jacketed guy was against it because he is an old war hero. Getting Ethan would be enough. Guess they don't know what the old boy has been up to," she grinned.

"Thanks, Jan. Appreciate it. Keep your ear to the ground, girl. We'll check in from time to time." The Sheriff left a couple of dollars on the table and walked out accompanied by his deputy.

As much as local militias had come into being in the years since World War III, the federal police forces blossomed into even greater bureaucracies. The multiple agencies continued to vie with each other to see which could create the largest organization of secret police to monitor their fellow countrymen, the ordinary citizens of the United States. Almost every facet of American's personal life was now in a federal dossier, available to any police agency, even down to which church they belonged and how many services they attended each year. The FBI, BATFE, U.S. Marshal's Service, Treasury Department, Postal Inspectors, even military intelligence agencies intruded in domestic intelligence activities where their individual services were involved. Legislation forced them to cooperate within the larger context of the intelligence community. All information is forwarded to a central collection and recording facility for dissemination for every request from any governmental agency at any level. For those in authority at state and federal levels, a clearance procedure was installed to protect those in power. The unelected directors of bureaucracies and government offices had unusual authority for access, rivaling that of the federal police agencies. Thus, the heads of certain intelligence agencies blackmailed certain Congressmen and Senators into supporting ever larger budgets and legislation favorable to their agencies.

Robert Bradley immediately phoned Ethan as soon as he hung up from informing the sheriff of the presence of the federal officers. Ethan's wrist phone rang. "Ethan, two feds were here looking for you. One was FBI and the other BATFE. One let it slip that it didn't matter that you weren't here; they would track you anyway via your wrist phone/GPS unit. I told them you were going camping for a week in the Big Horns for solace and reflection. That might have been bait to get me to call you; if so, it worked. I doubt though, that you are very far out of town. I suspect this call is being monitored, and they might have your current position because of it. Nevertheless, I felt you needed a warning. I don't know what they really wanted; they didn't say much, but I don't care. I don't trust them. Be safe, above, all and watch your back. Love you, Son."

"Thanks, Dad. I don't know when I will see you again, or under what circumstances, but I love you too. You take care of yourself, and watch out for them. They will probably want you next." Ethan turned off his phone, took it off his wrist, and started to throw it out the window, then thought better of it. When he reached the town of Basin, he pulled into the local supermarket. He purchased two five pound bags of rice, several one pound packages of dried, mixed beans, a two pound jar of peanut butter, two boxes of kitchen matches and a package of butane lighters, a box of quick oatmeal, a pound of sugar and one of salt and a box of Snickers candy bars. One of the shoppers left the engine of his car running while he dashed in for a moment. Bradley quickly opened the passenger door and put the wrist phone/GPS unit under the passenger seat. He loaded his groceries into the front seat of his pickup and headed west, towards the Absaroka Mountains. He turned off Highway 120 and on to 296 until he came to the gate closing the highway. It was always closed in the winter due to high snows. He backtracked until he found a place he could pull the truck off into the trees out of sight of the road. There he packed the backpack with what he thought would be required. He took the folding camp shovel, a small axe, a folding camp saw, backpacker's grill, his old Boy Scout cooking set, a one man survival tent, some fishing lures and the old spin fishing outfit to fish either in open water or through the ice. Almost as an afterthought, he lashed the lightweight Atlas carbon fiber backcountry snowshoes with crampons on the outside of the pack with a bungee cord. He felt like a bear when he put the pack frame on, and figured he had close to sixty-five pounds on his back. He smiled at the weight, remembering when he used to hump heavier loads up hill and dale in training and in the Congo. He took it off, removed his multi-layered parka and put on only the white outer parka shell. He fully appreciated one of the most dangerous things you can do in severe cold weather is sweat. He knew he had to avoid that at all costs. He kept the rifle in his arms, belted on the .44 Vaquero, put the pack on, and started up along Clark's Fork of the Yellowstone River.

The weather was clear but cool during the days, with highs in the twenties. At night the temperature dropped zero and below. He used the survival tent the first three days. On the fourth day he shot a nice mule deer doe. He figured he was far enough away from anybody who didn't have a pack horse outfit that it wouldn't be noticed. Hunting season was closed in the high country, and it would be hard to pinpoint the location of one rifle shot. He boned the deer, cutting the meat into dried strips which he smoked and dried over the fire on a large rack he built of green wood so that it would produce a lot of smoke. Only problem was, that most of the wood was coniferous which provided a lousy taste to the meat. On the fifth day an aircraft flew over only a thousand feet or so above him. It caused him some concern, but he figured it might be the forest service. Perhaps they spotted the smoke from his fire. Two days later he was cleaning his mess kit when he noticed movement across the valley floor. With his binoculars, he identified it as five men, all armed, wearing army uniforms. He immediately broke camp, packed his meat and left after circling around his camp and leaving foot prints in half a dozen different directions for at least twenty yards.

Bradley hiked carefully, staying in the timber as much as possible. Then the first snowfall came. He wasn't used to doing the snowshoe shuffle. He had to avoid the mal du raquette that comes with being out of practice with snowshoes. These are painful muscle cramps and in severe cases, tears of muscle sheaths and tendons. Bradley figured he was making two to three miles a day at the most on the snowshoes. The weather then cleared for three days before the blizzard hit. He made a large circle ultimately headed south as he carefully traveled to lower country with the unlikely hope of finding an abandoned cabin or some shelter which he could use as a base camp to hunt. At least he could find more meat to eat. He figured that they, whoever they were, had alerted the isolated ranches of his presence and possibility of his appearance. He suspected he was painted as a military deserter and an armed and very dangerous man. He didn't know, but his mind presented the worst scenarios. He dared not return to his truck because he anticipated that at the very least it had been bugged with a radio tracking device. He considered that they might have even booby trapped it or confiscated it. They might have even taken the battery or something, or however unlikely, were keeping it under observation. He stopped each day an hour before dark so he could gather wood and an adequate shelter for the now cold nights. By his map and compass, he figured he was about twenty five miles northwest of Cody.

He built his camp on the side of the ridge and was about to light his fire when he observed a light farther down in the valley. He observed it with his binoculars and saw that it was a working ranch. There was a ranch house, a barn, and another building the nature of which he couldn't determine. He broke camp and headed for the ranch.

He watched the house for an hour, moving around it on the hillside above it in three quarters of a circle before approaching the back side of the barn. He didn't want to cross the barnyard in the open. There was a three quarters moon which provided more light than he wished for. He waited for another hour after the lights went out and then slipped into the barn. He moved carefully in the dark, keeping the use of his mini-flashlight to a minimum. Several horses continued to snicker, and one kicked the side of the barn several times. He moved into the loft, took off his pack and pulled hay bales around himself to make a nest. He unrolled his sleeping bag, crawled in and quickly fell asleep.

He was awakened by the squeaking of the opening of the barn door. It was daylight. A voice from outside called in, "You can come out now. You're safe here. I expect you're cold and hungry. I know you're in there. Your tracks lead in and there ain't any other way out. Don't come out shootin', cause we'll shoot back. If you are Major Bradley, they are looking for you but you are safe here. You're among friends."

Bradley crawled out of his sleeping bag, rolled it, packed it, put on his pack and carefully climbed down the ladder, rifle lashed to his pack. He drew the .44 magnum from its holster and held it at the ready. Outside the barn door stood an old rancher, heavily bundled in a mackinaw. Bradley looked to both sides and saw no one else, so he stepped out into the open.

"Come on in, Friend; my wife is making a big breakfast and I suspect you could eat some." The man turned and walked away, with Bradley following. Bradley followed the man into the house through the mud room, where he dropped his pack, leaned his rifle in the corner, took off his boots, but left the belt with his .44 and knives on. They entered the kitchen where they lady of the house was pouring steaming cups of coffee at the table. She introduced herself. "I'm Sarah, and if this lug didn't introduce himself, he's Fred. We're the Wilkersons, and if you are who we think you are, you are most welcome. Now sit and eat, who ever you are, and if you can, tell us who you are and why you were sleeping in our barn."

Bradley smiled at the hospitality, and pulled up a chair. He picked up the coffee, smelled it, and smiled again. He picked up the pitcher of cream and poured a generous helping of half and half into his cup. She set a stack of pancakes with sausage patties on the side in front of him, along with a bottle of syrup. Fred and Sarah took their chairs.

"We say Grace around here, Son." With that, they all bowed their heads while Fred said a short prayer of thanks. Fred handed Bradley the butter for his pancakes while he added cream to his coffee and sipped it.

Just before he put the first fork full of pancakes into his mouth, Bradley asked, "Who do you think I am?"

"Well, the FBI was here about a week ago, said they had a Marine deserter roaming these hills. They wanted to question him but not take him into custody. Said his name was Bradley. Of course we didn't believe them. We read a different story in the Basin Newspaper a week or two ago, about how Major Bradley resigned his commission and came to visit his Dad. Paper said the real reason the government wanted him was because he was preaching adherence to the original Constitution and Bill of Rights, not the new ones Congress has been passing. If that's right, and that is who you are, you are welcome here. Most of us Wyomingites don't care for our U.S. government anymore, and are seriously looking about forming a new one, our own, with the original Constitution. Might as well, looks like that's what the Mexicans are doing from California to Texas. Something else, too, I don't know if it is a trap or what, but some fellas from the Wyoming National Guard came after the feds left. One was a captain. Said they wanted Bradley to join them. Said the Governor was offering him a Colonelcy in the National Guard; might be the beginning of the formation of an independent army.

Several of us western states here have been moving right along about forming our own government here, either an autonomous unit or completely independent of the east and west coast folks. They're nothing but a bunch of socialist elitists who think they should rule the rest of us. Those Guardsmen left us a phone number to call, or for you to call if you're Bradley. They'll come pick you up. I went into town last week and dialed it from a pay phone. Whoever answered said it was National Guard Headquarters in Cheyenne. I just hung up then. The National Guard Company in Cody is refusing to obey an order for federalization. The company commander there said they belong to the state and Governor of Wyoming now, not to the federal government anymore."

Bradley sighed. "What day is it?"

Bridgette said, "It's the twenty-eighth of December. Three days after Christmas. I don't suppose you had a turkey dinner out there, did you."

"If you're Bradley, I'll run you into Cody if you like, or Worland, or give you the phone number to call. Line here might be tapped but I don't know that. The one in Cheyenne most likely is. Whoever you are, if you like, we'll just give you some food and let you be on your way. If you're Bradley, you're welcome to stay a while, even a couple of days. You can shower, Sarah will wash your clothes, and you can get some good hot, home cooked meals into you. I expect you have lost some weight out there."

Bradley thought, "What the hell. I can't live out there forever. Even guerillas have to have the support of the local population. I really don't have a lot of choice." He shoved another bite of pancakes into his mouth, slowly shook his head yes, and said, "I'm Bradley."

Bridgette and Fred smiled, and Fred said, "Welcome home, Son!"

CHAPTER 3

FRED DROVE A SHOWERED, SHAVED, AND WELL FED ETHAN BRADLEY INTO CODY THE NEXT DAY. The first stop was at a barber shop where Ethan got a high and tight hair cut. Other patrons just studied him, and he stared back at them, but no one said anything. A few just smiled, figuring he was the wanted Ethan Bradley. All of them knew or knew about Fred Wilkerson as a conservation minded rancher with rumors of ties to some type of militia. Fred jabbered away with the usual barber shop talk with several of the patrons and the barber. Fred paid for the haircut and then they drove to the National Guard Armory in Worland .

Captain Ferguson eyed the individual through the glass of his office door as he strode across the gymnasium floor of the Armory. He rose from his chair and motioned for Bradley to come into his office. "What can I do for you, Mister?"

"I hear tell that you are looking for an individual by the name of Bradley. I know him. If it is good news or bad news, I can get it to him."

The captain smiled and held out his hand. "I'm Jim Ferguson, the company commander here. Welcome, Major Bradley. Oh, don't worry, you're safe here. You're in friendly territory with a few exceptions of émigrés. Your picture was published in the Basin Gazette a week ago. Some people even remember you from your high school days in Worland. Probably a dozen people have already recognized you. There are no federal agents left in this town. The only feds with badges and guns are the Rangers in Yellowstone Park, and they are all in with us. The State Adjutant General would like to have a few words with you, if you can find time in your busy schedule to pay him a visit. It's a 400 mile drive to Cheyenne, but I think it will be worth your time. When the feds found your truck, they stupidly reported it to the county sheriff. We put a note on the windshield asking you to come in. When you didn't return to it after the first week, we put another note on the windshield telling you we swept it for explosives and transmitters. After the second week we towed it in. If you didn't see it, it is sitting on the backside of the building on our parking lot. You can drive yourself down to Cheyenne, and we'll fill your gas tank, or we'll assign you a driver and even a guard if you like. We don't want to lose you, although the threat from the feds around here is really over, at least for the time being. You missed some of the political fireworks being out there in the boonies. There aren't any feds to speak of left in this state. You have impressed a lot of people staying alive out there that long, with just what you carried on your back. I'm authorized to give you $500 cash for travel expenses down to Cheyenne." Captain Ferguson opened his desk drawer and pulled out an envelope from which he counted out ten fifty dollar bills. He placed them back in the envelope, wrote the address of the Adjutant General on the outside of the envelope and handed the money to Bradley.

"Just what does the Adjutant General have to say to me that is so important that he's willing to spend five hundred of his precious dollars to have me come see him?"

"To be honest, I believe he is going to offer you a promotion, among other things. I suspect he also wants to discuss the political situation as well as the military situation with you. After speaking to him on the land line, I believe he would come to see you rather than asking you to come to him if he weren't so tied down right now. Things are happening very quickly. You can head down to Worland, check on your Dad, and leave for Cheyenne tomorrow. The Wind River Canyon is open, and the weather is supposed to hold for a couple of days."

Bradley stood up, didn't say anything, held out his hand which Captain Ferguson shook. He handed Bradley the money who accepted it, nodded affirmatively and left saying only "Thanks."

Bradley drove to south of Worland where he spent the night with his father. After a hearty breakfast, he drove his own vehicle down to Cheyenne. He checked into a motel outside Cheyenne using the name of Randy Gibson and paid cash for the room. The following morning he went to the Adjutant General's office at precisely 08:00. The secretary was opening the office door as he appeared, and he followed her in. He introduced himself. She immediately looked into her boss's office, knowing he had been there since 06:00. "General, Mr. Bradley is here to see you."

"Send the man in, Jean, send him in." The General stood up from behind his desk and strode over to Bradley as he entered the room. "Come on in Mr. Bradley, and have a seat. I'm John McIntire." The Major General pulled a chair up close to the lounge where he plopped down. "I'm sure glad to see you. We have all been hoping you would come in. Quite a few people figured you were dead out there in that country. You must be pretty good at field craft to survive that tough cold. You certainly don't look any the worse for the wear."

"Thank you General, I'm fine. What can I do for you? You paid me good money to pay you a visit."

"I don't know what you know and what you don't, so I'll start with the basics. First, the Governor has authorized me to offer you a Colonelcy in the Wyoming Army National Guard.

That will probably be upgraded to Brigadier General in the future, but it will do for right now. I will explain a few things to you so you will know where I'm coming from and what is happening. Things are moving very swiftly. Wyoming, Montana, probably North Dakota and South Dakota, are banding together as an autonomous region. Now, Alberta and Saskatchewan are also at the table talking, but there are things they don't like and we are hearing from them things we don't like, so I can't predict how or what their participation will be. You know Columbia formed an autonomous region and got away with it, being formally recognized by the federal government last year. We are trying to do the same.We are meeting stiff resistance however, from the federal government. They don't want to lose our agricultural production, our water, and what they consider federal land, which is eighty percent of the land in this state. There is a lot of federal land in the other states as well. They, the federal government that is, have other major problems, however, down south. With the flood of illegal Mexicans, and legal ones too, into the southwest over the last fifty years, the Mexicans are now the dominant force. Many if not most of them have NOT been acculturated into our Anglo type of western European society. Some of the third and fourth and now fifth generation Mexicans now still can't speak English because they stayed buried in their enclaves. The democratic politicians saw them as votes, republican politicians and employers saw them as cheap labor, and the Mexican government saw their immigration as a safety valve for their excess population. Everybody figured it was a good deal all around. Admittedly hard working and industrious, they still formed a very strong subculture. Nobody saw past them as individuals seeking a better life and economic opportunity, that political control was maintained by Mexican and Mexican-American politicians who used them as pawns for a power base. Those Mexican-American politicians, especially the Mexicans, encouraged them to maintain their cultural ties and ethnicity with Mexico while soaking up cash from our social welfare programs like Social Security, MEDICAID and MEDICARE, to which most of them never contributed. That's when the fireworks really started. When the administration cut back on MEDICAID AND MEDICARE a few years back because the government couldn't afford all of that socialized medicine, the immigrants felt it was owed to them. They really became politically active them. It was a motivating factor. They took over much of the system by working within the system, that is, the vote in the southwest. Those same politicians have formed a cabal with Mexican politicians and industrialists who are using them to gain access to American territory, wealth and other assets. The feds chose to ignore all the criminal activities; both organized and individually, associated with the immigration, especially the illegal aliens. They ignored the fact that many, if not most Anglos all along the border felt necessary to go armed most of the time in spite of laws to the contrary, simply for personal defense against robbery, rape and plain old physical assault for the fun of it. What we have done in the long term, is trade our northern European heritage for a Hispanic one.

These Mexican-American citizens, Mexicans really, are at the stage of open rebellion and warfare. The Chinese have armed these Mexicans in the barrios of our southwestern cities by the boatload. The feds found the Chinese were running arms shipments in through Mexico. Mexico passively supported it because they want the southwestern region back from us. They really covet the super port of San Diego. Mexico wants a repeal of the Treaty of Guadalupe of 1854; they are claiming land from central Texas to California and north to Colorado as part of Mexico, irredentism at its best. Irredentism, if you don't know the term, is making claims to territory based on historical ties to the land. If they owned land a thousand years ago, they claim it in the present. Obviously, the Palestinians are another example, just more recent that the Mexicans in our southwest.

Hell has broken out in some of the major cities. Mexican gangs out of East L.A. are taking over white neighborhoods all over the L.A greater metropolitan area. They are telling Anglos to get out and do it real quick, or they will be fertilizer in their own yards. Some of these gangs have had paramilitary training by Mexican and Chinese experts. It all seems to be coordinated. Congress repealed the Posse Commitatus Act of 1878 and all of its amendments last month which forbade the use of federal troops for domestic law enforcement purposes. That allows them to send the Army or any other branch of federal troops, including the Coast Guard, in even without a declaration of martial law. They're calling it civil disobedience rather than outright rebellion or secession. The Army is mobilizing to try and take back the streets and city of L.A. Same thing is happening in San Antonio. Houston is a mess; it's a tossup between the blacks and the Mexicans and the whites. That's a three ring battle down there. The Army isn't even going to try on that one. We figure the Army and the United States Marine Corps can't fight all along the border and southern cities and bother us up here at the same time. Some of those politicians intend to break the southwestern states away and either unite them with Mexico or set up an independent country with themselves as presidents.

Now, another unknown is how loyal individual members of the armed forces will be in this upcoming civil war. We hear reports that many are deserting. Most of the Regular Army is Hispanic and black, about forty percent each, and they are deserting in droves. National Guard and Army Reserve units composed primarily of Mexicans have seized Army Reserve and National Guard armories in a number of smaller cities and towns down south and in the southwest. Black Americans are rioting in Atlanta and a couple of other cities due to cessation of welfare checks.

While you were out in the bush, the Federal Government announced that it could no longer pay its debts; that the interest due on all its bonds and notes could not be met for

January. Foreign investment has been tapering off the last couple of years, dramatically this last year. Without that continued influx of foreign capitol to borrow, the government couldn't pay the interest on its financial instruments. Smart people were buying gold and silver numismatics when prices were low. Diamonds and jewels were less wise, because Joe Smith couldn't determine their value, and you have to buy retail and sell wholesale. Therefore, welfare payments of almost every kind will be greatly curtailed or eliminated. With fifteen percent unemployment at the national level, and so many dependent on government handouts, there was bound to be fireworks. Local police agencies of course are overwhelmed. A massive crime wave has already begun to sweep the country. The one bright spot out here is those Mormons in Utah and Nevada. They have driven all the Mexicans down to the southern most tip of Nevada, down around Las Vegas. Now there's a city in trouble. Man, the riots, looting, rapes and murders are occurring in broad daylight by the hundreds. The mayor down there just yesterday ordered the police to shoot on sight any perpetrators, announcing martial law to be in immediate effect. Looters were crashing the big hotels; guests were being assaulted in their rooms. Their security systems were simply overwhelmed. Most security guards wound up guarding the money, letting the guests fend for themselves. For a while, the police in a lot of cities borrowed the military's electromagnetic millimeter wavelength heat cannons for crowd control, but after a while they simply couldn't handle the crowds in the larger cities. Man, they sprayed the rioters with those cannon, and you should have seen the rioters dance. You know, it penetrates about one sixty-fourth of an inch of the skin with 130 degree heat. Makes them feel like they are on fire, but there were so many riots and so many rioters the police just gave up.

I just got back a couple of days ago from a meeting of States' Adjutants General in Minneapolis. National Guard units are being federalized by individual companies all over the country. Rioting isn't just limited to the south and southwest. Many of the larger cities in the north and east with large minority populations are experiencing such disturbances. Many of these National Guard companies are refusing to suppress the riots in their home states. Some company commanders have told their units that if you can't support the federal government, get out of uniform, making them sign resignations, or whatever documents they care to draft to cover their asses. Some Guardsmen reported to their armories, drew their weapons and disappeared into the population.

The Governor of Montana ordered all federal offices in the state closed two days ago. He enforced it with Montana National Guard troops in Billings. That is the proposed capitol of our new autonomous region. He ordered all the federal judges, federal marshals, FBI, Bureau of Alcohol, Tobacco, Firearms and Explosives (BATFE), Social Security, the Environmental Protection Agency and other bureaucrats to get out of town or go home and stay there. They no longer have any employment or authority in the state. The Governors of Wyoming and North Dakota have agreed to Billings being the capitol of the autonomous unit. State governments will remain at their current capitols, but they have expelled, or are expelling the feds there as we speak. We have determined that our National Guard units here in Wyoming, so far as we know, are loyal to the State and Governor of Wyoming. Same holds for Montana. Are you with me so far, Mr. Bradley?"

"How did Columbia manage to break away and make it stick? How did they manage to avoid invasion by federal troops to keep them in the Union?"

"The reasons are complex, but what it boils down to is that they are not completely independent. True, they have their own judicial system, law enforcement, education and other systems, all now independent of the federal government. They agreed to a mutual security pact for defense. All military installations remain in federal control with federal troops stationed there. Fort Lewis, the Navy and Air Force installations all remain so without a hiccup. The political philosophy of the great majority of the people there is similar to that of the east coast and southern California. They are the intelligentsia, the elitists, and the upper middle class and upper class liberals. A major part of the equation is money. They decided they wanted to keep more of their own money and quit supporting the lower class in the rest of the United States to a slice of the good life with such high taxes. The area is extremely rich in brains and money coming from Asia. Their autonomy was bought and paid for by the Chinese. British Columbia and Vancouver has been a toehold for the Chinese on this continent. The Chinese have been expanding south into the USA in this century. China and Japan have poured billions of dollars into the area, along with some of their brightest scientific talent. The Chinese in particular, have built and staffed with their best folks and the brightest American scientists that they could recruit, several state of the art research centers in physics, biology, and engineering. The region is rich in water, and could threaten southern California with shutting off the tap. Additionally, British Columbia is part of that ecological system and shares the liberal mentality, so invasion would have something of international repercussions. With the breakup of Canada, the U.S. didn't want to be seen as invading its northern neighbor, especially when the neighbor is enriching what was part of the U.S. Seattle is the center of Columbia, which is a financial, light industrial and research center all rolled into one. A lot of our Sierra Club types fled Wyoming for Seattle. They are welcome to them. A lot of southern Californians are also flooding into Columbia, which is beginning to cause Columbia some heartburn. That's their problem. A lot of our Mexican population has left Wyoming for parts south, like southern California.

The politicians from New England, New York, New Jersey and Massachusetts especially, don't understand what is going on or why. They can't conceive that much of the country wants to retain and live under, our Constitution and Bill of Rights as it was written. The welfare state has overwhelmed us, constantly growing ever larger since Franklin D. Roosevelt introduced it with his New Deal. Now the United States is bankrupt, financially, morally, and spiritually.

On a personal basis, Mr. Bradley, you don't have a job, your wife and her family has rejected you, as they are ensconced in Baltimore. Although that city is having its riots by its black citizens as well, your family is quite safe. You have no place to go, you have been out of engineering too long and are behind the power curve in your respective fields, but you are a superb soldier. I strongly urge you to accept this commission as a National Guard Colonel, Mr. Bradley. The pay is good, although not what you made as a Marine major; it is still quite satisfactory, all things considered. You will command a brigade of light infantry. Ordinarily, an infantry brigade as a Unit of Action would run around 3500 men. Yours will be as many men and women as you can recruit in your district. Your territory is the Big Horn Basin to include all of Park County and northwest Wyoming and Yellowstone Park. Historically, our combat unit here in Wyoming has been the 115th Field Artillery Brigade until we were reorganized in 2010 under the Army's Stryker Brigade concept. Your area of responsibility has several company sized units in combat, combat support and combat service support units that were assigned to support our single Wyoming Stryker Brigade. The muscle of our Brigade is in Stryker companies and battalions mostly headquartered on our prairie east of the Big Horn Mountains, in Casper, Sheridan and Gillette. You have engineering, medical, transportation, psychological operations, military police units and so on in your area. What we need now in your area are units trained in light infantry and mountain warfare and insurgency tactics. Our single Stryker

Brigade would be no match for a massive assault by the regular army. Your mission therefore, is to retrain and recruit for guerilla warfare, not only in your area, but for the whole state. Members from other units throughout the state will be attached to you for short periods for training. You must train to train others regardless of the environment they are in, mountains or prairie. If we are attacked, we will fall back into your area, the Big Horn Basin, and depend on you and yours for guidance and survival.

Your job then is to recruit, train, and lead an infantry brigade in the defense of our autonomous region. Your brigade will be as big as you can possibly recruit for it. What is left of the oil and gas fields are potential targets, as well as the irrigation systems that are left. We will try and equip you as best we can as light infantry. Heavy weapons will be something of a problem, but we will try to get you some heavy mortars, shoulder fired surface to air missiles, and crew served weapons. Armor is about to disappear anyway, but infantry fighting vehicles and trucks are something we are working on. They will be primarily dispersed among other regiments whose territory is our eastern prairie. Helicopter support for resupply and assault is an entirely different matter. In all honesty, it doesn't exist. What do you say?"

"What about the Native American population? Where do the Indians stand in this? The make up a significant portion of all of these states, Wyoming, Montana, North and South Dakota. There are several million of them. Will they stay with the U.S. federal government? Will they join us? What are, or will be, their demands? They are a sizable minority population in this proposed autonomous region of yours. I can see that they will quite likely demand complete control over what is now the reservations, and no white folks admitted. Hell, some of them would go back to living in teepees and expect the bison to return in sufficient numbers to return to the totally primitive life. There is still considerable animosity between some of the tribes!"

"The Indian question is an unknown. We do know that Native Americans from all of our involved states have held their own meetings, supposedly in secret, to hash that out. So far, we have not heard any kind of demands from them. I expect they haven't reached any kind of a consensus. They might be waiting to hear from us. You're right, in that they could be something of a fifth column for us. We'll have to wait and see."

"What about our Mexicans General, both those who have been here for years and generations, even centuries, and those seasonal migrants, legal and illegal? What do we do about them? Where do our American born Mexican-Americans stand? They are a big part of our Big Horn Basin population?"

"Mr. Bradley, I wish to God I could tell you. I think most of them are concerned they will be considered as foreigners, not supporting the autonomous position. Many who are American citizens get substantial welfare considerations, and they don't like losing it. I can't really give you any guidance there. There is no way to determine where they will collectively stand. I appreciate the position of those individuals who do support the autonomy movement, but fear wholesale violence against those of Mexican descent. You'll have to muddle through that one on your own."

"What will be your future role in all of this, General?"

"My position will remain the same. I'll be the Commander of the Wyoming National Guard Division, Brigade, really, of the new regional force, should our autonomous state become completely independent. It is much more likely that we will negotiate a defense treaty with the remains of the U.S., a mutual defense treaty with overarching strategic consequences. Secret discussions are occurring on that topic, among others. Nothing guaranteed, but that's probably the way it will fall out. Such an arrangement will have almost catastrophic consequences for U.S. foreign policy. It will almost certainly limit under what circumstances the U.S. can commit troops overseas. Under the proposed system all citizens of our autonomous unit are free to join the U.S. Armed Forces and serve under their command, officers and enlisted alike. By mutual agreement, such persons will be awarded dual citizenship and be subjected to the laws of the jurisdiction of their residence or place of their crime. They can't be prosecuted under both systems. That much we have already worked out."

"What General is your own personal philosophy, your political philosophy that drives you to this recourse?"

The general sighed, thought for a moment and replied. "The best I can do is to try and paraphrase Alex de Tocqueville. Democracy, like any other institution, has no inherent values of its own, but only what men make of it. A Republic in the hands of a benevolent government, a benevolent bureaucracy, serves the people. If the politicians and bureaucrats are primarily interested in their own entrenchment and enrichment, the people will suffer. Of course, it is the people's own fault for electing the politicians that create the bureaucracy, for becoming dependent on the government for their slice of the good life, for feeding at the public trough, for depending on the government for education, food, housing, medical care, jobs, transportation, and all other aspects of our society. There are those who blame multinational corporations and stockholders as insatiably greedy, and as displacing the state. It's been made worse by politicians who have surrendered so much of our national sovereignty to the United Nations and to whom we have sent so much of our money. That's it in a nutshell."

"What is your prediction for the outcome of all of this, General?"

"I can't say what will happen, how this movement will play out. Maybe Wyoming citizens will turn chicken at the last moment, but I don't think so. Perhaps it will be peaceful, but I don't think so. The politicians, the bureaucrats and their federal goons don't like losing part of their territory. It might be guerilla war, or a limited war or the heavy stuff might come out for a full blown conventional civil war, like the Balkans in the latter days of the last century. Much will depend on what military personnel do. If there are many like you, well, we stand a better chance."

"Who will be my immediate superior General? You?"

"You will be under my immediate command. We hope to have at least five other brigades like yours of no fixed size although that's probably a pipe dream. More likely they will be battalion sized, or perhaps slightly larger or smaller. One will be centered in Casper, one in Cheyenne, one in Gillette, in Laramie, in Sheridan and hopefully, one in Rock Springs, although that's pretty sparsely populated over there. We will accept anybody who is physically fit between the ages of seventeen and seventy into the militia. Right now the federal bureaucrats must feel assaulted from all sides. Riots in the cities is a result of failure to issue entitlement checks; sending federal troops in to quell the riots has resulted in mass desertions; bringing troops home from the Middle East to save money has destabilized the region and threatens our oil supply line by civil war in Saudi Arabia. Iran and Iraq are clashing all along their borders, the European Union is helpless and God knows what the Chinese are planning. Now the U.S. is breaking apart. They can't set priorities very well or very quickly. While we don't have a whole lot of energy left to export at least our autonomous region is self sufficient in oil, natural gas, cattle, grain and we control headwaters of the Missouri River system."

"Just how much leeway do I have in dealing with those who oppose our secession? As an active service member, what is my jurisdiction over civilians who resist our secession, short of martial law?"

"That's one question that has no resolution. If we are committed to secession we can't tolerate a fifth column in our midst. You'll have to decide that for yourself."

"I won't be prosecuted for whatever actions I take against the unionists, to use the civil war term?"

"Mr. Bradley, we are already in a civil war; the opening shots have been fired between federal police officers and several of our militia units. The only reason we haven't seen regular troops involved is because they are tied up in the cities and along the border. I can only quote old Ben Franklin when he said 'Victory gives the winners the right to hang the losers.' Running battles have occurred between platoon sized units of the BATFE and FBI in Cheyenne, Sheridan, Great Falls, and Billings. The feds have kept that pretty quiet. As we speak, federal offices are being closed and their officers are moving out under a window of amnesty. That window closes in a week. My personal opinion is that after that window closes, any unionist agitator is fair game. Of course, my opinion isn't worth a damn in any court, but this is civil war. I guess it really depends on who wins. My opinion is that you have authority to promote, demote, or even execute proven traitors if you feel it is critical for our autonomous unit to succeed. Of course, a trial would look more legal to future idealists of the ACLU persuasion."

"By traitors you mean people loyal to the federal government, General?"

"By traitors I mean people who swear allegiance to our autonomous state, which we have yet to name, who don the uniform of our autonomous unit guard, yet have fealty to the federal government. It does not include citizens who are sitting on the fence. Historians have estimated that in our Revolutionary War of 1776, about one third of the citizenry was patriots, one third Tories and one third fence sitters. We have to dispose of the Tories and keep a careful watch on the fence sitters. Tories, with the approval of the British murdered numerous patriots throughout the time of the Revolutionary War. One reference states an estimate 10,000 American patriots died of disease, starvation, brutality and exposure in the hold of the prisoner of war ship named the Jersey anchored off New York City."

"How do we deal with the Tories that we know about now, General?"

The Major General looked Bradley in the eye, and coolly responded, "Either we drive them out or we kill them. We have no means to incarcerate them and we can't have a fifth column in our midst."

"Now, Mr. Bradley, what is your take on our ability to defend ourselves and possibly our new nation?"

"The concept of distributed operations should really be termed disbursed operations. That is the strategy they will probably attempt to employ. Early in this century the concept came into being because of inadequate military manpower. Small teams of a few elite soldiers widely scattered over large areas relying on information technology won't work against us if we are capable. Nobody gave any thought to the possibility that a highly technological and competent enemy could counter their satellite and computer and radio communications. The teams are supposed to call in air strikes by unmanned aerial vehicles, manned aircraft or missiles. Well, they found out otherwise. These teams can be located when they communicate by satellite. Their radio beams were easily pinpointed and artillery was laid on them. Disbursed operations didn't work well in Military Operations in Urban Terrain- MOUT- either. We didn't have enough guys who could immerse in foreign cultures in the cities. They learned they appropriate language but not the nuances of the culture. Consequently they were soon identified and compromised. Most of them were tortured until they couldn't reveal any more information. They were usually killed in hideous ways when they were no longer thought to have any value. The

Muslims committed the coup de grace by cutting off their genitals, stuffing them in their mouths and taping their mouths shut. If they didn't die in shock they suffocated. They were then decapitated and their heads left where they were easily found by other soldiers. Dispersed operations work okay in the third world armies out in the boonies, where company sized and larger formations could be targeted. Where the so-called enemy melted into the civilian population and couldn't be identified. Distributed operations were useless. The liberals wouldn't buy into the real life fact that in a hostile culture there were no neutral civilians. In those situations every man, woman and child is an enemy soldier, at least a potential one. I lost several men in Africa to grenade carrying kids too small to carry a rifle. Some of them were girls as young as nine or ten. When people live in great fear, it is easy to control the great majority them. So, I think given the military situation of the U.S. forces today, that is what we will face. If we are technologically capable, we can certainly make them bleed and think."

"Will you take the job, Mr. Bradley?"

Bradley looked the two star general in the eye, and said, "I'll take the job."

CHAPTER 4

TWENTY YEARS EARLIER ANOTHER MEETING HAD OCCURRED. "General Chang, Mao Lin, Your strategy, while not a complete success was so overwhelmingly positive that you are awarded the Hero of the Peoples Republic of China medal. Your grandiose plan gave us the oil of the Central Asian Republics, expanded our arable land to feed our people, gave us potable water, new homes for our population, natural resources we so desperately needed, and a chance to reduce our pollution and attempt to reverse the environmental decline we have suffered for so long. It came so close to succeeding in its entirety. Only the meddling of the United States prevented us from establishing almost complete world hegemony through the control of natural resources. Yet your plan was so favorably disposed that we made enormous gains in territory, energy and mineral resources. It placed us on a par with the United States on the world stage. Your brilliance cannot be lauded enough. Now you come to us with a concrete proposal whose details you have heretofore retained exclusively to yourself. This General Security Council will listen for your next grand strategic plan with eagerness."

"Thank you, Mr. Chairman. Yes, we have accomplished a great deal, yet there is more that we can accomplish. I submit to you a long range plan. We cannot defeat the United States militarily at this time, but we can encourage The United States to defeat itself over a span of time, perhaps a generation, perhaps more, perhaps less. This can be accomplished by the orchestration of a variety of means."

"Tell us your thoughts, General Chang."

"The United States is a very large country. All is not well in North America. Quebec set the example by declaring independence, followed by the Canadian Maritime Provinces. We can encourage significant internal dissent by a variety of means within the United States. The U.S. is, and has always been, a heterogeneous population. Until the last few decades however, the ruling culture was that of the northern European immigrants. That is to say, what they call the WASPs, or White, Anglo-Saxon, Protestant culture. Now that culture is being challenged. Mexico has long strived for unification of the two countries. The influence of the Latino culture is massive and growing. We can encourage and support that challenge in a variety of ways.

Add to this the unrest of the Black American community. They feel squeezed out by the Latinos who have a stronger work ethic and compete with them for lesser skilled jobs. They are equally if not more so more prone to violence than the Latinos. The Black American family is essentially an anachronism. So many children are born out of wedlock, are raised in single parent families, lack an adequate father figure, are into drugs, teenage sex, lack adequate education and training in a marketable skill, relying on welfare for economic support, and have little hope for the future. This community can be exploited and encouraged towards violence more than the Latino community. We should finance and encourage their feelings of inadequacy, of second class citizenship, of discrimination, all the fault of the WASPs and not of their own doing.

We can highlight disparities, foment racial disorders, employ various economic tools and means to infiltrate their education system. We do not have to employ violence. Rather, we can seek to have them attack and destroy themselves, even by violent means. Class enmity will be the result, and it could be very violent. We encourage racial and cultural diversity; we support anti-firearms groups in order to disarm all but the criminals and make criminals out of those who do not surrender their firearms to the police; we bribe their politicians to support our plans without them knowing it; we encourage gang activity in all the various cultures, particularly in the sale of illegal drugs to support themselves which will also support our opium trade; and finally encourage the appointment of federal judges who share our views to legitimize our desires.

We already possess trillions of U.S. dollars in the form of their financial instruments. The current administration is acutely aware of the sensitivity of the issue. Therefore we should not play this card, but hold it in reserve until such time as other tools can be brought to bear. Multiple pressures, that is means, simultaneously applied, are synergistic whereas when they are forced one at a time, they are much more easily dealt with as independent issues.

Who knows where it will stop, if it stops at all. We must be very selective in our choice of agents, both our own and those we recruit in North America. Of our own provocateurs, we must choose those who will not succumb to western ways. Our Chinese agents must very carefully inculcate the love of Mother China in their children, so that as native born Chinese-Americans their loyalty will always remain with their native homeland of China. Americans we recruit as agents must have a deep abiding feeling of inadequacy, of persecution, and essentially hatred toward their society. While our goal is to cause the deterioration of the U.S. to military and political impotence on the world stage, it could conceivable go even further. If my proposed plan will succeed beyond our wildest dreams, the USA could fracture into regional entities, perhaps complete break apart."

CHAPTER 5

"Deon, here's five hundred dollars. I want you to go flying tomorrow," stated Jean Toussaint.

"Where do you want me to fly to, Colonel?" asked Deon Johnson. Deon Johnson was a trusted lieutenant of Jean Toussaint's.

"I want you to fly over the millionaire's village, that D'Arcy Estates that is about twenty miles northeast of here. Rent a plane tomorrow for a private flight from the usual company. Tell the flight service you are taking photos for advertising purposes. You wish to illustrate the enormity, security and recreational advantages of the estates. Take a camera, and get me some good pictures. I want pictures that show the entire layout, the whole clover leaf, and pictures of each individual leaf. Get some pictures at different altitudes and directions. Take a notebook and record what you photograph. Don't screw it up."

Jean Toussaint liked to be referred to as "The Colonel" although he never rose above the rank of Sergeant E-6 while in the U.S. Army. Born to immigrant Jamaican parents, he joined a street gang at the age of eleven. He proved to be quick witted, intelligent, observant, athletic and willing to follow orders without question. He was smart enough to remain in high school long enough to graduate. By the time he was eighteen he ran the equivalent of a squad of the gang.

The gang was composed primarily of Jamaicans and Haitians, although blacks from other Caribbean and South American countries were welcome. The makeup of the gang simply reflected the makeup of the neighborhood. Some members were also descendents of slaves brought to North American in the nineteenth century. The gang was commanded by a thirty five year old Jamaican who had founded the gang fifteen years ago as the result of a knife fight. He killed the leader and assumed the leadership. When he was eighteen and the week after his high school graduation, Jean Toussaint was ordered to join the Army to acquire military skills. He did well in the Army, in four years rising to squad leader. He attended as many Army training courses as he could, went through Airborne School at Fort Benning, GA and earned his paratrooper's wings. He re-enlisted for another three years. He volunteered for Ranger School, but was washed out after the second week of the jungle warfare training phase. When he completed his second tour he was a Staff Sergeant, grade of E-6. He returned to his ghetto roots in Baltimore's inner city where he quickly assumed the role of a lieutenant of the gang leader who had ordered him into military service. After two years of serving in this role, Jean Toussaint simply walked behind the gang leader sitting at the table while he was conducting a meeting and blew the man's brains out. Jean Toussaint then simply announced that he was the new leader. Were there any questions?

Now, ten years later he commanded a gang that really amounted to a small army. Under his leadership the organization expanded to over eight hundred members. They seized control of a larger section of the ghetto by eliminating the leadership of a smaller gang and either killing or co-opting its remaining members. Toussaint organized the gang along military lines. It approached a battalion in size and organization and continued with unabated growth. Astutely, Toussaint established a working relationship with the U.S. Congressman from the district, in effect, becoming a private army for the Congressman. Anyone who didn't vote for the Congressman could be severely hurt. At age thirty-seven, Jean Toussaint became a well dressed man who began to cultivate the necessary polish of a business man himself. He never married. He considered a family a liability. Instead, he more or less had his choice of women, either voluntarily or involuntarily. He established a system of brothels that utilized white slaves, mostly women imported from Eastern Europe and forced into prostitution, which he visited rather routinely, both to sample the girls and to insure that all was running smoothly. Any pimp or madam with their hand in the till found their hand, head or other part of their anatomy removed from their body.

Shortly after returning to Baltimore Toussaint was stopped for a routine traffic violation by a rookie state police officer just outside the Baltimore city limits. In reaching for his driver's license his sport coat flared open revealing that he was carrying a concealed handgun in a shoulder holster. He was arrested on the spot and taken to the county jail where he was booked. For his one phone call, he picked Nelson Bartlett out of the phone book as the attorney to represent him. Nelson Bartlett had a few private words with the judge who was a law school classmate, left a five thousand dollar bribe on the judge's desk, and confidently represented Jean Toussaint in court. The judge sentenced Jean Toussaint to sixty days probation. Thereafter, Jean Toussaint traveled with two bodyguards, who were gang members that purchased licenses to be private investigators licensed to carry firearms. Toussaint retained Nelson Bartlett as his attorney thereafter.

Juan Cartagena moved into the Big Horn basin five years before Ethan resigned from the Marine Corps. His assignment by the Director of the National Farm Workers of America was to integrate himself into the Big Horn Basin. It was part of a long range plan of the National Farm Workers of America. The NFWA was centered in the San Joaquin Valley of California and was a powerful political organization with a hidden agenda. Its mission was not only to insure access to all social welfare programs for Mexican-Americans and Mexicans in the United States, legal and illegal, but also to foment political dissatisfaction. Their ultimate goal initially was the unification of California with Mexico. Over the years the leaders realized that they were thinking too small. Their dream gradually expanded to include much of the southwest, extending north into Colorado, Utah and southern Wyoming. Money was funneled through a series of bank transfers from the National Bank of Mexico and private donations to hide their original source by China into the NFWA coffers.

Cartagena was either sent a money order from the NFWA each month to insure that he had adequate funds for his mission or a courier delivered larger sums. On occasion, the funds were used to provide bribes to local officials. It was a long term assignment. He took his wife and four children who provided the usual picture of another Hispanic farm worker moving into the area. He slowly established himself as a congenial, hard working Mexican-American. He was in fact, an illegal alien by virtue of having crossed the Arizona border as a ten year old boy with his parents. He never applied for citizenship, electing to remain an illegal alien. He had no difficulty in acquiring four years of college through the use of forged papers. He attended a junior college for two years and then moved to a small state sponsored university where he majored in political science and psychology. It was there that the met the woman who was to become his wife. Juanita was an American born Mexican-American. She shared his passion for Mexican nationalism and of a dream of a new Mexican state in the southern United States. He became an organizer for the NFWA after graduation. It was the only employment he could find where he could apply his education. Over the course of the years as a NWFA organizer in California, he honed his people skills to a fine edge. His persuasive skills were unsurpassed. Over the next fifteen years, he and Juanita had four children. He made sure his children were well behaved and did well in school. When they misbehaved, he did not spare their rear ends from a two inch leather belt. His wife was a true partner in his mission for NFWA. He slowly became a leader in the local community in Hot Springs County, even running for a seat on the county commissioners. He lost by only a narrow margin of a few votes. Quietly, without any fanfare to draw attention to his real activities, he built an underground organization, one or two individuals at a time. In effect, he created a cell centered on himself. It was a cadre that quietly supported agitation for political independence, although they publicly espoused multi-culturalism and respect for Hispanics through peaceful means. They were to support the political re-alignment movement of the southwest by political activities. Surreptitiously, they prepared to use violent means should it become necessary. The members were provided a means to acquiring firearms through an underground system. The criminal community, in effect the Mexican gangs of southern California and the Chinese together assured a ready supply of AK-47s to any Hispanic who wished to possess one. Hugo Chavez of Venezuela readily supplied them at cost from the factory he purchased from Vladimir Putin of Russia in 2005. Each assault rifle came with half a dozen magazines and a thousand rounds of ammunition. A second generation Mexican-American farmer was provided funds by NWFA to purchase both good farmland and desert scrub. The farmer believed in the cause and now owned a dozen sections of land, each section being a square mile, including several in the badlands that provided a training ground and rifle range for their practice.

Over the last four years, Cartagena began to slowly inculcate contempt for the Anglos of the Basin. He began a subtle campaign to discredit Anglo teachers in the public school system. He had Hispanic parents teach their children disrespect in the classroom by making derogatory comments about Anglo teachers at every opportunity, classifying them as racists. Parents in his organization who had school children attended teacher-parent meetings with the intent to harangue the teachers, accusing them of racism and favoritism and incompetence. This was a technique pioneered in Title 1 high schools in southern California in the early days of the twenty-first century. The students were encouraged to call their women teachers "puta" or whores, to assault their teachers when they didn't give them good grades gratis, or to trash the cars of their teachers who attempted to instill some form of classroom discipline. Food fights became common in the cafeterias. Food was of course provided free, that is, at tax payers' expense, with full meals at breakfast and lunch. Vandalism was at a devastatingly high level. The students put graffiti in Spanish everywhere, on the walls of the classrooms, the halls and even the floors of the gymnasium. The graffiti often reflected Mexican culture, such as "Viva Villa", or lewd comments about individual teachers or other ethnic groups, particularly whites, such as "Gringos eat shit". Every pregnant fourteen year old girl was looked upon as providing another vote, another increase in the family welfare check.

Cartagena began to encourage increased migration of illegal Mexicans into the Big Horn Basin. The increased population was to provide more political force and above all, more soldiers if required.

CHAPTER 6

"THERE IS BUT ONE SOURCE TO ALL OF YOUR TROUBLES, O ATHENIANS, AND THAT IS THAT YOU HAVE CEASED TO BE SOLDIERS." DEMOSTHENES

"Comrade General Chang, Wi Lang, we have found some of your proposals regarding the United States most interesting. One in particular shows much ingenuity. Our geologists tell us General, that your proposal to sink a nuclear bomb in Yellowstone Lake in Yellowstone National Park is most interesting. As an active volcano, with the lake filling the caldera, it would initiate a major volcanic eruption. Unfortunately, our geologists tell us that it might initiate a super eruption. While that could conceivably destroy half the United States, the world as a whole would suffer as a major ecological catastrophe. Such a catastrophic eruption might possibly result in the equivalent of a nuclear winter lasting several years through the magnitude of the billions of tons of dust and ash that would circle the globe reducing the sunlight equivalent to an arctic winter lasting for perhaps decades. No General, the Security Council rejects the novel but extremely interesting proposal.

Your father's first grand master plan twenty years ago was much more of a success than a failure. Almost all of the objectives were achieved with relatively minimal cost, considering the gains made. He realized at that time, twenty years ago, that we could not defeat the United States militarily, but we could encourage it to defeat itself over time, perhaps a generation, perhaps more, perhaps less. His plan to do so appears to have accomplished much of this. With the current state of world affairs, and internal turmoil of the United States, the opportunity for further gains according to your father's last plan has arrived. We lament his passing. Now, we recognize that you have inherited your father's brilliance in advancing his grand strategy. What have you to say?"

"Thank you Comrade Commissar, your praise to much too gracious. I did little to accomplish so much. It was a combination of your authority, of your building and allocating the resources, and the splendid performance of our agents in the United States over these last years. As this body so wisely determined, further expansion and completion of my father's first plan in the face of American and Japanese aggression would have cost us dearly. Now patience has awarded us with another opportunity, perhaps as much or more, that can be gained at minimal cost.

In this basic plan, we will assume strategic control of much of the Middle East's oil, reduce the truculent population to manageable numbers, eliminate the United States as a competitor and gain even greater control over the world's economy. Since our negotiations with the Iranians have dragged on over the years without favorable results, I will reveal my plan to you."

Maria returned the dinner to the kitchen. The customer at the Ram's Horn cafe got up and left in disgust.

"Maria that is the second dinner order you have screwed up this week and it's only Wednesday. For some months now you have been more and more distracted. I've seen it coming. You are not concentrating. You're more and more nervous. Something is terribly upsetting you. What's wrong? Has Tomas found another woman, or what? I don't want to lose a good waitress. You have been here for what, four or five years now? So what is going on?"

"No Jan, at first I thought it was another woman, but it is not. It is a cause."

Maria sagged into the chair in the now empty Big Horn Café and put her elbows on the table and her head in her hands.

"That labor organizer from California; he is here to cause trouble. Tomas goes to their house for meetings. He's been going for months. I think this man is a violent man. I think people have disappeared because of him. He talks crazy. He tells Tomas and the others that they are only campesinos here, that they should own the land together. He talks of a commune or communes. He talks not of buying land but of seizing it from rich farmers and ranchers. Tomas is beginning to believe it. He tells the men that the children should be taught in Spanish in the schools, that the white teachers are stupid and not qualified to teach. He says we should teach the children at home. The teachers lie about history, he says. Much of the USA from Florida to California belongs to Mexico, but the Gringos took it away from our fathers by force. He says he has guns for us, for us to defend ourselves against the Yankees when the time comes to drive them out. He tells the men not to worry. He will teach them how to use these rifles when the time comes. The time is very near, he says. Some of the men believe him. Tomas said many of the men are bringing their wives to the meetings. He wants me to go too. I think Tomas is beginning to believe him. We must not fight amongst our selves, the Hispanics, but be ready to fight the Gringos. We see things happening on television. We see people hurting and killing and burning because they are different. The government can't seem to stop it. Many say it will get worse, that there will be a civil war. What do you think Jan? If violence comes, what should we do? Where would we go? We have been here for fourteen years. We are citizens under the amnesty system, but we are not part of the bigger community. Rumors say and I believe them that he killed Jorge Robas last year or had him killed for repeatedly disagreeing with him. Jorge just disappeared. I think he made Jorge's wife testify that Jorge just ran away by saying he would kill the children if she did not. What should I do Jan?"

Jan put her arm around Maria's shoulders and gave her a big hug.

"I think you should go to the meetings with your husband Tomas. You should listen and think and learn exactly what it is that this man Cartagena wants. Why is he trying to do this? What will be his job or position if everything goes his way? Find out if Gringos are welcome to come to the meetings. I would like to hear myself. Don't ask right away. Go to a number of meeting first. Go until you are comfortable at the meetings and are accepted. There might be much truth in what he says. You will have to decide for yourself. Frankly, so many wonderful, hard working Americans are Hispanics, are of Hispanic origin. It is true some Hispanic families have been in North America for over four hundred years. Between now and then however, quit costing us money and customers. Be your old friendly self, no more wrong orders. Everything will be all right in the long term. Good people will not turn on good people regardless of their ethnicity or religion. This is not Nazi Germany."

The Chinese Ambassador to Mexico bowed low at the waist. He thrust out his hand as a broad smile crossed his face. "It is so pleasant to meet you again, Mr. President. I thank you for taking the time from your busy schedule to see me. I have directions from the Government of the Peoples Republic of China to put forth a proposal. I think you will find it personally and publicly most agreeable."

"The pleasure is mine, Mr. Ambassador, won't you please be seated. Tea or coffee, Sir, and my Secretary will serve us."

As their tea was served and as they sipped it, the Chinese ambassador made small talk for a few moments to put the Mexican President at ease. When he sat down his empty cup he stated "My government has authorized me to negotiate with you for a greater percentage of your oil production. We will pay ten U.S. dollars a barrel over the top of the daily market price for all of the crude oil you supply us. Alternatively, if you prefer, we will pay in gold at the market price rather than dollars. Now, three of those dollars will be paid directly to your favorite charity, one dollar to the favorite charity of your oil minister, and the other six will be publicly accountable, payable to the National Treasury of Mexico. Of course, there will be separate methods of payment. We pay in cash and will deliver to whatever accounts you specify on a weekly basis. We will load our tankers at Vera Cruz for the Caribbean production and ship through the Panama Canal. From the Pacific side, we will load from Mazatlan or any other port you designate. We will purchase as much oil as you are willing to sell us without arousing any suspicions. We wish to keep our agreement secret for as long as possible in order neither to disturb the world oil market nor to alert your northern neighbor of our purchase. If at some future date you wish to expand our agreement to include refined products, particularly gasoline, my government would look forward to such an arrangement. We do ask for one small concession in return. That simply, we are allowed to establish an import company on your border with your northern neighbor for the importation of our line of agricultural machinery. We believe we can offer a quality line of agricultural equipment at a substantial savings over other brands. We won't need very much, just a single modestly sized warehouse, perhaps a hectare of land all total. That will include the sales area, parking lot and the warehouse itself."

"Mr. Ambassador, I am absolutely positive that we can do business."

Bradley drove back to his father's home, arriving after dark. He unloaded his truck and entered through the garage which served as a mud room.

Robert Bradley was happy to see his son. Ethan grinned at his Dad, and said, "I took the job. It's Colonel Bradley now, of the Wyoming National Guard. Don't know what the pay is, but I don't care. I have most of north central Wyoming as my Area of Operations."

"Congratulations, Colonel. I was hoping you would take the job. Come quick and watch CNN, the Communist News Network. There are riots all over in the east coast cities. People are going hungry. Food isn't being brought into the cities, and the food stores have all been looted. Lots of fires are burning, too. Stupid bastards, burn down everything, even their own homes and stores. This is in Atlanta. Look at this! Hey, that reporter just got shot on camera! This is a live broadcast; now they got the cameraman too, unless he dived to the ground. He is down as well, but look the camera is still running. Man, look at those ghetto dwellers run. Where are the police and Army to control this? I'll bet the Army is guarding DC to protect those sorry ass bureaucrats. They should be guarding the people in their homes, not government buildings and their business hour inhabitants."

The television broadcast switched to Richmond, where the Governor of Virginia was holding a press conference. He declared that any and all citizens who used deadly force to defend their lives, their families and their properties against rioters and looters would not be prosecuted. Some smart ass reported asked, "Do you mean you won't prosecute anybody who shoots a looter? Who has any guns anyway?"

The Governor looked directly at the reporter and responded, "Any means of deadly force can be employed to protect yourself and your loved ones. If anyone is still fortunate enough to possess firearms and elect to use them for self defense, so be it."

The Central News Network colloquially called the Communist News Network, commentator then cut in with "Our helicopter is broadcasting live over New York City now showing multiple fires in Harlem. Several districts lost power and gas services earlier today with the consequence that people are cold as well as hungry. The Northeast Power Consortium spokesman stated that power will be restored within twenty-four hours. Power loss was due to a fire at a major substation."

Robert Bradley turned off the television and started for the kitchen to prepare their supper. "I can remember your Grandad predicting all of this around the turn of the century. I didn't want to believe him, and most people scoffed at him. Then, it became more and more obvious that he was right. I was reading Alexandr Solzhenitsyn's The Gulag Archipelago last night. God, what the Soviet people suffered. He asks a critical question with at what point to you begin to resist tyranny? Where do you draw the line? How do you resist it, passively and actively? We, like the Soviets were, are a nation of sheep, of wimps, for the most part. Like Solzhenitsyn said, we got what we deserved because we didn't love our freedom enough to stand up and fight for it. I think we are, or were anyway, headed in that totalitarian direction. Patriotism should not be considered or confused as or with loyalty to the state. Now with this new civil war brewing, we might be able to head it off. There are enough patriots left who drew the line at firearms confiscation. Your Grandad predicted our economic downfall would be a major factor. We continually overspent our budget, always borrowing more money in the form of issuing bonds and Treasury Bills and printing more worthless paper money in the form of Federal Reserve Notes. Most of those were brought by the Chinese. I remember we borrowed 600 billion dollars in the year 2003. Now we can't pay the interest on them. We're financially bankrupt. Just like the Weimar Republic of Germany after World War I."

"What about food supplies out here, Dad? What do you have in stock? Will you make it through the winter?"

Robert Bradley smiled at his son as he started peeling potatoes. "Son, I put up plenty of supplies, somewhere between one and two years' worth of staples. You know rice and beans in combination, any kind of bean, make more or less a complete protein. By complete protein I mean one which has all the essential amino acids in sufficient quantities for the human species. I always keep a hundred pounds each of rice, beans, flour, sugar, canned fruit, canned meat, dried potatoes as well as fresh ones, tea and coffee in stock in five pound packages. I grow many of my own vegetables. I just date and rotate my stock as a matter of routine. Lots of people now have their own gardens out here. Apples are the only fruit trees that grow in this climate, so lots of people planted them and make apple sauce for their winter fruit and vitamin C. I have fifty some odd quarts stored in the basement. In spite of the short hunting seasons, I always get two deer and can them in quart jars in barbeque sauce. I can always manage to afford half a beef if I want it, and this fall I bought a nice 220 pound pig from a local farmer and had it custom slaughtered. We're having pork steaks, mashed potatoes, cauliflower, and apple sauce for supper and brownies with ice cream for dessert. After that, I think a snort or two of brandy is indicated. Oh yeah, I always keep at least a case of spirits on hand. I learned that from your Grandfather. One other thing. A friend who is an electronics type, swept the house for bugs for me after the feds were here looking for you. He found one. It was the telephone. It was acting as an open microphone even when the receiver was in the cradle. We took care of that, in-house and outside, so to speak. He also swept the truck and found a bug in the radio. We can converse in complete security now."

After supper Robert Bradley poured them each a brandy in a snifter, then disappeared for a few minutes. When he returned, he handed Ethan a Government Model 1911A1 stainless steel .45 ACP. "It was your grandfather's Springfield

Armory .45 ACP. When the agents came to take my guns, they took them, but they didn't get very far. Ten miles out of town those agents met with a bad accident. I have recovered my collection, and now I have both your Grandad's and mine. You can have what you want from them whenever you decide what your needs are. Here's a Kydex concealment holster for the .45 for civilian dress, a shoulder holster if you want to wear it under your military tunic and an issue holster for your pistol belt. Here's a concealment magazine carrier with two extra magazines. They're loaded, as is the one in the gun. It is in condition three though, none in the chamber."

That evening Ethan Bradley removed the U.S. insignia and the major's gold leaf as his badge of rank from his Marine uniforms. His father handed him his old Velcro eagles as his new badge of rank. Ethan gratefully accepted them and velcroed one on the collar of his tunic and one on his field jacket.

"I got an ear full on the Mexican-American population from the Adjutant General today, Dad. What's your take on the problem with the Mexicans, anyway? Hell, they have been the agricultural labor force and the dirty job workers that the welfare sucking scum won't take."

Robert Bradley nodded slowly, "my problems with the Mexicans are several. They have changed, and continue to change the cultural makeup of this country. The U.S. now is damned near fifty percent Hispanic, mostly Mexican. We didn't shut the gates fifty years ago when it was a hot button issue. Now, our Anglo Protestant citizens can't stomach the Latin Roman Catholic cultural influence such as lack of birth control. That's another element in this catastrophe. The Mexicans are demanding dominance of their culture in values and religion, and the WASPS don't want to relinquish their power and become culturally subservient. I admit that most of them have a good work ethic, better than the welfare sucking scum as you call them. That doesn't change the fact though, that they are taking over the political machinery entirely through legal, legitimate means. That means they are drawing more and more out of the social welfare programs, running them down. We can't afford that. Their Hispanic criminal gangs are more vicious than the Chinese tongs or the Vietnamese gangs of the last decades of the last century. They rule the drug trade. There is little difference between the Mexicans and the so-called Native Americans anyway, at least genetically speaking. They all came from Northeast Asian stock across the Bering Strait twenty thousand years ago to settle the Americas, maybe in one wave, or maybe in several over several millennia. It doesn't really matter. They are really all Native Americans. The biggest single difference between Mexicans and so-called Native Americans is the greater infusion of European Spanish blood in the Mexicans. And that only had a two hundred year head start on the infusion of French and British blood on North American natives, at the max. Hell, disease got ninety percent of all Native Americans anyway. Mexicans just don't believe in birth control and have multiplied like rabbits. Don't misunderstand me; their influence hasn't been all bad. Many have a sense of family, of loyalty to their family that much of our Anglo and African-American populations lost years ago.

No, anybody who has any affluence at all today lives in a gated community or an apartment building or complex secured by private security personnel. Many of these guards are now well trained and armed. The better ones don't use rent-a-cops made up of newly arrived immigrants the way they used to. The middle of the middle class is struggling to maintain that, having to send their kids to private schools for a halfway decent education. With mom and dad both working for that , the security of that gated community and private school for their kids, the kids are pretty much left on their own, to their own devices which all too often means recreational drug use. That's the start down the tubes. Hell, better than half the members of both houses of Congress today use recreational drugs for that matter."

The next morning Ethan walked into the National Guard Armory in Worland, Wyoming. The Staff Duty Noncommissioned Officer recognized him from his picture, stood up and saluted him as he approached. Bradley smiled and returned the salute.

"Sergeant Thompkins, I'm Colonel Bradley of the Wyoming National Guard. I am taking command of all units in northwest Wyoming. Get out your pencil and notepad. We're going to make a list. The first thing I want you to do is to call a meeting for 11:00 hours on the morning of 10 January for all National Guard officers and Noncommissioned Officers (NCOs) at and above the rank of E-6. I presume we have a list of all of those units, their staffs, and phone and fax numbers?"

"Yes Sir, we sure do." "Excellent. Send a fax announcing the meeting here at Worland Armory and follow-up with a phone call to each unit. Then get me the personnel files on every individual in this unit. Then call Captain Ferguson and inform him of the meeting here so you two can make the appropriate arrangements for it. I will make Worland my office because of its central location. Therefore I will require an office for myself and my NCO. Then I want to discuss our communications system with our communications officer, or if we don't have an officer, your best communications NCO. I'll spring for coffee and donuts for the meeting on the 10th, but for lunch everyone is on their own. What bakery or donut shop makes the best donuts in this town?"

"The Krispy Kreme shop undoubtedly has the best donuts Sir. Have you seen yesterday's Cody paper, Sir? You are in it again." Sergeant Thompkins handed the paper to Bradley.

"Why should I be in Cody's paper, especially again, Sergeant?"

"Well Sir, they have been running stories about you off and on. According to them you're some kind of brigand. I don't know where they get their information, but they have been demonizing you for several weeks. It sounds like they have somebody, some point of contact in the Pentagon that doesn't like you, feeding them a lot of information. You are supposed to be a blood thirsty, rapist murderer, killing lots of innocent people to hide your crimes."

Bradley opened the paper and began to read. The story covered his duty in Africa. According to the paper, he and his men pillaged, plundered and raped their way across central Africa. Bradley thought to himself, *"I wonder if this crap came from my old battalion commander over there. That perpetually drunk SOB wouldn't even get out in the bush himself. He didn't give a rat's ass about the battalion or anybody in it. I don't know why he would do this, if indeed he is the source. He was a pretty weak character, not like a real Marine. Somebody higher up must be putting pressure on him."* Bradley threw down the paper in disgust and shook his head. I'll have to do something about that later. "Now, let's get on with business."

Bradley set up a folding table outside the Staff Duty NCO's office as a temporary desk. After reviewing all the personnel files in the unit, he set aside those of the NCOs at the grade of E-6, Staff Sergeant.

Promptly at 11:00 hours on 10 January, Captain Ferguson, Commander of Charlie Battery, Wyoming National Guard called the meeting to attention. Everyone stood at attention while Captain Ferguson simply said, "Colonel Ethan Bradley, Commander, The First Brigade, The Basin Brigade, of the Wyoming National Guard."

Bradley took the podium and spoke. "Be seated. First, we will dispense with a few basic rules. I do not care to be saluted indoors or out except when you report to me for the first time indoors. I don't care to be a sniper's target. Officers, it is up to you whether or not you choose to be saluted within your own units. Second, I expect appropriate military punctuality. Third, if you disagree with me, say so. If you think you have a better idea, speak out. I don't like sycophants or obsequiousness and will not tolerate it in subordinates. Fourth, I am not a micromanager. I do not like being micromanaged and I do not recommend my subordinates practice it. I prefer to see initiative within established guidelines. If you or your subordinates wish to go outside those guidelines, consult your chain of command. Fifth, I expect each and every one of you to be tactically competent. If you are not, you are hereby on notice that you better drill and practice until you are. We have a very short time span to achieve that goal. If you are not, when the time comes, I will relieve you of your command. Tactical competence will be your highest priority. We are to be a light infantry brigade and specialists for guerilla warfare for this environment and to act as trainers for other units in guerilla tactics. I expect every soldier to be an accomplished marksman. Every infantryman should be able to engage the enemy at three hundred meters with their individual rifle. As yet I do not know the extent of resources which I can provide you. Until then, you will have to practice the old Army adage of do the best you can with what you have. Utilize the training videos during the week. Spend the weekends in the field honing your skills. We will never have all the resources we desire. Time is a precious resource ladies and gentlemen, don't waste it.

Heavy weapons are another question. We do have two reserve artillery units as you know. Two batteries of the venerable 105 millimeter howitzers are in this unit of action. How much more artillery, armor or air support I cannot say. Those matters are concerns that are much higher than this unit of action. I am aware that they are being addressed, but no one knows of the outcome. Certainly, shoulder fired weapons other than rifles are critical. We do have a few of these but they are to be conserved for the most severe occasions. Practice with the simulators in your armories as much as possible. Frankly, I would just as soon have third generation man portable LAWs, Light Anti-tank Weapons, than tanks. I will request as many as I think we can use. Armor isn't much good in our mountains and snows. This is mostly infantry country save for the center of the Basin and that won't change for eons. Distances are considerable. The Adjutant General informed me he is working very hard on getting us trucks. If necessary, we will commandeer civilian pickup trucks, buses and vans. Also, I want to make use of our motorcycle riders as messengers in the event all of our electronic communications are jammed.

Should open warfare result, it is not unreasonable to expect the regulars to use all means at their disposal against us. I anticipate C4I will be our weakest area-Command, Control, Communications, Computers, and Intelligence. Our networks are all an integral part of the federal system. We must immediately disconnect and establish our own networks. I realize that any system we establish could, and probably will be, closely monitored. Nevertheless, there is no use in freely giving away intelligence. Intelligence is a vital concern. We cannot tolerate any federal sympathizers in our midst, particularly if they can communicate our situation, requirements, movements or anything else to the federal troops or government. For lack of better terminology, I will use the terms of the American Revolutionary War. We who believe in the original Constitution are the Patriots, those who wish to remain with what was the fifty United States are Tories, and the fence sitters are Neutrals. Neutrals are highly suspect. I would like to see Tories voluntarily resign.

Be particularly aware of those who are amateur radio operators and specialists in communications in our areas. If these radio operators don't have your complete trust, confiscate their equipment. I realize that they are a miniscule part of the problem of enemy communications, but they have a knowledge base of radio theory and communications that the general public does not. That makes them doubly dangerous. Hopefully, they will all be patriots. If necessary, take further action as you deem appropriate to insure they do not transmit information in any way. Micro-cell phones are potentially an even greater threat. At this time I don't know how we will screen Tory internet or telephone connections. Fifth columnists must not be tolerated. It was recently pointed out to me that when the former Soviet Union collapsed, and East Germany with it, German citizens seized the headquarters of the East German secret police, the Stazi. They found that fully twenty-five percent of the East German population was on the payroll as spies and snitches on their neighbors for which they were rewarded. I hope that is not applicable here. A totalitarian government drives everyone under its aegis to some degree of complicity. It was usually necessary for elemental survival. No more. Those days are over for us. Civilians are either with us, against us, or sitting on the fence. Those who are known to be against us cannot be tolerated. Neutrals deserve our disdain at the least. We have to some degree become a nation of wimps and cowards. Life has been too good, too materialistic, and to compliant. The test was the banning of privately owned firearms. Those who surrendered their firearms failed the test. They have little time to find their spine.

Understand that we are fighting for our freedom in no uncertain terms. The federal government has become tyrannical and is no longer tolerable. The United States is about to break apart and civil war is quite likely. Indeed, it appears to have already emerged in the southwest. If anyone here disagrees with that, or wishes to remain as part of the union, shall I say a Unionist or Tory, please stand right now. I will accept your immediate resignation and departure with no hard feelings. I will say however, that if you choose to be a Unionist, a Tory, you will have a very limited time to sell your home and depart from the state of Wyoming. Henceforth, your loyalty is to the state of Wyoming and not the former United States of America. Not if, but when we form an autonomous unit with other states, your loyalty should be transferred to that unit. The original Constitution and Bill of Rights will be restored as the highest law of the land in that unit. Anyone who disagrees with the transfer of their loyalty to Wyoming and a prospective new nation, now stand. You have two minutes to make your decision."

Bradley paused for a full two minutes by his new watch to give everyone time to mull it over. "Since no one is standing, henceforth, you are all members of a new organization that is no longer part of the United States. Anyone who changes their mind will henceforth be regarded as a traitor. Freedom, ladies and gentlemen, for us and even more for our children, is more important than property or our own lives. At the first opportunity you and all members of your units will remove the U.S. Army patches from all of your uniforms. I require you to give the same opportunity to every individual in your units to resign and move out of Wyoming. Any of those who balk are to be summarily dismissed and immediately reported to this Headquarters.

My job is to command the First Brigade of the Wyoming National Guard which will quite likely become part of a larger regional force. I say Brigade because a brigade has no fixed structure. Hopefully, we can build it to regimental size. We will call ourselves the Basin Brigade. It appears that Wyoming, Montana, and other states are on the verge of coalescing and forming some type of autonomous unit. Our district includes all of northwest Wyoming. Other brigades are centered in Cheyenne, Casper, Gillette, Laramie, Sheridan and perhaps Rock Springs. I have the task to recruit and train as many men and women as possible for this brigade. Not only will we recruit for active members of the First Brigade, we will also recruit and train a civilian militia. The biggest difference between the two is that you will be in uniform and hopefully get paid, the civilian militia will not, their training will likely not be as thorough, and when push comes to shove, they will either fall under your command or act independently in small groups or as individuals. My preference is that they act independently in squad sized units with loose coordination with you whenever possible or until such time as greater organization is indicated. One other factor of which you should be aware. I have been granted authority to courts martial, hold military tribunals, and summarily execute individuals identified as traitors if I deem it necessary for our cause.

Civil rights will be observed to the fullest extent possible consistent with the threat of compromise of mission or our individual and collective freedoms. In studying the history of civil wars, one factor becomes immediately apparent. Those who enter into civil war with grim determination, which are willing to pay any price, and are utterly ruthless, always win. Thomas Jefferson said the 'Patriots won because the Spirit of Seventy-Six was kept alive in the hearts of common soldiers and commissioned officers and a few dedicated generals and statesmen until the British recognized the impossibility of subduing such a people and acquiesced in their independence.' The same tenacity by politicians and the military of North Vietnam led to our defeat in Vietnam. If you have identified Tories beyond question, you might inform the civilian militia to take appropriate action. Otherwise, give them a few weeks to sell their possessions and leave or face the possibility of arson and execution. Some might consider this the first step to martial law or make us as guilty as the federals. Perhaps it is so. Time will tell. Make no mistake, ladies and gentlemen. This is not a table top exercise or a psychological drill. We are about to enter into lethal combat with *those who WERE* our fellow Americans. Some will be in uniform, some will not. Be prepared to kill them if it becomes necessary.

It will be necessary to develop a new political infrastructure consisting solely of Patriots. From a political perspective, our first targets should be the politicians and their goons; the federal security police, their informants and sympathizers. Tories holding public offices must be removed. Patriots must be appointed in their place. Work with the civilian leadership in your counties that you can trust. Judges, mayors, council persons, aldermen, police officers, sheriffs and their deputies, whatever office they hold or you choose to call them, they must be for us or they are against us. These people cannot be neutrals. In their positions, that is an impossible line to walk. Neutral people will bow to pressure from either or both sides. Again, a totalitarian government drives everyone under its aegis to some degree of complicity. It is necessary for elemental survival. The Chamberlains and the Quislings and the Vichy government of Petains always emerge. Some out of the genuine belief that they can ameliorate the harshness of totalitarianism, others out of grandeur and ego and some out of plain cowardice. Making the distinction on each individual will be difficult. Nevertheless, it is what we must do. I acknowledge that we will make mistakes and that some innocent people will wrongly pay with their lives. That is the cost of freedom. It is partly the fault of such victims, of their failure to make hard decisions on the part of their own freedom. If you make such a mistake, you must learn to live with it and the citizens of your community must stand by you and your decisions.

I repeat, from a tactical and operational perspective, we are to be primarily a light infantry unit with a flair for guerilla warfare. Everyone, regardless of their specialty, is to be first and foremost an infantryman, a rifleman. Our geographic disadvantage is that we are flanked on almost all sides by mountain ranges surrounding a relatively flat basin. The basin obviously, is amenable to vehicular type warfare; the mountains to guerilla warfare. We must be prepared for both as best we can. Guerilla warfare will be our specialty on the flats and in the mountains. The Basin is our operational base and primary source of support. We will hold the gates to the Bighorn Basin to the point of bleeding the attackers to the maximal extent, but not to the point of our own annihilation. We are not Leonidas and the three hundred Spartans.

The emphasis will be on mountain operations however, because we will probably not have the resources to hold the desert area of the basin if we are attacked on the operational level. I will work with the company grade commanders on our defenses at their respective gates to the Basin. Those companies guarding the gates, so to speak, will receive the lion's share of heavier weapons.

I repeat, one of our major problems is training to be trainers. We will emphasize small unit tactics in our own environment. Our bases will undoubtedly be monitored from satellites; therefore we will use the strategy of dispersion into platoon sized units. Plan dispersion of your units so that you can communicate with FM radio equipment most of the time. That requires line of sight, short range for use. You want to be far enough apart not to present a large target, but close enough to support one another. Build extra bases, essentially small mountain camps, and move from one to another on an irregular basis. Use outfitters and packers to build your camps so that it appears they are building hunting camps. Recruit these skilled people into the militia. I recognize that they will probably have a problem with the required discipline. Do the best you can with them because we need their skills. Have them build the camps to hold platoon sized units. Build those camps throughout all surrounding mountain ranges. Terrain and weather will dictate much of your dispersion. Practice winter exercises. Establish these camps over the weekends such that they are difficult to identify from the air by unmanned aerial vehicles. Certainly, utilize the cabins that exist on the U.S. Forest Service lands. If the owners object, inform them that their cabins have been confiscated. Make sure they understand the consequences of being considered a Tory if they report your occasional and future use of their cabin to anyone else.

Emphasize physical fitness. Battalion and company commanders are to organize local militias of known patriots only. No suspected Tories or fence sitters are to be accepted.

Urge each household within your area of responsibility to store at least a one year supply of food-flour, rice, dried beans, sugar, salt, canned fruit, canned and dried meat and vitamin pills. Train wives and teenage children in firearms basics and store a modest supply of ammunition for home defense in the absence of husbands and fathers and active members. Everyone should be trained in basic first aid. Have the citizens of your counties begin stocking their larders now. Offer evening training in the form of DVDs. We will supply you with them on request for specific ones. We will provide you with a list of what is available. Maximize the militia's attendance at these evening training sessions. Make spouses and children welcome. If we go hot, everyone will be involved whether they like it or not. At least they will have some idea of what is expected and how to perform. I repeat, it is critical to maximize the militia's training. Whenever possible, we will send militia members to the training center at Guernsey, Wyoming. Make a list of those willing to go and submit it to my office. Each member of your units is to have at all times, a field pack appropriate for the season, ready to go at a moment's notice. Soldiers are to draw their weapons from their armories and retain them in their place of residence. Ditto for ammunition. Many of us are hunters and shooters and have personal firearms so it shouldn't be any different having a military rifle or handgun at home. Crew served weapons will be maintained at the armories. Officers and NCOs are to be armed at all times. Acquire a handgun if you do not have one and carry it concealed when you are in civilian dress. It is reasonable to expect assassination attempts on your life by Tories or federal agents in the immediate to not too distant future. That certainly happened in the border warfare of the civil war. Certainly if we fail, we shall surely all be hanged. God Bless Old Benjamin Franklin when he said 'victory gives the winners the right to hang the losers.'!

Know your community. Who can be trusted and who cannot. Consider the possibility of the loss of electricity, both for short durations in hours, and longer in days. Plan for it. Encourage backyard gardens and home canning for fruits and vegetables. Hopefully this will be settled politically in a short time. If not, we must be prepared for the worst; civil war with bloodshed and of a long duration.

I will visit each of your units at the first opportunity. I intend to get to know each of you professionally and will judge your strengths and weaknesses. Be frank and objective with me. Nobody is perfect, especially me. I know that I have made mistakes and will undoubtedly make more. Just don't make the same mistake twice. Once I know your strengths and weaknesses I will do the best I can to assist you in strengthening your weak points.

In the immediate future I will place recruitment advertisements in all the local papers in the district. The ads will be for membership in the regiment but also for the civilian militia. The civilian militia will report to your armories the same as recruits for the Guard. They are to drill with you as much as possible. Since our medical and dental resources seem to be extremely limited, each member will have to seek medical and dental care as an individual. We don't have the people to provide it or money to pay for it. If you know any medical personnel, in any medical field, try and recruit them. Physicians, nurses, dentists, medical technologists, nurses aides, therapists of any kind, it doesn't matter. We can use all the expertise we can get.

Anyone who is not physically fit or capable of spending extended time in the field has very little time to get fit and deployable. If not, put them out. We can't waste resources on them. If they prefer, they can revert to the civilian militia. There are many who will fit into that category. There are many who can't make it on a physical basis as a full time soldier but will do very well as a militia person, both men and women. They can be of considerable value as intelligence gatherers in their community. If they balk at dismissal, they have one level of review-me. I will not tolerate obese or physically unfit soldiers. Everyone will have to be in sufficient physical condition to conduct their duties as active duty soldiers. I do not believe in double standards, so you ladies who want to be infantry will have to meet the same standards as the men. That includes being able to pick up an unconscious two hundred pound fellow soldier and run, and I mean run, carrying that soldier for one hundred meters. Ladies, get with the program if you wish to be infantry combatants. If you are clerks, then I am willing to concede to a lower standard. Frankly, in my study of military history, I have found that women make excellent snipers, equal to, or better than, men. If that is your forte, I am all for it. We will discuss standards for that at a later time.

Each unit will be provided with a progressive ammunition reloading machine. Save all of your brass because ammunition will be a critical factor. I will do my best to see that we have sufficient amounts of ammunition and or reloading components, but no guarantees. Individual weapons are to be utilized in semi-automatic mode only. No more spray and pray. Each round is expected to impact on the target. One shot-one kill is the standard.

My headquarters will be in this armory. Captain Ferguson, you will continue to command your unit as if I were a hundred miles away. Proximity is to be ignored. I am vitally concerned with communications. I want to be able to communicate with you and your units individually and collectively. I expect you to communicate laterally with your fellow units as well as up and down the chain. Again, expect electronic warfare attacks and plan on how to defeat it. Identify motorcyclists and plan to use them as messengers.

I realize this presents something of a dilemma for us all. We must keep our economy going. At this point, we are not full time regular soldiers, but organized Guards personnel. It will be quite difficult for all of us to juggle our jobs with these military requirements. Do your best. If and when the feces hit the fan, we will find out how well we juggled.

As I become familiar with you and your units, I might organize you into more appropriate battalions, albeit smaller than the current Army Table of Organization and Equipment standards. Some of you can therefore expect promotions. Some of you, and I hope it is very few of you, might well be demoted. Save any questions you might have for when I visit your units. If you have questions, you should also have thought through alternative solutions with their pros and cons. I want to hear your solutions to your problems. As soon as I get my office established here I will have separate communications channels from Captain Ferguson's company and will promptly inform you of them. I will require a very small staff. I will need a regimental Sergeant Major and an adjutant. If there are any volunteers among you, see me after the meeting. It will require your relocation to Worland because of its central location. That is all."

Colonel Bradley stepped from behind the podium as the group came to attention. Captain Ferguson took the podium and described the various restaurants in town and dismissed them.

Colonel Bradley's complete address appeared verbatim in every local newspaper in the Basin except one. That newspaper edited his address by inserting italicized comments to emphasize the loss of civil liberties and freedoms under the Patriots, replacing Tory office holders with Patriots, the forcible eviction of those who hold Tory beliefs from their home, and their possible executions, the very things they claimed they were supposed to be against. It omitted remarks concerning the necessity of such actions; it listed the names, telephone numbers and addresses of many of the officers and NCOs. The newspaper was published in Cody. A motorcycle messenger delivered a copy of it to Colonel Bradley's office the day of publication. After reading it, Bradley picked up the phone and told Captain Livingston of Powell to have half a dozen men armed with handguns in civilian clothes surround the newspaper officer at 11:00 hours tomorrow. He is to have several of his personnel who are the best shots act as snipers in civilian clothes in over watch of the newspaper office as well. They are to be armed with civilian rifles so as not to attract more than minimal attention. They are to pay particular attention to the possibility of neutralizing Tory snipers and security guards. The following day Colonel Bradley drove to Cody in civilian dress.

Colonel Bradley entered the newspaper office, removed his hat and unbuttoned his topcoat and sport coat, and approached the first desk where a young woman was seated. "Good morning, Ma'am. I would like to see the editor of the paper, please." She pointed to a door, and said "His office is in there. That is his secretary you see behind the glass door." Bradley replied, "Thank you, young lady." Bradley walked into the secretary's office and asked to see the editor. "He's busy, and not seeing anyone, but if you will leave your name, I will tell him you called." Bradley nodded, and simply walked by her and through another door into the office of the editor. He sat down in a chair immediately across the desk from the editor. The editor looked up from his desk and made eye contract as Bradley walked in and took the chair. As Bradley sat down, his sport coat flapped open for a second, revealing his Springfield Armory GM .45.

"I know who you are Bradley. You aren't a Colonel or anything else around here but a jackbooted thug just like the ones that you claim you are trying to prevent. I won't retract the story or anything else about you and your so-called Patriot movement to form an independent state and break apart these United States. No use arguing with me boy, that's the way it is."

"How did you acquire a copy of my address to the officers and NCOs of my command? That was privileged information."

"That, Bradley, is also privileged information. A journalist has to protect his sources. You have no need to know how."

"You have printed personal stories about me that are wholly untrue. Not only will you cease printing such lies, you will print a retraction stating that your source of information was conducting a personal vendetta against me. If I am correct, some those stories are coming from a former battalion commander of mine in Africa who was absolutely worthless. He is now a mailman, more or less, in the Pentagon, carrying papers from office to office. Without going too far down that road, I suspect he is being used as a mouthpiece for someone higher up. Nevertheless, those stores are fiction. You will make the corrections."

"Bradley, who the hell do you think you are? You expect me to print retractions when the official source I have is higher than you ever thought about, and I have only your word? Bullshit boy, I am not going to do anything like that."

Bradley rose from his chair, looked the editor in the eye, and said simply, "You have been warned. Stop it now." He turned and walked away. As soon as Bradley closed the door behind himself, the editor picked up the phone and dialed the city police.

"This is Tony Edwards, editor of the paper. Ethan Bradley was just in my office. He's armed, and he threatened my life with a handgun. He's on his way out the building now. If you can move fast, you can catch him. That will be quite a feather in your cap. The feds will love you for it."

Two city police squad cars pulled up behind Ethan as he was walking towards his car. Four officers jumped out, guns drawn. Ethan turned around as he heard the footsteps running behind him. "Don't move Bradley, you're under arrest," said one whose jacket had two stripes on the sleeve. Bradley just smiled at him. Bradley casually looked all around, in a 360 degree circle. The police corporal, with a big smirk on his face pulled out his hand cuffs. Bradley never took his hands out of his coat pocket. From all sides, half a dozen men converged on Bradley and the police with handguns in hand. The corporal suddenly heard the ratchet of the revolver placed in his right ear as Captain Livingston cocked the hammer. Others were disarming the other three police officers. "What do you want to do with them, Colonel?"

"Disarm them, handcuff them with hands behind their backs for the moment, put them in the back seats of their squad cars and we will drive them five miles out of town. There, strip them and their cars of their equipment and uniforms. Leave three of them handcuffed along side of the road, the fourth, hands free. Drive their cars a quarter mile or more past them with the keys in them. The one without handcuffs can walk barefooted to their cars and recover the other three. They won't freeze to death in that time, but they will be too cold, too embarrassed and unable to offer pursuit. The uniforms and equipment might come in handy later." Bradley turned and walked to his car as his orders were being carried out.

Cody's paper carried the complete story the next day of the kidnapping of their police officers. In the story was a detailed description of how Bradley had held a gun to the editor's head and threatened his life if he didn't print retractions on Bradley and the Patriots. The story alleged that they meant to leave the stripped police officers to freeze to death, but one of them had a handcuff key hidden in a sock that allowed them to escape. They should be charged with attempted murder as well as kidnapping and threatening the editor and the police officers' lives. A group picture of the four police officers in uniform accompanied the article. Several comments from the involved officers embellished the article with false statements of being beaten about their bodies with their own nightsticks. They all swore to arrest any Patriot and particularly Ethan Bradley at the first opportunity. Bradley read the article with utter disgust. He called Captain Livingston and inquired about the comments regarding the alleged beating of the officers.

"Sir, I personally supervised the release of those police officers. Not one of them was struck in any way. We left their squad cars with the engines and heater running only two hundred yards away to reduce the possibility of cold injury. I read the article this morning myself. The article is entirely false."

"Thank you, Captain. We will pay the editor a visit again tomorrow morning. I doubt that they will expect a visit so soon. Have your men ready as before. I will visit the editor once again. I don't anticipate a replay of the previous day, but you never know. Better put a rifleman or two in position to act as snipers."

Bradley walked into the editor's office without bothering to stop or to look anywhere but straight ahead. He unbuttoned his overcoat and his sport coat as he walked into the editor's office and sat down in the chair as before. The editor had quite a surprised look on his face. His mouth dropped open. He recovered, and said "Well, Bradley, back so soon? I am surprised that you had the balls to come here again. Perhaps I shouldn't be, though, as many people as you have murdered, and the insubordination you showed your Marine Corps superiors."

"Why did you lie in that article? I never threatened your life, those officers were never struck, and we took pains to insure they suffered no cold injury. Why did you fictionalize it so much?"

"Call it artistic license, boy. It sells papers. Hell, truth. What's truth?" Truth is what you believe it to be, and you boy, are a loose and dangerous cannon."

Bradley nodded, and said, "OK, I'll accept that. Where are you originally from?"

"California but that doesn't mean anything." was the reply as the editor opened a drawer on the right hand side of his desk and looking down, reached into it. Bradley didn't say anything. He simply snatched the Government Model .45

from his shoulder holster and pointed it directly into the face of the editor. A Smith and Wesson Model 686 .357 magnum revolver emerged from the drawer in the editor's hand. A massive look of surprise again came across the editor's face as he looked up into Bradley's automatic. Bradley pulled the trigger. The bullet went through the middle of the editor's forehead and out the backside, splattering blood, bone fragments and brain tissue on the wall behind him. The body shuddered and went limp, with the arms hanging over the edges of the chair. The revolver dropped to the floor. The empty cartridge case bounced off the wall and landed near Bradley's foot. He picked it up and put it in his pocket. He took the .357 and stuck it in his belt. Keeping his .45 in his right hand and placing his fedora over his automatic with his left hand, he calmly walked back out through the office, looking straight ahead, never glancing to either side. When he reached the door, he turned around and looked to see if anyone had drawn a gun. When he saw they were all stunned into immobility, he put on his fedora, reholstered his automatic, buttoned his coat, and walked out to his car. Captain Livingston was outside in civilian dress. "Everything OK, Sir?" he asked.

Bradley smiled, Why yes, thank you Captain, everything is just fine."

The next day's edition of the paper carried a description of the execution of the editor. No names were mentioned, and no one claimed to have recognized the murderer.

There was no comment from any of the police investigators, although the Chief of Police of Cody postulated that Bradley was the murderer. No mention was made of the fact that the editor had drawn a revolver. He lamented that no one would come forward to identify the man who pulled the trigger. The example was set.

CHAPTER 7

IT WAS AFTER DARK WHEN BRADLEY REACHED HIS FATHER'S HOME. Robert Bradley was watching the evening news when Ethan walked in. "Hi Dad, how are things going for you today?" he asked as he hung up his hat and overcoat.

"OK, Son, I hope your day went well. It's started big-time. It's worse than they have been reporting. The scattered riots are growing in size and number. They just had reports from Fort Bliss and Fort Hood, Texas. Lots of Hispanic soldiers are deserting. A number of arms rooms on both bases were overtaken by one means or another. A number of black and Anglo soldiers were shot trying to stop it. No mention of where the deserters went; home or to Mexico. Apparently some of them took armored fighting vehicles, though. Man, I sure wouldn't want to live in Texas now. I wonder how many of those Mexicans are going to become banditos with that kind of fire power. The President made a speech at noon today, calling for calm and promising that everything will be worked out to everyone's satisfaction. The Union will be preserved, he claimed. I don't know how he intends to do that. Hell, it's him and his party and socialist police state philosophy that have precipitated this whole mess ever since the end of the last century. They are a bunch of social welfare police state advocates. Your Grandad used to preach it would come to this. So what did you do today?"

"Well, it started here in the Basin today as well. I executed the first Tory."

"Really! Who was it?"

"The Editor of the Cody paper. I killed him in his office just before lunch. I figured he didn't need to die with a full stomach. That would be just a waste of good food. Tomorrow I need to work on who tape recorded my address to the troops and gave it to the papers. Then I will try to get a handle on the Mexicans here in the Basin. I don't want any coordinated action from them. Then I have to ascertain where the Native Americans stand. Then I have to address the Tories, or perhaps all three at the same time. I'm going to be on the road a lot for a while."

"Better not let anyone know your travel schedule. They will ambush you along the way. Lots of the new immigrants from the east and west coasts haven't left the Basin, although lots of them are up around Cody. Bunch of them think the anti-gun laws only apply to other people, not them. They don't think they're the bad guys. I don't know if they are ready to take violent action yet or not. That seems to be the center of their activity in the Basin."

"I can't allow them to get organized, or if they are, to terminate their organization and perhaps them. I hope there are not a lot of women involved."

The next morning Colonel Bradley telephoned General McIntire in Cheyenne.

"General, where does the state of Minnesota stand in all this? We could sure use that state with its transportation assets, the Twin Cities Army Ammunition Plant, its agricultural base, head of the Mississippi River, the brain power and medical centers it holds, and its population. My immediate concern is military logistics, with long term consequences for lack of manufacturing, computers and communications, transportation and a sufficient population base. We're supplying Minnesota and Wisconsin and maybe others with electricity generated from our two fast breeder reactors up on the Yellowstone and Missouri Rivers in Montana. That should be worth something. Incidentally, I have officially coined the terms Patriots for us, Tories for the federalists, and Neutrals for the fence sitters for our Basin."

"Colonel, we have been discussing very seriously that possibility with Minnesota's governor and leading politicians. They claim they are thinking about it, but we don't really know where they stand at this time. They have a lot of liberals, especially in the Minneapolis-St. Paul area. It will be tough. The University faculty there is full of Tories. I wouldn't hold my breath on it, one way or the other. Historically, Minnesota has been pretty far left by our standards. I agree it would sure anchor our eastern flank if we could bring them into the fold, but there is no way I can give any kind of assurance right now. How are things on your end?"

"I'm getting settled in General. I've laid down the rules and will start visiting what will be my companies and possibly proposed battalions headquarters, trying to get a handle on who can do what the best, what assets I have, what I can develop, and where I want to go. I might liaison with Billings later on with your permission Sir, so I'll know what's on my northern flank. Where the various segments of the population stand on secession, what logistics I have and what I will require to maintain order and support our independence are my first investigations, Sir."

"Very good, Bradley, I knew you could handle it. If there is nothing else, keep me informed of your progress. You realize that this phone call is undoubtedly monitored by the feds."

"Yes Sir, I do. It doesn't bother me at all. If you prefer, I will communicate by fax or by runner if you so desire. I can't guarantee the fax won't be monitored either though, Sir." One more thing, General. I assassinated the editor of the Cody paper for printing lies.

"Bradley, use your discretion. That's all."

Colonel Bradley then dictated a written order to Staff Sergeant Thompkins for all company commanders. You are to obtain a census of all Mexican-Americans, and all other Hispanics within your respective counties. Illegal aliens, those here legally, those in transit, or any other status are to be counted. Personal data such as name, address, age, place of birth, occupation, number in family, is to be gathered. All organizations which serve this subpopulation are to be contacted for their records for cross examination. Identify any with criminal records, suspect criminal behavior, users of illicit substances, and those who are not disposed to good order and discipline. Use of whatever force is necessary, including deadly force, to gather the information is authorized. Your reports are to be in those office thirty days from receipt of this written order."

"Sir, not to be insubordinate, but do you mind explaining something to me?"

"Certainly not Sergeant Thompkins, what is it?"

"Sir, do you have a problem with Mexicans and Indians?"

Bradley thought for a few minutes, about how to compose his thoughts such that Thompkins understood him. Nodding briefly, he slowly spoke.

"In reality, we are all immigrants here. None of us are true natives to the Americas. The differences are the times of our arrival. What we call Native Americans and the Indians of all of the Americas, and Mexicans are descendents of the peoples of northeast Asia. It is believed that they came in waves across the Bering Strait in the last ice age to populate North and South America, some 20 to 25,000 years ago. In the closing decades of the last century a trend in the change in the nature of the illegal Mexicans migrating here began. True, it was slow, but inexorable. Admittedly, much of this was the direct result of our insatiable demand for drugs, particularly marijuana and cocaine, but also opiates and methamphetamines and illegally imported pharmaceuticals. We began to see the criminal element of Mexican society enter our country in an organized manner. True, it was slow at first, but we ignored it. The great majority of immigrants were hard working and honest, but the percentage of bad folks kept increasing. Anglo-Americans along the border became increasingly alarmed. They started by putting bars on the windows and doors of their homes and businesses. More and more Anglos along the border acquired firearms and the skill to use them. At first, the guns remained at home; then they began routinely carrying them in their vehicles. I don't mean just the ranchers and farmers. They never stopped being armed, continuing from the nineteenth century. There is some historical precedent to the myth of the cowboy, particularly in the southwest. No, I mean urban and suburban folks, especially those on the fringe of suburbia. Concealed weapons carry became common. Bodies of illegal aliens who assaulted people began to appear along rural highways, dumped there by citizens who found it necessary to defend themselves or their property. Virtually 99% of shootings and such deaths went unreported. Many were also buried in shallow graves in the mesquite. 'Shoot, shovel and shut up' became the by-word in many rural areas. No doubt a lot of innocent braceros simply seeking a better life were murdered. Not much can be done about that. That was the chance they had to take in illegal immigration. The Mexican government has to share in the responsibility for that. If they would have a more equitable society and national birth control program to get their population crunch under control, if they had instituted a birth control program decades ago, the problem would not have such a magnitude.

Mexican-American politicians perceived a great opportunity in this. The more violent illegals either formed new gangs or took over existing ones. Financed by the drug trade they quietly morphed into regimented, highly disciplined private armies. These armies and the politicians have a common goal, and that is political control. They are gaining control of the political system by both criminal and legitimate means. If we don't do something now, we will be as corrupt as any South American oligarchy, the archtype banana republic. Your Constitution, Civil Rights and Bill of Rights will be meaningless, Sergeant."

Sheriff Brady walked into the Armory in Worland. The Sergeant Major rose and stuck out his and. "Morning Sheriff, what can I do for you?"

"I would like to see the Colonel for you few minutes if that is possible."

"Now is as good a time as any before he gets on the road." SGM Killian knocked on the closed door. The command "Come" came from behind it. Sheriff Brady stepped in as Bradley in civilian clothes rose from his desk and shoved out his hand. "Coffee, Sheriff?" he asked.

"I have a better idea. There is something I want you to hear first hand. It's down at the Big Horn Café. I buy the coffee."

At the café the Sheriff chose a booth that had an empty booth on each side. There was no one in earshot. Most of the morning regulars had already left. Brady noted that no Hispanics were present. Jan Neville served them coffee.

"Jan, tell the Colonel about Juan Cartagena. We don't want to arouse suspicions or alert Maria, just act like you're taking our order. "

Jan quickly related what she had learned through Maria. "I haven't learned where the guns are that he has mentioned."

"Thanks, Jan. We'll act at the appropriate time." After Jan left, Ethan said "We'll be at your disposal for whatever and whenever you want, Sheriff."

"I'd like for him to stick his neck out far enough so that there is no question when we chop it off. What do you think?"

"I think that is great. You call the shots" as he sipped his coffee.

"We'll let him initiate some illegal activity and then we'll nail him."

"Ok, ok, already! I know we won't make the mortgage payment again this month. What do you want me to do?" Simon Gray Horse poured another two fingers of Ten High bourbon into his glass and downed it in a single swallow. Margaret Gray Horse looked sullenly at her feet.

"We'll lose this trailer if we don't make the payment. Then where will we live? Our son quit school to herd cattle, our daughter at 15 already drinks and smokes pot. I think she rents her body for money for alcohol and marijuana. You wouldn't leave the reservation to attend school after your accident. All you do is drink and feel sorry for yourself because you lost an arm on the oil drilling rig. We have to do something to eat and save our home."

"Yeah, tell me what", retorted Gray Horse. "The company offered to send me to college to make a teacher out of me. That was the cheapest way out. No sir, they can pay me workers compensation forever."

"You know they won't. The time is up your so-called workers compensation is over next month. It was the same amount they would use to send you to college. Now it is all gone. You spend most of it on booze to assuage your self pity."

Simon Gray Horse hit his wife hard with a right cross that caught her on the lateral corner of her eye and temple. She fell over sideways and struck her head on the edge of the table. She laid sprawled unconscious on the kitchen floor. Gray Horse immediately regretted his action. If she reported it, he would be bound for prison. This was his third and final assault that the court had warned him against. His probation would be revoked and he would be sentenced to the state prison in Riverton. For an instant he thought of murdering her by strangulation or breaking her neck. On second impulse he picked up the bottle of whiskey and pushed open the screen door and stumbled outside. He realized he would be found guilty of murder by any judge and jury. *"Another drunken Indian,"* he thought. *"That's all the jury would see."* Half drunk, he stumbled the 50 meters down to the creek and leaned against a tree. He slid down the tree and took another drink from the bottle. Gray Horse didn't know what to think. He noticed a small cloud of dust raised by a sedan that turned off the paved highway and on to the gravel road. There were only six dwellings on the road and he watched as the car slowly drove by each of them to finally pull into his driveway. He sullenly watched as two men he did not know emerged from the sedan, each of them slowly looking in a 360 degree circle. His ancestral instinct aroused by their cautious behavior warned him to be cautious. Both men wore coats and ties. Gray Horse took an instant dislike to them. They represent somebody or something with some power, trained men, he thought. One remained by the car while the other walked to the trailer door and knocked. When no one answered, he called out. When no verbal response occurred, he opened the door and cautiously looked inside, calling out loud "Hello, anybody home?" He immediately observed the unconscious Mrs. Gray Horse on the floor. He knelt beside her, noting her respiration while he felt her pulse. He also noted the swelling and forming bruise between her eye and temple. He carefully sat her upright and from the sink made a cold compress from a wet dish rag. He held it over the bruised area for a moment when she moaned and raised her hand to her head. She opened her eyes and was surprised by the strange face.

"Easy Ma'am, I'm a friend, looking for Mr. Gray Horse. I presume you are Mrs. Margaret Gray Horse?"

She wasn't fully cognizant and didn't know what to say.

"Would you like for me to help you into a chair, Ma'am," asked the man. She nodded slowly and the man rather easily lifted her to her feet and guided her to a kitchen chair. He knew who she was from studying her picture. She held the compress to her head while the man to a seat opposite her. When her eyes cleared, she asked, "Who are you?"

"I have a business proposition for Mr. Simon Gray Horse. I believe the company I represent can offer a beneficial package to your family. Is Mr. Gray Horse in the area?"

"I don't know. I don't know how long I have been out."
"What happened," he asked.

"Oh, I tripped and hit my head on the edge of the table. I don't know where Simon is or when he will be back."

The agent nodded affirmatively, knowing once again Gray Horse had assaulted his wife.

At that moment, Gray Horse overcame his curiosity and staggered to his feet. He set the bottle behind the tree and walked unsteadily back to his trailer. The man guarding the car immediately observed the movement and that Gray Horse's hands were empty. Nevertheless, he leaned against the car crossing his arms across his chest and in a seemingly inoffensive position. What he really did was to reach inside his coat and place his hand on his Glock .40 S&W just in case Gray Horse had a concealed weapon.

"Who are you, what do you want here," hoarsely asked Gray Horse.

"There is a man inside waiting for you with a profitable business proposition, Mr. Gray Horse."

Without thinking to ask how the man knew he was, Gray Horse grabbed the handle by the trailer door and pulled himself up the steps, opening the screen door and stepping inside. The man rose from the table.

"Good afternoon, Mr. Gray Horse. Your wife seems to have had a bit of an accident here. We'll be happy to drive the two of you into Riverton to see a physician if you like."

"Oh no, that won't be necessary, I'll be fine," said Margaret.

"What do you want here," asked Simon. The smell of bourbon disgusted Agent David Many Horses, but he feigned ignorance of it.

"I have a business proposition that will substantially aid your financial distress, Sir. Could we discuss this outside?"

A fear went through Gray Horse. "No, you can say what you want right here." He wanted the security of his wife's presence.

"I'm David Many Horses, a federal officer. A militia group is forming here in the Big Horn Basin. We want you to join in that militia. Your job will simply be to identify its members. As a matter of fact, I will join with you to insure your safety. You are known around the Basin, I am not. I am to be your cousin from Hardin, Montana, up on the Crow Agency reservation. There is no risk to you, only to me. In return, all of your debts will be forgiven, that is paid for you, and your son and daughter will receive full college scholarships."

Martha inhaled sharply; all of her dreams could come true. Both men noted her reaction.

"So, you are a fed, and you want me to spy", said Simon.

"Not at all, you are simply my endorsement to join the militia. I'm the spy, not you. If and when you agree, your mortgage will be paid in full within 24 hours, scholarship trusts funds will be established with a local bank for your children and you will receive a monthly stipend for one thousand dollars for life."

"And I don't have to snitch on anybody asked Simon?

"Not at all, I'm the intelligence gather man, not you. What do you say?"

"What if I say no?"

"Then to prison you go. My partner and I just saw you slug your wife into unconsciousness. That's three strikes for you Mr. Gray Horse. You will do five years hard time. No booze, no sex, unless you want to peddle your asshole to your cell mate, or somebody younger, stronger, and homosexually inclined to rape you. The choice is yours."

"I say, why not?" In a moment of rare clarity and greed, he asked, "Can you put the $1000 a month in my wife's name so I can't drink it away?"

"Done", said Agent Many Horses.

CHAPTER 8

DR. MALIK, YOUSSEF IBN MALIK WAS A SECOND-GENERATION PALESTINIAN AMERICAN. His parents arrived in the United States in 1989, as refugees to escape the pressures of the Intifada and the retaliations of the Israelis. His parents worked hard to insure the education of his sister and himself. The family did not openly participate in any political activities. His father secured a job as a janitor in the Silver Springs, Maryland school system. After twenty-five years he was the Maintenance Director at a high school. Youssef attended the high school where he graduated at the head of his class. His parents forbade him to participate in sports, but let him join the chess, biology and debating societies of the school. Youssef won a four year scholarship to the University of Virginia where he majored in biochemistry and biology. The two fields really melded into the same discipline. His biology teacher preached "mathematics is the basis of physics, physics is the basis of chemistry, chemistry is the basis for biology and biology is the basis for human behavior." Youssef was accepted into the graduate program at the University of North Carolina where he took a Master's Degree in biology. He did his thesis on controlling mechanisms of virus penetration into cells. The theory was that if a mechanism could be found that prevented virus penetration into cells, then no viral infections could occur. He remained at Triangle Park to continue his studies as candidate for Doctor of Philosophy. After three more years of research on the interaction of virus particles and host cells post penetration, he was awarded his Ph.D. It was during his doctoral work that he met the vivacious and seductive Fatima whom he courted. She was working on her bachelor's degree in mechanical engineering when he met her at the local mosque. Fatima was extremely active in the Palestinian-American Society. She participated in demonstrations, wrote letters to her Congressmen and the President, and did her best to disguise an enmity for Israel and everything Jewish. They married the summer that she received her Bachelor of Science in Mechanical Engineering and Youssef his Ph.D.

At a meeting at Centers for Disease Control & Prevention the March prior to their graduations, Youssef pulled a copy of the announcement for a position for a bench level virologist at USAMRIID at Fort Detrick, MD. He applied, and was granted acceptance pending the award of his Ph.D. As soon as they graduated, the newlyweds eagerly moved to Frederick, MD where Fatima soon found a job with a construction company. At USAMRIID, Youssef Malik immediately took the nickname of Mark, since it was easier for people to remember, and it sounded more American. He began as a bench level virologist, examining newly discovered nonpathogenic virus DNA segments within the DNA of human lymphocytes. She designed heating and ventilation systems for buildings. They settled down to a nice comfortable life. Over the years they bought a modest home, had two cars and ultimately the couple had two children. The second childbirth resulted in a ruptured uterus, so the decision was made on the surgery table to remove the damaged uterus. Youssef was disappointed that they could not have more children, but he swallowed his manly pride and said nothing about it to Fatima, happy that he had at least two sons.

Youssef's work was very thorough and meticulous. After fifteen years at USAMRIID and four years after George Hoskins smuggled virus sample was received, he accepted the position as Chief of the Virology Division. His security clearance was upgraded from SECRET to TOP SECRET, as required for his position. The background check on Youssef Malik revealed nothing of particular concern. He was simply considered another outstanding member of the American community, a second generation Palestinian-American, as so many other second generation immigrants had done. Research revealed his wife's previous political involvements, but there was nothing to indicate any significant activity since the birth of their second child, Yassar. The appearance of being a thirty-seven year old working professional engineer and the mother of two boys was favorably regarded. Apparently she little time for any politics.

The Department of Defense outsources roughly ninety percent of its medical research by contract. There is simply too much on the cutting edge of medical and biological research for the Department's military laboratories. By this method, a great number of Ph.D. candidates in various fields are funded at a wide variety of institutions, public and private. The candidates get their degrees, the institutions the prestige, and the DOD gets the results of their work.

Any good research begins with a literature research to determine what has been accomplished and just where the cutting edge of research is and who is doing it where. In his new position, Mark Malik reviewed classified contracts on research of obscure viral diseases. A major mission of USAMRIID is to develop potential vaccines against possible biological weapons. He discovered that numerous contracts had been let to the Israeli government. Not only were viruses being studied, but a number of pathogenic bacteria and fungi were being studied as possible bioweapons. The rationale was that the research was for mechanisms to block the effects of these agents should they be employed as biological weapons. Much had been done earlier on the classical agents, tularemia, anthrax, the pneumonic form of bubonic plague, smallpox, and others. Malik was horrified that the Israelis should possess such knowledge and that the American government was keeping it classified. He did not mention his concerns to his superiors, but kept his thoughts to himself. Over the ensuing months, he became progressively depressed, not so severely as to interfere with his work or his ability to be a supervisor, but it was interfering with his home life. One night after sex that Fatima deemed more mechanical than emotional, she put her arm across her husband's chest and bluntly asked him. "OK, so what is it that has you disturbed all these months? Are you having an affair with one of your co-workers, or what?"

Malik took a deep breath and sighed. "Ever since I took this new position, I have access to work that I did not know existed, and very few people know about. It troubles me that much of the work has been done on biological agents that could be used as weapons by the Israelis, under contract with the U.S. Government."

Fatima said up and bed, "Do you mean that USAMRIID is funding Israeli research into biological weapons?"

"That's about it," admitted Malik. "I don't like it; it disturbs me, but I can see where they are coming from. The worst part about it is that the Israelis' could produce highly virulent agents in large quantities, in a very short time, a matter of weeks. To my knowledge, they have not, but they have that capability. It does not bode well for our ancestral homeland. Perhaps it is the source of the current flu epidemic in Israel that was on tonight's news. It is quite possible that one of their experimental agents escaped from the laboratory."

"Wow," said Fatima as she lay back down. "That is scary."

"It must never be mentioned, Fatima, by you or me to anyone. Even telling you is a security breach that could land me in prison. It must be our secret. Although I must admit I do feel much better having shared it with you. Do not be bothered by it; it is my burden and it will probably come to nothing better than good science." They lay there curled together until they drifted off to sleep.

A few days later, Fatima paid cash for a computer card at a convenience store. At a computer chat lounge, she sent an electronic mail message to her handler in Washington, D.C. In it she said "Have vital strategic information for major propaganda purposes. Meet me Sunday at 16:30 at the ice skating rink in Frederick. Samantha." Samantha was her code name. She did not meet with her handler on any regular schedule. Only when she had some useful tidbit would she contact him. Her handler knew enough not to try to contact her, that when she had important information about her husband's work, she would contact him.

A few years earlier, Engineering Genetics, Inc. of Seattle, Washington received their fourteenth cell line patent. The epithelial stem cells were first isolated in mouse embryos, then in domestic cat embryos, and then their biologists made the jump to a human morula, in their laboratory in Xinjiang, China. A morula is a ball of cells that develops from a fertilized egg and will continue to develop into an individual of that species. It is an early stage of an embryo. To avoid U.S. legal entanglements, they utilized Chinese fertilized human embryos to extract the cells and shipped the isolated cell lines frozen via first class air to their Seattle laboratory. The real work with human cell lines was done in China, but the tissue culture that resulted was flown to their primary U.S. laboratory for patent application purposes. The epithelial cells at the 256 cell stage of the embryo were sufficiently primordial that they were just beginning to differentiate via several pathways that could be identified. Once isolated and maintained in a variety of experimental culture media, those cells which developed into respiratory mucosal cells were identified. At this stage, various influenza viruses were introduced into the cultures. Viruses isolated from ducks, geese, chickens, pigs, horses, cattle and humans were introduced into each culture media to determine growth characteristics and survivability. Those tissue cultures were cataloged, along with the viruses and subsets were frozen for further research.

Dr. George Hoskins of Genetics Engineering in Seattle worked with avian tissue cultures for nine years. He was the Chief of the Avian Viral Diseases Branch of the Agricultural Division of Genetics Engineering. He experimented with cell lines from a variety of avian species. He particularly concentrated on wild species, as he correctly felt this was the natural home of avian influenza viruses. If he could find an appropriate cell line that would grow a variety of avian influenza strains, he had a most useful tool for poultry vaccine production. He requested that all of the zoos in the United States send him fresh chilled respiratory tissues from their deceased exotic avian species immediately upon necropsy. He had wildlife departments in various regions ship him songbird eggs for attempts at respiratory cell isolation. He found what he sought in the ubiquitous wild mallard duck. In the seventh generation of cell division he isolated a primordial respiratory tissue from the fertilized mallard egg. He established the cell line through twenty-five generations and found it to be stable. When he implanted selected strains of avian influenza into the plates with the cell line, he found minimal or no cytopathic effects, that is, the virus grew well without killing the cells. The cells recognized the protein of the virus as their own. In biological terms, this is referred to as "self". The cells apparently released the virus in large quantities without cell rupture. He reported his findings to his superiors. The cell line and the virus strain were immediately flown to China for further testing with strains of naturally occurring Asiatic avian influenza virus that they had isolated. To everyone's delight, the cell culture was easily maintained and could be grown in huge vats.

The Influenza A viruses have two primary surface proteins by which they are categorized, neuraminidase and hemagglutinin. Seventeen different proteins of significance, variants of neuraminidase and hemagglutinin, were identified on the surface of the various influenza virus strains tested from the different species, pigs, chickens ducks, horses and humans. These proteins are processed by a type of white blood cell called macrophages. The macrophages break the virus protein down into segments of amino acid chains called peptides. The cell packages them by combining these peptides with other proteins and projects them through the cell membrane so that they protrude from the surface. When these proteins project from the surface of a virus infected cell it allows them to be attacked by a type of white blood cell known as killer lymphocytes that destroy the infected cell. Viruses have no replication machinery of their own. They take over the host cell's means of division and cause it to produce more virus particles which are released when the cell ruptures. None of these protein variants of hemagglutinin and neuraminidase were common to all of the viral strains tested. Several types that were common to more than one species however, were identified. Several were host specific. As his next accomplishment, George Hoskins of Engineering Genetics, Inc. developed a unique virus that contained the proteins for a variety of avian species by adroit manipulation of the genes that result in their formation. The H12N1 strain of influenza virus had the genes removed which were responsible for the severe cell disruption and provoking a severe inflammatory response. The result was an infection with almost no clinical disease in all the domestic avian species in which it was tested. This unique virus caused minimal morbidity, that is, clinical illness, in the avian species but provided excellent immunity to all avian species against all naturally occurring strains of avian influenza found in circulation in the natural world. The result was a vaccine for poultry producers world wide that they could administer intranasally by simply aerosolizing it in their closed poultry houses.

The tissue culture thus produced provided the means to mass produce modified live virus influenza vaccines in test tubes or large production vats instead of eggs. Vaccines thus could be rapidly and very inexpensively produced. Without waiting for patents to be granted, they experimented with other strains influenza viruses. As soon as the patent for the cell line was granted, they applied for the patent for the avian vaccine.

In China, work continued with using the human respiratory mucosal cell tissue culture and human Influenza A strains by substituting and mixing the genes from the viruses of other species. When a virus so engineered appeared promising in terms of morbidity or mortality, it was tested on political prisoners.

Prisoner 287 developed a fever twenty-four hours post nasal insufflation. In 48 hours, a severe viral pneumonia developed that affected the lining cells of the alveoli of the lungs known to the medical community as type I pneumocytes. The mucosa lining the nasal passages and the pharynx were also affected. The alveoli are the terminal air sacs in the lowest level of the lungs, the terminal balloon-like structures of the lungs where gaseous exchange occurs. In 72 hours, Prisoner 287 was dead. The virus was tested on 25 more people. Four survived, but took weeks for recovery. Each prisoner was maintained in an isolated barrier cell equipped with High Efficiency Particulate Aerosol (HEPA) filters, and ultraviolet lights to prevent the escape of the virus. Death was due to respiratory failure by the death and shedding of the type I pneumocytes into the alveoli. The victims' lungs could not exchange gases due to being plugged with dead cells and tissue fluid. The immune response contributed to death with the responsive white blood cells and fluid rushing into the lungs. The victims literally died of drowning and suffocation in their own tissues and fluids. Since the virus also infected the lining of the upper respiratory tract billions of virus particles were introduced into the environment each time the victim coughed or sneezed. The virus strain was found to be particularly hardy, surviving warm temperatures and sunlight to some degree as well as freezing temperatures. The virus can be held for decades at freezing temperatures and remain viable.

Engineering Genetics, Inc., made hundreds of millions of dollars on their avian vaccine alone. It was hailed as a major break thru from the standpoint of tissue culture technology that allowed Influenza A vaccines that matched circulating viral strains to be very quickly and inexpensively made. Engineering Genetics, Inc. promised a similar human vaccine would soon be made that would prevent a world wide epidemic, called a pandemic, of influenza similar to that of the of 1917-1920 pandemic which was estimated to kill up 60 million people.

George Hoskins was delighted to receive the invitation to visit the company's major research laboratory in Urumqi, the capitol of Xinjiang, China. Many felt that his efforts were worthy of the Nobel Prize for medicine.

The night before his flight to Peking, a police car behind George Hoskins turned on its lights and a two second blast from its siren as he pulled onto the freeway. Not understanding why he should be stopped, he pulled over to the side of the freeway in the emergency vehicle lane. The police officers left the flashing lights on top of their vehicle on. Any car that was following Dr. Hoskins had to continue with the traffic. A helicopter hovering overhead kept a watchful eye on the traffic below for any unusual maneuvering of a vehicle behind Dr. Hoskins. A uniformed officer stepped out holding a clipboard over a shoe box. Dr. Hoskins rolled down the window.

"Relax, Doctor, this is a friendly visit. You haven't broken any traffic laws." He pushed the shoebox through the open window into George's lap. "You have been under intense surveillance by Chinese agents ever since you received the invitation to visit China. We have been very reluctant to contact you for fear of compromising you. We want the Chinese to believe that you are, shall I say, untainted? This is a very brief way of interrupting their surveillance and contacting you without compromise. We swept your car earlier for transmitters and temporarily removed what we found. We'll just let the Chinese think they malfunctioned. Inside you will find a pair of shoes just like the ones you are wearing; only they have hollow heels. They are radio opaque, so the hollow chambers will not be revealed by radiography should they choose to x-ray your luggage upon arrival." The officer pretended to be writing on the clipboard as he spoke. If you rotate them counterclockwise while pressing on the center front of the heel where there is a hidden switch, you can open them. They won't open without pressing hard on the switch. These tablets are for any notes or anything that will fit that you might wish to bring out of China with you. Rest assured your luggage and clothing will be curiously but thoroughly searched by the Chinese. We know the Chinese are up to some strange things in the lab at Urumqi, and we are curious as to what. Now, I am a uniformed civilian police officer, so you can truthfully say you have not been contacted by the FBI or the CIA." He handed George a completed citation with "WARNING" written on it in large letters and returned to the patrol car. At the first break in traffic, the police car nosed out into traffic with the lights on and the officer indicated for Dr. Hoskins to proceed. Before he got out of his car in the parking garage, he put the new shoes on and put his old ones in the box and put them on a shelf in the garage.

The concern of the Chinese management however, was their highly secretive research on human influenza A viruses. Every effort was made to conceal their work with the highly virulent strains of human virus from Dr. Hoskins. He had absolutely no knowledge of its being tested in humans. Dr. Hoskins was given the grand tour of the facility. It took an entire day to brief him on the various ongoing research projects and the layout of the laboratories, and then tour the various laboratories.

"We're working on a new vaccine for hoof and mouth disease, Dr. Hoskins. We have found a loop of core protein with a fair degree of antigenicity to it that is common to all strains of the cattle virus isolates that we have examined to date. We have isolated the gene for it and hope to incorporate it in an innocuous carrier or cassette virus. After that, we will see how well it compares with different strains of the virus we have in our virus library that we have isolated from swine. As you can imagine, a single vaccine for all strains of hoof and mouth disease that would be effective in all cloven hoofed species, cattle, swine, sheep and all the others, will be a tremendous boon to the livestock industry worldwide. Some day it might even be applied to wildlife. Tomorrow you will have the opportunity to perform some virus transfer in a newly designed safety cabinet, or hood. We have found it to be much more effective than the standard biosafety cabinet. We have applied for a patent on the hood. More importantly, we hope to patent the new hoof and mouth vaccine within two years. We are progressing very rapidly with it.

"Thank you Dr. Chu. I am very much looking forward to that. It would be a boon to African wildlife as well. You probably aren't aware that I have long been a supporter to save what little is left of African wildlife. With all the political turmoil, the civil wars and continued environmental destruction there, anything that will change peoples' minds about the threat of diseases that wildlife species can carry will be most welcome. Of course, I'm not sure how you would round up a million wildebeest to vaccinate them," he said with a chuckle.

The meals were all extravagant. Both Chinese and American foods were offered. George Hoskins never had food so good. Lunch was served in the executive dining room in the laboratory's main building. For dinner, he was taken to the finest restaurant in Urumqi. Two thirds of the way through the dinner, after the first four courses with the accompanying wine, Dr. Hoskins excused himself to attend the men's room.

The men's room was furnished in the finest western tradition. Dr. Chu, Soo Lu, joined him after a few seconds. Dr. Chu cautiously and nervously peered under the doors of the toilet stalls to see if any were occupied. None were. He stood at the urinal next to George Hoskins.

"Dr. Hoskins, I'll leave a specimen of a virus in an unbreakable 2.0 milliliter polyethylene test tube in the test tube rack tomorrow in the Category IV laboratory for you. It will be the one marked with an X on the rubber stopper in the rack. The stopper will be glued in so it will not leak. It is imperative that you get this sample to your government. It is a particularly virulent strain with some very unique characteristics. It was designed for very sinister purposes. I fear it is the leading candidate for weaponization. You must somehow devise a method to remove a sample from the hood without detection. The only way I can think of is to hide it in a body cavity as you go through the decontamination tunnel. Should you fail, our lives will be forfeit, perhaps along with millions of others. I cannot emphasize the importance of this specimen."

At that moment, a strange individual entered the men's room. Both Chu and Hoskins zipped their pants and washed their hands with soap and made small talk about the superlative food. Hoskins held the door open for Chu who bowed at the waist. Hoskins put his hand on Chu's shoulder and gently guided him first through the door.

"I will be delighted to try the dish you recommended, Dr. Chu. I find it extremely fascinating, not to mention exciting. You have no idea what a marvelous time I am having."

While in the Category IV laboratory George Hoskins glanced briefly at the television cameras mounted in the four corners of the room and determined that there was a blind spot in one corner of the hood. No camera was mounted in the hood, an oversight that the Chinese designer had not considered. In that blind corner, and out of the scrutiny of the television cameras, he managed to palm the only test tube with an X on the rubber stopper. He stuffed the test tube under the sleeve of his disposable scrub gown after loosening the tape around the surgeon's glove taped to the sleeve. There, it was invisible. As he attempted to remove the test tube rack from the hood, he deliberately caught the corner of the rack on the edge of the porthole used for placing and removing specimens in the hood. He dropped the rack of test tubes on the floor which broke every tube. The Chinese scientists watching on the closed circuit television panicked for a moment until they realized there was to be nothing in the rack that was really hazardous. The whole exercise was to demonstrate the state of the art laboratory to their visiting guest. "Not to fear," called out Dr. Hoskins. "I'm just a bit clumsy from being so excited. No need for anyone to come in. I know the procedures, and have used them on occasion in Seattle. I am sure everything will be fine. Awfully sorry for the mess. I'll clean it while I am here; no need for any assistance." Following the Standard Operating Procedure for laboratory accidents, he sprayed the entire area with disinfectant, waited fifteen minutes, washed it down the drain into a special chamber for autoclaving, and sprayed it a second time. In the process he slipped the vial from his sleeve under his shoe coverings and up the leg of his scrub pants Thus, even the virulent specimen was no longer in evidence. All the glass and stoppers went into the vat that was an autoclave below which was sealed with the throw of a switch.

In the first airlock of the disinfection tunnel he took a tremendous chance when he removed his scrub pants by swallowing the 2.0 milliliter test tube while pretending to cover his mouth when coughing. In the shower, he scrubbed with soap and water, rinsed, then stood under the disinfectant shower, then sat, quite uncomfortably, in the ultraviolet lights for five minutes wearing protective glasses. As soon as he emerged from the stall, he vigorously scrubbed his hands with hot soap and water.

The evening of his return to the United States, three strange cars cruised up and down his avenue of residence. They had kept the local traffic under surveillance for two weeks so that any strange vehicles, especially occupied ones, would be recognized. Local residents were carefully observed to determine if any of them might be of Chinese extraction. All homes from which George's house could be observed, were investigated. Two of the cars parked, one on each side of the street, facing in opposite directions and at opposite ends of the street. The third car parked in the next block and two men in casual clothes got out and walked to George's house. Two CIA operatives remained in the car to guard it while they also kept watch. One of the two men walking to Hoskins's house was a research virologist from USAMRIID at Fort Detrick, Commander Douglas McDougle in the Navy Bureau of Medicine. The other was a CIA officer, Robert Gilbert. Their job was to debrief Doctor George Hoskins. They introduced themselves and showed their identity cards.

CIA Officer Gilbert turned to Mrs. Hoskins, and said, "We would like a few moments of conversation alone with your husband, if you don't mind, Ma'am."

"Of course. I'll go make some coffee for you gentlemen while you chat with George." Mrs. Hoskins excused herself and proceeded to the kitchen.

Hoskins had placed the test tube in his home freezer after carefully wrapping it in newspaper and a larger plastic vial to protect it. He forced himself not to have a bowel movement until he returned. He was severely constipated after two days, but nonetheless removed the vial from his feces while wearing gloves as soon as he had the privacy of his own toilet in his own home. After a few moments of small talk, George went in to the kitchen and removed it from the freezer. The Navy scientist put the tube in a padded screw top aluminum tube, then in to a padded metal box and padlocked it.

"So it was Dr. Chu, Soo Li, who provided you with this specimen? Do you know why he did it?"

"No, I really don't. I never met Dr. Chu before, never even heard of him. I don't know what his role in the company is. I can only repeat what he told me. Apparently, this is a quite virulent virus that he felt threatened world stability or peace or something. I really don't know. I have no idea how the virus was affected by my body temperature after more than sixty hours of exposure. I never had the chance to talk with him again after the few words we had in the men's room. For all I know, even the men's room had a camera in it. Do you know anything about Dr. Chu?"

"No, but we will by morning. We'll do our homework."

"What of this specimen? Who will work on it and where? I am very curious about it. I don't even know what type of virus it is, whether it is a DNA or RNA virus, a vaccine strain or a virulent agent for sinister purposes. I don't know what media will be required to grow it. I know nothing of it. I presume I will not be allowed to work on it, even though I am very curious. Can I have some feedback at all?"

"Dr. Hoskins, you have already done enough. Probably more than you realize, and certainly we cannot divulge any information to you for your own benefit. Suffice it to say that we are extremely pleased with your efforts. Dr. Hoskins, we must ask you to refrain from ever discussing any of this with anyone, even your wife, let alone your colleagues. It is of course, all classified. Your efforts cannot be publicly recognized, but you have probably done your country yeoman service. For that your government thanks you. Should you remember anything else, please give me a call from a landline phone outside your laboratory or home." He handed George Hoskins a business card. It had his name on it, but it was for a furniture company, obviously a front. The two men said good night and casually strolled back to their car. The Navy Commander placed the specimen container in an ice chest in the trunk of the car. The specimen was flown to the United States Army Medical Research Institute for Infectious Diseases (commonly called USAMRIID or RIID for short) at Fort Detrick, MD, where it was immediately put into culture. Officer Gilbert launched an intense research study to determine just who Dr. Chu is.

"Attention." The Sergeant Major called the room to attention as Colonel Ronald Aspins and CIA Officer Robert Gilbert entered the secure conference room at the U.S. Army Medical Research Institute of Infectious Diseases. It was 14:00 hours on a Friday afternoon.

"Sergeant Major, would you leave the room please. Guard the door to see that we are not interrupted in any way. Ladies and Gentlemen, this is a classified briefing at a higher classification than any of you have been previously awarded. Due to the urgency of the situation, we have decided to dispense with the normal administrative requirements for reclassification. None of this is to be mentioned to anyone outside of this room. It is not to be discussed among yourselves in your offices or anywhere else except this room. If you need to communicate with each other, clear it with me and this room will be made available to you. Are there any questions? No? Good, then we will proceed. Allow me to introduce CIA Officer Robert Gilbert. He will provide you with this briefing and is coordinating associated efforts with this project. Officer Gilbert."

"Thank you Colonel. This information I am about to impart to you has the highest strategic national and international importance. It could affect the world order for decades or centuries to come. Therefore, I must stress what your commander has already told you. Colonel Aspins has informed me that each of you is a Division Director that will in some way be involved in the project with which you are about to be tasked. This briefing is provided so that you can initiate preparation for your tasks that are to come. We have received very credible information that the Chinese have as their ultimate objective the eastern Mediterranean littoral. They mean to capture the entire Middle East with its oil and gas reserves as well as the Dead Sea with its mineral wealth of potash and other resources. One of the weapons they will deploy, according to our latest information, is an artificial virus that they have created. It has some of the characteristics of Influenza A viruses, but has been built from scratch. There are no known vaccines against it of which we are aware. We can only speculate that the Chinese have formulated one against it to protect their troops and perhaps the civilian population. We have no word of a mass vaccination program in China, but that doesn't mean anything. The intelligence we have is that they will initially deploy this against the Palestinians and let it spread naturally. It has the genome to be highly pathogenic. If it doesn't spread well, that is, into the entire region, then they will also release the virus in Israeli, Egyptian and Syrian cities. Word is that their agents are already in place with the virus in cold storage and awaiting the command to release it. The initial release could occur in a few weeks to two months at most. We believe they are planning a winter campaign so that by early spring most of the damage will be done. Apparently the influenza pandemic didn't kill enough people in the Middle East to satisfy them. They want a clearer field, I mean less resistance, to seize the world's greatest reserves of natural gas and oil. I don't have to tell you what it would mean if China, or any other single country for that matter, controlled eighty percent of the known oil and gas reserves of the world. We expect to have a sample of this artificial virus in less than two weeks. All I can say is that I hope to God you can develop an effective vaccine in a crash program that requires no more than a month."

The division directors sat there stunned at what they just heard. Colonel Aspins rose and moved to the podium as Gilbert sat down.

"I am appointing Commander McDougle to head this research team. All of your thoughts, planning, requests for materials, even people, will be coordinated through him. Obviously, everything will have the highest possible priority. Start strategy planning with Captain McDougle on how we are going to solve this problem. The latest models of protein auto-analyzers are already on order and should be here in less than two weeks. It is quite appropriate if some of you wish to man your teams around the clock. Be thinking about everything you will need over the weekend, to include more laboratory technicians. That is all." Gilbert and Aspins strode from the room as the audience came to attention. The study and characterization of the virus was assigned to Commander McDougle and his team of virologists working in the Category IV laboratory. The Centers for Disease Control and Prevention of the U.S. Public Health Service in Atlanta was not told of the specimen.

By the time Malik reached home he was shaking. Fatima was not home, but the kids were. Considering himself something of a liberated Muslim, he poured himself a stiff drink of Johnny Walker scotch whiskey. One of his sons was playing a virtual reality game on the computer with a neighborhood friend. Irritated, and finding the boys' raucous laughter annoying, he walked into the living room, glass in hand and ordered the boys outside, raising his voice to the point of shouting at them. Admonished, they removed their headsets and dashed out the door. He drained his glass and poured a second two fingers of straight scotch. He finished his second drink and was sitting on the living room couch when Fatima came in. Feeling the effects of liquor, he looked at his wife, really glaring at her. Fatima immediately realized her husband was extremely upset. "What's wrong, Youssef? Did I do something I should not have" she said smilingly. She bent over the sofa and put her arms around Youssef's neck and kissed him on the cheek.

"We had a very important meeting today. Only the division chiefs were briefed. It seems that there are indications that the Chinese intend to use some new artificial virus as a weapon to depopulate the Middle East. You know the Chinese are on the march again, headed west. The powers that be seem to think their goal is to go all the way to the Mediterranean. We are supposed to get a sample of this artificially concocted super agent to try and decode so that we can build a vaccine against it, all in a few weeks. Already we are placing orders for extra equipment. A comment was made that we will probably work around the clock. That also means additional laboratory personnel at the bench level. They will have to perform their tasks without knowing the overall picture. The CIA seems to think this agent will be released in Syria and Egypt and Palestine within a couple of months, some time in the early winter for maximal transmission."

"That is absurd. No one would do that. It could threaten all of mankind. That is preposterous."

"Is it? I wonder where this influenza pandemic originated. Did it not serve China's purposes in eliminating much of the opposition to their westward march? How many millions of Palestinians died over the last year or two? How many Muslims? Perhaps this year's naturally occurring influenza strain did not kill enough of the Middle East peoples to satisfy them. The entire Third World has borne the brunt of it. I am beginning to wonder. Would it not be to the benefit of the Chinese if they controlled the major oil supplies of the world? They don't have to worry about world markets anymore. They are so huge all they have to satisfy is their own internal market. If this briefing is accurate, and if the Chinese carry through with it, all of our families in Palestine will be, shall I say, eliminated for the benefit of China. It makes sense to me. How many figures have you seen coming out of China about how many Chinese died? Why were they so spared? I have never heard any information coming out of China about their losses to influenza."

Fatima thought about it for a moment. She mentally balanced the absurdity of it against the possibility of it. The strategic gains China would make from such a disaster began to be apparent and grow in significance in her mind. She could not share the growing despair with Youssef as she thought more about it. Instead, she decided not to dismiss or make light of it, but to outwardly appear calm in the face of it and present a neutral stance.

"Well my husband, I haven't made plans for dinner. What would you like? Perhaps I should phone in an order for pizza, your favorite. I could do a little shopping I forgot to do on the way home and pick up two pizzas at the same time. It won't take any longer than it would if I took something out of the freezer. How does that sound? You have another drink and I'll phone in an order, go get some odds and ends, some soft drinks to go with it, and pick up the pizzas. They boys will like that as well."

Fatima purchased a phone card at the first convenience store she passed several miles from the house. Then she went grocery shopping for thirty minutes. Enroute to the pizza parlor she stopped at another convenience store where she used the phone card to call her handler in Washington, D.C. She requested an urgent meeting with her handler at 12:00 hours tomorrow at the Super Shoes store in the Mall in Fredericksburg. She knew there would be a crowd at that time. They never met in the same place twice. Two blocks away an old pickup with two men dressed as farmers in it photographed her. The resolution of the camera was such that it revealed the numbers she punched into the phone. When she finished her conversation, she tossed the phone card into the trash receptacle in front of the store. Immediately the pickup moved to the store where one of the men retrieved the card from the trash can. A second vehicle, this one a plain sedan, continued to follow Fatima to the pizza parlor and then home. Her fingerprints on the card along with the video of her telephone conversation would prove significant in her trial.

The date-time group on the videotape corresponded with the phone company records of time, date, place and number dialed. Hidden lapel cameras recorded Fatima's meeting with her handler the next day on a bench outside the shoe store while her sons selected new sneakers. Her handler could not believe what he had heard. He declared that it was absolutely absurd. Such a scheme could not succeed. He immediately suspected a trap but did not inform her of his suspicions. He instructed her to proceed home and never speak of it again. With that, he rose and walked away, knowing that he would not be arrested because he had diplomatic immunity. A dozen FBI agents were in place to observe and record the conversation. One sat on the front bench just inside the door pretending to read a book while his FBI female companion tried on a variety of shoes. Another on a bench twenty feet away from Fatima pretended to work a crossword puzzle in a newspaper. Small, pencil-like microphones picked up every word exchanged while Fatima relayed the conversation. The FBI team leader made the decision to effect an arrest upon Fatima's arrival at her home where Youssef could also be simultaneously taken into custody.

The virus survived at body temperature and was grown and characterized by sequencing the amino acids in both the capsule and the matrix of the virus particle. When the virologists had sufficient amounts of the virus to study, they sprayed it into the nasal passages of nonhuman primates which developed severe and fatal influenza. Using computer models to visualize the virus, they substituted amino acids within the molecule until they identified of several proteins from both the matrix and capsule that appeared highly antigenic, that is, immunity producing. With further testing in laboratory animals, they confirmed these proteins were strongly antigenic and resulted in protective antibodies, called humoral protection, and more importantly, in cell mediated immunity, from challenge with a number of influenza virus strains in the virus library. In a classified section of a commercial laboratory, development of a vaccine against the virulent strain of influenza began. It was with this vaccine that Bradley and other members of the armed forces were vaccinated on an experimental basis several years later.

Robert Gilbert stopped at the main gate of Fort Detrick, MD. The military police corporal didn't quite know what to do when Gilbert showed him his badge and told him that this was an unannounced visit to USAMRIID. The corporal, not knowing what to do, picked up the phone and called the staff duty NonCommissioned Officer, or NCO. The NCO told the corporal to record the license plate number, badge number and ID card number and allowed the CIA officer to pass without calling anyone else. While the corporal was busy recording the identifiers, the NCO called the office of the Commanding Officer, USAMRIID. When Gilbert drove the three blocks from the gate to the laboratory, the Commander was waiting for him in his office.

"What can we do for the Central Intelligence Agency today, Officer Gilbert?" asked Colonel Ronald Aspins, Medical Corps, commanding.

"I'd like to talk to Commander Douglas McDougle first, and then have an exit interview with you, Colonel, provided you have the time. I realize that my coming unannounced has its disadvantages for you, and for that you have my apology. I do not intend to disrupt your schedule. Rather, I am here for an informal update on the virus specimen that Dr. George Hoskins brought out of China six months ago. I am sure you are aware of our interest in this specimen."

"Of course. I'll take you to Commander McDougle's office personally. If you are not aware of it, the Commander has been selected for promotion. He will probably pin on his eagles after the first of the year. He has made considerable progress in studying the virus. He is in charge of it, and has a very small team of well trained personnel. He watches things very closely. All of his people have a clearance higher than

Top Secret, but we don't like to discuss that. Let's proceed to the lab."

Commander Douglas McDougle USN, (Promotable) was at his desk reviewing last week's progress when COL Aspins knocked on his door. He looked up to see Aspins and Gilbert.

"Hi Ron, didn't know you were coming. Welcome aboard. Can I get you a coffee? You know the Navy always has the best coffee."

"Sure Doug, with lots of cream. I just dropped by to chat with you on the progress regarding the virus."

Aspins said, "I'll leave you two to talk. I will avail myself for an exit interview Officer Gilbert, when you are ready to leave." With that, he left and closed the door behind himself.

"So tell me Doug, what about this virus? I do know a little virology. I initially was zoology major at the University of Missouri-Columbia, in the pre-med program before I got smart."

"Well, this is a most unusual strain of Influenza A virus. It is a human strain but it has genes in it from both bird strains and swine strains. It appears to be a genetically engineered virus. The avian strains of flu A attack different types of cells of the respiratory system than do the human strains. So this virus will attack both the ciliated cells of the upper respiratory tract, thanks to the bird genes, while the human characteristics attack the nonciliated cells of the lower human respiratory tract. That avian characteristic enhances the spread as the upper respiratory tree, the nasal passages, sinuses and upper parts of the pharynx and larynx have lots of ciliated cells. Every cough or sneeze is really going to release billions of virus particles into the air. The virus is unusually resistant to environmental factors. That's where the swine genes come in. This characteristic allows the virus to survive in the environment of the swine farm lots. Many if not most different types of viruses are damaged or killed by ultraviolet light, by sunlight, but this strain is quite resistant to ultraviolet light and to heat. That means it will linger in the air a lot longer than normal strains. It has the potential to be a real zoonotic problem. If it spills over into the wild bird populations, especially the migratory species, say, Canada geese, then it could become established and a chronic problem. Since Canada geese use waste lagoons and pastures that domestic animals use, it could potentially transfer to other species. Simply put, that means it could interact with domestic stock, swine, cattle, chickens and turkeys, in the barnyard.

Historically, and with recent discoveries, Influenza A viruses are thought to have 15 unique subtypes of hemagglutinin protein and nine types of neuraminidase protein. Each virus strain has one type of each, but they can occur in any combination. We found a sixteenth type of hemagglutinin. Another unusual factor is where the precursor of this hemagglutinin protein is cleaved. We're not sure what this means, but we strongly suspect that it will result in enhanced virulence. Virulence of course, is defined as severity of clinical disease. Lastly, we found a gene that is pretty uncommon, not one strain in a thousand of influenza viruses seems to have it. This gene causes apoptosis, which simply means programmed early cell death. The infected cells age very rapidly so to speak. They die in hours to days instead of the normal weeks to months. That opens the respiratory passages and lungs to bacterial infections and pneumonia. If we're right, this is one hell of a major virus, a real killer virus if it ever gets loose in humans."

"What I am hearing Doug, is that this is a genetically engineered biological weapon, a real weapon of mass destruction. Is that right? How much potential does it have for that?"

"Rob, let me tell you, if this virus ever gets out, and we don't have a vaccine for it, it could be the worst plague in the history of the human species. It could kill hundreds of millions of people of all ages, not just the old, the infirmed and the young, but everybody. Colonel Aspins has given the development of a vaccine the highest priority of this laboratory. Trouble is, we are going to need more money to do further testing. I don't know how we are going to test any vaccine in humans. This is such a hot virus I would be hesitant to expose anyone to it. If any experimental vaccine fails to protect the experimental subjects, they probably won't live. One other characteristic about it that we haven't deciphered is that it is not affected by amantidine or rimantidine, at least not in Petri dishes, the two classical antibiotics against Influenza A. We are going to have to find some very adventurous human subjects to test it in, after of course, we try it out in a number of different species of laboratory animals and then nonhuman primates. If a vaccine will protect most species of macaques, those are rhesus monkeys, it will almost always be an effective vaccine in humans. We are going to have to be very, very careful and very, very sure before we can proceed with human clinical trials."

"How soon will that be? Can you give me any estimate?"

"I would say in about two years we should have a good vaccine, provided there are no glitches. We have to be very, very careful that this thing doesn't escape from the lab. We have confined the work to the Level IV laboratory. There isn't a heck of a lot more I can tell you, unless you want to get into the enzymology of the virus and the amino acid sequences and the codons of the genes."

"No thanks. I'll leave that for you laboratorians. I'll go have a chat with Colonel Aspins and report our conversation to my boss. Based on what you tell me, I suspect that priorities will change, certainly for funding. I am sure that when you are ready your reports will go through the appropriate classified channels. They will quite likely reach the White House through the Chairman of the Joint Chiefs, the SECDEF, and the Director of National Intelligence. It's been good talking to you, Doug. Here is another of my calling cards. Give me a call if you have anything more that you think might be of interest. I'm really offering you another channel of communication outside your own. I trust your judgment and if you hit any stumbling blocks, let me know. I'll see what we can do from the intelligence side of the house."

"Say, if it not asking too much, can you tell me about Dr. Chu?"

"I can give you a little information, but nothing is to go outside this room. Dr. Chu did his basics in biochemistry in China. He came to Stanford for this Ph.D. While there he converted to Christianity. He has a wife and two kids. He is originally from Szechwan. Virology is his specialty; he worked on arthropod viruses for his Ph.D. That's about all I can tell you."

He sat down his coffee cup, and the two men walked to Colonel Aspen's office.

"Coffee, Officer Gilbert? I'm going to have one."

"No thanks, Colonel. I just filled up with Commander McDougle's excellent brew. From what he tells me, this is one hell of a hot virus. I deduce it was engineered as a biological weapon."

"That's what we think as well. The Chinese might have already begun work on a vaccine. In fact, I suspect they have. It would provide them with an enormous strategic clout if they want to depopulate the world."

"Doug didn't say anything about a vaccine for it."

"Doug is pretty modest. He has isolated several isotopes from the virus which appear to provide excellent immunity. He is just beginning to test it in several species. We will closely monitor their progress. Ultimately, we will have to test this in human volunteers. We have no choice. It is simply too severe a weapon not to do so. God help those volunteers if we don't get it right."

"Any predictions on a time frame, how soon a vaccine will be available?"

"No one can predict research at all. Sometimes breakthroughs occur very quickly, often through an accident, and other times it takes years, in spite of well laid plans."

"From a spook's point of view, wouldn't unleashing such a biological weapon require that your own population be vaccinated against it to prevent your own annihilation? I realize of course, that no vaccine is 100%, but certainly you would want a vaccine of extremely high efficacy. If this is a weaponized virus, wouldn't the creators vaccinate their own people first?"

"That is an excellent perspective. You can bet this will only be deliberately released when the home population is essentially complete vaccinated. God help us if it is accidentally released as a laboratory accident."

"Well, in that case, I'll get out of your hair. Best of luck to you and your teams Colonel, especially Commander McDougle."

In mentally reviewing what he just heard, Officer Gilbert found himself shivering uncontrollably as he walked to his car. Thinking to himself, we need to determine who has been vaccinated, if anyone at all. We need some blood samples. The people most likely to receive vaccine before the general population are the elites. How do we get blood samples from elites? Do we knock their embassy personnel in the head and bleed them? Do we try and pick ordinary citizens off the street for bleeding? Kill them for a blood sample so it looks like a murder-robbery? Who or what country has had mass vaccination plans in effect in the last few years? What countries are capable of this? Are they surrogates for a larger power? We need world wide blood samples. Somebody once said the *World Health Organization has a sample blood bank in Geneva, Switzerland? Maybe we could tap into it? Maybe if we hit one of their attaches in one of our major cities so that it looks like a street crime? If it tests out with antibodies we have proof. They all have their own prostitutes for the single folks within their embassy staffs so we can't use venereal disease acquired on the streets for a sample. They would see their own physicians anyway, not treatment in one of our facilities. What the hell! Automobile accidents happen all the time. Let's have a car crash! Candidates begin with the Russians and Chinese. I'll propose it to the Director and see what he says. No one will be the wiser for blood samples drawn in the emergency room. It will all have to be programmed, but it can be done.*

CHAPTER 9

THREE MONTHS LATER A MINOR CHINESE SECRETARY IN THE LOS ANGELES CONSULATE WAS THE VICTIM OF A NONFATAL HIT AND RUN ACCIDENT. He was rushed to Los Angeles General Hospital Emergency Room. In New York, a Palestinian consulate was wounded in a drive-by shooting near his apartment. A Russian chauffer was attacked by three hooded men in Washington, D.C. He received a minor stab wound in the leg and was rushed to a hospital. Blood samples from each victim were hand carried to Captain McDougle at USAMRIID.

A secret contract was let with the Israeli government to produce 350 million doses of vaccine to be stored in the U.S. against the possible weaponization of the virus. Israel lied about the initial production figures, siphoning off fifty percent of the first three months production to store for its own use. They claimed that some minor adjustments were necessary in the production procedures, such as minor temperature variations for the "soup," meaning the large vats of culture media in which the vaccine virus was grown. They kept enough for every Israeli citizen plus a fifteen percent reserve.

After the virus smuggled out by George Hoskins had been characterized, appropriate epitopes identified, and experimental trials conducted on human volunteers and administered to Special Operations Command and other selected military personnel, President Walsh, called the Director of the Food and Drug Administration into his office.

"Dr. Adams, in front of you is an agreement for secrecy. You are to sign it before any further discussion or proceedings. Briefly, it states that you agree to utmost secrecy in what you are about to hear, and that any disclosure under any circumstance, will result in you spending the rest of your life in solitary confinement. This includes your even telling your wife that you were called to the White House today. Do you wish to proceed?"

"Mr. President, what could possibly be so secret as to dictate such an agreement? Are we about to engage in biological warfare or something?"

"Dr. Adams, either you sign the agreement or you do not. You are under no obligation to sign it. Your position as Director of the FDA is not vulnerable if you elect not to sign it. If you do not, you will simply be escorted from this office and your deputy will be sitting where you are later today. It is that simple. You will be the titular head, but he will have the real authority."

Intrigued, Dr. Adams thought about it for a moment. Being both a veterinarian and a physician by training, he always felt he missed something in life spending so much time in school and research laboratories. He realized the President sitting across from him was a lame duck Republican who didn't have to worry about re-election. All the odds were that Senator Richard Newkirk would be the next President of the United States. A tingle of excitement surged through him as he considered he was going to do something that might come out of a spy novel. He leaned forward and signed the agreement placed in front of him by the President's secretary. The secretary took the document and left the Oval Office closing the door behind her.

"Dr. Adams, we acquired a sample of a biological agent from a foreign nation several years ago. My folks tell me that it is a genetically engineered organism, capable of wreaking devastation on the human population of the world. Without the knowledge and consent of you and your agency, we have proceeded with vaccine trials against this agent. While the initial human trials were limited, I ordered, under the utmost secrecy as Commander-in-Chief, to have selected members of our Armed Forces vaccinated with it by calling it by another name. This has been an ongoing program for several years. The fact that, as far as we know, none of your people know of it, should indicate the high degree of secrecy surrounding this agent and the vaccine. We have had no known adverse reactions from this vaccine manufactured at a secret facility. I have called you here today to inform you that I have ordered mass production of the vaccine, enough doses for every person in this country. The vaccine will be stored at a private institution under contract. If and when it is necessary, the President at that time will order a mass national vaccine campaign to protect our good citizens.

Given the risk of a break in secrecy of such a program, I have decided to incorporate you into the loop. It will be your job to stonewall any curious members of your organization regarding this agent and the vaccine or its production or storage. So far as you have been informed, it is an experimental animal vaccine with which your agency has no involvement. The less even you know of it, the better off we all are. Any of your folks who pursue knowledge of this agent or vaccine, in spite of your attempts at stonewalling, will find themselves in serious trouble. They might be the only person or persons on a deserted island in the middle of the South Pacific or perhaps even worse. I trust I have made myself perfectly clear.

One other aspect, much less serious, is that it might require one of our intelligence folks or one or some of our scientists to pose as members of your agency. In that regard, I also expect your full cooperation. You are to provide these people with complete cover for whatever it is they find it necessary to do. Do you have any questions?"

"No, President Walsh, I don't. I might have questions in the future should something arise. Who should I contact in that event?"

"In that case Doctor, you will have a direct pipeline to the Director of National Intelligence. With the upcoming elections, I cannot say whom my successor will appoint in that capacity. Nevertheless, whoever it is will be fully briefed and prepared to offer you whatever assistance you might need. If there are no further questions, I thank you Doctor, for taking time from your busy schedule to come."

President Walsh stood up and offered his hand across his desk to the Director of the FDA, who shook it and said,

"Thank you, Mr. President, for the confidence you have entrusted in me. I will do all I can to insure the secrecy of whatever it is that you have just not described."

Achieving excellent results in macaques, i.e., several species of rhesus monkeys at the U.S. Army Medical Research Institute of Infectious Diseases, the testing proceeded with human volunteers. All volunteers were conscientious objectors who wished in some way to serve their country and share the equivalent danger of the battlefield. All twenty-five volunteers of both sexes resisted challenge with a large exposure to virulent virus. The antibody response to the hemagglutinin molecule of the virus proved very significant. The cell mediated immunity was also quite impressive, as cytotoxic, i.e., cell toxic, lymphocytes demonstrated significant cross reactivity to different but related strains.

The political process began when President Walsh had two years left in office. A dozen candidates in each party either declared for the Presidency or formed exploratory committees to see if they could raise enough money and had enough charisma and support to gain their party's nomination. With one year left before the general election, the number for each party had dwindled to six. Deals were discussed behind closed doors. Positions between the candidates were clarified by the national committees but not made public. Who was electable? Who could raise money? Senator Kennely sensed an opportunity. The democratic junior senator from Massachusetts was handsome indeed. He learned he could present a great appearance, but had great difficulty in holding his temper. Kennely brought in the experts from different charm schools; psychologists for behavior modification, make-up artists, so-called tap dance artists to teach him how to field and glibly answer tough, penetrating questions. At the top of the list was temper control. As the field narrowed down, Newkirk's chances improved daily. Behind the doors a heated debate about a running mate took place. In order to provide so-called geographic balance and appeal to selected minorities, the Democratic National Committee chose as Newkirk's running mate Congresswoman Norma Cantor. She had her own baggage but for the most part it was considered an asset. She was a lesbian from San Francisco. Her mother was a white Jewess and her father an African-American. She attended the University of California at San Francisco for her undergraduate degree in economics, history and political science. She earned an LLB at UCLA. She was in the California State Assembly for two terms before running for Congress. She had been elected to the U.S. Congress twice before and sat on several significant committees in the House of Representatives. While their politic presented to the public was essentially parallel, she and Newkirk could barely tolerate each other behind closed doors. They were all smiles in public. She incessantly argued in private for a cutback in federal spending, a more balanced approach to the federal deficit. Newkirk would have none of it. The Chairman of the Democratic National Committee and Senator Kennely thought they could control the competition and friction between them. The liberal media came in swinging in full support of them. The liberal mainstream media refused to ask the questions that should be asked. They refused to make an issue of their personal lives as being unfair and un-American. Instead, the media dwelled on increased social programs, retrenchment in foreign policy, and budgetary cutbacks for the Department of Defense. Once elected, the gloves came off. In particular, the friction between Edward Andretti, President Newkirk and Vice President Cantor became extreme. Norma Cantor demanded a balanced budget, a cut back in welfare programs and protective tariffs. The shouting matches became louder and longer. It seemed that there would be no end to a three ring circus. Finally, after more than a year of internal friction, the DNC chairman and Senator Kennely said enough is enough. The President was afraid to fire her because of the political firestorm it would cause. Vice President Norma Cantor was relegated to the role of being the President of the Senate. She was excluded from the inner circle in the decision making process in almost all circumstances. She was informed of what decisions were made and told she was expected to carry them forward in public whether or not she agreed with them as befitting the office and the appearance of a unified party. She seriously considered resigning, the reconsidered when she decided she could accomplish some good in her role as President of the Senate.

"I'm Simon Gray Horse and this is my brother's son, David Two Bears, from Hardin, Montana. He's had a little marital problem up there and so he's thinking of moving down here. Nasty divorces are not fun."

Captain White Horse held out his hand. "Glad to meet you gentlemen. Please be seated. What brings you to the armory, especially you, Mr. Two Bears?"

"We heard there is much trouble throughout the land. We do not want the Army coming out to our reservations.

History has shown that to be very detrimental to Native Americans."

Simon Gray Horse nodded in agreement.

"I'm not certain of what is going on up in your country, Mr. Two Bears, but I wouldn't be surprised if your state units are not recruiting people up there. Have you checked with your Montana state militia?"

"My wife's family has driven an insurmountable wedge between her and me. It was a nasty divorce with threats of violence. We have no children, so I wished to depart the area before someone, possibly me, or her two brothers, become extinct."

"That's a pretty good reason. I understand the country up there is very desirable. I don't know how mountainous it is, but I hear it is good cattle country."

"Yes Sir, Captain that it is. It's quite lovely and the cattle industry is flourishing on the reservation. Some of our red brethren are successfully engaged in commercial bison operations. There is an excellent expanding market for bison meat and by-products."

"Have either of you had any military experience, even Boy Scout training?"

Both Indians chuckled. "We're Native Americans, Sir. We can still sneak up on white men."

Captain White Horse smiled. He pulled out two questionnaires, hand each one, along with a pen and said, "Please fill out these forms. I know it is dreary paperwork, but forms are the oil of the administrative machinery. You can fill them out at the table outside the door. Just give them to my Sergeant when you finished. We'll call you when we have our next training session scheduled. Thank you for volunteering. I think you will both make excellent soldiers. Good day, gentlemen."

Captain White Horse stepped out of his office door and caught the eye of the Staff Sergeant. With a nod of his head he motioned the SSG to follow him outside. When they stepped outside, Captain White Horse said "Don't touch those forms. Just have them put them in the in-basket. I don't want your fingerprints on them. Call Sergeant Divers in the Sheriff's Department to come over and lift their fingerprints off of them. Snap their pictures with your digital camera when they aren't looking."

"Colonel, Captain White Horse here in Thermopolis. How are you today, Sir?"

"We're hanging in here, Captain. What can I do for you today?"

"I just had two Native Americans in here to volunteer. One of them is known, the other I am very suspicious of. I have directed their fingerprints and photos be surreptitiously taken. One is not your typical reservation Indian as he presents himself to be. I'll forward his prints and photo to you ASAP. Perhaps you can have him checked out. He claims to be from Hardin, Montana, on the Crow Agency up there. He is obviously educated, much too sophisticated to be a reservation Indian as he claims."

"Outstanding, Captain. We'll see what can be learned. I'll get back to you when I have anything definite.

****

"Well, they don't trust any Gringos whatsoever. Maria asked last week but I am not invited to any meetings. I hope it didn't raise suspicions about Maria. I wonder if Maria has turned, so to speak. She has begun to ask me pointed questions over the last month or so. I'm rather uneasy about it."

"What questions, or what is she asking about?"

"Well, she is asking how you feel about Mexicans, Sheriff, and not just you, but your deputies. I ask her 'how am I supposed to know?' The Sheriff and I aren't friends. I only see you and your deputies in the café. She told me that perhaps Jim and I should get to you know better. I don't think that she would have thought of that by herself. Something else; she asked if I knew someone who would teach her and her husband how to shoot, 'how to shoot real good.' I asked if they were going to starting hunting. She said, "No, she didn't think so." They just wanted to learn about guns. I caught Maria looking on the internet on the computer in the library where to buy military manuals. She has become less communicative the last few weeks. I think she is torn between her husband and her conscience. She did mention that Tomas disappears for a weekend every now and then. She doesn't know where he goes, but it is with Juan Cartagena. Last time he went he brought home a rifle. He said it was an AK-47, but wouldn't talk much about it. He told Maria not to tell anyone, but she let it slip. She doesn't like it in the house."

"Colonel Bradley needs to know. This has gone beyond a law enforcement matter. Maria won't testify against her husband. The judge won't issue a warrant, search or arrest, based on second hand information-that's hearsay. We'll keep Senor Cartagena under surveillance. Sooner or later he'll make a slip and we'll get him. Thanks, Jan. You have been a bigger help than you know."

"Colonel, Major General McIntire is on the scrambled line for you."

"Thanks, Sergeant."

"Bradley here, General. I hope all is well there."

"Ethan, your suspect is from the Crow Agency all right. He is half Crow and half Sioux. He works for or against his own people; however you want to look at it. He is the BATFE agent for southeast Montana. By devious means we ran a security check on him. His files were initially blocked, but we opened an alternative line. We have two choices. I'll leave it to you as to which one. They are to eliminate him, or use him as a double agent, feeding him false information. I doubt that would last long in your situation. I consider it rather dangerous, but that is your call."

"Thank you for the trust, General. I'll dispose of the matter at the appropriate time and place. On another matter, we need a greater propaganda effort, General. There are too many people who won't accept the situation, too many fence sitters. We need some people like the political officers of the former Soviet Union Red Army, the Federation of Socialist Republics or whatever they call themselves these days. I have directed my more erudite folks to write letters to the newspapers in the Basin to sway public opinion and support our position. Cody and Jackson are our worst areas. A lot of good citizens over there don't know which way to turn. They see the results of liberal socialist policies and don't want to return to California. They are afraid to stay here because they are afraid of the Patriots. I have also decided, rightly or wrongly, to order the seizure of all firearms and reloading supplies from all the sporting goods and hardware stores over there in Cody. We need them to arm our patriots in the militia companies who are late comers to the cause."

"If you watch much TV news Ethan, you might have noticed that the very few television journalists who leaned toward us are no longer on the scene. The unofficial word is that they were told to retire, support the government 100 percent or go to jail. I don't know about TV reception in your area, but electronic aircraft flying high over the Dakotas have begun to jam some of the local news broadcasts from stations here in Cheyenne as well as Billings. A TV station in Pocatello was blown up. We think they put a 500 pound bomb from a predator drone on it. I don't know if President Newkirk is making these decisions or his SECDEF or his DHS head.

Certainly they wouldn't occur without his consent. On that other issue, let me know when action is completed."

"Will do, General, as soon as it is done."

"I'll be in Thermopolis most of tomorrow, Sergeant. I need to see Captain White Horse." Ethan dressed in casual civilian clothes, holstered his .45 ACP and rode his motorcycle to the armory in Thermopolis.

"Captain White Horse, how do you feel about assassinations?"

"Well Sir, that depends on who is being assassinated, by whom, and for what reason?"

"If I gave you a direct order to assassinate an infiltrator in your company, how would you feel about that?"

Sir, if I discovered a spy in my company, an order from you would not be necessary. I would kill him, or her, on my own authority."

"Your intuitive suspicion is correct. Gray Horse and his alleged relative are spies. The cousin is a BATFE agent from Hardin."

"No problem Sir. "I'll eliminate him as soon as I can work out the best way to do it with a minimum of fuss."

"It is in your hands Captain. I'll leave the details to you. Just don't take too long to do it. He's probably trying to identify everybody."

Captain White Horse called in his company sergeant. "Send a runner to Mr. Gray Horse. He and his cousin are to report to me at 20:00 hours at the road construction site on highway 170. I'll brief them there. Tell them we are holding night infiltration exercises and since they are not yet trained, I'll be using them as guards at that crossing point. Tell them it is absolutely critical to be on time. Punctuality is a military virtue that is a necessity. No need for them t come armed, as it is just an exercise."

At 18:00 hours Captain White Horse dug a trench with a back hoe six feet deep and four feet wide in the middle of the road bed. He stationed a trusted soldier at each end of the construction site as a flagman 300 meters in each direction. He and his Sergeant armed themselves with Remington 870 twelve gauge shotguns and sidearms. Gray Horse and Two Bears pulled up to the site at 19:55 hours. Sergeant Dempsey ordered them to park their car off to the side of the highway where construction workers parked. Gray Horse and Two Bears approached and sheepishly saluted, putting on a good act.

Captain White Horse said "a patrol will be coming through here sometime between now and 24:00 hours. We expect them to follow the wash over there, but we don't know that for sure. The corporal leading the patrol is a pretty good night warrior. I have some night vision goggles and have a prepared position for you over here. If you see someone you are to call out 'Halt! Who Goes There?' Then you should fire the flare pistol to identify them. They should respond with by calling out "Company Zebra". Now, your position is over here behind this pile of gravel," pointing to it. "I have laid a flashlight, the flare pistol and NVGs on a board behind it. Take your positions."

As Many Horse and Two Bears approached the trench, Captain White Horse unshouldered his shotgun and shot them both in the back. Their bodies fell forward into the trench. Captain White Horse jumped into the trench and searched both bodies. He removed all identification and keys.

"Sergeant Dempsey, fill in that trench. Tomorrow this section or road will be paved. He changed into civilian clothes, put on a pair of vinyl gloves and a baseball cap. He climbed into Many Horse's pickup and drove to the Riverton Wal-Mart, parking in the lot and pulling his hat down low over his face before he left the truck. He deposited the gloves in the men's rest room and met his wife and kids who were shopping for groceries.

"What in the hell are these people thinking? Where are their minds? What do they hope to accomplish?" exploded Richard Newkirk, President of the United States, letting his Irish temper get the better of him, again.

"Columbia set the example as an autonomous unit, Mr. President. Now, other states think they can do the same thing, either regionally or individually. It is the Balkanization of these United States," said Frank Stokes, the Secretary of State.

"Don't these people realize that Columbia is nothing more than another state? It's an amalgam of states that got together for economic reasons to form a super state? Hell, they still pay taxes to this central government! They're bound to this union by defense treaties, by the postal system, by transportation, by power grids, by water distribution and God knows what else. Their judicial system isn't all that independent. It is simply a super expanded state with a little more jurisdiction over the money we sent them."

"I would point out Mr. President, that they send us more money than we send to them."

"Damn it Frank, I know that! Why should all of a sudden a bunch of states in different parts of the country want to break away? Why are there race riots in the south and southwest? All this happened after we banned private ownership of firearms except by special license. Why do these people want to own guns anyway? We'll provide them with police protection. Look at the size of our national police forces. Why are the Hispanics and Black Americans deserting the armed forces by the thousands?"

Senate majority leader Naomi Campbell glanced around the room then spoke to everyone present.

"Successful nation building from separate political entities uniting is rare because it requires politicians to surrender power. The dissolution of our country is essentially the result of the same process. We politicians have usurped so much power from the people without their genuine consent, in the form of a tremendous federal self serving bureaucracy, or out and out theft of power through disguised, that is, misrepresented legislation, that many of the people of the middle class, especially the upper middle class, can no longer tolerate it. The lower class doesn't care as long as they get free bread and good circuses. We the people have lost so much of our individual liberties as guaranteed in the Bill of Rights to make that document meaningless. Of course, many of the masses are willing to trade these freedoms, those restrictions of choices of life and lifestyles, as long as the state guarantees them bread and wine and circuses and public housing. The riots that you see are the result of the failure of the state to deliver on those promised essentials."

President Newkirk just glared at Senator Campbell, but said nothing.

"The anti-gun law was just the straw that broke the camel's back, Mr. President, at least for the middle and western parts of America. Certainly that was the case for the white middle class in the Midwest and Rocky Mountain regions. It is much more complicated however, than just the demise of the Second Amendment."

"Oh yeah, Noami? Tell me why! What about you, Norma?"

Naomi Campbell spoke before Norma Cantor could compose her thoughts.

"Our liberal philosophy is about ten thousand years ahead of our conservative cultural and physical and mental disparities, Mr. President."

"What the hell does that mean?"

"It means that no multi-cultural, multi-ethnic nation has survived for very long, never in the history of civilization. Each of us belongs to his tribe or super tribe. We have developed so many cultural centers that we can no longer bond together as a single nation. As Frank said, it is the Balkanization of the United States. Language and religion are two of the most significant glues that bind a nation, and cultural values are so disparate now that there is little allegiance to any center. Spanish has gained equal footing with English. We continue to teach grade school kids in thirty different languages in Los Angeles to encourage cultural and ethnic pride. Roman Catholicism is stronger than ever before; multiple offshoot religious sects have sprung up all over the country. As a Roman Catholic, Mr. President, I am sure that you realize that faith should not be confused with loyalty to the Church. Particularly troublesome is militant Islam within the black community where the two are confused. Our laws have protected them collectively and individually while many waged sedition against us. It has become a major force throughout the black population of the southeast. We have more than a dozen major religions now active in this country, each clamoring for its share of recognition. Interestingly, Protestantism and Roman Catholicism are coming together on a number of issues, forming something of a common Christian base. Multicultural, multilingual, multireligious and multiracial societies have never succeeded for very long and probably won't for another thousand years. Who would have realized that our support for the United Nations Mandate on nationality and independence, that allowed regions to peacefully secede from original nations, would influence the disintegration of the United States? Remember when the sociologists all said that sooner or later the whole human species would blend together?" They said it took us white folks.100,000 years to evolve from our earliest ancestors when Homo sapiens was all one color, probably black, and expanded out of Africa. They said we would overcome all racism and all the races would meld and we would all be the same once again. They said it would only take a couple of centuries; so much for the mixing of the gene pools. I think they were wrong. It might take a couple of millennia.

Another factor is the perception these westerners hold of themselves. These people are an independent minded group, Mr. President. They liken themselves to the pioneers of two hundred and fifty years ago. They like to think they adhere to the original Constitution and to the basic tenants of Protestantism, at least for the most part. Attacking the religious center was a mistake. Eliminating 'One Nation Under God' from the Pledge of Allegiance, barring the Ten Commandments from public places, banning Christmas displays, and on and on, destroyed a lot of our national cohesion. That wasn't just limited to the west either. That offended a lot of people in the east. Neither do they care for the concept of a 'living Constitution.' As your opponent in the election said, 'a living Constitution simply means that the current crop of politicians can change it to mean anything they want it to mean.' That went down very well with most of them. Your opponent carried virtually every rural county west of the Mississippi and many in the Midwest on that concept. It is a real sagebrush rebellion,"

"Christ Naomi, you are beginning to sound like some TV evangelist. Well, Naomi, where do we sit with our armed forces to eliminate this sage brush rebellion?"

Naomi Campbell was born a Black American in the slums of Bayonne, New Jersey. She was raised by her mother as a single parent. She had five siblings, three brothers and one living sister. An older sister was murdered in their public housing building at the age of fourteen. Each sibling was fathered by a different man. Her mother had a constant stream of different boy friends, none of which remained to form a family unit when she reached the middle trimester of her pregnancy with his child. One night, when her brothers were out of the apartment and her mother was at work, one of her mother's boy friends raped Naomi when she was fourteen. When she was sixteen, she was cornered at the Laundromat and dragged into the alley, where she was gagged, and gang raped by six black youths. When her elder brother who was nineteen heard of it, he climbed into her bed, put his hand over her mouth one night and raped her as well. She became pregnant and sought an abortion at the neighborhood family planning clinic.

In high school, she was a very popular cheerleader. She represented her home room on the student council for her junior and senior years. She was on the girls' varsity volleyball and softball teams. Her grades were a perfect 4.0 although she could only read at the eighth grade level. Under the Scholarship for Promising Minorities program of the state of New Jersey, she was awarded a four year scholarship to the University of New York. She enrolled as journalism major. She struggled mightily the first two years, seeking help in virtually every course. She virtually lived at the library to study because the dormitory was so noisy and disruptive. Finally, she achieved the appropriate plateau of scholarship her junior year, and excelled her senior year. A few friends in the dormitory taught her the basics of grooming and dress. She jogged routinely and discovered tennis so that she remained in excellent physical condition. She was a very attractive young black woman when she graduated. She applied for and was accepted as an intern for the U.S. Congressman from her district. After two years, she decided to apply for law school. With a strong recommendation from her Congressman, whose bed she frequently graced, she was accepted into the University of New York School of Law. She graduated in the middle of her class and went to work for the Southern Poverty Law Center, working out of a store front law office in the slums of Bayonne, New Jersey. After two years, she ran for city council seat and won. After one term, she ran for the state senate and won. Her next step was to run for the U.S.

Congress. Her district was eighty percent black, with a few Hispanics and some Koreans and Vietnamese. No other candidate had a chance. On her first term she was assigned to the Committee on Transportation and Infrastructure. On her second term she requested and was appointed to the House Armed Services Committee. After three terms in Congress, she ran once again on the Democratic ticket for the U.S. Senate seat. She won handily. Because of her experience on the House Armed Services Committee, she was appointed to the Senate Armed Services Committee. She was re-elected to the Senate for her second term when Richard Newkirk was elected President. Now at forty-eight, having never taken the time to develop a long term relationship with one man and have a family, she was a dedicated, hardened Democratic liberal who knew nothing but politics and sex. She was always promiscuous but extremely secretive in her personal life and very discrete with her romantic interludes as she moved through a series of lovers. When she was elected to the U.S. Congress, she immediately decided that she would provide no one with the opportunity for blackmail or political ammunition for any indiscretion. She only conducted her sexual affairs on weekends, when she and her lover would travel separately and with disguises to distant rural locations for a lovers' tryst. As a politician she was extremely pragmatic and a shrewd negotiator. She could smell what was on the wind and act before the situation became a threat. Some people were talking of her being the first woman President and the first Black American President. She did nothing to dispel that position. In order to achieve the necessary politically correct racial balance and because of her membership on the Armed Services Committees, President Newkirk tapped her to be Secretary of Defense.

"I have ordered all U.S. naval vessels to immediately return to their home U.S. ports, Mr. President."

"Why did you do that, Naomi?"

"We will need those sailors to guard critical ports and port facilities, Mr. President. They and the Coast Guard are the forces most appropriate and familiar with our ports. The Coast Guard is simply too small and spread too thin to guard our major ports as a single service. The Navy will have to be the major force augmented by the Coast Guard. In particular, I have ordered the Pacific Fleet to guard the ports of Long Beach, Los Angeles, San Francisco and Seattle. Units of the Atlantic Fleet are to guard the ports of Galveston, Mobile Bay, New Orleans, Miami, Baltimore, Charleston, New York, Houston and Savannah. I have prepared for your signature the appropriate documents to bring the Coast Guard into the Department of the Navy as a military force under the Homeland Security Act. They will be integrated according to prepared plans. The Navy will patrol out to the 200 mile limit as well as provide off-shore security where indicated. God knows what these so-called Patriots are willing to do, let alone Islamic extremists. We don't want a ship loaded with Algerian natural gas to be detonated in Boston's harbor, or similar event anywhere, Mr. President. That would be the equivalent of a twenty-five kiloton nuclear weapon."

"All right, I'll buy that. How long will it take for these naval forces to reach their ports?"

"It varies, Mr. President. Those coming from the Arabian Sea, Indian Ocean, and the far Pacific will take two to three weeks. Too many of our ships are still oil burners, not nuclear driven."

"Now, what about our Army doing its duty in quelling these riots? What about these mass desertions? Why is this occurring? What troops can we count on?"

"Frankly, Mr. President, I am not sure you can count on any federal troops. The divisiveness runs so deep throughout America that I am skeptical. Our armed forces are nothing more than a reflection of the society that provides them, Mr. President, and that includes the schisms. I don't believe they will come together again unless there is an indisputable external threat. In Texas black soldiers will only fight against Hispanic rioters and Hispanic troops will only fight against black rioters. In some scattered units, platoons and companies, they are fighting each other. The chemical industry in Houston is coming to a standstill because of the riots and firefights. Those folks who want to work are afraid to go to work for fear of being ambushed by gangs of another race. Many of the blacks in units sent to the Houston area are deserting and taking their rifles with them. Whites are in a tough spot, caught between the blacks and Hispanics. White families are fleeing the Houston area as fast as they can. As we all well know, some of those white folks defending their homes have been overwhelmed and killed by mobs. Many young Muslims joined the military for training. Once they were trained, they withdrew back into the Muslim communities from which they came. Most of our enlisted ranks came from the lower class of our society; they joined to gain a foothold, training for a craft or for the college benefits. They then left. The flag ranks are politicized and the middle ranks are either careerists or a few mission oriented mercenaries.

The one bright spot is Fort Campbell, Kentucky. The 101st Division Commander there quadrupled the guards on all the unit arms rooms using only Caucasian troopers. He called for a meeting of only his Caucasian officers and instructed them to guard the weapons and vehicles areas. He then announced that all Black and Hispanic officers and men are on extended leave for an indeterminate time. Fort Campbell remains in federal hands through the exclusive use of white troops."

"Then will somebody please tell me how we are going to hold this country together?"

No one spoke for several minutes as Richard Newkirk looked at each member of his party's leadership in turn. When he reached the Senate Majority leader, Jacob Lippsitz, Lippsitz slowly spoke. "You probably won't, Mr. President. It is too late. The disparities run too deep. The best we can probably hope for is a confederation, perhaps something like the Swiss cantonments. Each new unit will be a separate state yet bound by defense and major infrastructure requirements to a central entity. It will take a great deal of work to make it a viable, feasible relationship. Yet, I am sure, every responsible person will realize that such an arrangement is in the best interest of all concerned."

"Naomi, can't we muster enough force to keep these states in line?"

"Mr. President, you would have to kill half the people in these regions that want to break away. As desirable as preservation of the Union is, we don't have the armed forces to initiate a major civil war. This is not just a major civil disturbance, Mr. President. It is the demise of the United States as we know it. It could be the Civil War of 1861 all over again. If you attempt to use force to maintain the Union, it will be just like the breakup of Yugoslavia in the 1990's. It would be better to allow the secession than the bloodletting that would follow. Who knows? Perhaps if it is a peaceful separation now they might petition to rejoin the Union later, after they see the error of their ways. Remember it took about a hundred years to overcome the enmity caused by our last civil war. There was still heartburn over flying the Stars and Bars Confederate flag into the 1990's. Maybe the European Union would send troops in here the way we did into the Balkans, although I can't comprehend the Europeans being that stupid. We are simply too large, too geographically diverse and civilians are still too well armed. Most of our rebels would look upon that as a foreign invasion. The rebels would no doubt wind up possessing many of the weapons of the Europeans; particularly worrisome would be the heavy weapons."

"What about a draft, re-instating selective service and training a new army?"

"That will take several years, Mr. President, assuming you have a definable base, a country, a nation, that will provide the population base from which to draft young people. Then too, their legislators will have to vote for it, and there is no guarantee that anyone will answer the call. Ever since we eliminated the compulsory military service as a result of the Vietnam War sixty years ago, a large segment of our population has grown into wimps and weenies. Youth as a class are no longer willing to serve in the armed forces except as a first step out of poverty. Our youth have nothing that they consider worth fighting for, other than materialism. Only volunteers have manned our services and only those who chose it as a career path are truly warriors. These careerists are for the most part, hardened soldiers, at least the enlisted men, Mr. President. Most first time enlistees chose the armed forces simply to learn a trade or craft and then don't re-enlist after their first three or four year term. As a whole, our society has become too soft and too materialistic to consider the harshness of military service and sacrifice. That is particularly true since they spend so much time out of country in places like the jungles of Africa and the deserts of Asia.

On top of that, training an army to sufficiently high standards will take several years. We have become militarily speaking, very dependent upon technology. Much of the lighter equipment and arms are disappearing from our military bases as we speak. Arms room after arms room has been raided. New equipment and arms will have to be procured. Even military vehicles have been stolen and continue to be stolen. Many have been driven into Mexico. Commanders are no longer obeyed. A number of officers have been shot when trying to stop the thefts. I have the fear that these arms and vehicles will be given to the Mexican Army, or large raiding parties of bandits will be formed. Who is there to stop raiders with infantry fighting vehicles come tearing through the countryside, perhaps even attacking small cities as well as the smaller towns? Remember in the Mexican Revolution, during the late 1910's and 1920's, numerous warlords arose and controlled various sized segments of that country. They raided and looted as they chose until central authority was restored. In that regard, this morning I ordered all heavy weapons and equipment remaining on military bases in the south and southwest to be immediately moved to northern bases, so as to save what hasn't already been looted. There are scattered reports of racially based firefights on some of our southern Army bases. In particular, Fort Bliss outside of El Paso and Fort Hood TX, near Waco, TX, armories were severely robbed and quite a number of gun fights occurred as you learned in your daily briefing this morning. Military police companies were relatively powerless to prevent the thefts. So far, the Marines from Camp LeJune that I ordered to guard the Capitol have proven loyal and are doing a remarkable job. Again, also this morning, I ordered all military stores removed from those states considering secession. In some of those states considering secession, National Guard units have already raided arms rooms on active component bases with bolt cutters, torches, and trucks and hauled off small arms, ammunition, and crew served weapons. Ditto for reserve component armories. You will forgive me, Mr. President, for acting without first consulting you, but I deemed timing crucial. When you gave me carte blanche authority on all defense matters, I assumed that authority I have done all I could to keep the national news media from covering these stories."

"Who are the leaders of these breakaway states? Why can't we have Navy SEALS and Army Rangers snatch these people and throw them in jail? Don't I have that authority under some kind of emergency law? What do you say, Pete?"

"You would make martyrs out of them and there are too many of them anyway. Look, why don't you let the House and Senate continue the debate on the issue of secession? At the same time, we can jaw jack the state governors involved. Repealing the elimination of the Second Amendment would certainly help the situation. Jake can continue to work behind the scenes to see what is required to keep these states in the Union. What do you say, Jake?"

"I say that I am beginning to hear rumblings about breakup from the citizens of New England. The de facto repeal of the Second Amendment did not sit well with Maine, Vermont or New Hampshire. There are a lot of hunters up there. New Hampshire's State Attorney General called and told me last night that their state senate is even considering recall of its U.S. Senators who voted affirmatively on the issue. That's a first, at least the first I ever heard of removing U.S. Senators from office because of their vote on a single issue. I don't think there is any legal basis for it. Even rural New York State is upset over it. Calling a telescopic sight equipped deer rifle a 'sniper rifle' and making those illegal just about the ultimate insult to the hunting community, even if there are only several million of them."

"I'll just freeze all the funds earmarked for those states under every federal program. We'll bring them back into the fold when they don't kind one red cent of federal funding."

I wouldn't advise that either, Mr. President. First, they send more money to us in taxes than we send back to them if you don't include our national debt in the equation. They were more fiscally responsible in their state budgets this last decade than we have been with the federal budget in the last century. Our deficit is crushing us and they know it. I wouldn't take that kind of action while there is any chance we can keep them in the Union through negotiation. You can use that as a carrot in those talks, but not if you withdraw it first. They wouldn't trust your word to restore them in the same amounts if you withdrew them first. Next, they won't agree to pay any share of the national debt if you do withdraw those funds. Some are now even calling for a 'Jubilee' as in the Old Testament of the Bible. That is when all debts, public and private, were forgiven. It happened once every 50 years," said Naomi.

"Pete, you find me a loophole in the law that will allow me to jail the governors and maybe the senators of these states that want to secede. Call it sedition, call it treason, call it whatever the hell you like. I just want it to look legal, I don't care if it really is or not. Now who are those senators and congress people who are for secession and who is against it?"

"Well, the senators from Montana, both members of your own party, are against secession, but the governor and people of Montana are for it. Wyoming's state senators and house members, the governor and the people are all for secession. Colorado is mostly for staying in the union, but there is considerable turmoil there with their large Mexican population in the southern part of the state which sympathizes with the southwest. The urban population wants to stay in the union. They don't understand why other states want to break away. These Colorado Mexican-Americans might well try to break off southern Colorado to join the Hispanic autonomous movement. The Dakotas, well, there's a couple of real pieces of work. Their Governor, Senators, and Congressmen are waiting to see how the wind blows. The Native American populations there like all the federal programs, but we haven't had the word out of the major powwow on what they want to do. Some indications are that they might want to form their own independent state out of the reservation system. They might offer to trade land so they can amalgamate one huge chunk of Indian Territory out of somewhere in the west or Midwest for all Native Americans. I find that hard to believe, but God only knows. They will sure have a hard time giving up all their money making casinos. I don't really see that as a viable alternative. Rather, the Navajos and related tribes, which is the largest entity, might try to break out the Four Corners area as a separate state; ditto for the Dakotas and part of Minnesota. Who knows at this point?"

"Hell, are they farmers? Some of them are ranchers, yes, but wheat farming? They don't know squat about modern agricultural wheat growing. I think that might be a trial balloon as leverage, to threaten to seize our wheat belt in return for something else. Jake, check with our Indian senator from South Dakota and have Dave feel out the Indian congressman from North Dakota and see what you can get out of them before the day is over. Those Indians have never really joined mainstream society."

"Mr. President, I suggest we use the remainder of this meeting to determine what our priorities are, and how they match the priorities of Congress."

"OK, Naomi, spell it out. What do you think they should be?"

"Our armed forces, especially the Army and Marines, are primarily composed of folks from the black and Hispanic communities; at least they exceed seventy percent collectively. We don't have a good handle on how many are deserting, as the desertions are not only continuing but increasing. We conceivably are or could easily approach a fifty percent loss right now of total manpower, and it could get worse. If we attempt to use them to quell some of the riots in the cities, many will probably refuse to fire or use any violent means against their own communities as is occurring in Houston. It might even encourage further desertions. Rather, we should have them guard critical facilities in states in turmoil, and possibly other than those considering secession, against any destruction or seizures. I am talking about chemical plants, power plants, power distribution substations, water and sewage facilities, distribution and food processing plants, and above all, communications facilities. We should be securing radio and television stations, newspapers and computer network centers. These could be weapons for those who are particularly well organized. I'm not sure how these facilities will continue to operate, but their continued operation is critical. Some of the gangs are essentially private armies, especially in the Los Angeles, San Francisco, Houston, and Baltimore areas. These gangs could seize them for propaganda purposes or to strangle selected neighborhoods. We have no idea how many foreign or even domestic Muslim terrorists are embedded in these gangs as sleepers, waiting for an opportunity to commit major damage to our infrastructure. I have alerted the Adjutant Generals in the northern states with a warning order that their National Guard units could be mobilized at any time for riot control duty and to guard those critical facilities.

Secondly, we can use the troops to establish escape routes out of the cities. We have to keep our road nets open so that those who want out can make it out. We don't want any mass killings on the highways that will close them down or function as choke points. That is not for or against any particular ethnic group. I expect though, it will be mostly the white population that will try and flee to the north, to the Midwest and Northeast.

Third, we need to insure the flow of food into the cities, and perhaps fuel supplies with the current season of cold weather. Our soldiers, especially the National Guard units, will go along with the humanitarian efforts. Our logistics capabilities will be strained on that one. Therefore, I suggest we prioritize which cities we will support and those which will have to be on their own."

"All right, Naomi, have your secretary record your ideas as regards to the use of the armed forces and give them to Dave Carlton in the House and Jake here. Let's see what our illustrious Congress persons think of them. I presume that you have a prioritized list of cities? What other proposals do you have in mind? Anybody?"

"There is not a lot to fight for from Texas west of U.S. Highway 87 across to Palm Springs. There are a lot of dry oil well holes, gila monsters, sand, rocks and rattlesnakes. I don't think we should fight for that, but let the Mexicans have it as a compromise. We'll keep all of California north of Monterey Bay, but let them have New Mexico, Arizona and Texas west of highway U.S. 62 and south of U.S. 40. That will give them the cities of Lubbock, Odessa, and Midland. Hell, they have had control of El Paso for decades anyway. Fort Bliss is really in the hands of the Mexicans from what Naomi tells me. We better be prepared to defend that line though, or we will be overrun," said Ed Andretti, Chief of Homeland Security.

"Do you mean to tell me General Singleton, that Mexicans will push farther north with military force"?

"That certainly is a possibility, Mr. President, but not as a strategic force. These last two weeks have been a hemorrhage of military personnel and equipment. As Naomi said, they are well armed, have dozens of Stryker infantry fighting vehicles they have stolen and driven to Mexico, could form small armies of company, battalion or even regimental size, and much more likely, will be the flow of ordinary middle class Mexican-American citizens who disagree with the revolution pouring north out of the southwest. Those Mexican-Americans could be in a world of hurt. They will be caught between the two forces and might be attacked by whites confusing them with Mexican interlopers. There will be those who are newly arrived from Mexico among them looking for any kind of opportunity. We all know Mexico is on the verge of its own civil war and that has resulted in an increased flood of illegal Mexicans. If they cross over the line expect bloodshed from the white community. The folks in the cities are pretty well disarmed, but the rural folks retained most of their firearms, or at least we think they did. They will be shooting Hispanics on sight without asking any questions first."

"Mr. President, I would like to point out a few things about the southwest that are not blatantly obvious. "

"All right Solomon, what does the Department of Energy have to say? You so rarely speak it, it must be important."

Solomon Lansky looked around the room at each cabinet member somewhat nervously, swallowing hard. He had no idea how many of the others really knew his personal involvement in government land allocation. He felt the little beads of perspiration forming under his collar and on his forehead.

"The threat of losing the southwest to Mexico is as much a strategic threat as losing the northern prairie states to the proposed Nation of the Missouri. The Nation of the Missouri with its coal is becoming less significant than the southwest with its deserts and sunlight as an energy source. We have spent hundreds of billions of dollars, both in and out of government, in the Department of Energy, with research, testing, and now in construction of solar energy plants. The technology is maturing in photovoltaic, fluid trough, and heated salt dynamics all of which will be on line in a few years. A consortium of power companies has very quietly put together a package, so to speak. They have been buying up private land for a song all around the federally owned land in the southwest and great plains. Power companies are half way through in completion of the Direct Current power lines in support of these technologies We can eliminate between three and four hundred coal fired electricity generating plants and as many natural gas plants. In a few more years, perhaps no more than a decade, the research will be mature enough to apply to motor vehicles to reduce our diesel and gasoline requirements. Experimental smaller commuter cars utilizing these technologies are in advanced development. Compressed air storage technology for generating electricity at night and peak hours of demand is mature and being constructed by power company consortiums. It is all interlocking into a grid, Mr. President."

"So you're telling me we have to keep the southwest as well?"

"Yes Sir, we simply cannot allow the southwest to break off. We have 30,000 square miles of desert in Arizona, New Mexico, West Texas and southern California we are filling with photovoltaic cells. We have kept the extent of this very quiet because it is considered a strategic terrorist target. This has to be a strategic thrust of Mexico. They want that investment, they want that solar energy. Mexico could be in control of the USA through control of our national power grid as it comes on line in the next few years. Building high voltage direct current power grid is necessary to replace the inefficient alternating current grid. The AC grid has been failing for many years now. It is too expensive to continue to maintain. Building it adjacent to the interstate highway system dramatically reduces the right of way costs. Maximizing economy of scale, photovoltaic farms are built at a fraction of the time and cost of coal fired plants, let alone the 15 years required for fast breeder nuclear reactors. We have kept the extent of this system pretty quiet because of it being a potential terrorist target. I can assure you, keeping the enormity of it secure has been a real headache. So far, we have been rather successful. We simply cannot lose it."

CHAPTER 10

"DR. HASSAN, THE CONTENTS OF THE VIALS, WHILE THEY REMAIN FROZEN, WILL BE VIABLE". Once thawed, they must be held at 40 degrees Fahrenheit for no longer than 72 hours and must distributed within twenty-four hours of reaching room temperature. The nebulizers will dispense the virus particles at the appropriate intervals. An innocuous orange fragrance has been incorporated in the canisters to disguise their true nature. Your people will simply attach them to the walls with the cyanoacrylate glues on the back of the dispensers by peeling off the paper and holding them in place for thirty seconds. That is all that is required. I suggest you select the most appropriate places and times for placement for maximum effect. The morbidity ratio is in excess of seventy percent. The case fatality ratio will be slightly in excess of five percent. Those deaths will be in persons who are immunologically compromised or in very serious life threatening health situations. Person to person transmission is a given. You realize of course, that it is almost inevitable that this will initially spread among your own people. As per previous agreement, we will provide you with all the necessary vaccine once the first case is reported in international channels. We will distribute it throughout the Muslim world the first week after cases suddenly appear. The vaccine has been thoroughly tested. The vaccine virus was grown in primordial human embryonic tissue culture and therefore has no allergenic component. It cannot cause the disease, yet bestows a powerful immunity. We can produce several million doses a week in tissue culture as required. I believe however, that we already have more than enough on hand. Rather, it is a question of distribution and administration. You must be organized and ready for a massive vaccination campaign among all your people. It will spread to Europe and North America quickly enough. You must not admit to its source, rather you must explain to the world that it is an experimental vaccine produced within your own laboratory that we built for you, and is being provided as an extreme emergency measure without adequate testing. Simply say that you selected certain genes from the influenza virus that provide powerful immunity and placed them in the canary pox virus that acts merely as a cassette or carrier for insertion of the appropriate genes. The canary pox virus of course will produce the necessary antibodies and a cellular immune response as well. It grows extremely well in the appropriate cell lines. They will probably not believe you, but then what is that to you or us.

The shipment of the pathological virus will arrive frozen in a CONEX, the Continental Express shipping container, of shrimp labeled as originating in the Chinese Province of Hue, Vietnam. Its value as a fresh frozen cargo of high monetary value will expedite its transit through Beirut to Damascus and on to Amman. Here are the identification numbers of the CONEX of interest. Your people should be on hand when it arrives and take immediate possession to insure its safe handling. Of course, those handlers should not regard it as anything but what it is labeled, fresh frozen shrimp. Under no circumstances is the CONEX to be opened by anyone but your people. We have already supplied you with sufficient vaccine to immunize all those who will handle the canisters. Those vaccinations should have been accomplished over the last six months. All should be in place. We will ship you the vaccine in the same manner. We consider the influenza season to be from late November through March. The peak is usually in January through February. Do not waste the opportunity."

"Thank you, Dr. Li, Yin Pao. The Palestinian people will be ready to do as you indicate prior to its release. This should liberate our land from the Crusaders and Zionists and return it to us, its rightful owners. We will be eternally grateful for your assistance. We cannot thank you enough for this wonderful weapon. It will also further erode American support for the Zionist cause; who knows, perhaps end it all together. What of your people, however? Certainly it has the potential to be a pandemic."

"An excellent question, Doctor. We have incorporated the vaccine into a mixture with our hepatitis A vaccine. We have been vaccinating our entire population with it for several years now. No one knows this outside of a few scientists and Security Council members, and now you. Guard this on pain of death. If it becomes known, we will know where it came from. It would mean the death of your entire clan. Make no mistake on that account. Now I must take my leave of you. My government and I wish you the most success." Dr. Li bowed at the waist, took two steps backward, turned, and left the hotel room.

****

Senator Kennely of Massachusetts, the grand old man of the Senate now in his early seventies, sat quietly in the corner and let his figurehead subordinate carry on in his usual manner. Kennely had always aspired to be the President. Realizing however, that he could never be elected, he strategically maneuvered his party such that he was the real power in the Democratic Party. He didn't have to hold the office to wield the power of the Presidency. His earlier womanizing, and later his alcohol abuse overcame much or his charm and wit of a decade ago. He was acerbic now when he chose, and charming as they come only when absolute necessity demanded it.

Richard Newkirk lacked the subtle nuance behind the scenes required of a true politician and worse, lacked the intelligence and judgment to make the best long term interests in his party's liberal philosophy. He did appear extremely handsome, was a skilled but superficial orator, and always smooth in front of the cameras. He garnered about 80% of the women's votes. Superficiality reigned over substance. Behind closed doors Newkirk was a different story. Newkirk managed to muddle his way through one of the ivy league colleges as an undergraduate majoring in political science. He acquired an appetite for women and whiskey which he had mostly learned to control by his senior year. After being severely beaten once by several masked members of a competing fraternity for being indiscreet regarding a young lady to which one of them was engaged, he learned the value of discretion. Henceforth, he never discussed his romantic affairs. It didn't take long for most of the co-eds he dated to see through him. He never found one with whom he felt he could be compatible. Besides, he thought a wife would get in the way of a political career. Then too, there were many attractive young women willing to share a bed with a rising politician. He applied for law school at the beginning of his senior year for entry the following year but was denied. He applied and was accepted the next year. He spent that layover year working as a graduate student in the political science department. He worked as a junior staff member for the Massachusetts Governor for two years after law school. After that he was elected to the House of Commons for one term, then to the Massachusetts state senate. Senator Kennely took notice of the young man and correctly deduced his aspirations. Kennely provided a moderate role as a mentor to him early in his career which was of enormous value. He had a very polished charisma, was always immaculately dressed, and was just beginning to learn to be a suave talker. He ran, and was elected to the U.S. Congress for one term. When the junior senator from Massachusetts was killed in an auto accident early his re-election campaign, Newkirk quickly placed himself in position for election to that office by taking over the campaign committee and running for the office with the blessing of the state Democratic Party apparatus. That was when Kennely began to seriously coach Newkirk. He never learned to control his temper when anyone disagreed with him in private and but only rarely lost it in public. That is why he refused to engage in one-on-one presidential debates. He became very vindictive in private whenever the opportunity arose to punish an opponent in some political way. Once in the U.S. Senate, Kennely's staff watched over Newkirk's staff which guided him like a mother hen according to Senator Kennely's requirements. Kennely guided him very carefully through all the bumps and elections necessary to reach the Presidency by the time Newkirk was forty-five. Having a front such as Newkirk was almost as good as being President himself. Kennely made it a policy never to correct his charge in the presence of others. He always attended the critical strategy meetings, but never made a remark. He would instruct President Newkirk only in private. This allowed Newkirk to present the façade of careful thought and reflection after having made initial temperamental remarks. Newkirk never invited his comments and others took the hint. Naomi Campbell had quickly figured out the relationship between Kennely and Newkirk early in their administration, but kept her insight to herself. She presumed others had as well. She knew some day it might become extremely useful.

"My illustrious colleagues of the Senate, we are entering one of the three gravest threats to our country in our history as a nation. Our Revolutionary War and its immediate aftermath was the first great test of this mighty nation. Our Civil War of 1861 bound the union together for another 160 years, and now, the threat has again arisen, to tear us asunder.

Why is this occurring and how do we prevent it? Why are our troops deserting our armed forces? Why are our citizens shooting our national police officers? What great tragedy has occurred that results in this upheaval? Are we so primordial a people that we cannot overlook each others' physical differences? Why can we not respect each others cultural values? So many wonderful contributions have been made to our society by so many cultures that we truly are the often described melting pot of the world. Why can't we live in harmony with one another? Surely, if this great nation breaks apart we will lose all that we have gained. We can not protect ourselves as smaller states. We are bound together by so many systems and infrastructures that will suffer irreparable damage from which we might never recover. It will be impossible to maintain our transportation systems, our communications systems, our water systems, our legal system, our educational system, our financial systems, and most importantly, our mutual defense if this fragmentation of our great country is to occur. Our European friends, our friendly competitors, are jumping with glee. They grew closer together as the European Union after the debacle of disintegration. They are approaching becoming the United States of Europe while we, the United States of America, grow apart. What compromises must be made so that, in the words of Abraham Lincoln, 'we can bind this nation together once again"? Jacob Lippsitz of New York paused at just the wrong time.

Senator Rockland of Wyoming stood up and shouted, "I'll tell you, Senator Lippsitz, return to the Constitution and the Bill of Rights as they were written. Abandon your nationalist-socialist welfare agenda and restore the government to the people! We are not part of Europe! We have elected a tyrant. And balance the budget." Rockland sat down as a startled Senator Lippsitz tried to regain his composure.

"Surely, Senator Rockland, you don't object to helping the less fortunate segments of our society in a land so rich as ours."

"Senator Lippsitz, our country is bankrupt. We are not rich, and a hundred years of feeding at the public trough has taught generations not to be responsible for themselves; that the government is responsible for them and will take care of them from the cradle to the grave. Socialism only works when there is a surplus and a Republic then can insure fair and equitable distribution of resources. What is happening is the natural outcome of that movement. Our, no, YOUR government no longer tolerates dissent. Political correctness rules our land. You send your secret police dressed in ninja suits burst into peoples' homes with no warrants in the middle of the night in the name of national security, you invade every aspect of our privacy and no segment of our lives is without federal scrutiny. You monitor every means of personal communication between and among our citizens. You have created a self sustaining bureaucracy that thrives on security of the state at the expense of the people above all.

This government is now philosophically no different than any of the forms of tyranny and is growing increasingly violent against its own citizens. That Senator is what must be changed. There is no way that the bureaucracy will oversee its own demise. Its underlying philosophy is bankrupt and until those change, there is no hope of reconciliation. The question now is will the secession be peaceful or violent. As Simon Bolivar the liberator of South America once said, Damned be the soldier who turns his weapons against his own people.'" Senator Rockland sat down. The senate chamber was ominously quiet.

"Tell me Senator Rockland, do you claim to speak for all of the people?"

"I speak for the people and the State of Wyoming. If you think I am alone, why not call for a national referendum on the issue? Ask if they are willing to allow states to secede to make entirely separate nations. Ask if they will approve of autonomous states within these United States, with entirely separate judicial and other systems, especially taxation, as they choose. Make sure that it asks if the people who are in favor of maintaining the union are willing to use force to maintain it. Ask those who sanction the use of force if they are willing to join the armed forces and fight to secure it. A similar referendum should be issued in the states seeking secession. See what the results of those will be, Senator. Certainly, any hypocrisy will not be lost on that farcical wanna-be world government, the United Nations."

"Perhaps Senator Rockland, complete secession will not be necessary. Is it not possible that some accommodation can be reached? After all, Columbia did not fully secede, but rather simply became more autonomous? A super state? Isn't that what you really seek? Do you really want to break completely away from the United States? Your region will be completely landlocked. Trade, commerce, communications, education, must all flow across through, back and forth, your proposed borders."

"I, and the state that I represent, are fully aware of all the ramifications, Senator. I am sure that the extremely valid points that you raised will be addressed in the process. We will let the people and the states they represent make the final choice."

"Perhaps I should refresh your memory, Senator Rockland. It was your party that introduced legislation requiring both thumb prints on ballots under the guise of eliminating vote fraud. You wanted morphometrics to verify identity for voter registration and voting. That denied the secrecy of balloting. Where are citizens' rights in that legislation? It was your Republican party under President Abraham Lincoln that denied the states the right to secede under the Tenth Amendment, resulting in our civil war in 1861. Now you wish to claim states rights that was denied by your party and resulted in that bloody war?"

The exchange between Lippsitz and Rockland played and replayed on all news networks for the next twenty-four hours. It played as well in Europe and the Middle East as it did in the North America. The illiterate populations of Africa watched it on their cell televisions. The Muslims danced in the dirt, the Chinese celebrated the most of all. It made a lot of people ponder just what the value of the Union is and what they were willing to personally pay to preserve it. It struck a cord with the populations of the states considering secession. It would, they felt, provide a view of the perception of the nation as a whole.

Two weeks later, Senator Lippsitz introduced a bill calling for such a referendum. Congressman Carlton introduced the identical bill in the House of Representatives. The President of the Senate and the Majority leader agreed that a vote will be called one week from this day for the national referendum to be held on April 15th.

As Colonel Bradley drove to Basin, Wyoming for a staff visit to the Army National Guard unit there, supposedly a company but really a platoon sized unit, he pondered the economic base of such a proposed new country or autonomous unit. Strategic thinking was something he began to appreciate at Command and Staff College and continued to develop, always trying to ascertain the long term consequences of any political or military action. He concluded to himself *"that the essential economic bases for the proposed new country are extractive and agricultural. The region is still rich in coal, has copper mining, although it is cheaper to import Chilean copper than to mine it in Anaconda, Montana; has some oil and natural gas that is quite expensive to extract, is a major wheat producing area, especially if the Dakotas join, timber is of some value, but there is little manufacturing. Wyoming continues to vie with West Virginia as the number one coal producing state. Billings was something of a center of light industry, electronics, optics, some metals, aluminum processing and manufacturing. There is some recreational industry, but that is severely disrupted in times of economic stress on the middle class. How serious are other regions in breaking away? The southwest is almost doomed to become the northern states of Mexico, provided Mexico holds together. Under the revised U.N. charter regions could now legally break away from a mother country if the citizens of that region supported it. The mother country that calls itself the United States has no recourse but to accept it under the international forum or admit their massive hypocrisy and use force to maintain the state. What about the Midwest and the Northeast? New England must be in turmoil as well,"* chuckled Bradley to himself. *"New York, New Jersey, Connecticut, Massachusetts, Rhode Island and Vermont are for the socialist police state model, while Maine and New Hampshire are more like the Montana-Wyoming model or are somewhere in between."* He still lacked information on how the Native American population would decide. Minnesota was another important unknown.

Bradley met with the captain commanding the National Guard Maintenance Company in Basin at 16:00 hours at the local armory, since Captain McCortle was a high school sociology teacher. He reviewed the personnel files of the officers and NCOs of the battery. The captain did not particularly impress Bradley. He seemed noncommittal and slightly on edge, which Bradley expected, but there was something more that Bradley couldn't define. He went through McCortle's 201 field personnel file a second time. McCortle acquired a Bachelor's degree in education from Colorado State University in Boulder in secondary education and sociology, a noted very liberal institution. He was married with two children, seemed reasonably well integrated into the community, had completed the didactic portion of the Maintenance Officers Advanced Course by computer and attended the field portion several summers ago. He graduated in the middle of his class. His class advisor ranked him as a middle to lower block officer, lacking in decisiveness and leadership. He couldn't give Bradley a straight answer on where he stood if the autonomous unit voted for secession. Would he support the autonomous unit or would he elect to remain in the union? Bradley decided not to force the issue at this time, but carefully observe his behavior as best he could. He gave Captain McCortle a reminder of his direct order.

"I tasked you in writing to develop a list of all the Mexicans and other Hispanics in the county. Coordinate your list through the social services offices, the county health department, and through all of the employers and farmers and ranchers of your county as required. I want you to identify those who are American citizens, those who are legal aliens, and those who are not. Personal information is to be provided. Names, addresses, phone numbers, age, marital status, family members, and so on. If necessary, take a couple of enlisted men with you as guards. Your county has one of the smallest Hispanic populations in the Big Horn Basin. It shouldn't take too long. I expect a compiled list on my desk in less than 30 days. What have you done to comply with is order?"

Captain McCortle took a deep breath, looked down, then into Colonel Bradley's face and shifted his gaze down again. "Sir, I haven't had the time to do much of anything with that. Really Sir, I think it is an illegal order. I don't think I should have to comply with it."

"Now, I will ask you directly, was it you that provided my initial address to my unit to the newspapers and or other media around the Basin?"

"Sir, no Sir. I did not do that." McCortle's face turned beet red.

"Do you have any idea who did?"

"Sir, no Sir. I have no idea."

"Have a good evening, Captain." Bradley dismissed himself and left. Bradley ate supper at a local diner and then visited the home of the company First Sergeant. Master Sergeant (MSG) Dale Longley was far more talkative, flattered that the brigade commander would visit his home. MSG Longley had served eight years active duty in the maintenance depots, acquiring a Bachelor's degree in mathematics at the same time. He taught high school algebra in the same school that Captain McCortle did. He had fourteen years in the National Guard, and so was eligible for retirement at the age of sixty. Longley had decided he was needed by the company and would stay until he had a total of thirty years. The extra time would supplement his retirement income as a teacher. CPT McCortle had not served on active duty, but was ambitious in terms of a National Guard career. While there was nothing suspicious about McCortle that MSG Longley could identify for Bradley, Captain McCortle had never gained MSG Longley's trust. He had not inspired his men, and seemed deeply troubled by the possibility of secession. MSG Longley identified Captain McCortle politically as a fence sitter. He refused to take any stand. Colonel Bradley asked MSG Longley to carefully monitor Captain McCortle's attitude, position, and as best he could, his activities. He specifically asked Longley to try and determine what Captain McCortle's final position on secession would be. MSG Longley did not know if it was Captain McCortle who provided the tape recording of the first briefing to the media. MSG Longley thought it was possible. Col Bradley also designated MSG Longley as the Recruiting NCO for the company and discussed holding a recruiting drive in the high school for the senior class.

Bradley checked into a local motel for the night. He drafted a recruiting advertisement specific for Big Horn County on his laptop computer after supper. The next morning he visited the local paper, a weekly, and placed the advertisement requesting that able bodied personnel who are supportive of the act of secession and are willing to serve in the Wyoming National Guard, see MSG Longley. The advertisement emphasized that the Wyoming National Guard might become part of the active force of the autonomous unit if secession occurred. The editor balked and demanded a cash payment when Bradley told him to send the bill to the Adjutant General in Cheyenne.

"I don't own the newspaper, and we are on a shoestring budget. All ads have to be paid in full before they are run." Bradley looked directly at the editor and calmly asked "If secession comes, where will you and this newspaper stand?" A bolt of fear went through the editor as he suddenly realized he was addressing the man who killed the editor of the Cody newspaper.

"I'll run your ad, Mr. Bradley, err, Colonel Bradley, and I will send the bill to the Adjutant General, just as you said."

"Thank you, Sir. I appreciate that as does the State of Wyoming. As a related topic, do you know how or who provided a copy of my address to my officers and NCOs to the Basin's media? If you do, I would appreciate the information."

The editor shook his head vigorously no, and stated, "I have no idea. I received it by fax. There was no return address on it. It was cut off the top of the fax and the text was placed on my desk."

Bradley chose to ignore the obvious fact that the address of the sender is always on a fax and the editor was quite likely lying. If he was telling the truth, then he had a Tory in his newspaper staff who removed the address. He thought he made the man sweat enough for the moment, but he would bear watching. Instead, Bradley responded "I appreciate your time and efforts on behalf of the cause of the State of Wyoming and the original Constitution. The media is the most powerful of tools. Ideas cannot be suppressed, but should be openly discussed. I am not familiar with any previous editorials you have run in your paper. Perhaps you should begin a series of editorials discussing all sides of the issue in an unbiased manner. Ultimately, you will have to make a decision to support one side or the other. In the meantime, I strongly suggest you reflect upon your own editorials so that you can decide where you will stand should the discussed autonomous unit, or an independent one, come into existence. Hopefully all will be accomplished in a peaceful manner, whichever way it goes. My purpose in this uniform is not to attack the United States, but to protect us from attacks by the United States in the event we decide to part company. Have a good day, Sir." With that remark, Bradley rose and left.

Captain Livingston out of Powell sent an engineering platoon to the armory in Worland the next weekend where they quickly built an office for Colonel Bradley and his sergeant. The signal platoon quickly had it wired for the necessary computers, faxes and telephone lines. The federal government still had not closed down satellite communications, but was certainly monitoring everything that came and went via satellite and telephone lines. Establishing secure communications except by runner seemed impossible.

Colonel Bradley received a fax the following week.

> FROM: Adjutant General, Wyoming National Guard, Autonomous Units
> TO: Brigade/Regimental/Unit of Action Commanders
> SUBJECT: Update on Political Autonomy
> DATE: 12 February 20XX

1.   Two names have made the final selection list for the subject unit.
   a. Republic of North Central America
   b. Republic of Missouri
   c. Republic of the Nation of Missouri
Since the Missouri River drainage is the only geographic feature common to all involved states save Idaho, "C" seems to be the favorite at the moment.

2.   The states of Nebraska, Kansas, and Iowa have sent representatives to our meetings to discuss their possible involvement.

3.   Idaho, Wyoming, Montana, North Dakota, and South Dakota have reached agreement to secede, pending

Referendum of 15 April 2026. All voting will be electronic and closely monitored. Votes will be instantly registered nationally and at the state capitols of the involved states.

4.   The United Nations has declared that individual states have the right to secede from the United States, or to declare autonomy, the same as other provinces in other countries.

5.   Unofficially, the states of Massachusetts, New York, Connecticut, Pennsylvania, Michigan, Wisconsin, New Jersey, Rhode Island, Ohio, Indiana, West Virginia and Minnesota are discussing the possibility of remaining as "The United States". Outside of that circle, they are also conferring with northern Atlantic coastal states of Maine, Vermont, and New Hampshire. They have formed a committee to draft something on the order of an unofficial constitution. The outcome is unknown.

6.   The Indian Alliance consisting of the tribes residing in Montana, Wyoming, North Dakota, South Dakota and Nebraska has decided to support the autonomous unit, providing their reservation lands are respected. The Board of Governors of the involved states has agreed.

7.   A raid by federal authorities to arrest the members of the Board of Governors during a secret meeting last week failed. A number of federal officers were killed, as were five members of the Autonomous Unit's security forces. The federal government's Department of Justice denies all culpability. President Newkirk of the U.S. claims total ignorance of the raid.

John McIntire,
Major General,
IN, Commanding

The month of February was unusually cold, going against the trend of warmer winters. Travel was more constrained, but Bradley made the rounds to determine the amount and success of winter training occurring among his companies. He was disappointed in Captain McCortle in Basin, who had not scheduled even a weekend outdoor exercise. He relieved Captain McCortle on the spot on his next visit to the armory in Basin. He called First Lieutenant Ronald Thorsen into the Armory and appointed him as Company Commander. MSG Longley typed the orders. "I will change my mind and grant you one level of appeal, Captain. You can appeal to Major General McIntire. I doubt it will do you any good, but do not let me discourage you from doing so. Decide if you wish to remain in the Guard and do it quickly. If not, submit your resignation to Lieutenant Thorsen. I am beginning to suspect your loyalty. It would perhaps be better for you and your family if you moved out of this region, and do it rather quickly." McCortle made no response. He saluted, did an about face, and walked.

Bradley drove to Powell, where, in civilian dress, he called on Captain Livingston at his workplace. He informed Captain Livingston of relieving Captain McCortle. He instructed Captain Livingston to have his signal officer Lieutenant Weir, a bright young computer engineer, somehow or another monitor the electronic communications emanating from Captain McCortle's home. "I don't care how he does it. Bug his phone, his cell phone, home and school fax, or whatever, but have your Lieutenant monitor him very closely. I must know if he is feeding information to the feds. Obviously, this is to be clandestine."

Back in his office, Bradley informed Regimental Sergeant Major Michael Killian to set an officer's call for the first Saturday in March.

The television news one early February evening carried the story of a massive epidemic of respiratory disease occurring in the Middle East. The outbreak, as the Centers for Disease and Prevention (CDC&P) prefers to call epidemics to avoid public panic, centered in Israel. Its eruption was sudden and massive, literally within twenty-four hours in multiple locations. All initial indications were that it was Influenza A, of an atypical strain. It seemed to have characteristics similar to those of avian and porcine viruses when examined with the amino acid auto analyzers. Since it was not reported in the Far East, speculation immediately arose that it was a mutant strain carried by migrating birds between Europe, eastern Africa and the Middle East that spilled over into the human population. The World Health Organization laboratories in Geneva, the Centers for Disease Control & Prevention in Atlanta all examined its DNA with sequential analyzers and characterized it. They all reached similar conclusions. It did in fact, have some genes almost identical to those of avian and porcine strains of Influenza A. No doubt existed whatsoever in anyone's mind that this was a unique mixing of the genes of influenza A strains characteristic of multiple animal species. It did seem unusual to the experts that such a melding of viruses did not originate in China or Southeast Asia. The first reports carried news of hundreds dying in Israel. In 72 hours, the reports carried news of thousands dying, particularly in the Palestinian refugee camps. Two crews of television journalists from the Central News Network and National Broadcasting Company were stricken and died while covering the epidemic in Tel Aviv.

All travel between the Middle East, Europe, and North America was immediately suspended. The economic effects were profound. Ships from across the Atlantic were not permitted into harbors to unload their cargoes until they had been anchored offshore for two incubation periods of influenza, and then only after each and every crew member was given a physical examination by a physician who was approved by the Public Health Service. Some tried to avoid the quarantine by sailing through the Panama Canal to the west coast ports, but they were immediately detected and prevented from entering the Canal Zone.

The Center for Disease Control and Prevention sent a team to Tel Aviv to collect histopathological samples and assist in whatever way their Israeli hosts requested. The mortality rate was soaring. The team pathologist participated in two autopsies of youthful Israeli citizens who died of the disease. The Israeli pathologists stepped back from the necropsy table to let the American pathologist collect tissue samples by himself. He selected tissues from virtually every organ, dropping them specimens in different fixatives or tissue culture solutions for virus isolation when they returned to the United States. He collected two separate samples of everything. Secretly he hoped the CDC was still standing, undisturbed by the rioting. Against his will, he was directed to share all specimens with the U.S. Army Medical Research Institute of Infectious Diseases, USAMRIID for short, at Fort Detrick, MD. USAMRIID would get one complete set of all specimens. Even though he wore the uniform of the U.S. Public Health Service which is considered a uniformed service, he had an inherent distrust of everything and anything military. When he returned to Atlanta, he handed the specimens over to a military courier. The specimens were flown by helicopter from the Atlanta airport directly to Fort Detrick.

"ATTENTION!" Sergeant Major Michael Killian called the Officers Call to attention as Colonel Bradley stepped up to the podium. MG McIntire assigned the Sergeant Major to Colonel Bradley as his brigade Sergeant Major because he trusted him. Killian had served MG McIntire well in various capacities for over fifteen years, and the General admonished Killian to serve Bradley equally as well.

"As you all know, there will be a national referendum on secession on 15 April. The outcome is anyone's guess. We are all aware of the ramifications. I have directed company commanders to get as much winter training in as possible. I am disappointed in those results. Let me give you a scenario. The country breaks apart, possibly into several new nations. We, the states of Wyoming, Montana, the Dakotas, and possibly Idaho will most likely be one of them. In order to preserve the Union, President Newkirk decides to use force to maintain all fifty states within the Union. We are invaded by military forces of the United States upon announcement of secession. We can expect combined air and ground attacks. Both manned aircraft and armed unmanned aerial vehicles attacks can be expected. The National Guards of the respective states are to resist where ever and when ever possible. When the U.S. military pressure exceeds our ability to hold or counter attack, our forces are to collapse into the Big Horn Basin. Our mission is to be prepared to support and train all such withdrawing units in winter and guerilla warfare in as short a time as possible. We must be able to train them in light infantry tactics in the mountains during winter. This war could last for several drawn out years. It could well be as bad or worse than what our forefathers experienced at Valley Forge. It will be just like our first civil war, only fought with modern weapons, including electronic warfare. In order to accomplish that mission, we must be proficient in winter mountain light infantry tactics ourselves. I have found it necessary to relieve one commander so far because of a lackadaisical attitude. I am quite capable of relieving each of you that does not understand or comply with the necessity of our mission. Spring is just around the corner. I consider us as having failed in our mission at this point. Make the best possible use of your remaining time. Time is a resource we might not have much of. Major General McIntire is doing all he can to garner heavy weapons for us in order to guard the entrances to the Big Horn Basin. That does not denigrate the possibility of airborne assault. If that is the case, each and every small arms round must count. That is why I have emphasized marksmanship as a fundamental skill.

Part of this scenario will be to preserve sufficient food and fuel for the civilian population as well as our military forces. Each of you must press this home on your respective communities and their leaders. It is unlikely that food and fuel will be able to reach the Basin during hostilities. We must grow our own and make do with what we have. Encourage gardening and livestock production. Everything from rabbits for meat and fur to cattle should be raised.

Captain Livingston, I am directing you to study the irrigation requirements, basin wide. I am sure much of that information is available from the appropriate civilian offices. What we will need for water to maximize our agricultural production. We cannot reduce the flow of water into Montana, as they will be part of us. Rather, we must maximize what resources we have on a regional basis.

Captain Gates, inventory medical resources throughout the Basin. Encourage all medical facilities to stockpile medical supplies and pharmaceuticals while they still can. Have all medical facilities and personnel order as much medical supplies as they can, even on extended credit. Get a complete inventory of all medical personnel in the Basin.

Lieutenant Thorsen, as a Maintenance Company Commander, try and get a handle on all the transportation assets in the Basin, to include state rolling stock, privately own pickups and trucks of all sizes. The county tax assessors' offices should help there. We need to know what we have, where it is and what condition it is in. Try and determine stockage levels for spare parts for the more common brands and models of trucks in the Basin. Encourage dealers to order the maximum amount of the most commonly needed spare parts.

Captain Ferguson, determine how much POL, petroleum, oil and lubricants can be stored in the Basin. Count every abandoned gas station as well as those in operation, old rusting service station tanks, and anything else you can find that will hold 100 gallons or more of fuel, especially diesel.

Each of you should consider encouraging the citizens of your counties and communities to having one wood burning or coal burning stove so that they can heat one room through the winter.

The next time we meet, ladies and gentlemen, we might all be full time soldiers on active duty for our new country that will probably be called the Republic of the Nation of Missouri. That is all."

CHAPTER 11

BRADLEY AND CAPTAIN WHITEHORSE, COMMANDING OFFICER OF THE 105 HOWITZER BATTERY IN THERMOPOLIS, DROVE THE WIND RIVER CANYON IN THE CAPTAIN'S HUMMER. Where Bradley thought the road could be easily blocked he pointed out positions for the placement of explosives. A few landslides could immeasurably delay an advancing mechanized force. Machine guns tactically placed could enfilade any blocked convoy with devastating effects. Sites for mortar pits for light mortars were marked on the maps and sprayed with paint. Locations where an overhang would provide some cover from attack helicopters were given priority. Locations for drill holes for the placement of explosive charges were marked with orange fluorescent paint. Green paint was sprayed on the canyon walls adjacent to the highway for easier identification of points higher on the cliffs. The paint markers would be spray painted over later in neutral colors after the emplacements were made so as to hide their identification.

"I'll have two gun sections on it this weekend, Sir. We'll have everything done by 18:00 hours Sunday. I have enough explosives for about six roadblocks. Light anti-tank weapons (LAW) can accompany the machine guns for direct fire on the armored personnel carriers, especially on their tops. We can delay them for several weeks in this canyon alone. If they try inflatable rigid hull boats in the river to flank us, one or two additional machine guns should handle that threat. I will need more shoulder fired anti-aircraft weapons to take out the threat of attack helicopters and the UAVs. I only have two in my inventory. They might try to bring in troops on trains although I don't think they are that foolish. I'll take care of that as well. We'll have charges laid under the tracks in several locations."

"Good. Be advised, that UAV drones might fly in here first, looking for your locations. Most of them have infra-red cameras on them which will pick up body heat of your troops. Take the appropriate counter measures. Now, I have had cutouts of Stryker vehicles made with kerosene space heaters in them to imitate the real thing. I'll give you half a dozen of them. Put them to good use. Place them where they are not easily seen but not so heavily disguised that drones won't pick them out. Have your troops light the kerosene heaters and get away from them, under cover, where they can still bring their fires to bear on the drones and the enemy. The cutouts can draw their fire and you can shoot down the UAVs or the helicopter gunships, if they send them. Now I have to start thinking about Shell and Big Horn Canyons. I'll order Captain Livingston to put camouflaged and concealed positions in both canyons. I'll have him take care of Shell first because it is the most rugged, easiest and he can do it the quickest. One platoon will cover Shell, and one, perhaps two companies will be necessary to cover Big Horn Canyon. I'll put Captain Ferguson out of Worland in charge of the defense of Big Horn Canyon. They should each hold at least one platoon in reserve. I'll have to coordinate with the commanders on the east side of the mountains to insure we are on the same track. Their forces will probably have to retreat through those canyons and we don't want to cut off and isolate our own forces in front of the enemy. We must make sure our folks on the east side can successfully retreat into our Basin. That will take care of the passes to the east and the south. The gate to the north is the one that bothers me the most. If federal forces and push their way into Billings and come down from the north, the terrain is not nearly as favorable for the defense."

As they stood talking on the shoulder of the road, six pickup campers full of Mexicans drove by.

"Call it in to the Hot Springs County Sheriff's office, Captain. Let's see what happens."

Twenty minutes later at the northern end of the canyon, two sheriff's patrol cruisers manned by the Sheriff and four deputies established a roadblock across both lanes. The deputies were all armed with repeating shotguns. They allowed all the two way traffic to pass until the Mexicans reached the blockade. The caravan of Mexicans came to a stop. The Sheriff approached the driver of the lead truck and told him to turn around and drive back south. The driver feigned ignorance of English and replied in Spanish. The Sheriff didn't know what he said so he put his hand on his pistol and made a circular motion with the other that the drivers should turn around. The driver became irritated and demanded in Spanish the right to proceed while jabbing his finger excitedly ahead. The Sheriff shook his head no, "Nada", he said. The Mexican opened the car door and took a step towards the Sheriff who took two steps backward while grasping his MACE can in his left hand. The Sheriff said "Get back in the truck and turn around," whereupon the Mexican took another step towards the Sheriff, the anger showing in his face. He was met with a spray of MACE to his eyes. He screamed. Two trucks back two men jumped out, one with a pistol in his hand. The opening of the truck doors caught the attention of the deputies. The driver pushed the truck door closed with his left hand, holding a revolver in his right hand. The Deputy on that side didn't say a word. As soon as he saw the revolver, he raised the shotgun to his shoulder and fired. The load of #4 buckshot caught the big Mexican full in the chest and toppled him backwards into the truck door. He slumped to the ground dead, with two dozen holes in his chest, his heart a ragged piece of muscle.

The Mexicans were initially stunned. Then they tumbled out of the pickup trucks. A teenage boy, perhaps sixteen, came out of the same topper camper with a pump shotgun in his hands at port arms. The same deputy yelled "Drop it" and pointed his shotgun at the boy. The boy panicked and brought his shotgun up to his shoulder whereupon he received a fatal blast of #4 buckshot into his chest. A woman screamed and bent over the boy. The Sheriff took advantage of the distraction and clubbed the Mexican he sprayed with MACE to the ground with his rosewood nunchaku. Then he cuffed him. The deputy who shot the two Mexicans motioned with his shotgun for the others to get away from the bodies. He picked up the revolver and then the shotgun. Together the deputies and the Sheriff herded all of the Mexicans down the road twenty meters away from the trucks. Two deputies then guarded them while the other two with the Sheriff searched all of the pickups. They found two ancient Winchester Model 94 rifles in .30-30, two more shotguns, another revolver and a dozen large knives and machetes. During this time about fifteen cars of routine traffic backed up.

"What do you want to do with the bodies, Sheriff?" asked a deputy.

"Call the county coroner, so there can be a proper investigation. We can hold some of these people as material witnesses if we have to."

A Mexican lad came forward and spoke in English. "It is not necessary to have a formal investigation. We will take our dead with us. We know what happened. It will probably happen again, sometime soon. We will remember you and yours, Sheriff."

The Sheriff walked down to the Mexicans under guard. "Does anyone else here speak English," he asked.

A boy, perhaps fourteen, holding the sobbing woman said, "Yes, I do, a little."

"Do you understand what was just said, and what it means," he asked the boy.

"Yes, Sheriff, I do. We want no more trouble. Just look at us. We are hungry, we have been cold, and we are scared. Let us be. We will take our dead with us."

The Sheriff turned to his closest deputy, "We'll let them take them with them, but I want a sworn statement from half a dozen of these folks, and each deputy."

"Tell your people to pick up their dead and turn around. As soon as they have made written statements, they can leave. They can go no further north. If any of you come back, you will be shot on sight. No questions asked. Tell them that."

The boy repeated what he was told. When the two bodies were loaded, the first boy who spoke told the Sheriff "This crying woman is my mother. The dead are my father and my brother. I will be back, Sheriff, and I will kill you."

The Sheriff drew his .40 Smith & Wesson in one motion and was about to shoot the boy whose mouth fell open at the Sheriff's immediate response. His mother frantically threw her arms around her son, not knowing for certain what was spoken, speaking rapidly in Spanish, but basically comprehending that another son was about to be killed. Keeping his automatic pointed at the boy's face, he said "Get in your trucks and leave now, or there will be more killing."

The boy told his people they can go no farther. They will have to go back south for a while and go someplace else. The Sheriff uncuffed the driver he clubbed, and several Mexican men helped him into the back of the pickup. After four had made written statements that were reviewed by two deputies who could read, write and speak Spanish, a deputy directed them to turn around, one pickup at a time, starting with the last truck. All of the waiting vehicles had Wyoming license plates and their occupants were Native Americans or Anglos. The Sheriff allowed them all to pass without further consideration. The Mexicans stopped to camp for the night just off Highway U.S. 20 east of Shoshone. There they buried the father and son in shallow graves and outlined the graves with what stones they could find before darkness closed upon them.

The Chief of Computer Operations for the Burlington Northern and Santa Fe railroad acquired his doctorate in computer engineering from the University of Minnesota even though his home town was Gillette, Wyoming. He declared Minnesota as his state of residence because that was where he was employed. He always felt satisfaction in voting against the continued big government schemes at the state and federal levels, but was frustrated in that he felt that his was the only vote to do so. From his office he controlled the computers that controlled the trains that flowed back and forth across the northern United States for the Burlington Northern and Santa Fe railroads. He met his wife at the University of Montana where they did their undergraduate degrees. She majored in communications and went to work for the railroad while he completed his Ph.D. in Minneapolis. She produced the propaganda that the railroad so dearly loved. From the Twin Cities Army Ammunition Plant outside of Minneapolis-St. Paul went the week's production of ammunition to the various military bases of the Department of Defense, according to their allotment. Carloads were assigned to various trains headed in the right directions. Every day fifteen coal trains originated in each state, Montana and Wyoming, on their way to coal fired power plants east of the Mississippi River. Each week he exchanged numbers of one of the railroad cars so that one carload of ammunition was attached to an empty coal train returning to Montana and to Wyoming, passing through Guernsey, Wyoming where it was detached at the Wyoming National Guard base. He made sure the train schedules were such that the train sat on the tracks for several hours so the cars could be exchanged. In the place of the boxcar of ammunition was an empty coal car. From Guernsey, a

National Guard truck distributed the received ammunition to each of the separate brigades or units of action.

Unknown to all but a few individuals on the receiving end, another computer engineer at the Lake City, Missouri ammunition plant began supplying ammunition to the Nation of Missouri. He was much more aggressive than his fellow patriot in Minnesota. He changed train routings, the numbers on box cars and shipping containers, rerouting carloads of small arms ammunition and truck convoys on a daily basis. Coal trains coming out of Wyoming and Montana returned interlaced with boxcars of munitions. In some cases, additional railroad cars were simply attached to the ends of empty coal trains with no accountability at all. The trains stopped at several locations allowing the box cars and shipping containers to be offloaded or switched out. Paperwork was forged with substitute forms going over the computer network. Neither computer engineer was aware of the actions of the other. Occasionally, the National Guard at Guernsey was confused by what appeared to be double shipments, but thanked their lucky stars anyway and said nothing.

CHAPTER 12

A SYSTEM WITHOUT JUSTICE BREEDS RESENTMENT, RESISTANCE AND THEN VIOLENCE. It results in a vicious cycle of greater coercion, repression, torture, greater injustice, and ultimately results in overthrow of the system or civil war.

Senator Lippsitz's bill on the Referendum for autonomy was written to grant states the right to join together to form a new unit for greater commerce, common good, to form new laws, but still be part to the United States subject to federal law. Senator Rockland's bill was written to grant complete secession from the United States by independent states or en bloc as they desire. The Vice President, in his role as President of the Senate, ordered a committee to work out a compromise as a stalling measure. The Chief Justice of the Supreme Court vowed the Court would immediately rule on any compromise passed.

Senator Rockland stood up and denounced Senator Lippsitz's bill. "In this", he declared, "there can be no compromise. The states have the legal and moral right to withdraw from these United States. You, Senator Lippsitz, even so stated in your fervent address regarding the United Nations Resolution of secession of states and national sovereignty. You can't have it both ways. To hell with the Supreme Court. The State of Wyoming will break away regardless if its citizens so choose. The will of the governed will not be denied."

With that, Senator Rockland walked out of the Senate Chamber, accompanied by the Senators from North Dakota, South Dakota, and Wyoming's other senator. One Senator from Montana joined the walkout. As soon as the news of the walkout reached the White House, President Newkirk ordered the immediate arrest of the Senators. The FBI took each of them in custody in the confines of their offices.

The walkout was covered by the national media. People watched it on their personal portable televisions. News of the arrests shortly followed. Some cheered, others choked. The Senators were charged with treason against the United States and taken to a classified holding facility.

The Governors of the states of the arrested Senators called for immediate emergency session of their legislatures. Unanimously and ominously, they declared the arrest of their politicians as an act of war by the federal government against their states.

The virologists at the U.S. Army Medical Research Institute of Infectious Disease quickly characterized the virus recovered from the Israeli autopsies as the same or a very close strain to the strain George Hoskins smuggled out of China several years earlier. Only a few pinpoint amino acid sequences had changed and they were not significant.

Initially, thousands of Israelis and Palestinians were falling ill on a daily basis. Hundreds were dying every twenty-four hours. Then, the Israelis initiated a mass vaccination program that brought the epidemic to a halt in two weeks. Within a matter of days of the initial cases the extremely virulent strain of Influenza A had reached Europe. It geometrically spread through the population. Stricken with fear at what they had done, the Palestinian propaganda machine began to grind to its maximum capacity. The Palestinians hysterically blamed Israel for the epidemic.

From the floor of the United Nations General Assembly the Palestinian representative claimed to have positive proof that the pandemic was a plot by the United States and Israel to eliminate the Palestinian people. Else why would the outbreak occur in their territory while Israel was launching a nation wide vaccination campaign to protect Israelis?

"Where did they get the vaccine? How could they have produced it so soon? The only answer is that they had it on hand. They had it because the United States had developed the Influenza A virus as a biological weapon and provided it to the Israelis. The two nations then produced vaccine against it for their own people. Here, here is written proof of the complicity of the United States and Israel. Here are copies of the contracts between the United States and Israel to produce the vaccine against this specific strain of the deadly disease. There is no doubt whatsoever. Hundreds of millions will die because of these two incredibly evil nations. They should be eliminated from the face of the earth, for that is what they are attempting to do to all other peoples. They want to reduce the world's population so that they can have more resources for themselves. What better place to start than in the land of the Palestinians? While it is very remotely possible that the virus escaped as a result of a laboratory accident, rather than a deliberate release, the result is the same. The United States had genetically engineered the virus and provided it to the Israelis where it escaped from their laboratory or was deliberately released to infect the world."

In the first political move he did halfway right, President Newkirk ordered the immediate release of the vaccine in storage and the initiation of a massive vaccination campaign on the Atlantic seaboard as soon as the circulating virus was identified as the causative agent. "By God, why should I give vaccine to all those break away states? Who the hell are they to tell me that they can no longer remain a part of the union of which I am President and then demand vaccine from me?"

"Mr. President, secession has not proceeded. The April 15 referendum hasn't been voted. They are all still Americans. I can assure you that if you do not distribute that vaccine, you will be the most hated, and possibly the most hunted man in North America. Those citizens paid for that vaccine years ago with their tax dollars. It was stored at their tax paying expense for five or more years. It was a virologist in Columbia that brought us the virulent sample out of China. That allowed us to genetically engineer it, to remove the genes from it that induce immunity and to put them into canary pox virus to produce an innocuous modified live virus vaccine. Recall that the canary pox virus is nothing more than a carrier virus, sometimes likened to a cassette. Now, if you withhold it, you will be accused of biological warfare, and rightfully so. You might be tried in international court. With the Palestinians claiming that we supplied it to Israel for use against them, we will have a hard enough time explaining why we have 350 million doses of vaccine against it in storage. Hundreds, if not thousands of cases are already occurring along our eastern seaboard, especially in New York. Pretty soon it will reach across the country. There is no stopping it. The sooner the vaccination program is rolling, the better for everyone, including you."

Richard Newkirk brooded over what his Surgeon General just told him. Unusually candid for a Public Health Service Admiral, David Rosenberg laid it on the line for his boss. Naomi supported him.

"Our troops have been vaccinated with it, Mr. President, at least some of them. As Secretary of Defense, I have ordered the vaccine out of storage and administered to all active duty personnel under the Military Immunization Program as soon as it was apparent that it was protective, that is, the same strain that is circulating the globe. Those who have already received it were those who served overseas, especially in Africa and the Middle East and the Far East. Now, everyone will get it. It was administered one year as an additional influenza shot to those troops. The troops were told that it was either a booster, or a new vaccine for one disease or another."

"Admiral Rosenberg makes political sense, Mr. President. As I understand what Naomi just said, we better have all of our remaining military personnel immunized as quickly as possible. It won't do to have the Army down in these troubled times."

"I would call to your attention, Mr. President, that the influenza outbreak in 1917-1918 killed more U.S. soldiers than died from all other causes in World War I, "added Admiral Rosenberg.

Richard Newkirk just looked from one to another of his secretaries. "All right, we have a written plan for a national immunization program, don't we? Surely to God we have thought that all out. Let's get it started. Military has first priority, and thank you Naomi for getting that ball rolling. Admiral Rosenberg will you please work with Homeland Security to get all these folks immunized as quickly as possible."

"What about our allies, Mr. President? Israel is the manufacturing facility for this vaccine. Surely they have secretly manufactured enough for their citizens. Perhaps they have enough left over, or can initiate manufacturing again as quickly as possible. Has anyone let them know this vaccine is protective against it? I suspect however, that they have already initiated their vaccination program."

Richard Newkirk looked to his Secretary of State, Frank Stokes. "Call the Israelis; let them know this is a vaccine against the circulating disease. They have probably already figured that out. If not, they can get started on vaccinating their citizens if they haven't already. See how fast they can gin up to start vaccine production for it again. In the meantime, Dr. Rosenberg, see what commercial facilities can mass produce the vaccine for us and the rest of the world. Provide them with what ever virus stocks they need to get started. Let's get this done in the next twenty-four hours. Announce on the floor of the United Nations; tell the world we will provide vaccine at no cost to all the countries in the world as fast as we can manufacture it. We will also share the seed virus to allow other countries to make their own vaccine."

"In the face of this crisis, or should I say multiple crises, Mr. President, may I suggest you vaccinate the truculent Senators and turn them loose? We don't need them dying of influenza in our care. That would really make martyrs out of them and might be misconstrued as deliberate murder or death through neglect."

Richard Newkirk glared at Peter Perkins, his Attorney General. "All right, damn it Peter, do it and let 'em loose. Get them out of here. Let them go back to where ever they came from. Maybe with them out of Washington, things will quiet down. At least the riots are greatly diminished."

"Yeah, everybody is afraid to congregate now, as they should be. This is a nasty strain. The epidemiologist for the City of New York tells me they have a pretty good handle on the clinical disease characteristics, now. Its incubation is only 48-72 hours, usually on the real short side of that. People are often dead after 72 hours after onset of clinical illness with this virus. I will inform all state epidemiolgists or health commissioner or whatever they call the head physician in each state, to send an armed escort to Stillwater, Pennsylvania to pick up the vaccine for their state. Each state already has a distribution plan for it. Each county will send a vehicle to get its share to the state capitol, and each municipality will get their share from the county seat. That plan was worked out twenty years ago. The distribution plan should all be kept secret so no shipments are high jacked, and all should be heavily guarded." David Rosenberg worked on the state plan for Virginia when he was in the bioterrorism branch of the Public Health Service.

"One other thing, Naomi, find out who and how copies of those classified contracts wound up in the hands of the Palestinians. Those are highly classified documents. Somebody broke security. Work with the FBI, CIA and Homeland Security. I want the balls of whoever did this. I'll castrate the SOB myself."

"There is one other point of considerable significance Mr. President that needs to be examined."

"And what, Dr. Rosenberg, is that?"

"What about the Chinese scientist that provided us with the virus to produce the vaccine several years ago? If this is a deliberate release the Chinese will know someone there provided us with the strain for culture and vaccine production. We need to rescue that scientist. If we don't, he and his family will be killed. If we can rescue him, he will be living proof that China is the source of this pandemic. The fact that no cases have been reported in China indicates that it is not the result of a laboratory accident. It might also indicate that China has vaccinated its population in advance of a deliberate release. Alternatively, China might be masking the real situation there, but as I understand our reports, there are relatively very few cases. I tend to dismiss them masking the real situation then. I think they have vaccinated their population."

President Newkirk thought about it for a minute, "We'll get him out. We owe him that much." He picked up the phone. "Get me the Director of National Intelligence, right now! I don't care if he is out of town." He put down the phone and turned to Floyd Mitchell, Secretary of Health and Human Services, Admiral Rosenberg's boss.

"Floyd, you and the Admiral generally aren't invited to these meetings. My purpose in asking you hear today is to hear what you have to say about where you would make budget cuts in the Department of Health and Human Services budget."

"Politically, Mr. President, there aren't any good places. The most efficient and one of the least popular cuts could be in the obesity program. I looked long and hard at MEDICARE/MEDICAID expenses related to obesity. They are enormous. We could use body fat measurements as a means of reducing MEDICAID/MEDICARE benefits. Twenty percent body fat would be acceptable. At twenty-five percent we could reduce benefits, payment for medications, for hypertension, for type II diabetes, but no treatment, hospitalization for strokes and so on. At thirty percent body mass index we could eliminate all benefits for obesity related diseases, including joint degeneration. The public hasn't responded to public health programs attempting to reduce the fat and lead healthier lifestyles. It will be tremendously unpopular, but save us a hundred or more billion annually."

By the end of the third week of the pandemic, Israel was vaccinating the remainder of its entire population. It essentially had stopped the epidemic by eliminating the susceptible population. The evening television CNN News scene switched to Tel Aviv, where the CNN reporter was broadcasting live from a vaccination station. All Israeli citizens were directed to report to their assigned vaccination station as their highest priority last night. The stations, of which there were hundreds, saw lines forming as early as 02:00. Israelis wanted their vaccination and wanted it right now, so they could get on with their daily routines. As he was speaking, an Israeli nurse approached the reporter and asked him if he would like to be vaccinated.

"Absolutely," he cried. He handed his microphone to the sound man and took off his long sleeved shirt to expose his deltoid muscle. The nurse smiled, and vaccinated him in front of the camera. She then went from one to the other of the camera man and sound man to ask if they too, would like vaccination. The cameraman laid down his camera; the reporter picked it up, and broadcast the vaccination of the rest of his crew.

Palestinians vaccination stations were similarly busy, although there were not nearly enough of them. Palestinians waited in lines hundreds long, for hours, to receive their vaccination. One week later when those vaccinated began to fall ill and die the Palestinians realized the vaccine provided by the Chinese was not protective within their borders. This further reinforced the idea that the release was a deliberate move by the United States and Israel.

Robert Bradley watched the evening television news with considerable concern. Now in its fourth week, the pandemic was racing through the populations in Cairo, in Tunis, in Nairobi and Damascus. Amman was being devastated at this point in time. The Egyptian reporter claimed the government was making provisions for mass burial. According to Muslim custom, the dead must be buried within 24 hours. Egyptian trucks formed a loop that never stopped running carrying bodies out to be dumped in mass graves in the desert. A fleet of bulldozers couldn't dig sufficiently deep trenches long enough to handle the dead. It was straining Egypt's resources to the maximum. Their laboratories are working around the clock trying to formulate a vaccine. News that the United States was willing to share its vaccine virus for seed production was wholly ignored in the Muslim world. The United Nations was trying to coordinate vaccine production so that that it could claim a major role in the pandemic without success. Anti-American and anti-Israeli riots broke out throughout the Middle East and Africa. European nations turned on the United States denouncing America as the greatest scourge of all governments in the history of the world. London, Paris, Rome, Rotterdam, Milan, Vienna, Berlin, every major city in the world was ready to declare war on the United States.

Muslims began to attack Jews on the streets of American cities. Mullahs in American mosques preached that the only justice in the world was to eradicate all of the Jews in the world, starting with those in America. American Jewry had to be responsible for this world wide epidemic that was claiming thousands of lives every week in every city of the world. It wasn't safe for an American to be on the street in any city in Europe. The Muslim population of Europe, particularly France, skyrocketed in the last thirty years. France was now over thirty percent Muslim in population due to their rejection of birth control methods. The philosophy of assuming power by becoming the majority and legally seizing power through the vote became their grand strategy in the more democratic nations of Europe. Muslims in France attacked everyone they thought was an American without hesitation at every opportunity. Many used it as an excuse to attack Christians in general. One month after making the decision to restart production in American laboratories, the first shipment of vaccine reached Mexico City. It took eight weeks for the British, Germans and French to produce their first doses produced in cell culture which allowed the use of very large vats. Violence accompanied every vaccination center. Vaccination centers were first established in the larger cities. Since Europeans had disavowed privately owned firearms, stabbings and cuttings occurred by the thousands all over Europe as people fought for places in line for vaccination of their families. Several fraudulent black market vaccination centers opened on street corners, offering vaccine for one hundred Euros per dose. They operated for 12 to 24 hours and then disappeared before Interpol or local police became aware of them and could take them into custody. People who thought they were receiving vaccine received instead distilled water mixed with polyethylene glycol.

Dr. Hassan traveled to Cairo for an emergency meeting with the Chinese virologist, Dr. Li. Hassan complained bitterly to Dr. Li that the vaccine the Chinese had provided was not working.

"Why are the Israelis no longer falling ill and dying as we Palestinians are? We are dying by the thousands and tens of thousands on a daily basis. Indeed, we cannot bury out dead fast enough. Did you provide us with faulty vaccine? Is the virus strain different from the vaccine? Even now as the disease spreads through Egypt, what can be done? What is your situation in China? The information that I have been provided said you have been vaccinating your population with the vaccine for years. Are they too falling ill? This disease is far more deadly than we were led to believe by your scientists. We have vaccinated most of our population without effect."

"The Chinese ambassador put on his best frown to mask the fact that he was laughing his head off to himself. "These stupid Muslims," he thought, "they are so easily manipulated. The world will be better off without them. They have been most useful in forcing the absorption of American resources by Israel to counter balance them. Now their usefulness is over, and what is useless should be discarded."

To the Palestinian he said, "We have not experienced any significant cases of the disease at this point in time so I cannot tell you how well we are faring. It is true that we have vaccinated our entire population over the last five years with the same vaccine. We anticipate that the disease will arrive in China shortly, within a week or so. Therefore, I cannot answer your question at this time about its effectiveness in our people. I do not understand however, why it is not effective in protecting your people. If it is not protective, this will be of greatest concern to my government. I will immediately report what you have told me, and our scientists will begin to research the problem before the day is out. I am sure that blood samples from your people who have been inoculated at various times will be most helpful. It is possible that many of them have not had time to respond to the vaccine before they became ill. It takes ten to fourteen days for most vaccines to elicit the response. Perhaps many of them were in the incubation stage, already infected before they were vaccinated, the consequence of which is that the vaccination was useless. We need more information. Perhaps you can have your medical personnel collect say, one hundred blood samples of persons who were vaccinated every 24 hours for the first ten days? I realize that is 1000 blood samples, but that way our scientists will have plenty of material for study and can measure the development of antibodies in your people. We will compare that data with similar data from our own population. Then perhaps we can give you an answer. *"No doubt those serum samples will show a high titer to measles, but nothing to influenza!"* he thought to himself. Similar studies in our population indicate that a minimum of ten days is necessary to mount a response that is detectable. Let us hope that is the case, and that those who have been vaccinated do not come in contact with the disease for at least ten days. They will be protected. I will have one of our couriers pick up your samples as soon as you have acquired them. If you merely call this number our couriers will collect them and we will have an aircraft at the Amman airport within the hour to fly them to our laboratory." He scribbled a telephone number down on a piece or notepaper and handed it to the Palestinian.

Somewhat mollified, the Palestinian stated, "Let us hope so. We do live in such crowded conditions that perhaps the disease spread among us too quickly for the vaccine to be effective. I will immediately telefax my government with your recommendations. I am sure we will comply with that. We do very much appreciate your assistance and are grateful for all that you have done for us. Now I will send the fax." He bowed at the waist and left the room. The Palestinian's response saved his life. If the Chinese delegate had picked up his phone, an assassin waiting outside would have killed the Palestinian in the street.

The early spring weather was wonderful. It was April 1, April Fool's Day and that was not lost on Ethan Bradley. Bradley wondered if it wouldn't be a tremendously ironic joke if Congress had decided to hold the referendum today. He was still perplexed as to who had delivered a copy of his initial staff address to the press. He still had no clue. No similar instances had occurred since he relieved Captain McCortle. Still, he was reluctant to consider him guilty without more proof. McCortle had placed his home on the real estate market, primarily he admitted, out of concern for the safety of his family. His relief had brought suspicion on him as a Tory. He felt it best if he left Wyoming. He interviewed for a high school teaching job for the following fall in a small town in Michigan. He made it clear that he would leave as soon as his home was sold.

Recruitment was slower than Bradley had hoped. His entire brigade had recruited only 126 people throughout the Basin since he took command. The militia was doing somewhat better. He had 215 men and women who had volunteered. Most of them were middle aged and older. He felt the people really weren't involved as yet, and would fall asleep at night trying to think of a way to involve them. He continually reverted to the Boston Tea Party. The British response to the dumping of the East India Company's tea before it could be offloaded from three ships and taxed was to close Boston Harbor as punishment for the Massachusetts Bay Colony. The event united the people of Massachusetts and more or less began to bind the other colonies to Massachusetts. The colonies realized the British strategy of attempting to bring the individual colonies to their knees, one at a time. Lord North's desire for revenge and the infliction of economic pain on the colony was perceived as a greater threat than quartering British soldiers in American homes.

After supper one night, Ethan said, "Dad, I have yet to get over to Jackson. What's your take on the folks over there? I haven't been able to recruit nearly as many people as I would like from the center of the Basin. Think I can get a couple of hundred folks over there/"

"Son, the billionaires in Jackson have driven out the millionaires. The millionaires have all moved to Cody. Most of the Jackson Hole population is of the Hollywood and California variety, with a sprinkling of east coast elites and foreign billionaires thrown in. Jackson is a far more liberal town than Cody. Jackson has more or less become a large gated community. Tourism has dropped dramatically, but the billionaires don't care. They support the necessary local merchants and work force required for their comfort. The grocery stores, upscale clothiers, skilled building craftsman and some professionals do okay. These rich folks have created an enclave for themselves, with what is a small army of private security personnel. You just about have to know someone to even get in the area. The security apparatus even set up road blocks in the last month. The state police don't go in there any more. They have left law enforcement to the locals. The judge and county sheriff are owned, more or less, by the coordinated security agencies. The various security agencies owners' were smart enough to morph into one organization for chain of command, equipment, communications and control, a uniform pay scale for personnel and so on. They are several thousand strong. The only way to break that enclave is to completely isolate it. Cut off their public utilities and all traffic in or out. When they have no fuel, electricity, food or heat in minus twenty degree cold, it'll open. It will break open as they escape. Most of them will leave by their private aircraft. You can starve them out."

"I think I'll head that way, as soon as I'm sure the weather won't be a factor. Think I'll ride my motorcycle over, posing as a tourist. I'll take camping gear and see about a disguise and pretend I'm somebody else and just scope out the town."

"Well, you better not go as Colonel Ethan Bradley. They will probably shoot you on sight. The security forces over there are autonomous, and they are in the employ of the Tories from California. It is really some enclave over there. I don't know what to tell you as a disguise." Ethan Bradley didn't shave for a week. He borrowed a theatrical wig from the local Shakespeare in the Park players. He borrowed a motorcycle from a friend and had the Department of Motor Vehicles make him a phony driver's license. He packed a sleeping bag, mattress pad, a change of clothes, ditty bag, and a collapsible spinning rod, a plastic box of lures, a reel, and a mess kit in the saddle bags and on the passenger's seat of the motorcycle. He put his .45 ACP in its holster and three loaded magazines on a pouch on the backside of the saddle bags. The road was clear of snow all the way through Riverton where he checked into a motel. After breakfast the next morning at the motel's restaurant, he paid his bill and then donned his disguise. He took his time driving northwest on U.S. 26 so that he arrived at Jackson at 15:00 hours. He was stopped on the highway just outside of Jackson by security guards where a guard station had been built across the highway, complete with blocks of concrete barricades. Traffic was forced to slow to a crawl to get through the gate. A few cars and two trucks were ahead of him in line. When he reached the guard house he was stopped by the guard who asked for identification. Bradley chewed gum and acted nonchalantly as the guard examined his Wyoming driver's license.

"Kind of early for you motorcycle tourists to come up here. We won't have a spring thaw for a couple of weeks. Here it is the first week of April, snow is all over the ground, and there isn't any place for your kind to camp here anymore. You come from Wyoming, so you should know that. I see you have fishing tackle, but fishing isn't open here until June. Kind of out of season, aren't you?"

"Hey man, never know what opportunity might open up. I just try to be prepared. Don't mean to cause no trouble, can't afford any. Just want enjoy the snow and the mountains.

Who knows, maybe I'll ski over at Teton Village for a day. I don't want no trouble."

"Do you have any weapons, guns, knives, nunchakus, brass knuckles or anything like that?"

"No man, I am peaceable. Oh, I do have my little pocket knife, but that's about it. It is just a little stockman style." With that, Bradley pulled a pocketknife out of his front pocket to show it to the guard. The guard eyed it and just nodded.

"This is an expensive town, just how do you expect to pay for a room here? The campgrounds aren't open. You aren't selling dope are you?" The guard thought to himself *"You would be mighty welcome if you are, especially quality stuff."* Recreational drug use was very prevalent in the area, but the security guard didn't want to take any chances with Bradley being an undercover narcotics officer. Bradley pulled a wad of money from his wallet, and flipped through it under the guard's eyes, demonstrating that it was all fifty and one hundred dollar denominations. The guard memorized the name and address on the fake driver's license and handed them back to Bradley who pocketed them. The guard waved him on, and Bradley waved back as he pulled away.

The guard went into the shack and typed the name and address on the driver's license on his computer to Security Central. In a few minutes the replay came back, that such an individual was not in the database. The guard then called Security Central and informed them that a motorcycle rider with a driver's license with that name and address is on U.S. 26, riding a Honda 1700 cc. black motorcycle. Security Central put out a fax to all guard stations and a broadcast to all guards over the radio. The report on Bradley returned that he is a suspect to be observed and whereabouts reported when seen but not to be apprehended.

Bradley parked in front of the Rainbow Trout Café and walked in. Quite a few heads turned to watch him, with his phony pony tail wig protruding from under his helmet and week's growth of facial hair. He went to the men's room to remove his helmet, so he wouldn't pull his wig off when he removed his helmet. When he emerged, he found a seat at the counter. He slowly pivoted on the stool and returned the gaze of all who were watching him. Most returned to their meal or conversation, further ignoring him. He was an impressive figure in the leather motorcycle jacket and chaps; people thought he just might be the violent type. Bradley ordered toasted cheese sandwich and coffee. He listened to conversations around him as he munched his sandwich. After he consumed his sandwich and his third cup of coffee, he left money on the counter and returned to the men's room where he relieved himself and donned his helmet. He slowly rode down to Hobart Junction and back into Jackson where he took a room at the Holiday Inn. He paid in cash for one night. The security guard outside noted his arrival and reported it. After showering and changing wigs, a phony moustache and donning dress wool slacks, dress shirt and sweater with a down vest and knit hat, he walked the streets, observing and listening. He did not look at all like the same man who rode in on the motorcycle and walked past the security guard without being recognized. Bradley drifted from nightspot to nightspot, alternating bars, discos and restaurants. The nightlife establishments appeared to be oriented to particular patronage. The great majority catered to the twenty to fifty year olds. Ethan never used marijuana or any other mind or mood altering substance other than modest doses of alcohol. He was quite familiar with marijuana from the military classes on drug abuse he had as a company grade officer. He occasionally found marijuana in the possession of one of his enlisted Marines and in barracks sweeps. In nightclub after nightclub he could detect the odor of cannabis. In some, it was overwhelming. Many people were actively, openly smoking pot. In one corner of one establishment a circle of people were heating something in small container over a small alcohol lamp.

Bradley moved on. Somewhere around the fourth or fifth nightclub Ethan began to feel a little euphoric from the second hand marijuana smoke. He went outside and just walked up and down the streets until he felt he was back to his usual clear and alert state. He heard a little talk of politics, more on snow conditions, fashions and who was sleeping with whom. Of the political discussions, several centered on how the breakup of California would affect Hollywood in particular and southern California business in general.

One interesting conversation came from two elderly men, well dressed, nursing cocktails at an upscale bar that catered to a slightly older crowd. "We have not learned our lessons on war in the past fifty years. It is a truism that armies don't go to war, only nations go to war. Our politicians have never served; their children never have nor ever will serve in the U.S. Army, so they have never or will ever have any qualms about committing other young people to the horrors of war. Only when the rich, the politicians, the elitists and their children serve should we go to war. Well, this is a war of their making, and they can't escape it. It ought to be a constitutional requirement for every Congressman and Senator to have to serve 3 years active military duty."

His friend responded along another line of thought. "We've become like the Muslims, Sunni versus Shiite, although we're splitting along political philosophies and cultures rather than religious lines. Religion has played a significant part in cultural aspects admittedly; God versus the godless. The American Civil Liberties Union drove to remove every vestige of religion from community life. Those bastards at the ACLU still don't realize that religion is one variety of glue that holds a community together as a nation. It is unbelievable how quiet the Roman Catholic Church has been on this." After that comment, the speaker leaned over to peer at Bradley and noticed Bradley's attempt to unobtrusively listen. He nodded in Bradley's direction to his listener who turned around and looked at Bradley. The two men moved off to a booth.

At 01:00, Bradley ordered a sour mash bourbon and Coca-Cola at one of the bars and then walked back to his hotel. The night spots were still going strong. At 05:00 Bradley awoke with a vague feeling of uneasiness. His sixth sense alerted. He looked out the window to watch two security guards go through his saddle bags. They did not notice the .45 ACP in the false compartment on the back side of the saddle bag. It was cold, below zero Fahrenheit, and they were anxious to return indoors. Bradley quickly dressed in his motorcycle costume without the wig and went out a side door. He started his motorcycle and rode away without letting it warm up as was his usual habit. He headed towards the eastern gate by which he entered Jackson. He pulled off on a side street, put his hat over the hard wired headlight, and took the .45 from its pouch. He put the holster on his belt, checked the .45 to make sure it was loaded, cocked and locked, holstered it, pulled his jacket down over it and put the magazines in his motorcycle jacket pocket. He was about to pull the knit hat off the headlight when he noticed two security guard cars headed towards the gate. He drove down a parallel side street to approach the gate. There was no other way out other than through the gate. The road had been deliberately narrowed as a choke point, and deep snow on the shoulders of the road provided additional security to prevent any attempts to bypass the gate. There were three security guard cars parked in single file behind the guard station. The engines were running in the last two He counted five guards inside the station. He put the knit hat back on his headlight, put it in first gear, and as quietly as he could, crept towards the gate. He was directly opposite the guard station and through most of the barricade when they noticed him. Bradley saw them jump out of their chairs and set their coffee down so he stepped it into second gear and sped on. In his mirrors, he saw the headlights of the patrol cars come on. He reached down and pulled the hat off his headlight, quickly accelerating and reaching fifth gear and eighty miles an hour. He hugged the gas tanks, down behind his windshield. The wind chill factor was tremendous; it was below minus 100 degrees Fahrenheit. The patrol cars didn't have that problem. He didn't hear the shots fired at him because of the roar of his engine, but one of the bullets clipped his windshield, passing just over his left shoulder. He went faster. Suddenly, one of the patrol cars failed to make a curve and flew off the road. The other car stopped fifty meters later. Bradley slowed down so as not to overdrive his headlight. The night was still pitch black and he was tired. By dawn he was at Moran Junction. By 09:00 he was in Dubois where he stopped for a breakfast of pancakes with an egg on top, bacon, and coffee. A look in the mirror in the men's room revealed an area of each cheek not covered by his helmet had a small area of frostbite.

A deputy sheriff entered the café and sat down next to him. The deputy smiled, "Looks like you got a little frostbite there, Colonel. Hope it's not too serious."

Bradley looked the deputy in the eye but said nothing. "Oh, they put out a bulletin that some bike rider was wanted in Jackson for crashing a bar. They traced the serial number on the bike to somebody whose name wasn't on the driver's license. So, they figured at least they had a stolen motorcycle charge they could hang somebody with. They put together a composite sketch from several descriptions, and then somebody recognized you from your pictures in the paper. You're among friends here in Dubois. We've had enough of the Sierra Club and Southern California and New York politicians to last more than a life time. There aren't many citizens left around here; most just make a living on the traffic to and from Jackson and tourism. Those who are here however, are your supporters. I'm Jim Reeves, Undersheriff here."

Ethan held out his hand and said, "Colonel Ethan Bradley, Wyoming National Guard; pleased to make your acquaintance, Undersheriff Reeves." Bradley made it back to Worland about the time the sun was going down.

"Hi Dad, what's for supper tonight?" Ethan asked as he came in from the garage where he parked the motorcycle until he could return it to a friend.

"I'm grilling pork chops, with apple sauce, frozen mixed veggies, and an ice cream sundae for dessert. What do you think of that?"

"Sounds delicious Dad, I'm hungry and cold."

"Then pour us both a sour mash bourbon and turn on the news." Ethan did so without further comment and stood there watching the television reports coming in live from around the country as he sipped his bourbon. The CNN reporter was describing how gangs of black Americans were pouring out of Detroit to forage for food in the surrounding countryside. Farmers were helpless when half a dozen carloads of young black men burst into their homes to search for food and loot, and often rape of girls and young women. Similar gangs were allegedly working out of Chicago, Illinois to pillage into Wisconsin and Indiana. Gang warfare was expanding between black and Hispanic gangs in the Carolinas. It was becoming full fledged guerilla warfare. From the reports, no quarter was given and none taken in the border states between the south and the west. It was over economic dominance as much as ethnic cleansing. The agriculturally based dominant population of second and third generation Hispanics was eliminating Black American farmers and workers from the west by one means or another. Historically, whenever a minority with a serious grievance, real or imagined, turns violent on a national or regional basis, the majority against whom they have directed their violence retaliates in a massive and extremely violent way against the civilian population from which the rebels came. This occurred time and again during the last decades of the twentieth century in Africa, in Rwanda-Burundi, in Darfur, in Nigeria, in Uganda and other places around the world. The Black Americans who stayed rather than flee to the southeast suffered with no mercy shown. A brief report came out of New Orleans. The reporter cut and ran as bullets began to chip the buildings around him. In his minute of broadcasting, he stated that black Muslims now lived in enclaves within the city and were butchering their non-Muslim black neighbors.

President Newkirk gave the Patriots their equivalent of the British closing of Boston Harbor. Later in the same day he ordered the national immunization program implemented, President Newkirk had a change of heart. He called Floyd Mitchell, the Secretary of Health and Human Services and Dr. Rosenberg in a three way call. He put it on his speaker phone as he paced around the Oval Office. He ordered that no vaccine is to be released to the states that are considering secession. "We'll say that there are insufficient vaccine supplies for the moment, and that the threat is greater on the east coast, so they have priority. Those break away states will get vaccine later-maybe!"

"Mr. President, you don't dare do that! Those people are citizens of this country. They have every right to that vaccine, as much as you or I."

"I don't care, damn it. Let them get sick and die. They aren't going to break the United States apart on my watch. Maybe they will realize just how much they need to be a part of the United States. You two keep your mouths shut about it. Just say that their vaccine will be released in due time. Highest priorities are to go to the urban areas, specifically those of the northeast. I'll determine what is due time for those that want to secede, and it might not be until a year from now." His secretary overheard his comment and was greatly disturbed. Newkirk slammed the phone down in anger. An hour later, the Surgeon General Dr. Rosenberg, Floyd Mitchell, the

Secretary of Health and Human Services and Secretary Andretti of Homeland Security appeared in person at the Oval Office demanding to see President Newkirk. His secretary left for home at 17:00. At 19:00 hours, he finally admitted them to his office.

"I know why you three are here, and I am not going to change my mind. Those people will learn that the Union will be preserved, even if it costs them their lives. I'll teach them that they cannot secede. I don't give a damn what the United Nations, the Senate, or any body or organization says or thinks. They won't get the vaccine until they renounce the idea of secession."

"Mr. President, if you go through with this, it will be the end of your Presidency, possibly the end of the Democratic Party as an entity; expect to be impeached and you might just be labeled a mass murderer. Expect the potential illness of tens of millions and the loss of several million lives. Do you want to be responsible for that," asked Dr. Rosenberg?

"Good, let the bastards get sick and die. Maybe the survivors will recognize this government, its power, this office and we'll be better off without their treason."

"Mr. President, if you attempt to withhold vaccine, you will leave us no choice but to make it public knowledge that you are deliberately withholding vaccine from a segment of the nation and the American people. You are risking the potential loss of tens of millions of lives."

Secretary Andretti remarked, "As a student of history, Mr. President, I see a parallel in your position that is remarkably similar to that of Lord North during the American Revolution. He attempted to punish the American colonies, particularly Massachusetts, for considering secession. The results were that it hardened the position of the colonies and united them against Great Britain. That is quite likely to happen again if you don't release the vaccine."

"If you sons of bitches go public, I'll fire every one of you, if I don't have you killed first! Now get the hell out of here, I'm hungry and am going for supper."

The three looked at each other, and without a word, turned and left. On the portico of the White House the three stood silently for a moment. Floyd Mitchell spoke first. "Well, gentlemen, what do we do?" Go public now or later, or see if we can get him to change his mind tomorrow?"

Secretary Andretti said "Let's get Senator Kennely in on this. He has more power over Newkirk than Newkirk will ever admit. Newkirk is merely his puppet. He should be able to make him see the error of his ways. What do you say, Dr. Rosenberg?"

"I'm willing to give Senator Kennely a day or so to make him change his mind. I can stall off the rebellious states that long, but not much longer. If Kennely isn't successful in 48 to 72 hours, I don't think I will have a choice but to go public. We can't have all this blood on our hands. Failure to go public would confirm our duplicity."

He turned to his boss, Floyd Mitchell, "Floyd, why don't you try first with Senator Kennely, and if you don't have any success then you Ed, and I'll go last. If we can't get Kennely on board separately we'll go at him together. I am sure that he will recognize Newkirk's folly. I've no doubt he will influence him."

At that moment, Senator Kennely was enjoying a candle light dinner with a vivacious co-ed in the back booth of a very exclusive restaurant. The veal cutlets were delicious, and the Merlot was the best. The young lady was extremely attractive, twenty-two years of age, and a senior undergraduate majoring in pre-law. She could talk the language and had enough experience to use body language to its fullest. She began to attract boys at age thirteen, and never stopped. She could have her pick of almost any man. She knew how to look her best in candlelight. Her aim was the Senator's backing, first as his aide for a year then his endorsement as an applicant for law school. She would grace his bed if that would be necessary. When he placed his hand on her knee and began to run it up her thigh, she knew it would be necessary.

The Senator was overweight, although not grossly so with about 35% body fat. In fact, he was probably in pretty good shape for his age. He had a fatalistic view. He didn't expect to live forever. Kennely adopted as his motto the saying of an old Greek king "I have been a king, and as long as I have seen the light of the sun, I have eaten, drank, and paid homage to the joys of love, knowing that the lifetimes of men are short and subject to much change and misfortune, and that others will reap the benefits of the possessions that I leave behind me." That in fact, had become the Senator's modus operandi for the last fifty years.

One of the Senator's bodyguards sat quietly a few tables away, observing all the activities in the restaurant. The other remained in the Senator's car along with the chauffer. After they finished their dinner, the Senator and his date casually strolled outside to where his limousine was waiting. The one bodyguard followed in a second car driven by another security type. They drove to the Senator's home where he told the chauffer not to retire because the young lady would need a ride home in a few hours.

He slowly and completely undressed the young lady, while she stood motionless. Neither said anything, although she forced herself to have a modest smile. He admired her anatomy while he undressed himself, and pulled back the bed covers to the sheets. He seized her by both arms and guided her backwards onto the bed. He needed all the help he could, so he hung her head over the edge of the bed and entered her mouth until he was sufficiently erect. He placed his forearms under her knees raising her legs, pinned her arms with his hands and penetrated her. He became more and more excited and was so stertorous that the sounded like a heaving race horse. As he climaxed, he collapsed on top of her, apparently asleep, breathing heavily. She rolled him off of her, and proceeded to the shower. She dressed without saying a word, ignoring the sleeping senator. She walked outside to the waiting limousine, thinking to herself, "I hope it was worth it, and I hope it doesn't happen too often. At least he wasn't violent. It was an easy one thousand dollars." She had been paid at the beginning of the evening. The chauffer drove her to her apartment. She opened the car door and walked out without looking back.

The Washington Times scooped every other news media in the country. The morning headline ran "President Withholds Vaccine from All States Considering Secession." Within minutes telephones began to ring. The White House press staff denied any such knowledge. The Secretary of Health and Human Services refused to take any phone calls on the issue. His press secretary denied everything. It was simply too ridiculous to have any credibility. Dr. Rosenberg's office was swamped. He said it was best to contact the White House for clarification. The Homeland Security Chief said publicly he had never heard anything so ridiculous. Rosenberg, Andretti and Mitchell frantically scrambled to reach Senator Kennely by phone. At 08:00, Senator Kennely's maid entered his bedroom, to find him sprawled across the bed naked and unconscious. She phoned for an ambulance.

Within hours, all other news agencies began demanding proof of accuracy from the Washington Times. At noon, the Washington Times held its own news conference. For the entire world to hear, they played a tape recording of President Newkirk's outburst during the conversation of Mitchell, Rosenberg, and Andretti had with him the previous evening. By 18:00 hours, it had been played and replayed and broadcast around the world a hundred thousand times.

Forced to admit complicity, the trio of Mitchell, Rosenberg and Andretti separately confirmed their conversation on the portico that they would attempt to enlist the aid of Senator Kennely before going public. If the good Senator failed to persuade the President to release the vaccine, they would make a joint press release. At 13:30 hours a reporter pigeon holed Dr. Rosenberg and shoved a microphone under his nose and asked, "Do you think Senator Kennely will confirm this, provided he lives?"

"What are you talking about? We couldn't get a hold of the good Senator last night and it was on our agenda the first thing this morning. I called him at 07:00 hours this morning, but couldn't catch him. Why shouldn't we try further persuasion for a day or two before going public? What do you mean, 'provided he lives?'"

"Are you aware Admiral that Senator Kennely is at this moment in the Bethesda Naval Medical Center Coronary Intensive Care unit with a myocardial infarction? The prognosis is grave."

President Newkirk exploded when he saw the news on CNN. He denied everything. He had been misquoted, the tape is fraudulent. He ordered his press secretary to immediately call a press conference to deny all allegations. Vaccine would be provided for everyone in all fifty states, regardless of their current political recalcitrance. Mitchell, Rosenberg and Andretti stood before his desk and denied that any of them, individually or collectively, had made such a recording. None had any contact with the media until the media contacted them that morning. None had any idea where or how the tape came from. Experts outside the government quickly compared the voice prints of President Newkirk, the Admiral and the Secretaries with previous recordings and declared them genuine. There were no splices in the tape; nothing had been edited in or out. The case was damning. His political opponents were jumping up and down with glee. President

Newkirk ordered a sweep of his office for listening devices. A voice activated frequency modulating microphone four millimeters in diameter was found glued to the front under edge of his desk. No fingerprints were on it. Newkirk ordered a review of all personnel who stood before his desk in the last two weeks. No one had any idea who placed it there or when. Sweeping the building, no FM receiver could be found. The experts were convinced that the receiver with its tape recorder had been in the immediate vicinity of the Oval Office, probably quite close to the President's desk, and had been removed. Suspicion immediately fell on the White House staff.

The influenza epidemic hadn't really reached the Basin, but was clearly spreading quickly through the urban areas. The concern was travel to and from Denver, Billings, and Salt Lake City. In a stroke of inspiration, the County commissioners ordered all flights in and out of the Basin cancelled. The epidemic jumped from the Atlantic seaboard to the west coast, igniting in Chicago, Dallas-Fort Worth and other major cities enroute. Perhaps this was a concern, although it shouldn't be, Bradley thought, since President Richard Newkirk had ordered a complete release of the vaccine to all Americans. The greatest problem was vaccinating large urban areas that were being contested by various ethnic groups. Several Hispanic gangs in the Los Angeles, Houston, San Antonio and Phoenix areas refused to allow any vaccinations in the areas that they controlled unless the citizens were charged five dollars per immunization, which immediately went into their coffers. Admiral Rosenberg argued that it was better to suffer the blackmail than suffer the thousands of deaths. The gangs could be dealt with after vaccination while the threat of the disease was immediate and lethal. The vaccination program took six weeks to complete. The entire nation was vaccinated, more or less. Certain leaders of the black community began to scream that "white folks got the good vaccine, while the black community got old, lower quality vaccine". That of course, was vehemently denied by the administration, the Surgeon

General and all associated with the program, right down to state and local health departments.

Accordingly, ten days after the vaccination clinics closed, President Newkirk ordered the Army, now consisting mostly of white soldiers, into Houston. The President and the Governor of Texas jointly issued a statement of martial law. A hollow Army Unit of Execution out of Fort Hood was ordered to Houston to reclaim areas of the city. It was at less than half its normal personnel strength. The Unit of Execution consisted of five units of action, each of brigade size, each of which would normally be about 3500 personnel. As expected, many of the gang members melted into the population, claiming no knowledge of gang activity, let alone extortion. Patrols began to stop Hispanic youth on the streets and examine them for tattoos that were the hallmarks of some of the gangs. Any resistance or objections was met with a rifle butt. Those who were identified as possible gang members were taken to a central holding facility in the sports stadium for questioning. They were photographed, fingerprinted, a blood sample drawn for DNA analysis, and a retinal scan made. Those released received a single warning. "If we find that you are involved in acts of violence against the Army or civilians, are engaged in gang activities or criminal activities of any kind, expect the harshest of punishments under martial law."

The FBI assigned an agent to each army battalion in each unit of action, to assist with interrogation and intelligence. The FBI however, had done some of its homework. It furnished the names and addresses of ring leaders and their major lieutenants who were rounded up in raids, often in the middle of the night. The word that gang leaders were being sought spread like wildfire, and many disappeared into the underground. Resistance was slight from those captured, and President Newkirk determined that any resistance at all could be met with overwhelming force. On a few occasions, several rounds from the main gun of the Strykers, the infantry fighting vehicles, settled the question of resistance. The American Civil Liberties Union was unusually quiet about the tactics and "the rights of the suspect Mexican-American citizens or other minorities."

Major General John McIntire and his driver, Private First Class Richard Carter, were on Route US 20/26 headed west towards Shoshone, Wyoming.

"General, may I ask you a question, Sir?"

"Certainly, Carter, if it isn't out of line, I'll be happy to answer."

"Sir, how did all this mess get started; I mean, why is the United States breaking apart, why all these riots and things? I didn't have any civics courses in high school, I don't know much about government, Sir."

"Well, it's pretty complicated, Carter. Successful nation building in the form of, or by separate political entities, uniting or remaining together is rare because it requires politicians to surrender power. The dissolution of our county is essentially the result of the same process in reverse. Those who crave power see opportunities for greatness and wealth. The politicians have usurped so much power from the people without their genuine consent, in the form of a tremendous self serving bureaucracy, or out and out theft of power through disguised, that is misrepresented legislation, that many people of the middle class, especially the upper middle class, can no longer tolerate it. We the people have lost so much of our individual liberty as guaranteed by the Bill of Rights to make that document meaningless. Of course, many of the masses, that's the lower class, are willing to trade those freedoms, those restrictions of choice of lifestyle, as long as the state guarantees them bread and wine, free medical and dental care, clothes and circuses and public housing. The riots that you see are the result of the failure of the state to deliver on those promises. Secondly, is economics; we're bankrupt.

Over 60 percent of our national debt has to go into the black hole of welfare in attempts to keep those promises. I first became aware of it thirty years ago when it was published in 2003 that we borrowed 600 billion dollars a year just so the government could pay the interest on its loans. Now we borrow over a trillion dollars a year just to keep the government operating. China loaned us most of it through buying our bonds and treasury notes. Now when they cash them in, we can't pay, so we crash, real hard. We can no longer even pay the interest on these debts. Not only are we fiscally bankrupt but in other ways as well. Third is the demographic shift. We're becoming Latinized. It's a different culture and they want their share of power, even dominance."

"General, isn't a lot of this based on physical differences, I mean genetics, all this racial strife?"

"Oh hell, Son. The genetic difference between man and bonobos, the pygmy chimpanzee, is only about four tenths of one percent. We share about ninety-nine point six percent of our genes with the chimps. These differences aren't genetic, they're cultural and economic and power driven."

PFC Carter drank a 500 milliliter soft drink when they stopped for a break on the west side of Casper, so to relieve himself he stopped at the campground short of the village of Hiland. Carter pulled the car under the trees. Slightly amused, the General got out of the car and walked across the road. A second before MG McIntire exited he car, the Predator III drone operator turned away from his screen to call his superior's attention that the target had stopped at a picnic area. It was a perfect opportunity. The Major in charge had orders to "eliminate" the secessionist leader if an opportunity presented itself. The television camera in the nose of the Predator III did not reveal any other vehicles in sight. The Major only said, "Kill the son-of-a-bitch!" The operator released a Hellfire III missile that struck squarely on the roof of the sedan. Metal fragments, some in huge chunks, blew in all directions. MG McIntire had just stepped behind a tree to relieve himself when the missile struck. The Ponderosa pine stopped a six by twelve by four inch chunk of the passenger door chest high on McIntire. Immediately realizing what happened, McIntire knew enough not to expose himself. He hugged the tree rather than crouching down. It was harder to identify him standing. Even if Carlson were seriously injured, he couldn't help him. The loitering drone operator would identify that the missile failed to kill him. If the operator knew he wasn't killed with the first missile strike, he could always launch a second, and a third if necessary. The General stayed hidden for thirty minutes. He then removed his uniform tunic and hat and ventured over to the remains of the portable latrine, hoping the drone had left the area. There wasn't much semblance left of the structure. It had been literally blown away. The portable latrine was perhaps only ten meters away from the car. Carter's body had blood pooled from his nose and mouth as a result of ruptured lungs. Splinters of metal were embedded in his back. He was face down in the dirt, dead. He had lived a few minutes at best.

General McIntire kept to the very few trees there as best he could, and began walking back towards Casper. In his uniform, a single car passed him and refused to stop when he stuck out his thumb. General McIntire noted the license number and jotted it down in his notebook that he always carried in his breast pocket. The second vehicle gave him a ride to the National Guard Armory in Casper. From there he used a land line telephone to call his office and informed them of the attack and PFC Carter's death. He ordered another car to immediately leave from Cheyenne and meet him in Douglas, at the National Guard armory there. The Casper National Guard First Sergeant ordered a car and driver to drive the General to the armory in Douglas. There another staff car took him to his home. He instructed the driver to go buy his own supper and be back in forty-five minutes. The General showered, put on a clean class A uniform, and went to the home of PFC Carter's parents. By now it was 22:00 hours. Even though it was late, he felt obligated to inform Carter's parents of their son's death. Informing the bereaved parents that their son was dead while he survived was one of the hardest things he ever had to do. He had written many letters to parents and wives and families of subordinates who were wounded or killed in action under his various commands when in the Regular Army, but none that were ever murdered by their own government. Such tasks are extremely difficult, and are a significant reason that officers must maintain an aloofness from their enlisted subordinates. Maintaining a hard exterior shell is a necessity for emotional survival. An officer cannot become emotionally involved with his men. It is too difficult and heart rendering when they are maimed and killed. Such involvement can, and has, influenced tactical decisions that should be made on a rational, objective basis.

Mr. Carter half carried his wife to the bedroom, where she lay down on the bed sobbing that their only son was dead. Returning to the living room, he thanked General McIntire and volunteered to join the militia on the spot. The Major General informed Mr. Carter that a militia recruiter will contact him in the immediate future. Mr. Carter owned and operated a furniture store in Casper. As soon as he arrived at his office the next morning, the General sent a fax to all units informing them of the attempt on his life and that all brigade commanders should henceforth exercise due caution. It was unknown how far down the chain of command attempts at assassination would extend. He then faxed the Wyoming Governor's office so that his office could alert the governors of the proposed Nation of Missouri so that they could alert their National Guard commanders. An hour later he received a reply back through the political chain of command. The Adjutant General for the state of Montana had been wounded during the previous evening by an assassin's bullet. It appeared that President Newkirk had activated assassination squads to eliminate the higher ranking military and political personnel of the states favoring secession.

The good Reverend James Winston had been brooding for several weeks. He watched his congregation that he had sheparded over for thirty years at the Seventh Black Baptist Church of Detroit dwindle as the influenza epidemic took the elderly, the HIV infected personnel, the drug addicts, and others that for one reason or another refused to get the immunization or were severely immunocompromised. Now, with the race riots, the violence in the streets, he was prepared for what he felt he must do. That Sunday morning when he climbed into the pulpit, he realized that this would be the last sermon, if you could call it that, he would preach in his beloved church. As he looked out over his congregation, he realized that for the most part these were the good people, the ones who still had some moral fiber and conscience. He decided not to mince words but to be direct and as blunt as possible. He delivered a short sermon on Moses leading his people out of Egypt, across the Red Sea and into the wilderness where they wandered for forty years. He thought it appropriate.

"Brothers and Sisters, the time has come. The time of turmoil, of racial strife, of division of our country, and sorrowfully, of our church, is here. Look around you. The riots are occurring all over the country. Many of our black citizens, especially from the eastern cities, are migrating south by the millions. White folks from the south are migrating north to escape the violence directed at them by Hispanics and some of our black brothers and sisters. Our black folks in the northern cities are essentially in enclaves. Already most of the food stores are out of business, looted until their shelves are bare and then burned. It isn't safe to be out on the streets in our neighborhoods, much less outside of our neighborhoods. We are in a grave situation. Most of us are peaceable, law abiding citizens. A few of us are not. Nevertheless, we must look toward the future. What I see is terrible. It is terrible because we will not survive if we stay here. Most of us have held out the hope that these troubles will cease. I do not see that. I see our once great nation becoming three nations. Remember what happened in the Balkans? Enclaves such as ours ceased to exist or became centers of murder, rape and starvation. There is no longer any U.S. or UN cavalry to come to our rescue; the cavalry that was us for others is no more. Our infrastructure is failing and soon will be completely lost. We only have electricity a few hours a day. We only have water a few hours a day. What do you think it will be like when you can no longer flush a toilet? What will life be like when you turn on a tap and there is no water to drink? Where will you get your food? Many of you are now living on rice and beans for two meals a day. What happens when there is no food at all? Listen to me, my Brothers and Sisters. Why take the risk of remaining here? It is hopeless in my opinion. It is time for us to leave. I have conferred with many of our fellow Baptists in the south, in several states. Their communities are willing to assist us in moving into their areas. We have offers in Georgia, Alabama and South Carolina. What I am proposing is that we give up our homes and caravan to a safe haven where the Lord will help us resettle. If we stay here, we will ultimately starve, be overtaken by the white community who will drive us out with fire and brimstone, or die of disease in our weakened state. Summer is fast approaching and fall and winter will not be far behind. It is almost here. When winter arrives it will be too late. Put your houses up for sale. Consider anything you get for them a blessing. We should not debate long, but most quickly before the situation collapses in upon us. I have a plan. I will appoint leaders who will help marshal us along our way. The Lord provided Moses to lead the people out of Israel. Now, I am no Moses, but I propose to lead this congregation south before it disappears into the dust under the feet of the Egyptians. We will caravan out of here on the Sunday one month from today. We will hold a ballot at prayer meeting Wednesday night as to which state to go. When we make that decision I will visit the state and the congregations that have extended invitations to us. I will prepare the way as best I can. I will return to lead all you brothers and sisters to what I pray will be a safe and happy haven. In the meantime, each family must prepare. Bottled water, water in polyethylene milk jugs and bleach bottles, dried and canned foods, clothes, limited cooking utensils and small items of high value such as jewelry, gold and cash are all that can be taken. Gather all the gasoline and diesel fuel you possibly can in approved containers. Fuel is already in short supply. Stockpile food, fuel and things here in our church basement for our journey. Those of you who have SUVs or trucks and trailers should consider renting trailers and driving them here to church on that Sunday to load as much as possible. Plan to haul what might be of value to the congregation as a whole; water, clothes, bedding, food and fuel. With trailers you can haul portable BBQ grills, fuel drums and propane tanks, bedding and suitcases. Do not think you will be able to drive your cars all the way south unless you have enough fuel to drive them without additional sources. There will no room for furniture, televisions or anything of the sort. For those of you that have weapons of any kind, you are a Godsend. You gun owners will ride shotgun, like the stagecoaches of yore, to protect our people in our march south to safety. Make no mistake. If we stay here, we will die of starvation, disease or violence. If the good Lord is with us, we will have our lives. I will try to have buses here to provide for the majority of us. Go home, pray, and think. Thank the Lord for this opportunity and come and vote Wednesday night."

Sitting comfortably in his living room, Robert Bradley tuned in the evening news as was his habit. The largest news report of the day was that the Senators from the states that now comprised the proposed Nation of the Missouri agreed to postpone the referendum until September 15 in order to allow greater debate among both the people, the administration and the members of Congress in hopes that a settlement could be reached.

The Central News Network, colloquially called the Communist News Network that night also featured reports from several major cities in the east and south. In Houston, the Unit of Execution was making slow progress. The chemical industrial plants were secured, as was the airport and most of the major roads, public utilities, and government buildings. All of the media announced that any armed citizen would be immediately disarmed and detained. If they resisted, they would be shot on the spot, no questions asked. Stryker vehicles accompanied foot patrols. Drones patrolled the skies over the patrols. Any sign of snipers, an ambush or guerilla type activity was met with 7.62 mm. machine gun fire from a drone. The drones could hover like a helicopter or fly like an aircraft. They carried lightweight twin .30 caliber machine guns and 300 rounds of ammunition for each gun. They could circle for up to six hours. Unfortunately, they could only cover a modest portion of the massive urban area at any one time. It was difficult to shift from neighborhood or area to area. The logistics capability made that impossible. Therefore, they were directed to concentrate on the major elements of the infrastructure of the city. It would have taken 500,000 troops to cover the entire area.

In Atlanta, the African-American reporter stood in front of city hall and remarked that the nature of the struggle for the city was changing. "Many of the whites of this great city have fled northward or northwest to the Midwest and points farther north. Destinations seem to be cities that are not in such severe turmoil. Louisville, Frankfort, Chicago, Cincinnati and Columbus were destinations mentioned by fleeing whites whom I interviewed earlier in the day. Many of them loaded their vehicles with their most valuable possessions and started driving. It now appears that urban guerilla warfare has morphed here, it is shifting its target from the fleeing white population, once the target of both Hispanics and blacks, to inner city gang warfare. Hispanic and African-American gangs are now fighting over territory abandoned by the fleeing white populations. Many areas of suburban Atlanta are almost wholly deserted. Sporadic gunfire is still occurring, but it is impossible to determine who is shooting at whom. Roving bands of armed men are now driving up and down Peachtree Street in downtown Atlanta, where I am now standing, in pickup trucks they took from automobile dealerships. They have spray painted their gang's symbols on the vehicles so there is no fratricide. They are engaging other gangs similarly equipped in lethal combat on sight. There is no indication of a viable National Guard here to restore order. From what we have witnessed, it seems to be primarily racially oriented, Black-Americans versus Hispanic Americans. Department stores and shops here have been looted throughout the area. Little normal activity remains here, and corporate offices in the inner city appear to have been ransacked for anything of value. Who knows what valuable records have been lost or destroyed. No one knows how long this anarchy will last or how order will be restored. It is obvious that no federal troops from Fort Benning outside of Columbus, or Fort Stewart outside of Savannah, will be forthcoming. Back to you, Chris."

With us now is Theresa Sanderson in San Antonio. What is your situation, Theresa?"

"Chris, things seem to have stabilized quite a lot here the last few days. The Anglo population of San Antonio has fled to Austin, while the Mexican-American population of Austin has fled to San Antonio. Although the two cities have grown to within twenty miles of each other in recent years, there seems to be some kind of undemarcated line between them. The shooting across that line, just a few miles north of here has stopped. San Antonio is now primarily Hispanic in nature, while Austin is essentially Anglo in nature. Violence in San Antonio has dropped considerably. San Antonio never had a large percentage of black folks relative to the other racial communities, so a lot of what John saw in Atlanta isn't happening here."

Chris: "How is the black population of San Antonio doing there? Have they experienced much violence or have they left the city?"

"Chris, from what I have seen, many of the Black Americans left early in the conflict for cities or areas of the southeast. Some have gone to New Orleans, some to Alabama or Georgia. Also the few remaining here are staying indoors and off the streets where they might be considered targets. There are few people on the streets. Those that are out and about are on missions of mercy, first responders or they are seeking some essential requirements such as food or medicine. That's all from here. Things here are very tense, but relatively quiet. Back to you Chris."

"We have one more report, that coming from Houston. Are you there, Bill? Can you hear me? How do things look there?"

"Chris, things look pretty bleak down here. Many people of European descent are fleeing this town as quickly as possible. There are long lines of traffic attempting to get out of the city, headed north. I have a couple here with me, a Mr. and Mrs. Friedkin. They were carjacked just a few moments ago, as they attempted to get on the freeway that you see just behind me. Mr. Friedkin was slapped around, but not seriously hurt. They lost their car and their most prized possessions that they packed in it. They were headed to Mrs. Friedkin's sister in Illinois. Mr. Friedkin is a chemical engineer here for one of the chemical plants that are now closed. Tell me, Mrs. Friedkin, were you very frightened during this carjacking? Do you know the perpetrators?"

"Of course I was frightened! They all had guns, those assault rifles or whatever you call them. At first I thought they were going to shoot us. They were a bunch of Mexicans.

When they dragged Charles out of the car, he told them to leave us alone. They just laughed and slapped him. Now we can't get home. Where are the police? Where is the Army? Aren't they supposed to protect us? Why aren't they here? Why doesn't the Army shoot those people? Hasn't martial law been declared?"

Bill moved the microphone to Mr. Friedkin. "What do you say, Sir? Are you all right?"

"I am not hurt. I am sure the police are overwhelmed, but I am disappointed the Army isn't here. I heard martial law was declared for the city. I will never again demonstrate against the Army recruiters coming on to college campuses. I was there with our son at the University of Houston last year and threw a tomato at them during a recruiting day. I didn't know our Army was so small. Now I guess I am paying for my sins. I wrote letters to my congresswoman about the Department of Defense's budget being so large. Now I see we can't even defend our own cities against our own rioters. What is this country coming to? Where are we going? What will we do?" Mr. Friedkin looked around in despair, and flapped his arms at his sides. The cameraman panned to the freeway above and behind the Friedkins to show the bumper to bumper traffic fleeing north.

"This is Bill Hernandez live from Houston. Back to you, Chris."

Chris Blackwell looked at the prompter for a few seconds, and then spoke. "This just in. The Mayor of Los Angeles, Roberto Juarez has just declared for the state of New California. Again, the Mayor of Los Angeles is proposing a new state called New California, with himself as Governor. We are going to Carlita Hermosina in Los Angeles where the mayor has called a press conference. Go ahead Carlita"

"Chris, in a surprise move not five minutes ago the Mayor of Los Angeles has announced that the southern half of

California is splitting off from the northern half of the state. He has declared himself as a candidate for Governor of this new state, which he calls New California. We interviewed some of the state representatives from the northern part of California. They had no idea that Mayor Juarez was going to do this. They claim it came as a complete surprise to them. We have his news conference here on tape from a few minutes ago and will roll it in a few minutes.

He claimed that the people of southern California will support the concept of a new state based on historical ties with Mexico, the demographics of the proposed state, the economy of the proposed new state and the political realities. He declared for the office based on living his entire life in southern California, being a direct descendent of Benito Juarez, whom you will recall, was a full blooded Indian who was once President of Mexico in the nineteenth century; the close ties of the proposed new state with old Mexico, and above all, the desires of the people. He has proposed a referendum to vote on splitting the "old" state of California at the same time as the national referendum on secession of the proposed Nation of Missouri. He proposed the dividing line to be from Santa Cruz to Fresno to along the northern border of John Muir Wilderness area. He expects the northern part of California to petition to join the autonomous unit of Columbia."

The tape rolled and showed Juarez standing in front of a map of California with a red line drawn through it.

The tape began with a reporter calling out "Do you really expect such a proposal to be acceptable to the people of California and to the United States?"

Roberto Juarez smiled and replied, "Of course. To the citizens of California and to the citizens of the United States, the people of southern California, from Monterey Bay south, I propose a declaration of autonomy. Our population is now overwhelmingly of Hispanic origin, Spanish is now the primary language of southern California. We seek greater political freedom and the right to control our future. We have the demographic, economic and political base to form such an autonomous sate. The numerous Hispanic parties have come together, coalesced under a rainbow organization to form a united political front against the Washington, D.C. based political powers. There are some in our coalition who wish to completely separate from the United States. We have watched the erosion of states rights as more and more power was usurped by a strong federal government, a bureaucracy that ignored the wants and needs of the Hispanic people. We do not stand alone in southern California. Our brothers and sisters of Mexican origin in other states have expressed a very strong interest in joining us. If other states decide to join us, it is possible that together, this unified front will renounce the treaty of Guadalupe of 1854 when the United States usurped land that was rightly part of Mexico and now ours as Mexican descendents. We Native Americans occupied it for 20,000 years before the arrival of the Europeans. Indeed, our Native Americans had lived in harmony with the land before Europe brought us her diseases, swords and gunpowder.

Political harmony within the United States is quite probably a thing of the past. The northern states of Mexico have a great deal more in common with us than they do with the states of Central and Southern Mexico. It is possible that the states of Sonora, Baja California, Chihuahua, Coahuila, Nuevo Leon and perhaps others with join us. If this occurs, such a political coalescence could form a strong union, an independent state between what remains of the U.S. and remains of Mexico. Such a state will rival or exceed what remains of Mexico. Think of it! It could be a nation that extends from the Pacific Ocean, from Monterey Bay south, east through New Mexico, Arizona and southern Texas, through Houston, to perhaps Vera Cruz.

Such a state is agriculturally self sustaining, with fruits, vegetables, rice, wheat, cattle, and maize. We have oil, copper, silver and uranium mines. Our population will be relatively homogeneous, a blend of people united in the common cause of determining our own political and economic future. The closed convention of Hispanic parties in Los Angeles last year resulted in the agreement in principle with the formation of such a state. The population of southern California in this proposed new state is now over sixty-five percent Hispanic, mostly of Mexican descent. The Asian population is fifteen percent and the WASP population is only fifteen percent. The people will vote for it. As for the northern part of the old state of California, I have no doubt they will opt to join Columbia. After all, while Columbia is an autonomous unit, it is still a part of the United States. I have no doubt those good citizens wish to remain U.S. citizens. Both halves of California are economically viable. After all, all of California and the southwestern U.S. was once Mexican territory. We lost it when gold was discovered in California, in the war for Texas Independence in 1836, in the Mexican-American War of 1845, and under the treaty of Guadalupe in 1854 which was forced upon Mexico. All of these events resulted in a massive inflow of people of European ancestry. Now, the situation is reversed. Repeated immigration from Mexico, Central and South America has made an irreversible demographic change favoring the Hispanic cultural heritage. We are a great majority, speaking a predominant language, and sharing a common religion. Why should be not form a new state that adequately reflects political realities?"

Another reported shouted "Will this proposed state of New California be a democracy, a republic, or other form of government?"

Roberto Juarez again smiled and declared "This state will continue in the classical form of democracy and government we have had in California for the last two hundred years. It will be with elected representatives for the people, senators representing the subdivisions of the state, an independent judiciary, and will adopt the Constitution and Bill of Rights under which we have labored for so long. For now, we are simply tied too closely with the United States by trade, financial institutions, education, transportation, defense, water, the postal service, utilities grids and a myriad of other ways to form a new and completely independent nation. That is unthinkable at this time but who knows what the future holds. We will have to wait and see what the future holds regarding my earlier comments. No, the state of New California will retain the same political flavor."

Robert Bradley laughed out loud at Roberto Juarez. "Hell", he said to no one in particular. "It will be like the Italians, Yugoslavians and the Rumanians joining forces to fight on the side of the Germans in World War II! Ultimately, many of them turned on each other. Those Mexicans are abysmal failures. Those people won't know what hit them. The next thing you know they will adopt the Mexican constitution and be part of Mexico and wonder what happened to their individual freedoms and corruption will overwhelm them. Those sexios (Presidents of Mexico are elected for a single six year term and colloquially called sexios) and other politicos down there are going to take those people for a real, long hard ride. I reckon this country we have known as these United States has about had it. What was the U.S.A. will be four, five, or six autonomous units now. Perhaps like the old Soviet Union when it broke up and formed the CIS, or Confederation of Independent States. Perhaps so, except for New California, Texas, New Mexico and Arizona when they become part of old Mexico. This is the Balkanization of what once was the United States of America."

At that moment his son walked in the door. Robert Bradley greeted him with "Hey Ethan! Did you hear? The Mayor of LA just declared for a new state, the southern half of California, with himself as Governor! Wants to call it New California." Robert Bradley pulled a bottle of brandy from the lazy susan and poured them each two fingers of brandy into snifters.

Ethan sipped his brandy, and said "There will be hell to pay in watching and closing all of these new borders. There's going to be a tremendous number of people moving around. They are going to shift everywhere. Kind of like when India broke into Pakistan and India after India achieved its independence from the British Empire in 1948. Hundreds of thousands of people died in that one. There will be a lot of violence associated with abrupt and massive population shifts. Hope it is not as violent as was India and Pakistan, kind of like the Balkans in the 1990's, only I hope without the internment centers. I guess we will have to wait and see. I have considerable concern about these people trying to escape into Wyoming. I don't think we can keep them out without killing them by the thousands.

Say, any news about assassination attempts anywhere around the country today? Newkirk tried to make a hit on General McIntire and barely missed with a missile. The Adjutant General of Montana stopped a bullet yesterday, but it wasn't fatal. Things are really heating up before the election."

"Hmm, haven't heard anything, nothing on the CNN tonight. I imagine they are keeping such attempts as quiet as possible. Of course, Newkirk and his storm troopers will deny all knowledge or complicity in such attacks if it ever comes into the open."

Secretary of State Frank Stokes, watching the television in the White House briefing room, jumped out of his chair. "That whole speech was a bunch of crap! On second thought, there is some truth in it. We've known for twenty years that Mexico was in deep trouble as a nation. They have a caste system that is damned near as bad as India's. People can't break through from the lower levels to the upper ones. It is based on skin color and birth. You're doomed to the caste you were born in. Mexico is even less homogeneous than the USA. The Indians of Yucatan and Quintana Roo have about as much in common with Mexico's northern states as they do with the Puritans of New England. Homogeneous my ass! They are a blend of European Spaniards, Indians, descendents of black slaves and all possible crossbreds in between. Mexico has an undiscussed caste system like that of India. It just isn't talked about. The wealthy peninsulares, those of who are of pure Spanish descent or close to it, are at the top of the heap and the Indians at the bottom. Everybody else is in between. They can't break through those class barriers regardless of their abilities. That's one reason the poor of Mexico have been pouring in to the USA. At any rate, the Mexican Army won't be able to prevent the northern states from breaking away if they choose any more than we can keep southern California in the union by invading it."

"All right", said President Newkirk. "What are the odds of such a state making a go of it, at least initially?"

"Frankly Mr. President, the odds are not better than fifty-fifty. The Mexican Revolution between 1910 and 1925 was a multi-ring circus. Numerous leaders emerged in various states, most wanting to be President of Mexico. Ultimately, after Porforio Diaz's departure, and Madero's murder by Huerta, four major leaders emerged, Carranza, Villa, Zapata and Obregon. There were dozens of local bandit leaders and warlords all over Mexico. A lot of backroom deals and assassinations resulted in their constitution which is full of deliberate contradictions. It was written to mean everything to everybody. The political party the PRI ran the country for 80 years as a private political club. Every president was expected to leave office a multi-millionaire if not a billionaire."

"Okay Frank. Naomi, what about the Mexican Army keeping the Mexican states from joining southern California?"

No way, Mr. President. The territory is way too big, the Mexican Army isn't prepared to fight guerilla warfare in the mountains, the Sierra Madre Occidentalis and Orientalis, the western and eastern mountain ranges that run north and south, and that's a lot of country. The deserts are mountainous; it is not much country for mechanized warfare. Horse cavalry would do almost as well, maybe better. The government attempted to suppress Indian uprisings in the last century through terror tactics of their own without a lot of success. It just incurred greater enmity of the Indians in the southern Mexican states. As Frank said, banditry, brigandage, rape became major problems. Bandits in company sized units raped and killed and robbed in many Mexican states involved in their revolution. Don't forget Francisco Villa started out as a cattle rustler and bandit."

The camera turned to another reporter outside of El Paso.

"Juan Hermosino here of KKXY, with some of the people of Brownsville. Why Sir, are you rioting?"

"Amigos, this land belonged to our ancestors. Only after gold was discovered here in California did the gringos flood into the land. They took this land from our forefathers in the Texican-Mexican war of 1836, in the Mexican-American War of 1846, and forced our fathers to ratify it with the Treaty of Guadalupe. They lied about the boundary even then, extending it south to the Rio Bravo which they call the Rio Grande. Now we are peasants and serfs, working lands that are rightfully ours for a few dollars a day. The wealthy gringo owners are millionaires living in luxury while they dole out a few paltry dividends, such as the influenza shots."

"Senor, as a representative of the United Farm Workers of America who refuses to state his real name, but goes by Raphael, what specifically are you advocating?"

"Simply that you take what rightfully belongs to you. That is the land."

"Do you think, Senor Raphael, if that is your real name, the gringos who now own the land will surrender what they have owned for 200 years? Why would they do that?"

"Seize the land. Drive them out. If they do not leave peacefully, let them leave violently. Our forefathers owned it before gold was discovered in California and the gringos flooded in."

"How will you do this? Are you telling us you plan to murder these people, the gringos? Are we not better off here, now, than when we left Mexico? I do not condone murder. Even if I did, we do not have the guns to do as you suggest."

"You will have the guns. In the back of my truck are the guns that you will need as well as the ammunition to go with them. If you are cowards and will not claim what belongs to you, others will come who will claim the land from the gringos and you will be no better off. If you act, each of you will have enough land to farm as your own, to grow and sell and live a comfortable life. Form a commune and share the farm equipment. It belongs to no one but to every one. Certain religious sects such as the Heuterites and the Mennonites have done this as successful communes in various regions of this continent for two centuries. That is your answer. You have individual farms with shared equipment. People will always need food and you know how to grow it and can sell it. As the Chinese say, 'Food is heaven.' When the gringos in the rest of the country get hungry enough, you will do well. This is occurring all over the Valley. See how the President of the new state of California, Senor Juarez has acted. Do you think I am acting alone? For my behalf? There are many more such as I, all over this new state of ours. We will band together to ensure our rightful heritage. We will take back our heritage. President Juarez is taking control for all of us of Mexican ancestry. It will soon start along the Rio Bravo as well. Take the guns, take your land, and seize your economic and political freedoms."

The next day Colonel Bradley faxed all his subordinates to remind them to contact the political leaders of their communities. He announced a meeting in ten days to discuss the ramifications of the possible inflow of people in to Wyoming, how and what to address it, and organization of their militia units. The meeting will begin at 10:00 hours in the Worland National Guard Armory. All interested parties are to be invited, and it is open to the public. A published agenda will shortly follow. The influenza epidemic might be of major concern if many of the people attempting to gain entry into the Basin are in the incubation stage of influenza, and the people of the Basin are not vaccinated in time or inadequately vaccinated.

The Commanding General, Fort Bliss, Texas, a dedicated African-American soldier who came up through the ranks, gave the order. All troops remaining on duty, that is those which haven't deserted, are to be armed at all times, and be prepared to defend themselves and the base. He established routine perimeter patrols around the built-up areas of the base and closed the base to all unnecessary traffic. His Hispanic troops had mostly deserted. About half of his Black American troops remained on duty. Anglo soldiers now comprised an equally large racial segment of his command. With now about one third of his original manpower, he called General Frank Sedgley, the Army Chief of Staff. "Sir, things are entirely out of control here. There is no way that order can be restored, even with martial law imposed. I simply don't have the troops. I am pressed to hold the housing and main base areas of Fort Bliss without major bloodshed. I would like to evacuate the civilian dependents and as many other civilians who are not engaged in civil strife as soon as possible. I will fax you an outline of a plan within the hour Sir." When the Chief of Staff of the Army reviewed the outline, he called Naomi Campbell for a video conference with the Joint Chiefs. After a brief verbal outline to all by General Sedgley, Naomi Campbell called MG Scott at Fort Bliss along with the Army Chief of Staff on a conference video for a first hand report.

"Madam Secretary, the situation is out of hand in El Paso. It is open racial and border warfare down here. Some of my deserters are now looting and murdering in El Paso. I want to ask you through the chain of command to have the President ask the Governor to declare Martial Law in the area and allow me to cordon off temporary safe zones. Anglos are at particular risk, Black Americans only slightly less so, although there are so very few of them. The white civilians are fighting back as best they can, but they don't stand a chance. We either need to evacuate them, or provide security for their departure, or establish enclaves which we can defend. Frankly, I don't have the troops to do very well at any of them, especially guard enclaves other than on a temporary basis, no more than 48 hours. Most certainly I cannot guard the base and divert troops to do any of the above for any longer than that. I recommend we attempt to get them to evacuate themselves by privately owned vehicles northward and eastward as quickly as possible. We can give them perhaps advance notice to move in 48 hours, thereafter they are on their own. I can provide convoy escorts for perhaps one hundred miles. I don't think any Anglos in their right minds would not take advantage of the opportunity to get out while they can. What do you think, Madam Secretary?"

Naomi Campbell contemplated his words and then said "I'll pass your recommendations on to the President. I suspect he will go along with that. What do you think, General Sedgley?"

"I'll have to go along with General Scott, Madam Secretary. He is one of our best and brightest. I trust his judgment implicitly. I strongly recommend we accept what he says. I expect the Joint Chiefs will go along with it."

"General Scott, I'll get back to you through the Joint Chiefs and General Sedgley if the President agrees and calls the Governor of Texas. That will serve as your warning order to get organized."

Naomi Campbell called to her secretary, "Get the President on the phone for me."

Naomi Campbell outlined what Major General Scott had suggested to her. She added that perhaps it would be even better to order the entire base closed. First, get the white civilians out of El Paso and then organize for a complete evacuation of Fort Bliss, taking everything that was possible. Military dependents followed by civilian families would have first priorities; two suitcases per individual. All forms of transportation are to be utilized. Securing weapons systems at Fort Bliss would have priority over other government properties. Evacuation will be to Fort Sill, Oklahoma, where the division would reinforce the units already there. If necessary, MG Scott can run a 24 hour shuttle service to evacuate the weapons. She suggested that Fort Sill elements support Fort Bliss by sending empty trucks and troops to guard the convoys, of which there would be many. The Army Chief of Staff would direct coordination.

"Mr. President, the situation is worse in El Paso than anywhere else because the population there is overwhelmingly Mexican. The population of the region is over 90% Mexican, they number in the millions and they have the mass to overpower anything. If they attempt to overrun the base, it will be a bloodbath. The Base Commander will have no choice but to put mass fires on any mob trying to breach the base. Overrunning the outlying areas of the base will require little or no effort, Mr. President, but the General will have no choice but to defend the built-up areas, the housing areas, the weapons storage areas, and all the military families within them. I recommend that General Scott proceed first with evacuating the civilians from El Paso that wish to flee, along with the military dependents, because they are in the greatest danger, followed by the military defenders of base itself, Mr. President."

"How is Fort Hood, TX holding out Naomi? Do we need to order their evacuation as well, or of the Air Force Base outside of Austin?"

"Mr. President, I think they are OK for the time being. They are not an island, so to speak, as Fort Bliss is. They can hold their own for the moment. I am going along with Bliss's evacuation to Fort Sill so that if Fort Hood falls, we won't have to evacuate the same people twice. I believe that Fort Sill, Oklahoma is relatively safe compared to our Texas bases. Indeed, if it becomes necessary, Fort Sill then can provide reinforcements to Fort Hood to either hold or evacuate with the extra troops and their families will still be safe. Evacuate all the Air Force bases in Texas as well. Priorities are to fly the aircraft out with as much maintenance equipment as possible. Then truck out then all the maintenance equipment that is left. Lastly, everything else is to be prioritized by the base commanders."

President Newkirk concurred, and thus began the evacuation of El Paso and Fort Bliss, Texas. It was completed in 96 hours. Anglo-Americans began to flee from other southwestern cities. Santa Fe, Albuquerque, Tucson, and Phoenix all experienced massive outflows. There were a lot of shootings at gas stations as Hispanics did not want to sell the fleeing Anglos gasoline unless it was at greatly inflated prices. Friends and neighbors driving together in convoys of twos, fives, and tens, often settled the issue with force. It wasn't a question of money, but simply of getting sufficient supplies of gasoline to leave.

The influenza pandemic was wreaking havoc throughout the Middle East and spreading more slowly through Africa due to differences in population density. Africa had already lost a sizeable population due to AIDS. The disease spread rapidly through the Islamic world as Muslims gathered in mosques to pray. The larger cities of Damascus, Tehran, Shiraz, Baghdad, and Riyadh began having difficulty of disposing of the dead by the end of the second week of the pandemic. Medical personnel were among the first to die as a group. Many fled into their deserts, to be plagued with thirst and hunger.

"Mr. President, I think it would be wise to postpone the national referendum, to be on the safe side of course, because of the influenza pandemic. While vaccination has protected most folks, there will be those whose immune systems are so compromised that they will be at risk in going to the polls."

"What percentage of people are we talking about, Dr. Rosenberg? Why weren't these people vaccinated, or isn't the vaccine good enough?"

Oh, the vaccine is plenty good for healthy people, Mr. President. It is those whose immune systems are compromised that I am considering. Those folks, who have AIDS, are infected with the HIV virus but don't know it, those who have bad immune systems from cancer treatment, or have their spleens removed or are genetically unable to mount a good response to the vaccine. I don't know how many that is for certainty, but our statisticians estimate that it is around 10% of our population. That would be about thirty million people or more, Mr. President. Of course, that doesn't indicate how many will be infected. We don't know how much of the virus is circulating out there. We haven't been able to detect much in our monitoring systems. Apparently the vaccine is of such high quality that we don't have enough susceptibles to maintain the epidemic. No, it will be the individuals out there who lack good immunity that will suffer. They need to be aware of the risks of vaccination. A public announcement by you should inform them of the risk, or by the Secretary of HHS, or the Surgeon General. It is a hard call, Mr. President, but I would be negligent if I did not point out the risk to you that these folks will experience. It really is a hard decision, Mr. President."

"What do you think the political fallout would be if this administration made such an announcement? Do you think it would be accepted? Believed? I don't think so. No, you have done your job, Doctor, but the election will go on. I dare not cancel it. That would result in open civil war."

As influenza spread through Mexico, more and more Mexicans fled into the United States, demanding vaccination. Mexico's cities suffered the most. The slums built on hillsides filled with the dead. The stench became overbearing as the volume of corpses that could not be removed grew exponentially. In most U.S. border towns and cities, public health services continued as vaccination clinics that were part time, or in some cities, ceased to exist. In El Paso, they continued to some degree because most health care workers were Hispanic, until their vaccine supplies were exhausted or people stopped coming. Sensing an opportunity to help halt the flow of illegal Mexicans seeking vaccination into the United States, President Newkirk ordered that less new vaccine production would be diverted from supplying Europe as it became available. Only large cities in southern Mexico would receive vaccine claiming that it would save more lives. He ordered a public announcement of it. When the announcement was made at a specially called news conference from the White House that new vaccine production was being flown to Europe as soon as it was produced rather than to the border states the sense of rage along the border and south of it was further increased. No Anglo appearing American that had not fled north was safe on the street in any border city or town. The unforeseen consequence was that Mexicans attempted to flee farther and farther north in hopes of gaining access to vaccination. Even Mexican-Americans who had been citizens for their lifetime began to look upon the invading immigrants with a considerable degree of fear and distrust. By the busload, by the pickup truckload, Mexicans tried to move north. Some simply stopped when they ran out of gas and could find no more. They then tried to scavenge or steal gasoline, food and water from any source, sucking it from gas tanks of parked vehicles with garden hoses they found and cut into pieces, trying to force gas stations to sell it, or in some cases, at gun point.

"Mr. President, there are ominous signs along the borders in southwest Asia. It appears that Chinese convoys are moving at night into the western border areas of what was Afghanistan and Pakistan and Turkmenistan and Kazakhstan," said Harry Strother, Director of National Intelligence. Strother had brought General Dewey Singleton, USAF, and Chairman of the Joint Chiefs of Staff with him to the Daily Presidential Briefing, the first time a military officer had been present during Newkirk's morning brief. Newkirk detested the military and those who chose military service as a career. He had the deep, inherent fear that dominated the left, the fear of a military coup seizing the United States Government. Newkirk glared at General Singleton for a moment, the realized that there must be a reason that Strother brought him along.

"What do you think it means, General Singleton?"

General Dewey Singleton, United States Air Force, Chairman of the Joint Chiefs of Staff, dreaded the thoughts that plagued him.

"If it means the Chinese are on the move again, it couldn't come at a worse time. Europe has no forces to confront them, the entire Middle East is being depopulated by influenza, our Navy has vacated the Persian Gulf and Indian Oceans in order to guard our ports and harbors, Africa is in famine, disease, civil war, and general chaos, and we are faced with a civil war with no military forces ourselves, reliable military forces, that is, Mr. President. The Chinese can walk in and seize Iran, Iraq, and perhaps in Saudi Arabia if they chose and the only way to stop them is with massive nuclear fires. Apparently they are not suffering very much from the influenza pandemic."

"And what makes you think they are not suffering as much as everyone else?"

"Mr. President, our agents there indicate that there have been very few deaths associated with the pandemic. Illness from the disease is uncommon. Our embassy informs us that their hospitals have seen only a slight increase in the number of hospitalized cases, most the very young and the elderly, but are not anywhere overwhelmed or beyond their carrying capacity. It seems that they are immune for some reason."

"And why would that be, General?"

"Mr. President, it strongly suggests to me that they were prepared for this pandemic and vaccinated their population ahead of time."

"Harry, are there any indications that the Chinese have held any special vaccination clinics for this over the last year or two?"

"No, Mr. President, none that I am aware of. Perhaps Secretary Rosenberg might know something about it. Perhaps we should have a little session with him later this morning and see what he knows. Certainly it is most unusual. With their troops massing on the border, there is no way that they can escape exposure, yet they continue to mass in spite of the flu without suffering mentionable casualties.

One other subject I should mention, Mr. President, the results of the European Union Conference I returned from yesterday. It is being almost wholly ignored by our media as a result of our domestic troubles. Britain has refused to honor its commitment to the Quick Reaction Force. London, and especially Manchester, but other cities as well are burning from the Muslim riots. Only Ireland in the British Isles is relatively calm. Muslim rioters are demanding the entire British Army, all three undermanned Divisions, be seconded to the Quick Reaction Force for the defense of Saudi Arabia and its Islamic holy places. The French high command wanted to deploy to Kuwait's eastern border. The eastern European countries, especially Hungary, Romania and Greece want to block the Dardanelles against the Turks. Germany, who has the largest and best equipped force, advocated a strategic in-depth defense to draw the Chinese armies into tactical nuclear fire zones. Italy and Greece want to block the Balkans and patrol the Adriatic for fear of infiltration of Albanians and Bosnian Muslims. Crete is a mess. Iran was pledging death and destruction to infidels and invaders alike on the air waves again last night.

Four man patrols are now roaming British streets with orders to shoot any British subject who is in violation of the 21:00 to 05:00 hours curfew or who refuses to submit to questioning by or direction from the patrol leader. Whole neighborhoods are disappearing in smoke. White British subjects are cowering in their homes in fear while gangs of Muslim youths prowl the streets armed with clubs, knives, axe and pick handles, and semi-automatic nine millimeter handguns and some AK-47s. China supplied, really sold, thousands of handguns to Iran who smuggled them into Britain on oil tankers. Iranian agents then distributed them through the mosques. Russia fears Siberia will be the next major strategic target. Russian leadership however, refused to align itself with Europe out of fear of offending China. It declared neutrality while it is massively building its military arsenal of small arms and artillery battalions, armor and ground attack aircraft. They let it slip that they are reworking their nukes from strategic megaton size to tactical kiloton range. They admitted they are uncertain if their older tactical nuclear arsenal will still function. Still, it was a saber rattled by the Russian President. President Chertoff announced Russian territory was inviolate. Any force crossing into Russian territory would be met with maximum resistance and annihilation. Clever these Chinese, sowing violent dissent among potential adversaries."

"General Chang, your past grand strategy has resulted in tremendous gains for the Republic of China. Yet again you have acted without the express consent of this Central Committee. You have ordered more or less a massive mobilization of the Peoples Liberation Army Navy along the western borders. Is it your intent to move farther westward, is this just a show of force to influence certain governments to the west or do you intend to demonstrate your power to this Committee?"

"Comrade Secretary, I most humbly and sincerely apologize for my actions. It is most certainly not my intention to insult any member or the Central Committee as a whole. I have acted with the concept of maintaining the utmost secrecy. Very few knew exactly what was happening outside my general staff. Even the commanders of the various armies are not fully aware of what is happening. I have ordered that there is to be no communication between the armies, only within their respective organizations. That way, there is less likely to be an intelligence break. Western powers will not realize what is happening, whether we will advance or are merely conducting routine maneuvers. Today we are presented an unparalleled opportunity. The United States is in the middle of what will most likely be a breakup of that country, with the formation of several independent states. We have anticipated this and prepared for it. Technological intelligence gathering can never replace human intelligence gathering. Our hundreds of agents in every region of that country have reported the growing moods and economic difficulties in their respective regions. As such regionalization and cultural difficulties expanded, the Americans will have lost the political will and organization to inhibit any of our movements or objectives. They will be far too concerned with their own difficulties. Indeed, there is a complete re-alignment of global order in the making. We must take advantage of it. There is no way that I see that we can fail. Resistance will be minimal or non existent. What is there to stop us? The United States owes us trillions of dollars. We hold most of their financial instruments. All we have to do is mention that we will call in all of their debts, their Treasury bills, their bonds and so on and we will completely bankrupt them. There will be riots in the streets. It will be worse for them than it was for the German people of Weimar Republic of Germany at the end of

World War I. Starvation could well stalk the United States. It is too late for Europe to do anything but cry about their soft power or scream and gnashing of teeth at the United Nations. Who cares what the UN says or does? Europe only has a 60,000 personnel quick reaction force which is composed of lightly equipped elements taken from each of their national armies. They will not be able to offer any significant resistance. They have no significant arms industry anymore capable of mass production, even of small arms outside of Belgium let alone heavy armament. There is no one to resist us. From Iran, we can always choke off the oil pipeline of Europe and they know it. We will seize the region before they can mobilize or industrialize. We can move once again into Africa around the Horn. Who is there to impede us? No one will risk nuclear war. China will be the world hegemon."

"Officer Gilbert, to what do we owe the honor of this surprise visit to USAMRIID today?"

"Good morning, Colonel Aspins. Thanks for giving up your day this fine Saturday. We notified the base commander and you. Only you two know of our presence. We would appreciate that you kept our visit in confidence. If some of your folks come in for whatever reason, tell them we are upgrading the communications system or whatever seems appropriate to you. We need to take a look at your security. I brought a team with me; the Army is represented by Colonel Johnson, Army Intelligence, who is team member. It is primarily a CIA investigation today. We want to review your security operations, access to your classified files, your copy machines, and so on. Your security officer should be with us until we complete our survey."

"Seeing as how you have a dozen people on your team I take it that you suspect something is seriously wrong."

"We won't know that for a while. We have to investigate, then analyze. We won't have any immediate answers. If you can detail your security officer to us, we will get started. We might be here for several days. If that is required, we will leave several of our officers here overnight to insure that nothing is disturbed. Several team members will start with your classified documents and the records to their access while others will review your personnel files."

The contracts with the Israelis for vaccine production were first scrutinized and dusted for fingerprints. Records of copy machines dedicated to classified documents were duplicated for initial inspection and review. Several were dismantled to search for hidden components that could be regarded as transmitters, for the presence of duplicate programs that would reveal copies being surreptitiously made or transmitted. Hidden bar codes within the classified documents revealed the time and date they were copied. The magnetic tapes for electric card key accesses to doors and file cabinets were reviewed and copied. Twelve hours later the team folded its operations. Colonel Aspins remained to be debriefed by Officer Gilbert who gave him little more than a thank you.

Analysis of the fingerprints lifted from the documents, key access codes to the files and copy machines, and copy machine records revealed that the contracts with the Israelis had been surreptitiously copied by Youssef ibn Malik. Teams of FBI agents were immediately detailed to initiate enhanced surveillance of the Malik family to include their children. Their phone lines were tapped, their trash thoroughly analyzed, their medical records reviewed at the offices of their physicians, all rooms of their house were wired with hidden microphones and cameras photographed their every move from long distance. They couldn't sneeze without it being recorded.

Ethan decided that he would stop for a late lunch in Thermopolis. He pulled into parking space in front of a café on the main drag in the middle of town. He took a seat at the counter and scanned the menu for something other than the usual hamburger and fries or chili. He decided on the club sandwich and a milk shake. He watched the waitress pour a customer coffee at the other end of the counter. She was tall, lean, with long legs, slim hips and long hair. He couldn't see her face. The waitress, a late twenties or early thirty-something, poured him a cup of coffee with several servings of half and half on the saucer without asking as he reread the menu. Bradley looked up from the menu to see an attractive gal with a slight smile looking at him. Ethan returned her smile and placed is order while he poured the half and half into his coffee. "How did you know I like so much cream, Miss?"

"I recognized you, Colonel. I have even thought about joining your National Guard Brigade, but decided I would go for the militia instead. I am still working on my Master's degree and don't have a lot of time that being in the Guard would require. I'm a working gal, too, supporting myself, so time is very vital to me."

"What's your Master's in, Miss?"

"Physics. I am still in the coursework, although I have 28 hours of that out of the way. I haven't really decided on the main thrust of my thesis, but I am thinking it will be on light, on methods of changing or manipulating wavelengths at will, with the type of a computer key."

"Where do you get physics courses in Thermopolis, Wyoming, particularly on the Master's level?"

"I'm doing it online. I did most of my B.S. at Ohio State University, all but my last semester. My husband at the time, now my ex, is a petroleum engineer, so we moved to the Basin. I did my last semester's work on-line and got my B.S. Since hubby started globe trotting to far off corners of the world where I was not welcome to accompany him, I decided I needed something mentally constructive, so I explored getting my Master's. The University of Washington does offer a unique program on-line, so I thought I would pursue it that way, since I got stuck here."

"How did that happen?"

"Well, Tom's first job was to explore opening old wells here in the Basin, but then the company needed a traveling engineer, and he started moving around. First it was six months in Alaska, then it was to Iraq for a year and then to Africa. Following that, he went to South America where he met up with some Brazilian chicky-pooh. I haven't seen him since. We more or less got a divorce by mail. I didn't contest it. Last I heard he was somewhere in the upper Amazon Basin, looking at the possibility of opening some smaller fields. There are jihadists and cocoa growers in that region, as well as some uncivilized natives. I don't even know if he is still alive. I really don't much care any more."

"May I ask your name, Miss?"

"If you promise you won't laugh. I have had to bust a few cowboys in the mouth for their smart ass remarks about my name."

Ethan Bradley held up the three middle fingers of his right hand. "Scout's Honor, Ma'am, I won't laugh."

"It's Gypsy Lee, Gypsy Lee Perroud, and pronounced per-row. I don't know why my mother had to be such a smart ass as to hang such a moniker on me, but she did. Mom married a Cajun from New Orleans who migrated after the hurricane Katrina disaster. That gave me the Perraud part. He abandoned Mom when I was little"

Bradley allowed himself a slight smile. "It seems to me that you should be teaching high school physics rather than being a waitress. I would think that would be a better use of your talents."

I thought about it, but there are reasons why not. First, I make as much or more money being a waitress than I could as a high school teacher. Second, it takes a lot of time to be a teacher, with grading projects, tests and the extra-curricular activities you are supposed to do. I sat in a couple of classes in the high school here in Thermopolis, and in Worland as an observer to see if I wanted to do it. There are three groups of kids out there. One group wants to learn, about the upper ten, no more than twenty percent, and they will make it. The middle group, about a third of the kids, doesn't care one way or the other, and the bottom half seem to be down right resentful. On several occasions the younger teachers tried to assign homework to the kids. They kids resented it and there was such an outcry from the parents about their kids having homework, that the teachers resigned themselves to no homework and adopted something of an 'I don't care attitude.' The smarter group of kids did extra projects for credit. The parents and kids of the lower 50% don't have much of a value system and seem to think the world is going to take care of them without much effort on their part. It is really a shame. They aren't smart enough to realize the world is crashing down around them. I have zero tolerance for that kind of attitude."

"Aren't you married, Colonel?"

"Yes, legally still married, but my wife took our sons and quit the country, so to speak. They went to Baltimore, where she is doing very well in international law I understand. I hear rumors about her activities, shall I say, both professionally and personally. We don't have the same value system. She is a United Nations, internationalist system-world order oligarchic kind of person. She would surrender all of the sovereignty of all nations especially that of the United States, to international bodies, with the masses controlled by an oligarchy of the elitists from on high. I am for the United States, or more accurately, for what it was, and what I hope the union of states forming the Republic of the Missouri will be. She came to believe that only those with a stake in the economy, people of property and intellectuals should be able to vote. Those who are unemployed, own no stocks, bonds and so on, those on welfare, should have no voting rights. Hell, I never did figure out who she thought voted in those idiots we call politicians."

"And what is that, Colonel, I mean what is that you think the United States should stand for?"

"For starters, we will return to the Constitution and the Bill of Rights as they were originally written. Our courts will recognize them as the highest law of the land. No longer will judges and politicians and lawyers impose their concept of social engineering, ruling in favor of what they think is best for the masses, but uphold justice as opposed to upholding the system. As attorneys like to say, if you don't like it, change the system. Unfortunately, they control the system. Very few lawyers and politicians seem to think the way our Founding Fathers did, certainly I don't think the way today's legal eagles do."

"Colonel Bradley, I get off at 21:00 hours tonight. Would you like to go somewhere else later for a cup of coffee? Since you will be driving, you can't have any alcohol. That's against your own policy."

Bradley smiled. "Gypsy Lee, you have a date." Gypsy Lee brought him his club sandwich and chocolate milk shake.

CHAPTER 13

THE IRANIAN REPRESENTATIVE TO THE UNITED NATIONS APPROACHED THE PODIUM.
He had strict orders from the Supreme Revolutionary Council to compare Iran to the United Kingdom in the early days of World War II. He vowed, as Winston Churchill did, that Iran would not cave in to the threat of or an actual invasion by China. Iran would conduct guerilla warfare from every possible terrain. Iranians would fight to the death or until every last invading Chinese solder was killed. Any contributions of small arms by any nation for the citizens of Iran would be most gratefully accepted. It was the same request made decades earlier when United States citizens donated their privately owned firearms to Britain when Hitler's Operation Sea Lion threatened invasion of the British Isles. Britain was saved only by the Royal Air Force in the Battle of Britain. There would be no respite for the Chinese if they invaded his country the Iranian stated as a matter of fact. He requested that the United States, Western Europe and Russia form a triumvate as they did in World War II to repel any invasion of Iran by China. His country he claimed had only a limited nuclear arsenal, not one of sufficient size to deter the Chinese. Only the proposed triumvate had sufficient nuclear forces to compel the Chinese to withdraw from the positions of attack. Only the threat of massive nuclear fires would stop or repel the Chinese or force them to withdraw. He requested the United Nations pass a resolution requiring China to return to its original borders, the borders before they invaded the

Central Asian Republics for their oil. He declared there could be no other purpose for the massing of millions of troops in their newly conquered Central Asian Republics except for the invasion of his homeland. The U.S. ambassador to the United Nations abstained from voting on the resolution. So did the representatives of the United Kingdom, France, and Germany. Russia initially did not know which way to turn. The Kremlin realized that mineral rich Siberia could easily be the next target of China, but their lucrative business contracts with the Chinese worth hundreds of billions of U.S. dollars won the day. In the end, they voted against the resolution. Eastern European nations and many African nations supported the resolution because they could see themselves in the same situation in a decade or two. The Chinese ambassador to the UN stood, bowed to the General Assembly and walked out smiling.

Ethan Bradley wrote his father-in-law and requested the best way to proceed with filing for divorce. Would Martha contest it? Should he file in Wyoming or in Maryland? What would be the best grounds for divorce? Mutual incompatibility? Infidelity? Desertion? He received his answer in forty-eight hours by FEDEX. *"At least the international delivery companies were still working, thought Ethan."* Martha had just filed under Maryland law ninety-six hours earlier on the ground of mutual incompatibility. Earlier attempts to contact him by registered mail simply had not found him due to the current political turmoil. If Ethan would sign the necessary papers when they arrived and return them by FEDEX overnight express he would receive a check for $500,000 by FEDEX. Three days later the package of papers arrived at his father's home. Ethan Bradley poured himself another scotch as he worked his way through the morass of paper. He knew Martha would never again be his. As difficult as it was to accept that, he wondered what was really best for their sons, Josh and Sam. He gazed into his crystal ball to portend the future. He saw his older son Sam becoming a man of character, a modest success in several endeavors, but no center stage, earth shaking player. Sam too, would be warrior. Sam would earn his second star and retire as a division commander. From that base, he would develop several modest but successful enterprises.

Of his younger son Josh, his oracle presented him an entirely different picture. Josh was brilliant, but also utterly ruthless, arrogant, a bully, physically and every other way possible. He was to be a man without scruples, without conscience. You were either one of his supporting subordinates or an implacable enemy to be totally crushed at the first opportunity. Sam would be a happy man, a loving man. Josh would never be happy and never understand why. With that mental image, Ethan signed all the forms and drained his scotch, knowing all of the advantages his ex-father-in-law and his ex-wife would bestow upon Sam.

He was about one third back through the Wind River Canyon headed north when he observed the car barely off the road. A young woman was flagging at him to stop. "Hell, thought Bradley, nice place for an ambush. A rifleman up there in the rocks could take me out without any difficulty. No way to tell if it is a genuine breakdown or a trap." Bradley drove two hundred yards past her and pulled off on the shoulder of the road. He took out his binoculars and first scanned the cliffs on each side looking for a possible sniper. Then he observed her for a few minutes as she attempted to flag down two other vehicles, both of which continued past her. Bradley decided that it was probably a genuine breakdown. The woman occasionally glanced in his direction, "probably cursing me or wondering what I am doing," Bradley thought to himself. The next car came to a halt behind her car. Three men got out of the car and approached her. Bradley watched as they talked for a minute. One of the men grabbed her from behind around the waist, another grabbed her hands and they began to carry her, kicking and yelling towards their car. Bradley opened his pickup truck door and leaned on the horn. The long, loud blast momentarily attracted the attention of the men. Bradley got in and turned his truck around, driving slowly towards the woman's car. He pulled over on the left shoulder of the road, the river side of the road, just in front of her car. The men just stood there, still holding the woman. Bradley climbed out of his car and put his hand inside his jacket and grasped the butt of his Government Model .45 in its shoulder holster. "Good afternoon, gentlemen, are there any problems here?" Bradley noted that the three men were Native Americans.

"You just go on down the road Mister, and mind your own business," spoke the one man who wasn't holding on to the woman. He took several steps in Bradley's direction. Bradley took a few steps towards him.

"It seems to me that there is a damsel in distress here, and you gentlemen have something on your mind other than assisting the lady. Perhaps I can relieve you of any such notions of harming her and allow you and her to be safely on your way."

The larger man took another two steps towards Bradley and drew back a fist as he did. He suddenly found himself looking down the muzzle of Bradley's .45ACP Government Model, clasped with both hands at eye level, with Bradley's cold blue eyes looking into his just over the top of the slide of the .45. He heard the snick of the safety as Bradley thumbed it off. The man took several steps backward; he looked at his companions, glared at Bradley, and said only "let's go." The other two released the girl and got in their car. Bradley stepped in front of her car so they couldn't run over him with their car, keeping his automatic focused on the driver all the time, pivoting to follow them with the pistol as they drove past him. He holstered his automatic and approached the woman who had just opened her car door. She retrieved her purse and lit a cigarette. After she took a heavy drag she faced Bradley and said "Thanks, Mister. I owe you sometime."

"Forget it Miss. What seems to be the problem with the car?"

"I don't know. It suddenly died on me. I don't know much about cars. Can you give me a lift to someplace where there is civilization?"

"Sure, I am headed towards Thermopolis, where there are several good mechanics and a towing service. Get in." Bradley turned the truck around as she locked her car, crushed out her cigarette and then climbed into the passenger seat of Bradley's pickup.

"Where are you from, young lady? By the way, my name is Bradley, Ethan Bradley." Bradley noticed her Nevada license plate but didn't mention it. The young lady was quite curvaceous and her method of dress accentuated what was a lean, long legged frame. She had a very nice figure. She had jet black hair that was straight and cut so that it framed her obviously Eurasian features.

"My name is Paula, Paula Jean Darnell, lately of Las Vegas, Mr. Bradley. I very much appreciate what you did back there and for the lift. Would you really have shot those guys?"

Bradley looked at her and grinned. "Yes Paula Jean Darnell, I would have killed all three of them without a moment's hesitation if I thought it necessary."

"Since you are smiling while you said that, I think that you must be kidding or you enjoy killing."

Bradley continued to smile. "Neither is correct. I haven't killed anybody over a damsel in distress in some time, and I find that amusing."

"Oh, you have killed to protect some poor damsel in the past?"

Bradley sighed, the smile fading, thinking back to Africa. He didn't initially respond as the memory flashed through his mind. During one of his long range patrols, he and his platoon came to the edge of a village where John Fullbright's troops were raping and killing. Sporadic gunfire erupted as people were executed.

He entered one hut on the edge of the village where five men where holding a teenage girl, perhaps thirteen, spread eagle on the ground. Each arm and leg was held by a man while a fifth was raping her. Bradley stepped in and shot each of them in the head as they stood up. He inserted a loaded magazine in his issue .45 ACP Colt then and moved to the next hut. Two of his snipers were taking out targets of opportunity as they appeared in the open. Other members of his platoon were similarly killing Fullbright's men as they came across them, hut to hut. Their gunfire was mingled with that of Fullbright's men shooting the civilians as they infiltrated through the village. The enemy didn't realize the presence of Bradley's platoon until it was too late. It was possible that one or two escaped into the bush.

Bradley, with a more somber look, simply said, "We won't go there. What did you do in Las Vegas? From the looks of you, I would guess you are a dancer."

"Close enough," thought the young woman. "Hell, he doesn't need to know I was one hell of a high priced Hooker, at least not this minute. Let's see what transpires with this guy. He is a pretty good looking, rugged fellow. He might even by a cop, she thought to herself."

Bradley thought about asking about her ethnicity, but he decided against it. She had slight epicanthic folds and a light copper toned skin. Her lips were small and straight, her eyes black and flashing. Framed by her square cut hair, she had a definite pixyish look that was quite fascinating.

"So, Mr. Ethan Bradley, what do you do in this world to earn your bread? It looks to me like you and that gun of yours are old friends."

"The bottom line is that I am a soldier, Paula Jean Darnell. I am with the Wyoming National Guard here, full time duty."

"Aha. That explains everything. That is why you are armed, and why you didn't stop the first time you went past.

The chivalrous knight, the paladin protecting the damsel, and leading the freedom fighters against a despotic government that's what you are. I have read about some of you guys in the break away states. We certainly could use a bunch of you in Las Vegas. Things are pretty rough in Las Vegas. The Mexican and Asian gangs are battling each other over all the loot they can rob from everybody else and each other. The territorial wars over the rich white man are pretty violent. Pay or die, that's their code. Man, there is blood running down the streets. People can't get out of there fast enough. I'm lucky to have made it out. I hope it is a lot safer here. A gal can't run and hide forever."

"I would have thought you are Asian or part Asian, Miss, from your looks. I guess that would not have made a difference to the violent types though. By the way, are you always so incisive in your perceptions of people? You scoped me out pretty quickly."

"Yes, I am of Asian extraction. My grandmother was Thai, my grandfather a black American airman at Utapao Air Base in Thailand way back when. Grandad brought grandmother to America, California to be exact, where my mom was born. Mom married another half Thai-half Anglo-American husband in Los Angeles and here I am."

"I hear things are pretty bad in Los Angeles as well, with the mayor trying to split off the bottom half of California to make a separate country with himself as President."

Paula Jean was silent for a moment. "Yeah, things are pretty rough, but not as bad as Vegas. The Mexicans simply overwhelmed everybody else in L.A. And yes, Juarez wants to be President. We should have started killing all those illegal Mexican bastards when they started pouring across the border en mass decades ago."

Bradley looked at her. "You sound bitter, Ms. Darnell."

"Yeah, I am. The bastards murdered my parents last year. The Mexicans turned on the Asians as their nearest competitors. They initially went after Anglos primarily because of their wealth."

"I'm sorry to hear that." They were both quiet for some time.

"So, soldier boy Ethan Bradley, just what is it you do in the Wyoming National Guard? What rank are you?"

"I command the Basin Brigade, the rank is Colonel."

"Well, nothing like making the big time, Colonel. What are the employment opportunities around here? A girl has to eat, you know. I would also like to find a nice comfortable, cozy little place to safely lay my head. Do you know where that could be, Colonel?"

"Job opportunities are pretty scarce, Miss. You can inquire in Thermopolis, but you would probably have better success in Worland. Thermopolis is on the edge of the Indian reservation. They get a lot of non-technical jobs. You just came through Shoshone, where you no doubt saw two or three Indian owned casinos. They might be able to use a dancer or cocktail girl. Nothing like that is in Worland. Do you have any other talents, of sorts? Perhaps you could get a job dancing with the local five piece country and western band in Worland, but all the members also have other jobs."

"Is there a whore house in the area, Colonel? You soldiers are always horny?"

Bradley choked on that one. "Are you a prostitute Miss? Surely you don't make your living on your back?"

"A girl has to eat, Colonel. I make my living any way I can, on my back, on my tummy, or standing up. One thing though, I am delicious but I am not cheap. What about you? Are you married?"

"Sort of in between, Miss; I guess a divorce will be in the works very shortly."

"Hmm, any local girlfriends?"

"Not yet. I guess there is always hope.

This is Thermopolis. I'll drop you off at Freddy's garage. Fred has a towing service and is a pretty good mechanic so you can get your car repaired." Bradley eased his truck into the service station lot and stopped. Paula opened the door, climbed out, wiggling her butt at Bradley in the process. She turned around and looked at him, "Well, I am beautiful, intelligent, and if well kept, am supremely loyal. Look me up when you feel the urge, Colonel. I'll make it worth your while. Thanks again for the rescue and the ride." She slammed his truck door. Bradley watched her walk into Fred's garage, she knowing he was watching and he knowing that she knew he was watching. Bradley grinned, almost out loud.

She walked into the first bay where Fred standing under a car on the lift and was screwing the drain plug back into the engine oil crankcase. He lowered the lift and asked Paula Jean "What can I do for you, Miss?"

"I broke down on the road about fifteen miles back. I need a tow in and a good mechanic who is not too expensive to retrieve and repair my car; unless of course, some mechanic can get it started there so I can drive it in."

Fred turned to the man behind the counter in the office part of the garage, "Hey Tom, take the rollback and see if you can get this lady's car started. If you can't start it, haul it in."

Ninety minutes later Tom pulled into his garage with Paula Jean Darnell's car on his roll back. Just behind him came a caravan of two pickup trucks, an old station wagon and an old Ford sedan. Each was crowded with people, mostly children from a small baby to several teenagers. The pickups had toppers on them and there were four or five people in the bed in each of them. They were all Mexicans. They vehicles pulled up to the gas pumps and began pumping gas, filling each in turn. Fred warily watched them as he unloaded Paula's car in front of a garage bay door. When the Mexicans had filled all the gas tanks, they got out four five gallon gas cans and filled them. Fred checked the meters behind the counter and punched them into the adding machine. The bill for the two regular gas pumps totaled $364.55. A teenage boy approached Fred after looking at the price of gas on the two pumps. A man came in behind the boy. Fred didn't say anything, but slid open the door under the counter and he put his hand the butt of the revolver hidden on the first shelf. The boy simply said, "How much?"

Fred tore the tape off the adding machine with his left hand and simply said "$364.55." The boy turned to the man and told him in Spanish. The man grimaced, pulled out a trucker's wallet, carefully counted out the exact amount of money, which he handed to Fred.

"Where are you headed," Fred asked the boy.

"We are going to stay with relatives who live outside of Worland," he replied. The man spoke in Spanish which the boy answered in Spanish. Fred surmised it was a reprimand of some nature. Fred didn't say anything but just nodded. The man and boy went to the rest room, which everyone else in the convoy had already done. As soon as all of the Mexicans climbed back into their vehicles, Fred picked up the phone and called the Washakie county Sheriff's office.

"There's a convoy of Mexicans in two pickup trucks, a station wagon and Ford sedan down here in Thermopolis, headed your way. They have Arizona license plates on two of the vehicles and Mexican plates on the two pickups. They said they were going to stay with relatives outside Worland. You might want to check them out. Colonel Bradley went through here about two hours ago, so he should be in the neighborhood up there by now."

Ethan's cell phone rang. It was Sheriff Brady. "Colonel, Fred Townsend just called me from Thermopolis. There's a caravan of Mexicans coming up Highway 20 to stay here in Washakie County. I'm setting up a roadblock south of town. You want to come and observe or participate?"

"Thanks, Sheriff. I'll head out now. Where are you going to set up the roadblock?"

Between Kirby and Worland, where it's the narrowest between the river and the hills."

Two of the Sheriff's deputies had parked their cars diagonally across the road, stopping all traffic. One deputy stayed in his car in the southbound lane so he could back it out to allow southbound traffic to proceed. Bradley followed the Sheriff down the highway to the roadblock. In less than ten minutes, the Mexican convoy approached the roadblock and then slowed to a stop. The deputies, each with a pump shotgun, approached the lead vehicle, the sedan, from each side. They just stood there until the Sheriff and Bradley walked over to its driver.

"Where are you headed?" asked the Sheriff in English. While he understood and spoke Spanish, he didn't want them to realize it.

"We have relatives who live outside Worland. We are going to stay with them," said the boy driver in English.

"And who are they and where do they live?" asked Sheriff Brady.

The Mexican turned to the woman next to him and asked her in Spanish. She responded, and the driver replied, "Guterriz, Manuel, he is my brother-in-law. He works in the fields, in the farms and ranches around here. We will stay with him."

"Just how many are there of you in these four vehicles, and do you all plan to stay with the Guterriz family?"

"Oh, Si, we will all stay and get jobs here."

Sheriff Brady asked for some identification, to include a driver's license with morphometric data; thumbprints, picture, or retinal scan in digital language. The driver had none.

Sheriff Brady walked to the next car. It was driven by a young man, around twenty years of age, Brady guessed. He asked him for some identification. The young man produced a driver's license issued in Nogales, Arizona. Brady looked into the station wagon. There was one other adult in the front seat, and three kids in each of the rear seats, a total eight people. The children appeared to range in age from about three to perhaps twelve

"Do any of you speak English?" asked Sheriff Brady.

:Yes, I do, my aunt here understands a little, and the children in back understand some. The two boys in back speak a little; they learned in school. Many people in Mexico now learn English."

Brady moved to the other two vehicles and asked the same thing. All said they intended to stay with their relatives, the Guterizzes. One driver of the pickup trucks had a Mexican driver's license; the other driver had no license.

Sheriff Brady had one deputy move his patrol cruiser back so the rest of the traffic could bypass the Mexicans. Brady turned to Bradley. "Well, Colonel, what do you suggest we do with them?"

"I'm afraid they are just the beginning. Can you verify who it is they are staying with? The county, the Basin can't absorb these people. We're going to have to make some hard decisions. There is no work for them; no way can we provide health care or anything else for them. They probably haven't been vaccinated for the flu; they pose a potential hazard in every way. We need to make some hard decisions at that meeting in two days. The entire Basin needs to come together for a uniform policy. Potentially, there could be several thousand or thousands more of these people attempting to come in. I don't want to tell you your business Sheriff, but I would probably escort them to the courthouse and fingerprint and photograph them and confirm they are who they say they are. If this relative Guterriz of theirs does exist, hold him accountable for them until a policy decision is made on how to handle them. Ultimately, extreme measures might be required."

"How extreme, Colonel?"

"Bluntly, run them out of the Basin at gun point, or, if they resist, kill them, all of them. It is something we better be prepared to do or this will turn into a mini-Los Angeles."

Ethan pulled into the parking lot of Neville's machine shop and garage. It was considerably larger in the days of maximum extraction of oil in the Basin. Nevertheless, Jim Neville ran the best garage in the Basin and did the lion's share of automotive repair business in the county. He still had a very large machine shop capability. Now in his late sixties, Jim was still an active outdoorsman and occasionally worked on vehicles himself as well as running his business. He was a self made man.

"Hi Jim, how are things going here?"

"Well, Colonel, times are a lot slower than they were, but we're still putting bread on the table. What brings the illustrious military genius to our humble establishment?"

Ethan grinned. He enjoyed the ribbing Jim always gave him. Ethan had known Jim since he was a small kid and Jim helped him rebuild an old wreck of a pickup truck when Ethan was in high school. Ethan always held the man in high regard and a little bit of awe because of Jim's mechanical genius.

""Well, I want to enlist your establishment in the fight, if it comes. You believe in the freedom of the individual and abhor the welfare police state as much as I do. I also know the feds, the Bureau of Alcohol, Tobacco, Firearms and Explosives, have been on your butt, suspecting you of making illegal weapons but have never been able to pin you down. I need a major repair and service depot for what vehicles and weapons I have and hopefully will receive in the future. My maintenance company in Basin is oriented towards military vehicles and heavy weapons. You're the best mechanic in the Basin and have a superb machine shop. I need a repair depot for mostly small arms. I'll get the local gunsmith to come under your wing and work with you. What I need in trucks I will have to commandeer from the civilian pickup truck fleet; not legal, but necessary. I'm afraid my tactical fleet will consist primarily of confiscated civilian pickups and farm trucks. I'll need your support for them. My mission is to train and conduct guerilla warfare. The Prairie and Laramie Brigades will really get the Strykers and other vehicles."

"You think it will go hot, a real shooting war, a civil war, Colonel?"

"I'm afraid it is far more likely than a political solution that avoids armed conflict. Nobody really knows how it will pan out. Anarchy has already started in some of our cities. I have to prepare for all contingencies. Can I count on you?"

"You damned well know it, boy. I got rid of everybody around here I couldn't trust. Your dad and I go back a long, long way. I would do more if I could, but my back won't let me."

"Jim, you become our small arms repair depot and civilian truck repair depot you will have done more than your share. By the way, who is a wood work shop person that I can trust? I need some carpenter things done in preparation for defense."

"Yeah, Ralph's Woodworking, Cabinetry and Joinery over on Fourth Street. Just speak privately with Ralph. I am not sure about some of his help."

Ethan proceeded to Ralph's shop where he asked to speak with Ralph. Ethan didn't know Ralph, but he knew Jim wouldn't recommend him unless he could be trusted.

"Mr. Ralph Ebersoll, I would like a few words with you privately. I was just over at Jim Neville's and he recommended you."

"Come on in, Colonel. Can I offer you a cup of mud?" said Ralph, as he poured himself a cup of coffee.

"You wouldn't want to pass on one of those gals that the whole town is talking about would you? That oriental gal sure is a looker. Anyway, what can I do for you?" "Sure, the coffee sounds good. Cream if you have it. Regarding the girls, one is mine, the waitress, and you can't have her. The other is available for hire, if you have the money."

"Ouch, I heard some rumors to that effect. Unfortunately, pros have always scared me, and Mama would put the shotgun to me. Anyway, I don't think this is a personal visit. So, enlighten me."

"First, I need some frank answers. I need to know where you stand if our political situation goes hot. If the federal government sends troops in here, are you willing to fight?"

"Yes, but I am a little old for the physical bit. Can't run up and down the hills very well like you younger guys can. You must be desperate to be recruiting old farts like me and Jim Neville."

Ethan grinned. "You guys aren't old farts, and your contributions require your labor and money, but not your physical exertion. Can you trust all of your employees? Do they all feel the way you and I do? Can they keep their mouths shut about what I am about to ask?"

"Well, if they can't, they won't work here any more and if it is bad enough, they won't say anything to anybody any more ever again. Now, what do you need done?"

Ethan pulled several sheets of paper from a folder. "Here are the dimensions of a Stryker vehicle. What I am asking is for you to make several dozen cutouts of them in half inch plywood. They must be true to form, very quickly and easily assembled at the site, painted, and stored dismantled out of sight until called for."

Ralph studied the diagrams for a few minutes. "Me and the boys can do this, but you're talking about a couple of thousand dollars in plywood to do these right."

"If money is the problem, all I can say is buy the plywood, build them, and send the bill to the Adjutant General's office. I have no idea whether or not you will be reimbursed. I wouldn't count on it. If you are not reimbursed, call it your contribution to the cause if you like. One other detail that is not on there, and it is also an expensive one. These cutouts must produce a heat signature. I have discovered that a stovepipe from a kerosene heater projecting a foot or two above the rear of the cutout over what is the engine compartment in the real one will produce something of a similar infra-red signature. Can you do that?"

"Building them will be no problem, but if you want two dozen of these, with the kerosene heaters, that might be a problem getting the heaters. Summer is almost here and nobody is stocking them right now. I'll see what I can do. How soon will you need them?"

"I can't say when they will be deployed, but the sooner they are built and stored out of sight, the happier I will be. The troops will need to assemble them in a matter of minutes, perhaps in the dark. The simplest way you can fit the individual pieces together, preferably without tools, maybe hinges and hooks, the better it will be. Obviously, you recognize them as decoys. They could save the lives of some of out troops."

Ralph Ebersoll looked at Ethan and said, "Consider it done, Colonel."

"Come in General, come in. General McIntire, I believe you know Senator Rockland," said Governor Bridger.

"Yes Sir, we have met. How do you do Senator? Glad to be out of Washington, D.C. and easy reach of Newkirk?"

"You can bet on that, General. I never trusted that man from day one. He is a very charismatic, extremely handsome lowlife. He is run entirely by Kennely, but I guess everyone knows that. Anyway, how are our National Guard units progressing, General McIntire?"

"Well, better than I expected, but not as well as I hoped. We are desperately short of equipment, most units are half trained, and I don't see things improving much, even with summer just around the corner. Our people can't quit their jobs and be a full time Army, at least not without a massive influx of money. It amounts to us being like the Revolutionary War Minutemen. If Newkirk attacks with heavy forces or a combined arms operational maneuver force, we will be in a world of hurt. The best things in our favor are the influenza epidemic that tends to discourage large bodies forming, and the race riots all over. California wanting to break in half certainly has helped a great deal. I must admit though, I agree with the fed's priorities of guarding strategic assets and maintaining open corridors so people can flee as in literal mass migrations. Bradley is doing about as well as he can and as well as expected with his Basin Brigade. The two brigades on the east side of the Big Horns aren't really ready for heavy combat. Our strategy will be to stall and retreat into the Basin, keeping open our corridor with Montana. We will be otherwise shut off from the west, south and east."

"Well, if you haven't had the word, the Chinese are up to something again. The word hasn't leaked to the media yet, but it could at any hour. The Europeans or Japanese will probably scoop it. Chinese battalions are massing along their held territories in the former Central Asian Republics. It appears they are about to make the jump from what was the Central Asian Republics into the Middle East. Newkirk will have his hands full with that. Europe wanted us to be the world's policeman but under their control, or at least controlled by the United Nations. The European Union's Quick Reaction Force (QRF) has been hollow for years, with each nation pledging part of its own military force to a structure that never rehearsed, drilled, exercised or even had a staff much above what amounts to the Corps level. Their Quick Reaction Force really got the crap kicked out of them by guerilla forces from all sides in the Balkans. Croats, Montenegrins, Serbs, Albanians, Kosovovars, they all turned on the European Quick Reaction Force. It was almost like World War II again.

They didn't learn from our experiences in Iraq. The Europeans as individual countries are still smarting over that and are reluctant to put more of their forces into the EU's quagmire. Their 60,000 troops in the QRF isn't much over a 5,000 mile front if they have to face the Chinese. They don't have the aerial or even the ground hardware to resist the Chinese seizing all of the Middle East's oil fields. The Chinese are actually ahead of the European nations in the fielding of state of the art military technology. Their concept of a United States of Europe is going to bite them in the ass, because they all thought they could contribute a minor piece of their military establishment to a larger European force that could handle anything that arises and thus get by on the cheap. They have believed that their 'soft power', that is, their economic clout and moral attitude was superior to "hard power", or military force. Now, there is no way we are going to be able to contribute anything to the EU or to NATO or any other endeavor. We will probably sink to a second rate nation, maybe even a third tier. Winston Churchill, way back in 1946 said that 'if the states as distant and diverse as Texas and Massachusetts, Alabama and Oregon can share a sense of citizenship within their national framework, then surely the Europeans could form their own.' Old Winston would roll over in his grave if he could see the breakup of the United States. We are losing our common ground, our sense of unity of one nation. The dichotomy is severe, the question is whether or not we can or will regain our sense of one nationhood. It seems most unlikely to me. Old Winston just might consider it a harbinger of what will happen to his beloved concept of a United States of Europe."

"Please go on, Senator. We would like to hear your take on how this will play out and how it will affect us, especially as the Republic of the Missouri," said Governor Bridger.

"The European Union didn't learn its lesson when we pulled out of the Balkans and handed it over to them for peace keeping. I reckon we learned from that experience, and some from Iraq, that the American flavor of democracy just wasn't exportable to very many other places in the world. Europe, in the form of the European Union, worked against us even then. After China expanded in to Southeast and Central Asia, Europe still made it deliberate policy to wage economic competition against us. I will not say war, we while continued to protect their sources of oil, energy and raw materials and sea lanes of communication open for them. They think they can jaw jack the Chinese into behaving and being nice neighbors. I guess they just played us for the fool that we were. The Chinese might just change that for them if they take off a big chunk of Eastern Europe. The rest of Europe can't stop them. Of course, it might unite them, but they would have to use weapons of mass destruction, nuclear fires, to stop the Chinese, and I don't see them doing that on their own territory. Who knows, maybe the Chinese are behind this pandemic of influenza anyway. That's the way I see it, General. They could march right in to a depopulated Middle East and Europe and who's to stop them? Right now, the riots in Europe are as bad as they are here in the U.S. The Muslims are demanding that the Europeans defend Iran, defend Islam against the invading Chinese. The news broadcasts aren't really conveying the depth of it. Riots are especially bad in France and Spain, but Germany also has significant problems. The French and Spanish white folks don't have any means of self protection, but somehow the Muslims there all seem to have guns. They are giving the average Frenchman absolute hell, demanding they recognize the Sharia, the body of Islamic law, in declaring Jihad against the Chinese. The Frogs are getting what they deserve. Lots of districts in a variety of French cities have burned to the ground. Germany, on the other hand, somehow seems to have provided some small arms to its citizens and the Muslims are up against it. Turkey as you know went clerical in their last elections and is now demanding Jihad as well.

Anyway, now, we are an economic eggshell. Our cutbacks in the military expenditures to preserve our social welfare fabric over the last eight years have left us with a quite hollow military as well. Our withdrawal from Eastern Europe, the Balkans, Poland, Hungary and Romania left us with no capability for immediate response. We certainly lack sealift and airlift. Besides, Iran is a very rugged, mountainous country. The Chinese will have a hard time of it with Iran. This time, Governor, there is just no way we can help stop the Chinese if they cross into Europe. Consider it like the Mongol Hordes of yonder year. Europe will have to sink or swim on its own. All we can do is to continue to buy foreign oil from wherever we can at whatever price we have to pay as the Alaskan fields played out and the Permian Basin fields dry up as a result of fracking. When the Alaskan oilfields played out, the pressure from the environmentalists made us take out the pipelines to the sea by which we sold oil to the Chinese as well as the pipelines themselves. Guess where they will re-assemble them! Removing those pipelines was financially just about a break even proposition. The Middle East peoples are now going to have to pay for their sins. Let's see if Allah will protect them against Chinese aggressions. We have our own troubles. Right now, our racial problems are causing us a world of hurt.

The Black Americans in our southern cities, Atlanta, Birmingham, Tallahassee, Charleston, Houston, are now rioting over influenza vaccine. It seems the Reverend Samuel Mordecai Jones through his evangelical television network and through his network of churches and gangs has spread the word that all the white folks got the good vaccine while black folks got bad vaccine or no vaccine at all. Whitey had first call on it, and then and only then were the black communities vaccinated. He claims the vaccine was diluted when it was administered to black folks, so there would be more vaccine for white people. That would result in black folks having a greater chance of contracting the disease and wouldn't have as good a chance of survival. That has caused riots that Newkirk had blacked out on our national news media. He threatened to have any journalist who reported it shot and their television offices burned. Of course, it is all locally known. No doubt some of the Europeans will be reporting that very shortly as well. Newkirk can't stop them. Some parts of the D.C. area really had serious riots. Marines had to be posted at the vaccination centers in D.C. and Baltimore. Black families have started moving south in large numbers. Chicago, Pittsburgh, Philadelphia, Cleveland, even New York are losing a lot of their black folks. Philadelphia, now there is a city in trouble. So is Baltimore, although not as bad, at least not yet."

I take it you don't think there's much of a chance that the United States will come out of the referendum relatively unscathed, Senator that we will remain as one nation, perhaps as autonomous units with an overarching central government?"

"Governor, the folks from Nebraska, Kansas, and at least the upper half of Missouri, are thinking of joining the Republic of Missouri if it forms. I'm talking about the state of Missouri on the north of the Missouri River. The Senators from those states have discretely approached me about it. The city of St. Louis will most likely stay with the southern part of the state if it splits apart, as it is primarily populated by black citizens. The dividing line there will be somewhat hazardous, as the St. Louis suburbs, especially those to the north and west, are pretty well off and that just deteriorated into a battle zone. I can't say where the line will be drawn, as I don't know who and where and how many are willing to fight against those odds in that area. I can't say much about Kansas City. K.C. Missouri could go either way, but K.C. Kansas will go with us. Iowa is an unknown. They could be a wedge in the center. I don't think Minnesota will join us. Those folks are really of a 'blue state' mentality, they love the European Union model of social welfare. So many of them are of Scandinavian descent anyway, or at least the initial European settlers were, that it has carried over.

Lots of people are in a real quandary, particularly in those areas that will be border line between the disaffected. People don't know which way to jump. Most folks don't want anything to do with violence, but they don't want to lose their homes and property, and especially their lives. It is the areas where the racial and cultural lines are being drawn that are the most dangerous. You have probably been following the television news, watching the Mexicans and Mexican Americans flow north. That's not good, and where the violence is and will be the worst, that is, those areas where the populations are relatively mixed, where no one ethnic group dominates to control the polity. I pity those Mexican Americans and upper middle class black Americans who really are caught in the middle."

"Senator, what if the Iranians blow their oil wells the way Saddam Hussein did in Kuwait way back in 1991? How will the Chinese handle that? What an environmental disaster. The atmosphere still has dust in it from the nuclear fires of the last Chinese expansion, the Korean peninsula, and the India-Pakistan war. What if the Iranians decide to use their limited nuclear arsenal on the invading Chinese, if they do in fact invade? What would happen then? Do the Chinese have the expertise to put them out? What another global disaster that would bring. How much of the polar ice caps would melt and flood coastal cities around the world? China has over 200 cities with over a million people in each along their coastline. That will hurt the Chinese as much as anyone else."

"General, those are almighty good questions. If the Chinese retaliate with nuclear fires, what will that do to the oil fields, the possession of which is undoubtedly their objective? Nobody knows how this will play out. At least the previous Democratic administration had sense enough to fund massive research in wind power, ocean wave energy and solar farms in our deserts in spite of the environmentalists' protests. That research has paid off handsomely in reducing our need to burn oil and coal to generate electricity. We still need carbon based and fossil fuels for vehicles though. All we can do is speculate and plan for the worst. I sure wish somebody would genetically engineer a bacterium that would take carbon dioxide out of the air and make gasoline from it. One thing is for sure; I am glad to be back home here in Wyoming and will probably head for the Basin myself rather than stay here in Cheyenne. Cheyenne is just too close to Colorado. Those people down there in Colorado have the same mentality as Newkirk, a bunch of oligarchic elitists.

Governor, I strongly suggest you make all preparations for both civil and international war. Tough times are ahead, and I don't see any way around them. We need to think in strategic terms for the long run. Anything and everything that might possibly help our people would be most beneficial. If the Chinese cross the line into eastern Europe, wherever that line is, the Europeans will probably go nuclear. The closest thing I can relate it to is that it will be like the Revolutionary War again rolled into World War III."

Governor Bridger thought for a moment. "You're right, Senator. The first thing I will do is order all crops to remain within the state or at least within the Territory of the Missouri. All of our corn and sugar beet crops will go either for human food, animal fodder or for our biodiesel and ethanol plants here in Wyoming. I'll put the word out that no crops are to leave the state without approval of the State Secretary of Agriculture, which means no crops! I'll call Governor Johnston and suggest that he have the other states do the same. We can't afford to let the Dakotas and Nebraska supply fuel to the son of a bitch Newkirk. I'll also order our Treasurer to start buying gold on the open market and suggest to Governor Johnston he make the suggestion to the other states. Paper currency, ours or theirs, won't be worth anything like gold will. We'll start buying it in small but steady quantities. I'll order our Treasurer to do it through various dealers and banks so it won't appear to be a run on the gold market from one source. If they advise it, I'll send agents to the larger cities on both coasts to buy gold coins from all the dealers they can find. We'll send them with cash and body guards. I'll have our agents start with Columbia and Minneapolis and buy from local dealers as a trial run. Also, I'll order that no more federal taxes be withheld from anybody's paycheck. No funds are to leave this state for the federal government."

A similar situation was developing in Austin, Texas.

"Colonel Carlson, the Governor is on the phone for you."

"Thanks, Mary, tell Dick to step in and put it on the speaker."

Colonel Matthew Carlson, Texas Department of Public Safety, Texas Rangers, Headquarters, punched on the speaker. Carlson worked his way up through the ranks, starting as a DPS state trooper, making sergeant after five years. He attended night school for five years and earned a Master's Degree in criminology. He made lieutenant after another three years, and then transferred to the Texas Rangers. After four years in anti-narcotics, he was promoted to captain of that division. He discovered and brought to trial several senior DPS officers of Mexican heritage who were found to be involved in smuggling drugs and illegal aliens into the United States. Two years later he stumbled into a well developed ring of Muslims using mosques as drug smuggling and distribution centers bringing in Middle Eastern heroin to finance terrorism in the United States. They were in part responsible for the assassinations of prominent Jewish American citizens. In frustration, the Governor of Texas appointed him as head of the Texas Rangers at the ripe old age of forty-three. Lieutenant Richard Barston was his second in command.

"Good morning Governor, I hope you have some good news for me."

"Matt, I wish to God there was some good news somewhere. The Secretary of Defense called the Secretary of Homeland Security who called me. Now I am calling you.

First, satellite reconnaissance has picked up a company sized unit of U.S. soldier deserters out of Fort Bliss. I'm sending you the satellite photos via video on your computer as we speak. They have two dozen or so vehicles, HUMVEEs, light armored personnel carriers, a dozen trucks for logistical support and two M1A3 tanks. It appears they are about 150 to 250 personnel strong. A real company sized operation. They are poised just across the border. It looks like they are planning a raid into the U.S. I am afraid it will be a lot more sophisticated and dangerous than the one you helped break up fifteen years or so ago. I asked for military assistance, but there won't be any. The National Guard is in shambles. The Hispanic guardsmen have mostly split. There is no intact National Guard unit of any suitable size any more. Most of the essentially Anglo guard units are busy protecting their home towns. Hopefully those in the southern part of the state will recognize the futility of that and organize evacuation of their communities. After evacuating Fort Bliss, it looks like the SECDEF is planning to evacuate Fort Hood and other military installations to the north of the Red River. She has issued their commanders secret orders. I think the strategy will try to hold the line either in north Texas or in Oklahoma. I honestly don't know what to tell you about this potential raiding party. We don't know their target, although they could move from objective to objective and we can't provide you with any resources to stop them. Our best guess of their axis of advance will be Odessa, Midland, and up to Lubbock. It is up to you to either try to evacuate those who haven't already fled or try to stop these deserters on your own. It's your call.

Tangentially, I have just given orders to the major universities, hospitals and other state institutions, along with strong advice to private enterprises, south of Dallas to immediately plan for evacuation of as much of their libraries, computers, laboratories, staff and instruments as possible. How the hospitals handle their patient load is up to them. I have ordered the universities to head for Kansas State

University in Manhattan, as that appears to be relatively safe territory. I've cleared it with the President at KSU. The University of Kansas is too close to Kansas City. KSU is just down the road from Fort Riley, so they have close military support. Indicators are that Kansas City is definitely having some serious racial problems. They will probably have to leave a great deal behind, but hopefully they can get it together to get the major resources and people out. The student bodies will be asked to volunteer to help as much as possible before they head for home or points north. I am afraid that once evacuation starts it will snowball into a disaster. Mexicans can easily push out of San Antonio into Austin which must appear as a very rich prize to them. Let me know what you decide after you think through it.

On another subject, for your information, I have ordered the immediate execution of all inmates on death row at the state penitentiary in Huntsville. I have also ordered the release of those incarcerated who are serving time for nonviolent offenses. I haven't decided what to do with the in-between group, those convicted of serious, violent crimes. Two thirds of them are Hispanics. I don't want to turn such men loose during a civil crisis that might erupt into full scale civil war, although that is most likely. I am open to suggestions on that one."

"Yes Sir, I certainly will give it immediate, highest priority. I don't have a lot of hope either. I fear our great state of Texas is about to meet its demise as we know it. At least Santa Anna's army had some semblance of discipline when they invaded in 1836. I'll call as soon as I can develop something; and I agree with you on your decision regarding the inmates at Huntsville."

Colonel Carlson thought for a moment and called in his deputy and secretary. "Maggie, issue a blast fax to all units. All weapons and equipment are to be immediately removed from all arms rooms of the Ranger companies and issued to all

Texas Rangers. Send a copy to each Ranger in each county sheriff's office to draw as much as he can from their respective arms rooms. I don't want a single round of ammunition, vest, helmet, or anything else left in there. Everything is to be issued, even if you have to give some Rangers multiples of an item, weapon, or ammo allotment. If the Rangers want to, they can give extra items to the local state trooper. Dick, we have a problem on how to stop an outlaw armored company from raiding north from Mexico. Let's start thinking."

CHAPTER 14

INSIDE CHINA, SENIOR OFFICERS, VIROLOGISTS AND POLITICIANS WERE WONDERING HOW THE UNITED STATES AND ISRAEL HAD ACQUIRED SO MUCH VACCINE THAT MATCHED THE VIRUS SO WELL SO QUICKLY. Virologists at Urumqi convinced the politicians that there was or is, a traitor in their midst. The vaccine could not have been produced so quickly without first researching and categorizing the agent. Only after identification of adequate epitopes, that is, parts of the virus surface that induce immune reactions, could a vaccine be formulated. Even then, the tissue culture requirements would have taken months to years for identification and maximum production. The odds of coincidence of Americans and Israelis pursuing and developing a vaccine with such effectiveness are so low as to be ridiculous, somewhere in the odds of one to millions. As the briefing came to a close, General Chang was absolutely seething.

"Who, how, or what happened that allowed the Americans and the Israelis to have such an effective vaccine so quickly? I want a review of everything, everyone, every possible contact that might have allowed the Americans to acquire the virus or our vaccine. I want answers and I want them quickly. All tapes of all visitors are to be simultaneously reviewed by an officer of the military security force and a laboratorian. Leave no possibility uninvestigated. Apparently it takes several years to research, develop and manufacture a vaccine in such quantities. Therefore, start ten years back and work forward in your investigations. I will have a hundred intelligence officers here in the morning to begin their investigations. Your staff will assign a laboratory technician or scientist to each of my officers to work as a team. They are to spare no one in their investigations, not even you, Dr. Li, as General Director of this facility."

Dr. Li, greatly fearing for his life and that of all of his relatives, bowed low, and stated "It shall be as you say, General. No one will be exempt under any circumstance." It was all he could do to control the tremor in his voice and the subtle quivering he was experiencing.

A classified fax from the U.S. Embassy in Peking was received at the Office of the Director of National Intelligence. A flurry of personnel activity was noted at the biological research laboratory in Urumqi, Sinkiang. The nature or cause of the activity is unknown, but over one hundred personnel investigating officers have been dispatched to the laboratory from the Chinese Secret Service in the last twenty-four hours.

There weren't many visitors to the highly classified laboratories at Urumqi. All communications with the laboratories in the United States were reviewed. The digitally recorded and preserved faxes, telephone communications, notes and visits to and from the United States were scrutinized.

CIA Officer Gilbert phoned ahead for an appointment. He was a little tired from his transcontinental flight, but he had managed to doze a little. The front desk at Genetics Engineering, LLC, in Seattle had been told by Homeland Security to expect a visitor of some importance from Washington, D.C. without being told whom or what agency he represented. Since he was to conduct an interview with the Chief Operating Officer of the Seattle Branch, the receptionist understood that he was important; probably somebody from the Food and Drug Administration or the U.S. Department of Agriculture. Since the company manufactured vaccines for both livestock and humans, he could represent either agency. He was directed to the appropriate elevator which he rode to the sixth floor. There he emerged to take a second elevator that ran only between the sixth and ninth floors. The top three remaining floors had the offices of the directors of the individual research and management divisions and directors of each of the special projects. In his secure telephone call, Robert Gilbert made it expressly clear that he wished to speak with the COO and the director of the "experimental" vaccine project 686. The fact that experimental vaccine 686 didn't exist was wholly irrelevant. No questions over the phone, please.

Robert Gilbert stepped into the office of Director Mark Tomlinson. He introduced himself to the Secretary as Mr. Gilbert of the FDA, presenting his credentials as an investigative officer of that organization. At that moment, George Hoskins entered the office. Without hesitation, Gilbert pivoted to greet Dr. Hoskins.

"How do you do Doctor. I'm Rob Gilbert of the FDA. I recognize you from your picture Doctor Hoskins. I am so delighted to meet you."

Gilbert stepped forward offering his hand and a large smile. Hoskins, somewhat taken aback for a second, recognized Officer Gilbert. He took the hand offered, and replied, "I'm very glad to meet you, Mr. Gilbert. I heard you might be coming. When the boss called me, I figured something was up."

At that moment, the intercom buzzed, and the secretary showed both of them into the inner office of Dr. Tomlinson. Dr. Mark Tomlinson stepped around his desk and greeted the men,

"Welcome, Mr. Gilbert, George. Please have a seat. Can I get you some coffee? I know how you like it George. What can we do for the FDA today Officer Gilbert?" as he buzzed his secretary for three coffees.

"Dr. Tomlinson, we have a request, rather unusual perhaps, but we wish a favor from you."

"Hmm," thought George Hoskins. "He isn't going to reveal who he really is. This is going to be interesting."

"It has come to our attention that a scientist of your company at the Urumqi laboratory in China has some interesting information. Dr. Hoskins has made the acquaintance of Dr. Chu, Soo Li. We want you to invite Dr. Chu to the United States to confer with Doctor Hoskins on a particular strain of avian visceral velogenic Newcastle Disease. I understand that Dr. Hoskins is now working on a new vaccine for that disease. You will of course be refunded for all expenses, but that is an inconsequential thing. As a matter of fact, we want you to invite not only Dr. Chu, but his entire family as a vacation at company expense, perhaps as a reward or a winner of a contest or something. Realizing the nature of your company, being Chinese owned, this might be difficult for you. Please consider some rational excuse within your research program here to bring Dr. Chu and his family to the U.S."

"Mr. Gilbert, I am immediately struck that an FDA investigator is interested in a vaccine for chickens and other avian species. That is the realm of the USDA. What is this really all about?"

Robert Gilbert grinned, mostly to himself. "Very astute, Dr. Tomlinson. All is not as it appears. Time is of the essence. We are talking hours here, not days. I am obviously not from the FDA. I didn't take the time to have the appropriate credentials developed through the USDA bureaucracy whereas I already had them for the FDA. It is an urgent situation to get the man and his family out of China as quickly as possible with the least amount of suspicion. Their lives are in immediate danger and they have been of great service to this country. You can be of assistance in this matter by lending your weight to the invitation. There is not a day to lose. I will leave the scientific details of the cover story to you and Dr. Hoskins. My agency, which shall remain unnamed, and I only ask that you be very, very quick about it. Getting the invitation out tomorrow, or even tonight will not be soon enough. Needless to say, there is considerable secrecy around this, and I cannot tell you any reasons about it. If it becomes necessary, you will be briefed after Dr. Chu reaches the United States. Dr. Hoskins has some inkling of what this is all about, but he is sworn to secrecy as well, so please do not ask him. I will check into a local hotel and will visit you tomorrow morning to determine your progress. I hope I don't interrupt your schedule too much. Thanks for the very good coffee."

"Your request for leave for a family vacation to Hong Kong is approved, Dr. Chu," said the Head of Security. "Your company is most generous, but then your contributions to China and to science have been enormous. How does your wife and children feel about such an all expense paid vacation?"

"She is absolutely delighted, Mr. Director of Security. She cannot wait until next week. The children are very excited as well."

"It does seem unusual that the company insisted on your children accompanying you. How will they make up their studies at the university?"

Dr. Chu shrugged and grinned. They are both exceptionally bright. They will take some text books along, but how much benefit that will be I cannot say."

"I understand that your company has made arrangements for the theater, the theme park, and several fine restaurants, a classic opera, and you will be staying at the Hong Kong Hilton Hotel."

Dr. Chu was very excited about this trip; he was also considerably ill at ease about it. Something was not quite right. He was unsure that he deserved it. Others had made significant contributions, and this was the first time the company had ever sponsored such a vacation for a Chinese national. It was most unusual that the company insisted on their son and daughter accompanying him and his wife.

When they opened the closets in their respective hotel rooms, they found clothing for each of them of the proper sizes for every occasion. In the late afternoon of the day, after attending the theme park, tickets for Dr. and Mrs. Chu to attend the opera the that night were on the table. Tickets for two to the hottest disco in Hong Kong for the son and daughter were in an envelope with their names on it. Even though they were tired, they knew better than to miss the opportunities. So, with a quick supper in the hotel restaurant, they assumed the appropriate attire and went their separate ways. Just prior to their arrival and unknown to them, arrangements were made for a special event in addition to their reservations at the Hong Kong Hilton. The gentleman sitting next to Dr. Chu at the opera introduced himself with a simple "Good evening, Dr. Chu. I hope you and your wife enjoy the opera; I am Mr. Lin, Xi Phe," just as the curtain opened.

Chu's anxiety increased ten fold. He did not know which security agency Mr. Lin represented, or if he was with the company. As the curtain descended for the intermission and the theater rang with applause, Mr. Lin simply said, "We must talk, Dr. Chu, in the men's room," and departed.

Dr. Chu accompanied his wife to the ladies room and then sought the men's room. Lin was waiting in a tactical spot near the men's room where he could observe anyone possibly following Dr. Chu. Chu glanced at Lin as he passed him, and

Lin appeared not to notice. Lin waited for a moment and then followed Chu in. At adjacent urinals Lin said "You will find tickets in your room tomorrow for a boat ride. It is imperative that you and your family be on the boat. Once aboard you will be contacted with further instructions. Do not mention any of this to anyone, especially to your family. It is critical that your entire family be on board. Identity cards are included that indicate your children are of age. Do not fail, Dr. Chu." Lin zipped his pants, washed his hands and departed independently of Chu. On the third evening of their vacation, an all night outing on a luxury junk that was a floating hotel, house of prostitution and gambling casino was made for the whole family. Lin did not return to his seat. Instead, another man who closely resembled Lin occupied the chair.

The junk was actually a floating pleasure palace. The finest cuisine, wines and liquors of the world, all games of chance, and the most beautiful and expensive prostitutes from all over the world were on board. Again, the appropriate attire was hung in the closets of their state rooms. On the table Dr. Chu found an envelope addressed for the eyes of only Dr. Chu. It contained 500,000 renminbi and a note. It read: Have the entire family at roulette table #3 at 24:30 hours. No absences. Chu pocketed the note without his wife seeing it, but he showed the money to his wife and said "A little bird has informed me as to how we are to spend this money. We are to be at a certain gambling table at a certain time tonight-all four of us. The children should see this."

"We will be there, my husband. The company is being too kind to us."

At 24:15 hours Dr. and Mrs. Chu gather their children from the dance floor, both of whom were slightly inebriated. They wanted to continue dancing, but Chu insisted they come with him. Chu, Win Ho, was having a particularly good time dancing with one of the beautiful prostitutes. He was negotiating a price with her while wondering how he could persuade his father to give him the large sum she was demanding. On the other hand, the girl was thoroughly enjoying the tit for tat barter with this bright young man who obviously was still dependent on dear old dad. "I have a surprise, you must come," he told them. The beautiful prostitute promised him that she would be waiting and watching for his return. Unwillingly but consenting, they followed their parents to the gambling salon. Chu looked at his watch. At 24:30 he put 5000 renminbi on red. He lost. He put 5000 renminbi on black. He won. He bet on black again and won. The children watched with little interest, wondering if this was the surprise. Chu bet on half a dozen numbers and lost. He put 5000 renminbi on #24 when a hand reached down and put chips on the same number. Chu looked up into the eyes of Mr. Lin across the table. They lost. After the "ooh" subsided, Lin nodded slight to his left and began to work his way around the table to Chu.

"We did not do so well on that last number my friend," he said in a rather hushed voice. Then quietly, he stated matter-of-factly "gather your family and quietly follow me."

Lin slowly wound his way through the crowd without looking back. Chu told his family "Come with me now and ask no questions." They all followed Chu who followed Lin who led them to the top deck, portside stern. He leaned against the rail. Chu walked up beside him. "Dr. Chu, in two minutes a boat will pull alongside right here." He flicked his cigarette lighter three time, then pulled a cigar from a breast pocket and lit it. He turned to face them all so that they could hear him, but he addressed Chu. "You and your family must get on that boat immediately without discussion, fanfare or hesitation. If you do not, all four of you will be dead tomorrow. We are getting you out of China." A man standing along the wall walked up to them and handed Lin a large duffel bag. Two minutes later an inflatable Zodiac riding low in the water appeared from nowhere. From the duffle bag Lin drew a rope ladder that he hooked to the rail. Then said, "Get down it now!," pushing the son to the rail. Don't stop, don't look up or down, just go." As soon as the boy was four steps down he guided the daughter over the rail next. People began to watch; a few giggled, thinking they were trying to escape gambling debts. Finally, Dr. Chu and Mrs. Chu started down. As soon as they were in the boat Lin unhooked the ladder and let it drop into the sea. As the Zodiac pulled away, he climbed over the rail and dived into the water much to the astonishment of the onlookers. He swam to the Zodiac where he was quickly pulled aboard. Ten kilometers into the open sea the Zodiac rendezvoused with an eighty foot yacht that pulled the Zodiac upon on deck and deflated it. It sped out to sea, its twin diesels pushing it at better than twenty knots an hour. Fifty miles out into the South China Sea the yacht rendezvoused with a U.S. Navy DDX destroyer that took the Chu family, the Zodiac and Lin aboard. The yacht took on 500 gallons of fuel and headed for the Philippine Islands.

St. Louis erupted into a vicious civil war the same as cities along the east coast and southeast. It was mostly gang against gang. Descendents of the Vietnamese refugees from the Vietnam War and Muslim Bosniaks who were allowed in as a result of the Balkan War of the 1990's clashed in the southern parts of the city, while Blacks in the northern and central parts of St. Louis were the primary protagonists. Not only were they fighting each other for the inner city, but they all began to raid the suburbs for food and loot. White families began to flee from the suburbs northward to Hannibal, Kirksville, and Marysville, Missouri, into Iowa, west towards Columbia and Kansas City. They stopped when they ran out of gas or food or both. Most were unprepared. Kansas City followed suit in a few days, with race riots erupting. At the same time Black Americans fleeing from Chicago headed south towards St. Louis, Louisville and Cincinnati. Any sojourner who failed to stop and fill the gas tank at every opportunity regretted it sooner or later.

At that moment, the former Reverend Alvin Hemmings, a former black Baptist minister, now head Muslim cleric for Houston, calling himself Mohammed bin Abram bin Selim, was declaring for the establishment of a black Islamic state in east Texas. With the tremendous growth of Islam in the Black American community, a number of mosques became established in the Houston greater metropolitan area. Selim's was the largest. Since the beginning of the new century, the Black Muslim population in the United States had grown from six million to over twenty million. Many of the converts, especially Black Americans, were former prison inmates. All around the rice and cotton fields of south Texas and Louisiana disenchanted Black American former agricultural workers flocked to Islam. Most were displaced by Mexicans willing to accept poorer conditions and lower wages and living on welfare. The message of paradise with its houris, the seventy virgins in heaven that go to each martyr, resonated particularly well. Selim preached against the Godless society of the world and of Houston in particular. Conversion to Islam or death was the only way to salvation, to redemption. From his mosque he coordinated with other mosques from Houston south to Corpus Christi and west to San Antonio. Hidden in boxes labeled prayer rugs and copies of the Koran in the basement of his mosque were five hundred AK-47 rifles, one thousand magazines for the rifles and five hundred thousand rounds of ammunition. With oil money supplied by royal Arabian princes loyal to Wahhabism twenty years earlier, two hundred thousand acres of land had been purchased between Yoakum and Edna, Texas. The land was actually a working cattle ranch offering adequate cover for its true purpose. Black Muslim cowboys patrolled the perimeter to maximize security. They carried rifles and shovels. Mexicans illegally entering the U.S. who attempted to cross the ranch found themselves buried under three feet of south Texas sand. A training camp was established there where teenage boys trained through the week and adults on weekends in what the

U.S. Army calls MOUT, military operations in urban terrain. The AK-47s with their select fire modes and moderate power cartridges are true assault rifles, ideal for the urban environment. Along with the AK-47s they were trained in rocket propelled grenades, booby traps, and small unit tactics such as ambushes and urban raids. The smaller mosques formed raiding parties in the outlying areas that began attacking ranches, farms and the smallest of the towns surrounding Houston. They were attempting to seize and hold by force what they intended to be a Black Nation of Islam. The mosques of Houston began to expel or kill all others who had not already fled the metropolitan area. Within the black community Muslims began to clash with followers of the Reverend Mordeciah Jones. The black Christian community was wholly unprepared for the alternative of convert to Islam, leave or die. Death squads of Muslims began to raid homes of known Christian blacks who refused to leave. Bodies were left in the streets as examples to neighbors to hasten their decision process. Those black Christians who wished to flee were not interfered with as they loaded their vehicles and drove east to find haven in the southeastern region.

In most cases of the isolated ranches and farms owned by Anglos, the owners were offered the opportunity to pack their vehicles and leave in peace. Some of them were raped and murdered as they attempted to do so. According to Mullah ibn Abram ibn Selim, Islam should not allow infidels to continue to exist, even on their borders. Not quite all Muslim brothers agreed with him.

"Deon, I want you to take your camera and telephoto lens and get some good pictures of the D'Arcy subdivision from the ground level. You took some aerial photographs of it last spring." The photographs revealed the subdivision was laid out as a four leaf clover. It was huge. Each leaf had six houses on it. Each property consisted of five to fifteen acres. A few had barns for horses and riding stable and arena. The entire area encompassed almost a square mile. The Nelson Bartlett family lived in one house on the easternmost clover leaf.

"Now I want you to get photos of the main gate, some of the houses if you can and especially of the guards. Change vehicles from day to day. Note the time the guard shifts change. Write down every car that comes and goes, the time and the license plate number, make and model. Especially get pictures of the guards."

"Colonel, are we going to hit some of these houses?" These are rich folks, but they ain't stupid. They got guards, and probably got guns and dogs and alarm systems and all kinds of things."

"Yes, Deon, you are undoubtedly right in some of those points. We can neutralize all of them. I will inform you of the details at the appropriate time. As for guns, some of them probably have guns for hunting; they are the elites, so they probably have some shotguns for duck hunting, and maybe some rifles for deer and big game hunting. You can bet however, that those guns are kept in a gun safe according to the law. That delays access to them. That is, if they have any guns at all. Remember us common folks can't legally own them. If they have any hand guns they will be in the bedrooms. You shouldn't let them get into the bedrooms. Most of these houses probably have a hidden safe room. Surprise is a major tactic. You should surprise everyone before they reach their bedroom or their safe room, which are probably one and the same. You have to take them before they can use a cell phone. Now, do as you are told and get those photographs."

Deon Johnson watched the main gate from the battered old car parked against the curb two blocks away. Every once in a while he would get out and stretch. He was too stupid to wonder if his movements would be noticed by the gate guards. He really didn't care anyway. The boss just told him to watch the gate and write down everything and everyone who came or left. How many guards were on duty at one time, and what they did in their little guard stand. For that the boss gave him a notebook, pen and small pair of binoculars. One of the brothers would drive up and replace him so that they have six hour shifts, with four observers to provide round the clock coverage. They used two different cars so that the local residents would get used to seeing the cars parked there all the time. After two weeks of recorded observations, Toussaint had a good idea of the routine traffic in and out of the gated community. After midnight on weekdays, only one guard was on duty until 06:00, at which time two guards replaced the one. On weekends two guards were on duty all night long. The guards usually carried their meals with them in coolers serving as lunch boxes which they placed in a small refrigerator. A small heating and cooling unit kept them comfortable according to the climate.

The details Deon Johnson snapped of the guards revealed the details of their uniforms. Three of the gang members took the photos to a men's tailor shop in downtown Baltimore just before closing. The tailor and his family were known to Toussaint. The tailor was a middle aged African-American who had done well. He apprenticed early in an upscale shop, quietly learning the skills of the craft. Well measured customers and quality cloth neatly cut and well sewn sold well to rising young men, ambitious brokers, bankers and lawyers and business men. After fifteen years of measuring customers, then doing the cutting and sewing in the back room, he made his move. At age thirty-five with a young family he opened his own shop a few blocks from the edge of the ghetto. He rented the bottom store front floor of a four story apartment building, put his family in the back rooms and started his own business. Business was good. Capable, young ambitious African-American men found the combination of the quality of cloth and workmanship and prices unbeatable. Since his shop was still outside the ghetto he also developed a clientele of white men. After fifteen more years of skimping he bought the building, refurbished it the three upper floor apartments, moved his family on to the second floor and hired two apprentices. One of his best clients was the leader of the gang that ruled one half of the Baltimore ghetto, Toussaint. Drugs, prostitution, muscle for hire and murder were the standard businesses of the gang. Attractive but poor young women in their late teens and early twenties of all races were observed then stalked until their habits were known. At the appropriate opportunity they were kidnapped. They were held as prisoners in an older building that had been refurbished into cells. They were addicted to cheap Chinese heroin, repeatedly raped, beaten and abused until they were completely submissive. It was enforced prostitution, they were white slaves whatever their race.

Jean Toussaint entered Franklin King's tailor shop just after his three gang members one cold February evening. Franklin King now had two daughters, sixteen and eighteen years of age, and a fourteen year old son. Franklin King looked at the photos handed to him by Toussaint.

"You will be well paid to make these uniforms. Tomorrow four more young men will come into your shop at various times. You are to make each of them a custom uniform according to these photographs. In addition, there will be no labels or identifying marks made on these uniforms. Merely identify the customers as A, B, C, and D or 1,2,3,4, if you like. You and you alone will make these uniforms after your shop is closed you will paid a substantial bonus for your efforts."

Franklin King looked at the photographs then into the eyes of Jean Toussaint. "This smacks of criminal activities. I want no part of it."

"My dear Franklin, you do have a choice, but it will cost you. Your daughters will disappear one day soon and not emerge from one of our brothels for years to come, if ever. Your son promises to be a fine athlete, making the varsity football team as a freshman. It would be a shame if one day he was found castrated. Then you would never enjoy any grandchildren. No one to carry on the family business or name, so to speak, but the choice is yours. Who knows, you might even experience a fire in your building late one night. It is rather old, isn't it. Certainly your family will suffer these severe consequences if you should mention this conversation or these uniforms to any one, especially police authorities."

Franklin King looked at Toussaint and said, "I will do as you ask. Tell your young men to wait until the shop is devoid of customers and then to come in well dressed, not in hip-hop or plain street clothes."

"Thank you Franklin, I knew we could count your cooperation. My men will appear as you request. Don't forget, you will be well rewarded."

Aerial pictures of D'Arcy Heights were thumb tacked to the bulletin board along with pictures of the gates, the guard house and the individual houses. Toussaint stood on the stage with a pointer. Pointing to the house of Nelson Bartlett in the picture, he spoke. "We will take every house there except this one. It is the center house in the third cul-de-sac, the eastern most one. That one is off limits. Anybody who does anything to that house or its occupants will answer to me. All the other houses will be hit. Each of you and your men will be assigned a specific house. Keep the killing to a minimum. Use only silenced weapons or a knife or a garrote. I don't want any major alarms going off. We will take each clover leaf simultaneously to prevent any widespread alarm. The back gate will be covered by one crew. It opens onto the country club which has its own gate and guards. Normally there is no one there, but we will have a team there just in case there is anyone returning from the country club. This is a share-and-share-alike operation. Everybody will share in the spoils regardless of how rich the house is that you take. Be thorough in your searching. Make the occupants talk, but quietly. The fire will bring the phone company guys in about an hour or two after the lines go down. Work fast but efficiently."

Charlie Bidwell was habitually late on the evening shift, usually around fifteen minutes late. This night he would be much later. Two cars boxed in his parked car, bumper to bumper. He yelled out "Whose cars are these?" He leaned on the horn of his car repeatedly bringing the neighbors to their windows. A cell phone call to two young black men resulted in their walking up to him and profusely apologizing. They moved the car in front, allowing him to drive away. One of the black men got into the second car, the one parked behind Charlie Bidwell, and began to follow him to D'Arcy Heights.

A young black man in a guard's uniform pulled up to the D'Arcy Heights gate. He got out of the car as the guard on duty stepped out of the guard shack. "Charlie Bidwell called in sick an hour ago. I'm the new kid on the block and your relief. Where do I park my heap?"

"I'm not surprised, he's usually late anyway. Just park behind our little stall here and come on in. Have you been briefed on the operation here?"

"Yeah, they are all pretty much the same. You can take off if you want to, I won't have any difficulty."

"Thanks, I'm Bob Withers," said the guard, holding out his hand. Deon Johnson seized his hand and firmly shook it. "I'm Jesse Stoner. You have a good night." Bob Withers put on his hat and coat, took his lunchbox from under the counter and said "The emergency switch is the red one next to the bottom of the entry window. That'll let the boys at the office know you have big trouble. The gate switches are on the counter; green is open of course and red is closed, on for each gate, coming and going. Have an easy night, Jesse Stoner."

After Bob Withers drove away, Deon Johnson made a simple phone call. "Come to the party." When Charlie Bidwell finally arrived, Deon Johnson walked up to his car as he opened the door. Johnson shot him in the middle of the forehead. Bidwell fell backward; Johnson put his legs back in the car, closed the door and returned to the guard house. Bidwell's car is part of the appearance of normalcy. The first fifty feet of fence on each side of the main gate entrance into D'Arcy Heights was a ten foot high brick wall. Beyond that was a ten foot cyclone fence with razor wire on the top and along the bottom three feet. The fence stretched around the back side of the entire complex, all four clover leaves, where a back gate led to the country club. The first van Deon Johnson let in immediately proceeded to the land line telephone switching unit just inside the fence. Two men emerged from the van and quickly removed the cover. They poured a gelatinous substance all over it and set an incendiary device time for three minutes at its base. They then drove to the first of the four clover leaves where the second van Deon Johnson admitted was waiting in front of the first house on the leaf Six men approached the house, one to each side, two to the front and two to the back. The telephone box fire eliminated all alarms connected by phone in the subdivision as well as all possible land line calls. One ski masked man inserted a titanium jimmy into the front door, heaved and grunted as the door lock gave way and the door sprung open. The two men entered the home holding semi-automatic handguns with silencers taken from canvas bags. A middle aged couple jumped up from their living room chairs.

"Scream and we shoot," said the ski masked man waving a silenced .380 automatic at them. "Cooperate and you won't get hurt. Lie on the floor and put your hands behind your back." The couple looked at each other, and the man said "What do you want?" facing the masked man covering them. "I won't tell you again, lie down now with no talking or die." The man and woman did as they were told. While the first ski masked man covered them with a gun the second used plastic binders as handcuffs to secure their hands behind their backs and similarly bound their ankles. "Call them in" said the first man. The second man made his way to the back door and motioned for the four on the sides and rear of the house to come in. The man with the gun asked the bound couple, "Is there any one else in the house?" "No, we're retired and live alone" said the man.

"Good, now tell me where your cash, jewelry, expensive works of art, guns and other goodies are and you won't get hurt."

"Why should I help you?" asked the man.

"Because if you don't, you and the wife get hurt real bad."

"The police and guards are already on the way," said the man triumphantly.

The masked man knelt beside the woman and took out a roll of duct tape. He rolled her on her back and taped her mouth shut. Then he rolled her back on her stomach. He took out a pair of pruning shears and without saying a word cut off her finger just in front of her diamond wedding ring. A muffled scream emerged from her mouth as he made the cut. He removed her ring from the stump as blood spurted over her back. "Now, I will amputate other things, fingers, toes, your dick and maybe your heads if you don't start talking. Where is your safe and your hidden room and what is the combination." The man talked his head off as the masked man took notes.

Two more vans arrived at the center of the cul-de-sac of the clover leaf. Six men emerged from each. Six of them went to Martha Bradley's house. Martha was just finishing a VSOP brandy in the library looking over some papers when her front door opened with a loud crack.

"What the hell the boys are doing now," she muttered as she started for the stairs. The noise which she presumed came from upstairs ceased as suddenly as it began. As she emerged from the library she found herself staring at two men with ski masks. "Don't scream or you're dead," said one pointing a

silenced automatic at her. The other brushed past her and opened the back door to let in four more men. The masked man appraised Martha's beauty. If anything, at thirty-three she was more beautiful than ever.

"Who else is in the house?"

"My two sons, who are asleep upstairs unless you woke them," said Martha.

"Any others?" asked the man.

"No, only the three of us live here."

"Where are the boys upstairs?"

"In the first two doors on the left," answered Martha. One of the four men climbed the stairs, listened for a moment at each door before opening it. In each case he saw a sleeping boy.

"Now Mama, here's the rules. We won't hurt your boys if you cooperate. You scream or cause us any trouble, and we will hurt them real bad. You understand?"

"Don't hurt my boys. I'll cooperate."

"Tell us where everything of value is and they will be fine. You shore are one fine looking Mama. Turn around and put your hands behind your back." Martha did as she was told. He bound her hands with a plastic tie. He duct taped her mouth shut from behind. Then he seized the front of her blouse and ripped it down off her shoulders along with her bra straps. He seized her breasts with each hand and felt their firmness. Martha had a sickening feeling. The man pushed her into the library and bent her over the table at the waist. He pulled down her pants and raped her from behind. The other five men ransacked the house, and then observed what their leader was doing with Martha. The next man laid her on the floor and raped her. They took their turns. The last held her by her hair and punched her hard in the solar plexus paralyzing her, then sodomized her on the floor. When they finished, they bound her ankles and left her on the living room floor.

"Tell the other boys from the other houses that there is one fine Mama that is real tight in here. They might want some fun too. I gave them my word no harm would come to her little boys if she cooperated. Make that a condition." The word spread among the crews robbing the other homes. More than a dozen men violated Martha that night. The last was Jacques, known as Jake, the Jamaican Snake. He was a recent arrival to the United States, an illegal alien. He was also a sadist. He severely beat Martha before he raped her. He beat her again leaving her face bloody pulp. She was unconscious when he strangled her.

The wail of multiple sirens very close awakened Nelson and Elizabeth Bartlett, and Sam and Josh Bradley. The boys looked out their windows and could see some of the emergency vehicles with their flashing lights. It was still dark outside. The boys ran to their mother's room only to find it empty. Nelson and Elizabeth looked out their windows and saw numerous ambulances, EMT vehicles and police squad cars. When the boys found their mother's bed was empty, they went downstairs. There they found their mother, her clothes mostly torn off, her face a bloody mess, with bruises over much of her torso, and lifeless. Sam ran to the phone and found the line dead. He and Josh dashed back upstairs and dressed as quickly as they could, then ran towards their grandparent's house on the next cul-de-sac. A policeman stopped the boys short of the Bartlett home and asked them why they were running outside. Sam blurted out "Mom is in the living room, all tied up, and she isn't breathing. We're going to Grandpa's house for help."

The policeman said "Point out which house is yours, Son, show me, then point to your Grandpa's house and go there." Sam pointed to their house. The front door was open with the light on. The policeman left the boys to investigate. They ran to the Bartlett home where Nelson and Elizabeth were standing in the front yard. When the officer saw Martha, he felt for a pulse. He cursed silently, and then stepped outside to report it and verbally file for a forensics unit as soon as one was available. When Charlie Bidwell didn't answer the routine check telephone call after the third call in fifteen minutes, the security agency dispatched a team of two men to investigate. When they arrived, they parked next to Charlie's car which they recognized. The bullet had splattered blood on the passenger window. The two security men immediately called their office for assistance to report Charlie's murder and drew their guns while they investigated the guard shack. The phone company arrived and called the fire department for investigation of the burned out switching unit. Meanwhile, the security agency sent more officers as backup. They began to explore D'Arcy Heights. They discovered several open front doors, whereupon they knocked and called out. At the first set of bound victims, they put in another call to their office for more police units. By dawn the size and scope of the raid was apparent. News teams converged on D'Arcy Heights. By 07:00 it was being broadcast live on network television. Until this occurrence, the raids had been limited to less elite suburbs in many cities, in more rural areas, and frequently outlying farms and isolated homes. Now the rich and famous no longer felt secure. Hollywood sat up and took notice.

"Grandpa, Mama's hurt bad. I don't think she was breathing. She's all tied up in the living room" said Sam.

"Elizabeth, you stay here and take the boys inside. I'll go see to Martha." Nelson Bartlett ran to his daughter's house where he encountered the police officer on the front walk. The officer stopped Nelson, and said "Who are you?" knowing full well that Nelson was Martha's father.

"I'm the father of the woman who lives here. I want to see my daughter." The policeman held him back. "No you don't.

She is beyond help. It will not serve any purpose to go in there."

"Let me go!" That's my daughter in there. Nelson struggled against the officer who held him firmly. An EMT approached them. The officer nodded towards the house to the EMT who went inside and closed the door. Nelson Bartlett began crying. The EMT emerged and drew a gurney from the ambulance, asking two others to assist. Martha's body was wheeled came out on the gurney in a body bag. The EMT and officer together guided Nelson Bartlett back to his own home. The press showed up and began broadcasting live and videotaping as much as the police would allow.

Many of the victims of the raid testified on live television how they were assaulted by the well organized gang of blacks. Several swore to get a gun and start shooting every black person they saw. "White America isn't safe any more. We have to take back our country!" shouted one irate middle aged man. "I'll buy a gun of any kind and every kind if I can find someone to sell me some!" He shook his fist at the camera. The raid left more than half a dozen dead, a number severely beaten, and several rape victims as well as Martha. The Baltimore newspapers carried a very detailed report of the raid. As a result of the television broadcasts of the D'Arcy Heights raid, the flight of the well-to-do white community northward from all areas of the central Atlantic coast states substantially increased over the next month, joining those fleeing from the southeast. They fled to the New England states and the north central portion of the United States. Bank accounts, cash, numismatics, valuable artworks and other forms of liquid assets went with them. Few whites were now left in the southeastern and southwestern U.S. except some pockets in southern California. Most had already fled north out of Texas; Arkansas was still a battleground. Southern Californians looked upon their television screens with dismay. Hollywood began to consider migration northward into Columbia.

Nelson Bartlett picked up the phone. His tears had ceased for the moment. He called his former son-in-law and informed him of Martha's murder. Ethan didn't say anything at first. Then, slowly, he asked about Sam and Josh. "The boys are physically OK, but in something of a state of shock in seeing their mother's body. Thank God the boys didn't witness her assault. They were asleep upstairs. Sam is handling better than Josh. I wouldn't want to be a black boy around Josh. He's liable to attack any black person he sees. God knows how strong that kid is for his size. Your teaching them some karate might have an adverse outcome, but I must admit, if I could get a gun right now I would kill black people too. Ethan, I don't know what else to say. Will you come for the funeral?"

"No Nelson, I won't. It wouldn't be appropriate. I am something of a target myself right now having just survived an assassination attempt. The Feds might try to take me out if I came. Transportation is a secondary problem. I want you to know that I loved Martha with all my heart. I always will. She was the love of my life. Take care of the boys for me Nelson. I'll come for them as their parent as soon as the political situation will allow it. Don't try to take my sons from me. That's something I will not tolerate and I think you can read and understand between the lines what I am saying. Those are my sons and I want them and I want them as soon as possible, and that means as soon as it is safe."

Nelson was silent for a moment. He understood perfectly that one way or another, Ethan would kill him and perhaps Elizabeth as well if they tried to keep the boys against his will. Of that he had absolutely no doubt. He knew that Ethan fully appreciated and resented his failure to accept him as a son-in-law over the past years. "I understand Ethan. For right now though, I think it is best if the boys stay with us."

"I agree Nelson. I appreciate you taking care of them until I can come and safely bring them home, to my home, here in

Wyoming. Until then, take care of them and yourselves."
Ethan hung up the phone and began to cry.

Nelson Bartlett watched the television replays with tears in his eyes. He read the more detailed account in the Baltimore papers. The papers detailed how DNA samples were being collected from the several rape victims. The Baltimore papers carried stories of the raid and the on-going investigation as front page news for days. Nelson read and re-read them. Ninety-six hours later the television news reported the police had a DNA match from the federal DNA library of convicted felons. One of the perpetrators was identified and his mug shot was displayed on television. Nelson Bartlett recognized him as a member of Toussaint's gang. Bartlett almost vomited. Did the involvement of this individual indicate that Toussaint's gang committed the raid? Is that why his house was spared? Did this individual belong to another gang? It seemed unlikely to Bartlett. Loyalty can only be to one organization, to one person. No gang member can belong to any other, and loyalty to the gang is paramount. Bartlett realized that his most infamous client was responsible for the murder of his daughter. *"What is my best course of action,"* he thought. *"Do I go to the police? If I indicate to Toussaint that I suspect him in the raid and murder of Martha, he will probably kill me, Elizabeth and the boys. He is the most vicious son-of-a-bitch I have ever counseled. I think getting Elizabeth and the boys out of his reach and then going to the police is the wisest move."*

Toussaint read the newspaper accounts, laughing out loud. The raid had netted several million dollars in cash and negotiable assets. He laughed until he read that Nelson and Bridgett's daughter Martha Bradley had been killed in the raid. That caused him some concern. He did not want to lose Bartlett as his attorney, but he knew that if Bartlett ever discovered his complicity, that Bartlett had enough information on him to have him convicted and sentenced to life imprisonment. Maryland had long since done away with the death sentence. Toussaint had three large wreaths, the largest available, sent to Martha's funeral but he did not personally attend. The more he thought about it, the greater he perceived the risk that Bartlett would find out his gang committed the crime. It preyed upon him until he decided he could no longer afford any chances. He could always find another lawyer. *"Lawyers are hungry as locusts, swarming over the land, devouring resources and clogging the courts. I can find another as good, perhaps better, than Bartlett"* he thought.

Ten days after the funeral Toussaint called in Jake the Jamaican Snake. He laid a dossier on Nelson Bartlett with half a dozen photographs of Bartlett in it on his desk in front of Jake. Toussaint had the good organizational sense to build something of a file on all those with whom he dealt. Their habits, their homes, their proclivities were included. Somehow his lieutenants failed to take note that Martha was Bartlett's daughter. Perhaps it was because they had never entered the D'Arcy Estates before the raid. "Take at least two others and kill this man on a dark street somewhere. Do it soon, before this week is over. Make it look like a street crime, a robbery. He is usually well heeled. Make sure he doesn't live more than a minute. Keep whatever you find on him as a bonus. Take sufficient help that there is no screw-up. He is a major threat to our organization. When it is done, burn the file."

A morose Nelson Bartlett sat at his desk. He had reread the week old newspaper on his desk the account of his daughter's death a dozen times. He also read in the morning's newspaper of the movement of troops from Fort Carson. He decided to call a meeting of the law firm partners tomorrow to discuss moving out of Baltimore. He drafted a short memo on his computer and sent it to all concerned. That evening he stayed late in his office debating with himself what to do about Toussaint and about moving. He realized that if Toussaint figured out that he knew it was his gang, his life was worthless. No one was more calculating and a cold hearted killer than Toussaint. That evening one of Toussaint's gang was watching the office building from across the street; another was watching the rear entrance. A third gang member was in the garage down the street where he kept his Porsche. It was a quite warm spring evening in Baltimore and a lot of daylight at 18:00 hours, so Nelson was wearing a light suit. He walked dejectedly down the street looking at his feet. He was at the mouth of the alley adjacent to the parking garage for his building when a black man stepped up behind him and shoved a gun in his ear, pushing him twenty feet into the alley. "Quiet man, if you want to live" were the last words he heard. At the mouth of the alley two other gang members grabbed him, one by each arm. A fourth suddenly shoved a wad of cotton in his mouth. The man behind him who had the gun stabbed him in the kidney with a double edged dagger that had a seven inch blade. He pushed it in up to the hilt and twisted, immediately destroying the kidney. The kidneys receive twenty-five percent of the stroke-volume of each beat of the heart. The hemorrhage is tremendous and immediate. The pain is unbearable. The man who shoved the wad of cotton in his mouth stabbed him directly in the heart with a similar knife. Nelson Bartlett was dead before he hit the ground. The four men leaned him against the brick wall, quickly wiped their knives on his suit and quickly but thoroughly rifled through his pockets. Then they just strolled down the alley and went various ways when they reached the other end of the alley.

At precisely 09:00 hours, Ethan Bradley walked on to the podium of the National Guard Armory in Worland. "If everyone will take a seat, we will get started. First, some house keeping chores. The restrooms are in the back right hand corner of the building behind me. There are half a dozen fast food restaurants in the city and half a dozen cafes, all of which I am sure, serve good lunches." That brought a chuckle from the crowd.

"Second, I wish to welcome all of you and thank you for coming. For those who could not make it, I hope you will carry the results of this discussion home to them. I have called this meeting to discuss how we will handle a potential influx of people into the Basin, particularly those from Mexico. One caravan came in two days ago. It will undoubtedly be followed by many, many more. Most of you have seen the massive population movements the United States is now experiencing. Our vote on regionalization, autonomous or independent, is not far away. The Basin does not have the resources to absorb even small numbers of people, let alone thousands or perhaps tens of thousands, coming from the southwest, south and Mexico. We need to make some hard decisions and make them very, very quickly as to how we will handle this problem. Our alternatives include sealing off the Basin, by use of force, if necessary. We can allow limited numbers, mostly relatives of folks already here, or we can do nothing and let the influx, which has the potential to destroy us, go unchecked. You have all seen what has happened to El Paso, San Antonio, Phoenix, Tucson, and the border cities.

Letting selected folks in has its own problems. How do we screen them to prove who they say they are? What resources can we provide them? How many of these select persons should be allowed into the Basin?

I am speaking to you first, as Commander of the Wyoming National Guard Basin Brigade. I have limited military resources at my command. Second, I am speaking to you as a fellow citizen addressing a problem universal to us all in the Big Horn Basin. Bloodshed is occurring all along what was the southwestern part of the United States. I do not want to see that here, but it might become necessary. We have the problems of continued food shipments into the Basin. With thousands more of people, we will not be able to feed them, especially if President Newkirk attacks us. The roads will not remain open. The Basin will be isolated and we must depend upon whatever resources we have at hand. Heavy weapons and severe combat will come into play. How will these non-Wyoming citizens react? Would they fight on our side? I doubt it. Would they fight for the federal cause? Possibly, because they see that as a door to resources they think the federal government can provide in the way of socialized medicine, housing, education, and general welfare. I don't know how to answer these questions from a political perspective. I can answer them militarily, but in order to be effective, the political and the military must be as one. Therefore it is up to you, as leaders throughout the Basin, to make some hard decisions and do it very soon. We have very, very little time for debate. I anticipate that within a week, maybe even a few days, hundreds to thousands more of Mexicans and others from the south and southwest, will attempt to enter the Basin. That is what I see. I will step aside now and turn the meeting over to the Chairman of the Washakie County Commissioners, Mr. Harrison. Mr. Harrison." Bradley stepped away from the podium as Jared Harrison stepped up to the podium.

Jared Harrison was a rancher from a long standing family, going back 150 years of living in the Basin.

"I don't know about anyone else Colonel, but I am not convinced with your argument about the possibility of serious violence here. We're relatively peaceable here in the Basin. Are you really convinced that we might be attacked? Many of us don't believe that we would be if we voted for secession. Not only that, but we employ Mexicans; have for decades, to work in the sugar beet and cornfields and feed lots and occasionally as cowboys. What's the harm in that?"

Colonel Bradley sighed and returned to the podium. "I'll be blunter about it. The issue is cultural dominance with its associated economic decline. Are you willing to accept the ascendancy of the Mexican culture and its subjugation of the white Anglo-Saxon culture? Look at Mexico. Are you willing to become the northern part of Mexico? If you are, in twenty years the only difference between here and Chihuahua, Mexico will be that the summers are cooler and the winters colder. The culture will be the same as it is in Chihuahua. Be prepared to accept that graft and corruption on a scale that you cannot imagine will replace the rule of law, at least what is left of it. Be prepared for Mexican squatters to claim your ranches as the politicians demand your land for their citizens in the name of land reform. Their overwhelming numbers and demands on the social safety net will tear it to shreds. You will have no social security checks when you reach retirement; that system will collapse, as close to bankruptcy as it already is. Health care will decline to a minimum, as their numbers and demands for health care which they cannot pay for crush that system. Learn Spanish, or Tex-Mex, because it will be the language of your children and grandchildren. Plan to become Catholics, as that church becomes dominant and will likely be state supported. Expect the educational level to decline as schools become ever more crowded and teachers must be bilingual to teach in both Tex-Mex and English. Expect history to be rewritten even more than by today's revisionists. It will be rewritten to reflect the Mexican perspective. Expect the drug problem to expand. Can any of you name a single Central or South American country that has not been wracked by political and economic stability in the last fifty years? Where graft, corruption, drug lords, political coercion have not ruled? Where elitist oligarchies, one to five percent of the population own eighty percent of the land and control the economy? Where elections are free and fair? That is what you can expect here as their culture becomes dominant. The Mexicans illegally immigrating here over the last decades have not adopted our culture, but rather demanded we accept theirs as an equal and independent entity. That is what you can expect. Many of you believe accommodation will work. Tell me how? Look at the last twenty years, at the marked changes that have already occurred. Look at the southwest, from southern California to Texas and tell me how accommodation has succeeded there. I contend it will not succeed any better here than it did in the southwest. The only other alternative is to resist. Resisting means turning them away at our borders. Many will try to force their way in. That must be met with violence. Once they learn they can force entry by violence or the threat of violence it will become their standard technique, their modus operandi. Many of you will shun the necessary acts of violence. You will refuse to defend yourselves and your homes and families and property because you have been fed the bilge that it is necessary and correct and your only legal recourse. Those of you who believe that and act accordingly will survive on the coattails of those who are willing to fight for that they believe and what they have. Some of you might try to flee? Where will you go? Canada? Possibly. That might be your only recourse. Given enough time, this immigration will reach Canada, perhaps even Alaska. 20,000 years ago northeast Asians crossed the Bering Strait to populate the Americas. They founded several empires. One of them, the Aztec, is now rising from history and expanding northward. If you don't stop it here, where will it stop? Part of my mission is to train the Wyoming National Guard Basin Brigade. Another part is to organize and train a civilian militia. Our National Guard mission is to defend Wyoming. It is not unreasonable to expect two invasion forces, one organized and military, and one a wave of illegal immigration that actually began peacefully decades ago. As southern California, Arizona, New Mexico and Texas convulse, and break off we are witnessing the beginnings of a mass exodus of white folks out of that region. Many will remain to see what happens, refusing to leave their homes and businesses. I cannot predict what would be the right choice for others, only for me. As they of the southwest must choose, so ultimately must we, collectively and individually. You have watched your television news for weeks. You have observed what is occurring in Los Angeles, San Antonio and Houston. If the United States breaks apart, and several nation states arise, the possibility arises that President Newkirk will attack us to retain us within the Union. He can't possibly hope to retain California and the Southwest in the union, but I am sure he thinks he can force us to remain. It will be our second civil war. Part of this will be a massive influx of civilians seeking safety and shelter and support in our Basin. Most of them will be Mexicans or of Mexican descent. The choice is yours. Fight, run or be overrun. It is the Balkanization of what was the United States."

Juan Cartagena rose from the back of the room. "This is crazy! You are crazy! You are no commander here! We are all good United States citizens! We abide by the law. We have harmed no one. We do not ask anything from anyone, especially not land. It is you and others like you who crave power that are causing the country to break apart. It is not we Mexicans. It is you soldiers, and the rich and powerful Gringos who are destroying your own country. You should be put on trial for treason! Your own country has refuted you. They took away your commission. You are a hunted outlaw. Any acts of violence against us Mexican-Americans or our Mexican brothers and sisters will be met with ten times the violence you provoke!"

Bradley rose with a smirk on his face. "Thanks for the accolades. You sir, are an illegal alien, a representative of the National Farm Workers of America, a political organizer who preaches disrespect for Anglo teachers in the classroom, who has organized separate cells to conduct guerilla warfare against Anglos when you feel the time is right. You have armed them illegally with automatic small arms. You have put a lid on the Mexican against Mexican violence in the Basin using force and even murder when you felt it necessary in order to present the appearance of a perfectly quiet, law abiding subculture and community. You are not the only individual to have an intelligence network. I suggest you immediately leave not only the Basin, but the Territory of the Missouri, perhaps head for California where others like you are fomenting the dissolution of these United States. Take your illegal compatriots with you but leave your AK-47s at the armory."

The room was stunned into silence. No one spoke for two minutes. Finally, the mayor of Worland took the podium. "Thank you, Colonel. I think Colonel Bradley has expressed it rather well in pretty basic terms. We should weigh his remarks very carefully. We have some very hard decisions to make and very little time in which to make them. What do you see, Colonel, September 15th as the defining moment?"

"Yes, Mr. Mayor, I do. I am sure a great many people, if not the majority, are waiting to see the outcome of the September 15th referendum. I anticipate it will pass. We will become part of the Republic of the Nation of Missouri, and the southwest will break off to become part of Mexico. If the latter occurs, expects thousands, if not tens of thousands, to flee that region, both Hispanic Americans and Anglos. There is no direction for them to flee but north. We must not allow the Hispanics in. Do we let the Anglos in or turn them away as well?"

"What is your suggestion, Colonel?"

"Turn away all comers. I am not responsible for the area south of the Wind River Canyon. If I were the Governor, I would close our state's borders to all except those of the Republic of Missouri."

"Why would you turn away Anglos from the south, Colonel?"

"Why? First, because we cannot absorb them or support them, even temporarily. Second, because it was their politicians reflecting their philosophy and policies that allowed this situation to develop over the last five decades. If they had closed their borders, had not looked for cheap illegal labor, had not developed such a bloated social welfare system, if they had the foresight to see the long range outcome, we would not be having this meeting."

"What are your specific recommendations, Colonel?"

"We establish roadblocks to all entrances to the Basin. Only shipments are allowed in, shipments of goods, foodstuffs or whatever. Only people from other states that will constitute the Republic of Missouri be allowed in. All others should be turned away. Federal identity cards with morphometric data should be sufficient to establish their current residences."

One of the audience stood up and asked, "Just how do you propose turning them away, Mister?"

The "Mister" was spoken with such a slur and with a somewhat sarcastic tone that most keyed on it. The not too subtle insult of using mister instead of the military rank of Colonel was not lost on Bradley.

"Our roadblocks will be armed and fully prepared to use any means necessary, including deadly force. Our Wyoming National Guard troops will man them, along with at least one deputy sheriff from the individual county. Understand me, Mister! We are repelling a foreign invasion; there are few friendlies and no neutrals. There are no civilians. Immigrants, men, women and children, all ages, both sexes are the enemy. If you aren't prepared to engage in the application of deadly force to protect the Basin and its people, I strongly urge you to migrate else where and do so very rapidly. Perhaps sunny southern California will be more to your liking."

The man sat down. He found Bradley's not-too-subtle hint of possible vigilante action by the militia a bit disturbing. So did a few others, most of them from the Cody and the area around Yellowstone National Park.

A woman stood up. "I suppose Colonel, that you will initiate such actions on your own authority?"

"I called this meeting Ma'am, to encourage discussion or debate, if you like, to consider alternatives, present my perspectives and possible plans of action. One of the principles of our original Constitution is that the military always remains under and subordinate to civilian control. I adhere to that principle. I will act independently on what I have presented only as the last alternative. By the last alternative I mean in the absence of orders or general direction from my superiors. The present chain of command runs from the Governor to the Adjutant General to me. I am awaiting my orders on these issues as we speak. If the people of the Basin wish some input-I will not say control at this point in time-then I suggest you contact your state legislators and the Governor's office. Of course, if the Referendum of September 15th supports remaining within the United States rather than an independent state, one of the two possible invasion threats is removed or at least reduced. I have a harder time with the idea of fighting against my former comrades in arms who remain in the United States military than I do in repulsing the invasion of a foreign culture, even if it is composed of unarmed foreign civilians, men, women and children. I trust that is clear enough."

The mayor asked, "How soon do you need a decision, Colonel?"

"The sooner the better, Mr. Mayor. We already had one caravan of four vehicles and fifteen Mexicans come into the Basin with the intent to homestead here. How many more are coming through that we have no knowledge of us anybody's guess. I just happened to become aware of that one caravan by a phone call from an astute citizen of Thermopolis. Perhaps 100 or a 1000 have already arrived that I don't know about."

The Mayor asked, "Are there any more questions or comments from anyone, on any aspect of this discussion? No? Then I suggest we all go home and ponder on what has been presented here. If we are to act at all, I suggest it be very, very soon. I would like to meet with the county commissioners of Washakie, Park and Hot Springs Counties immediately after this meeting, if you all would remain here for a few minutes. Without further questions or comments, I declare this meeting closed."

As the crowd dispersed, Washakie County Sheriff Brady took Hot Springs County Sheriff Joe Johnson by the elbow, "got a few minute, Joe?"

"Sure, but I can guess what you're thinking."

"Yeah, we ought to close the canyon without any further discussion and do it today. If you agree, I'll talk to the Colonel. He can assign some men to it and we'll have a deputy there 24/7. How does that sound to you?"

"Like a damned good idea to me. We should have done it weeks ago. Let's do it. I'll have a couple of deputies down there tomorrow morning. I hope you can persuade the Colonel can get some men down there for support, maybe an infantry fighting vehicle with a chain cannon for maximum effect."

CHAPTER 15

"GOVERNOR, I SEE NOTHING THAT WE CAN DO TO STOP THOSE PEOPLE WITH THEIR TANKS AND INFANTRY FIGHTING VEHICLES". It is a job of the Texas National Guard. We simply don't have the manpower, weapons, training to engage in this kind of warfare. I suggest Governor, that you order a complete evacuation of Texas south of Dallas-Fort Worth. Also, a declaration of Martial Law that is statewide, not just limited to Houston or other large cities. My Rangers and Department of Public Safety Officers need all possible authority to discourage violent crimes and looting. The best way to announce it I think is from whatever television and radio stations are still broadcasting. If you like, I'll fax some suggestions regarding the recommendations and wording. We want to avoid panic but at the same time impress our citizens of the urgency to evacuate north, even out of the state. From what I can see of the political situation, the upper Midwest would be the most desirable destination. Fuel for individual vehicles will be a problem. Service stations will make massive profits if not supervised. I'll assign a DPS officer or Ranger to each station along the major routes north to help insure people good out and they are not price gouged."

"Good Idea, Colonel. Fax your ideas and my staff will get started on it. I'll include an order that all service stations selling fuel are to maintain current prices and are to remain open until all fuel supplies are exhausted. What will you do, Colonel?"

"The twins are out of the nest, they finished college last year and both are working up north. I'll pack the wife and dog in our two pickup trucks and we will head north along with everybody else. I think Texas is done for. Perhaps I can get a job up in the northern Rockies or Great Plains states. Somebody up there should need the services of an old experienced Ranger."

"Good luck to you and all of your officers, Colonel."

"Thank you, Governor. It has been a privilege to serve in your administration."

Colonel Carlson, Texas Ranger, Texas Department of Public Safety, Commanding, issued the following recommendations to the Governor.

ONLY THE FOLLOWING ITEMS SHOULD BE CONSIDERED IN EVACUATION

1. Take your warmest clothes.
2. Firearms for protection enroute especially if you have to abandon your vehicle.
3. All the fuel for your vehicle(s) you can carry in certified gas containers.
4. Water and nonperishable foods.
5. Only small valuables such as jewelry, cash, negotiable bonds, items that require little room.
6. Critical documents such as birth certificates, marriage licenses, health and vaccination records.

A pickup truck with a topper or SUV is preferred to carry as much as possible. Plan on traveling as far as Kansas as a minimum; if at all possible, form a caravan with your friends and neighbors for supply and defense.

"Maggie, you go home to your family, pack, and get the hell out of here. Go as far north as you can. If your husband isn't already at home, be ready to leave the moment he arrives. I have enjoyed working with you. You have been a wonderful secretary. As of now, this office is closed."

Two Cadillacs stopped in front the mine resistant personnel carrier that straddled both lanes of the highway in the southern mouth of the first tunnel just north of Boysen Reservoir. The soldier glanced at their license plates. They were both from California. He motioned for the driver to roll down the window.

"We are not allowing any nonresidents to advance any further Sir. You will have to turn around and go elsewhere."

"Now see here, Mac, I'm a U.S. citizen and I go where I please. You have no right to stop me. Now get the hell out of my way, and move that damned tank or whatever."

"Sir, is that car behind you with you? You are not allowed to proceed. The Basin is closed to all outsiders. Only Basin residents and critical supplies are allowed in. We are authorized to use deadly force to prevent your entry. Make no mistake, we will open fire if you attempt to force your way in. If you are stupid enough to try, we will shoot to kill. Now, turn around and leave. Go back to California or wherever else you wish, but you aren't coming in here. Now, you can talk it over with the rest of your party in the Caddy behind you, but you aren't going any further."

The driver got out of his car cursing, and walked back to the car behind him, accompanied by the soldier who kept his rifle in at port arms across his chest.

Ethan showered and shaved. It was almost 20:00 hours. Ethan put on a short sleeved dress shirt and tucked it into his pants. He threaded his two magazine carrier on his belt as he threaded it through the belt loops, followed by the high ride concealment holster. He press checked his .45 ACP, put it in the holster, and slipped a bulky, all wool cable knit Cornish Chunky sweater over the sports shirt. The sweater admirably hid his .45 ACP in its holster as he checked himself in the mirror. The medium weight wool slacks hid the top part of his combat boots, the only part of his casual dress he failed to yield to fashion. His father eyed him with a slight grin as he emerged from his room.

"Going somewhere, Son?" he asked, his grin morphing into a smile.

"Well, I thought I might check out the social scene tonight Dad."

"I hope you're armed."

Ethan patted his .45 and nodded.

"I suggest you take a long gun too, Son. Can't be too careful these days. Better to have and not need."

"OK Dad, I'll take the short barreled pump shotgun. It will fit right behind the seat of the pickup, right at the top in the gun rack. Are you OK, Dad? You look a little different to me." Ethan looked a little more closely into his father's face.

"I'm fine, just indigestion. It acts up every now and then. No need for any concern. I'll swallow a couple of gulps of antacid and be good as new."

"I noticed that your library has grown quite a bit since I left home. Much of it seems to be history and politics. You have been reading quite a lot."

"Yup, and the more history I read the more I could see what was coming. The demise of democracy, or a republic for that matter, comes when the citizens realize they can vote themselves support from the public treasury. Everything from food to housing to clothing for school kids, to medical care, to education, you name it. As Dr. Robert Q. Steinman said early in this century,

'From bondage to spiritual faith

From spiritual faith to great courage
From great courage to liberty
From liberty to abundance
From abundance to complacency
From complacency to apathy
From apathy to governmental dependence
From governmental dependence back into bondage
From bondage into tyranny.

That's where we are today Son, fighting back from governmental dependency. We will win this fight or plunge into the bondage of a police state. Tyranny exists today as it always has and always will, as long as there are little people. Little people are those who will suck up to those in authority for a little money, an exchange of small favors, or something to their benefit. Little people do not realize or care or both, for the consequences of their duplicity. Little people who are willing to betray a fellow citizen, a neighbor, perhaps a friend or even a family member, no matter how severe the tyranny; little people who care for nothing but themselves. Little people have no value system, no integrity, no honor. Perhaps they should be eliminated with the tyrant."

Ethan pulled on his snow packs as he spoke. "You know Dad, I really find this troubling in the sense of leading a civil war. I have seen so much that I never gave much thought to until my last active duty tour. I saw the extreme of political correctness, of how much of our society has degenerated into welfare recipients with no concept of integrity, of self sufficiency, of responsibility for themselves, voting for whichever politician promised them more handouts. The parallels to the Roman Empire are remarkable. The majority of our politicians are just like those of the Roman Senate, arrogant bastards, concerned only for their own position and power, willing to continue to feed the mob that makes up so much of our society even though they know it will ultimately cause our demise. I wonder sometimes, if it isn't better to have an extremely strong central government that controls every aspect of our lives, from birth to death. Yet, I know, I have read, how it never works. The early days of the former Soviet Union and China under Mao are very illuminating of the disastrous consequences of that course of action. I wonder if we will ever recover. When Martha was still in law school she used to argue that we are an aberrant, an unnatural political system. Only oligarchies or tyranny could effectively rule. According to her, the ideal system that will endure for centuries in modern times has not been devised. It somehow must allow the best of the best to arise from the lowest rungs of society. Somehow those who are intelligent and ambitious must have a way to achieve an excellent education, opportunities for broad experiences and leadership development. If not, they turn to criminal activities to achieve their luxury and status. Those of mediocre talents and little or no ambition must somehow be made to be productive. The latter must have a modest standard of living, be comfortable and secure, have some social security net, in order to keep them from being restive, or downright rebellious that can lead to civil war. Obviously, we set the social net higher than our economy could stand, borrowing to support it and bankrupting us. Our politicians squashed our ideals too far for some of us. Now we are really in civil war. So, what Dad, have you discovered in your study of history all these years?"

Robert Bradley looked at his son, thought for a moment and said. "You cannot make the decision to go to war based on an algorithm with complete objectivity and rationality as some politico-military theorists claim. You can never adequately judge intent, perceptions, history and factors of which are not even aware. One thing that most theorists refuse to acknowledge is that a nation is not composed of just a government. Even in totalitarian states the will and demeanor of the people must be taken into account. To defeat a nation you must defeat the people as well as the government and its armed forces. The people must be psychologically crushed to the point where they believe that further resistance is useless and that will be crushed to death if they continue. In short, there really are no civilians in war. That is especially applicable in insurgencies. An oligarchy would probably be best if only some way Martha's comment about the rising of the crème de la crème could be found. We, like the Romans, evolved into such a soft society we refused to even physically protect ourselves, hence only the volunteer armed forces. A primary purpose of government is to protect the weak from the strong, internally and externally. The masses came to demand cradle to the grave care from the government instead of self sufficiency. No, until such a system can be found that is productive, old Winston Churchill probably had it down when he said 'Democracy is the worst form of government except for all others.' I'd make that a Republic though, instead of a democracy. Oh, to hell with political theory. Enough of my lecturing, I'm going to eat! Go have a great time with this new gal or whomever."

"Anyway, I don't know how this evening will develop. If all goes well, I'll see you tomorrow. My paycheck arrived from the National Guard so I am set for funds until the market for U.S. dollars collapses. I would really like to buy some gold. Ethan slipped on a light weight down parka with a hood and a knit hat on his head. "See ya Dad!" he called as he went through the door and into the cold of the night. It was 20 degrees Fahrenheit and the stars were intensely bright. *Not bad for a late April evening,* he thought. The road was dry so he drove to Thermopolis in thirty minutes. He entered the café where Gypsy Lee was continuously rebutting passes from two cowboys. Ethan took off his hat and unzipped his parka and took a seat at the counter one stool away from the two slightly oiled cowhands. *One beer too many in each of them,* he thought. He smiled at Gypsy Lee who smiled back.

"I'll get my coat and I'll be ready," said as she poured him a cup of coffee and set down a saucer full of half and half servings.

The two cowboys looked at Ethan, looked at each other, and back at Ethan.

"How come she'll go out with you, and not with us, Mister?"

"Not to be rude about it, Gentlemen, but you are out of your league. The lady is a quite bright scientist, about to complete an advanced degree in physics. I doubt that you have much in common with her other than current geographic location."

Ethan sipped his coffee, set down his cup, and smiled at them. The nearest cowboy came off his stool and glared at Ethan, who just looked at him, smiled, and sipped his coffee holding it in his left hand so his gun hand was free.

"You think you're better'n us or sumpthin' Mister. Cause you ain't. If you think you are, I'll teach you otherwise, right here'n now."

"Morons most likely", thought Ethan, *"but it might be a trap."* Ethan looked at the two of them with a steady gaze and spoke.

"I'm here to pick up my date. I don't want any trouble and neither do you. If you are looking for a fight, I suggest you join the Wyoming National Guard. They have a big one coming up and I am recruiting for it."

The second cowboy asked, "Who are you, Mister?"

"I'm Ethan Bradley, Colonel Ethan Bradley gentlemen, and now if you will excuse me, I see my date is ready."

With his left side to them, he took a last sip of his coffee with his left hand while he lifted his sweater with his right and grasped the butt of his pistol, just in case. The second cowboy, still seated, grasped his friend's arm to prevent him from doing something stupid.

"You and the lady have a good evening, Colonel," he said.

"Thank you, and you gentlemen as well," replied Ethan has he picked up his hat and coat from the counter with his left hand, keeping his right on the pistol grip. Gypsy Lee walked to the door. Ethan took several steps backward toward her, turned and pulled his sweater down over his gun. The standing cowboy's jaw dropped when he realized Ethan had his hand on the butt of a gun. Gypsy Lee opened the door and Ethan closed it behind them. The seated cowboy pulled his friend back on the stool. "That's a man you don't want to mess with. He'll kill you and never even get arrested, let alone go to trial. He's the main military man around here and messing with him will get you hung. We don't want to mess with his woman either."

"I figure there are a couple of decent restaurants in town, which do you prefer, the Cactus Rose or the Antelope Inn?"

"Neither. I have supper already three quarters prepared in my apartment. It is not a pretty place, but it is what I can afford. I keep it neat and clean and its private. I have rented a disk of a good movie I have wanted to see for some time. I have a good wine, a red rose chilling in the fridge to go with supper, and popcorn and soda for a snack during the movie. I want to curl up on the sofa and have a nice quiet at home evening. Please don't disappoint me. "

"Lady, you have a sucker for a nice quiet evening at home."

Gypsy Lee curled up against Ethan on the sofa, stretching out her long legs and putting her head on a pillow in his lap. Ethan pulled the folded blanket off the back of the sofa and spread it over Gypsy Lee. Half way through the movie, he simply bent over and kissed her on the cheek. She smiled, reached up and put her arm around his neck and pulled him down and kissed him on the lips. She was warm, full of energy and excitement while Ethan was so eager he was trembling. He realized it had been several years since he had such an exhilarating sexual encounter with Martha. The ray of light on his face woke Ethan and told him it was at least 08:00 hours. He looked at Gypsy Lee whose face was half covered with blankets. *She truly is beautiful,* thought Ethan, *and absolutely delicious.* He smiled and snuggled over against her. She purred an "mmmm" and rolled over on her side and backed up against him. He slipped his upper arm around her waist and the other under her pillow. She smiled but didn't open her eyes. They snuggled even closer under the two Hudson Bay blankets. The 40 F temperature in the bedroom made them all the more happy to snuggle against each other, contented. He realized she couldn't afford to set the thermostat any higher because of the cost of heating oil and natural gas. He appreciated that she purchased the finest quality beef steaks, more than she could afford, to please him. Ethan couldn't remember the last time he was so fulfilled and so happy.

The Washakie County Sheriff's office and the local town police organizations throughout the county decided to hold a combined meeting of all officers. By mutual agreement, they decided to address what everyone saw in progress-a racially based civil war. A fourth of the police officers were Hispanic. Several were lifetime residents of the area, but several were relative newcomers to their respective force. The senior officers regarded their new Hispanic officers with some degree of suspicion. The Sheriff, commanding the largest department spoke first. "I'll be blunt. The continent, the nation, the region, the state, this county and community are in turmoil. We are all aware that much of it is racially based. For those of you of Hispanic origin, the choices are limited. You are most certainly welcome to stay, but I cannot say at what cost. If you stay, I do not know if your fidelity to the community, the state, and probably the new nation will be recognized, let alone rewarded.

Neither can I predict your future should you choose to flee the Basin and the new nation. I do know that your skills will be a major contribution to whatever polity you choose to give your allegiance. You are all aware of the turmoil, the fighting, the dissolution occurring all across the southern half of what was the United States, between those of Hispanic descent, African-Americans and those of European descent. Your choice to leave or stay will be strictly up to you. Monetarily, the coffers are empty. Now, no one has any funds in the retirement account. The retirement plan is defunct because it was based upon U.S. bonds and Treasury notes. Therefore consideration of retirement benefits should not be a factor in your decision. Go or stay, the choice is yours in an indefinite future for all of us. Whatever you choose, I wish you the best in all circumstances. We are going to close the Basin to all comers except those from the states which will constitute the Republic of the Nation of Missouri."

"Mr. President, the representatives of the European Union are here. Shall I show them in? They are right on time as are the Secretaries of Defense and State and the Chairman of the Joint Chiefs. They are having a coffee in the anteroom chatting animatedly."

"Yes, thank you, show them in please Janice." President Newkirk placed his pen down and rose, walking around his desk to greet his visitors.

"Welcome, folks. Sorry to keep you waiting. Janice tells me you had coffee but can I offer you some more, along with some fine Danish? Please, pull up a chair and tell me what is on your collective minds," knowing full well why they had asked for an emergency meeting. Representatives of Germany, France, England, Poland, Austria, Hungary and the Czech Republic found seats around the coffee table. Not in the European Union but accompanying them was the Russian ambassador.

The EU's delegation's spokesman was from the Serbian Republic. His country would be one of the first to be over run if the Chinese expanded beyond the Middle East. "Mr. President, the European Union implores you to postpone the referendum regarding the secession of the various regions of the United States. Collectively, we have come to realize how critical a stable and unified United States is to the world order. Your military might far exceeds ours. Our concept of soft power has not come to fruition with the Chinese. A united United States, united with Europe is the only hope to withstand further Chinese expansion. Without the United States, a United States leading NATO type coalition, we cannot stop China without weapons of mass destruction. No doubt the Union's deployment of nuclear fires will result in Chinese massive retaliation. This is potentially far worse than the World War III in 2025 or World War II of the 1930's and 40's. This would be a nuclear winter from which our civilization would take thousands of years to recover, it at all. For the sake of humanity, put global concerns ahead of nationalism. Without a unified front, we are all lost. Even if the Chinese do not proceed across the steppes of Russia, into the Ukraine, the Balkans and Europe, China's control of Middle Eastern oil would still be sufficient to bring us to economic collapse. They could dictate any terms they wish."

"You make two interesting points, Ambassador Sloboda. Are you willing to make the same presentation to a joint session of both houses of Congress? I must point out to you that the odds are extremely unfavorable for a reversal of the course upon which we seem to have launched. We are experiencing massive internal immigration of which I do not see a reversal. Perhaps with the dust has settled we will be able to remain one country composed of several autonomous units. That is the best I think we can hope for. Nevertheless, if you will address a joint session, I can only hope all can agree on a postponement of the referendum, perhaps until the fall. That would provide more time for debate and preparation for whatever action might be required to hold the Union together. Right now, we are in the middle of quite a lot of turmoil, as you are all aware."

"Mr. President, we would be more than willing to make such a presentation. If you will schedule it, we will all attend, and I will personally address your Congress. We are grateful for the opportunity. Let us hope your Congress will agree."

"Ed, is there anything you would like to add to the conversation?" asked Newkirk of Ed Andretti, his Chief of Homeland Security.

"Yes, Mr. President, I would. I see quite a bit of hypocrisy here I feel compelled to mention. About half you gentlemen are Muslims. You Muslims have coerced your own European countrymen to convert to Islam in subtle and not-so-subtle ways. Now you come to us with a concern of fear, of being overwhelmed by a foreign culture when you are guilty of the same thing, only by political gudgels rather than by brute force. You have riots in your major cities, burning and killing and looting of people of other faiths by your Muslim populations. You kill Christian young men when you can catch them all alone. It is known as "The Curse" in the Balkans where it has existed for hundreds of years and led too much of the strife in the Balkans in the 1990's. All of Europe has already become somewhere between a quarter and a third Muslim, you invoke religious intolerance there, you demand adherence to the Sharia, the body of Islamic law, you have your mullahs preaching separation for a black Muslim America in our southern states, yet you ask us to hold the nation together on your behalf, ultimately for your defense."

"All right Ed, that really isn't appropriate here. I've mentioned to you before that I'll make the policy and the policy statements. Gentlemen, we'll discuss your concerns, but you must understand our desire is the same as yours in holding our country together. I thank you for your visit."

The convoy of six eighteen wheeled trucks left the Army ammunition plant at Lake City outside of Kansas City at 24:00 hours. Their destination was Fort Sill, Oklahoma. The entire convoy stopped at a large truck stop for breakfast near the Kansas-Oklahoma border. Two plain sedans, one in front and one in the rear, escorted the convoy. Each was carrying four Department of Defense civilian guards. Each truck had a driver and a co-driver. All of the personnel entered the truck stop for breakfast except for one guard who remained in each escort car. The trucks parked parallel in a row on the backside of the truck stop along with forty other trucks. Ten minutes into the break, two men stepped down from each of two trucks not associated with the convoy. After seeing the men dismount and chat for a moment alongside their trucks, the two guards in the escort cars closed their eyes when one of the men who had dismounted from two trucks walked over and tapped on the window. Not knowing all of the drivers and co-drivers or recognizing the dismounted truckers, the guards sat up and rolled down the driver side windows to inquire what the man wanted while their accomplice approached from the other side.

"Don't look now, but someone has a gun pointed at you from the passenger door," said the men. When the guards turned to look at the other passenger window they were struck a paralyzing blow with a tazer. The guards were quickly disarmed, their uniformed shirts stripped off, and handcuffed. They were placed in a van which quickly pulled along side of each guard's car in turn. At the signal from both cars, the convoy trailers were unhitched from their tractors, the tractors pulled away allowing other tractors to be pulled in their place. The substituted tractors were hitched to the ammunition laden trailers and drove off. Identical trailers pulled in their place and the original tractors were then hitched to the substituted trailers. The operation didn't take ten minutes. It was obviously well rehearsed. The on board computers of the tractors with their built in transponders did not reveal any changes in the location of the convoy. The switch was not observed by the tazed guards. When the drivers and relief guards emerged from the truck stop, they found their dazed and handcuffed cohorts in a van with its side door open parked next to their trucks. Panic ensued. A quick investigation revealed nothing except two stripped and handcuffed guards. The seals on the trailers were all intact. They deduced the objective of the attack was to acquire the uniforms and side arms of the assaulted DOD guards. The incident was immediately reported by radio to their superiors and then to the state highway patrol. No one interviewed saw anything out of the ordinary. A nation wide report was not issued. The incident of two uniforms and two sidearms was so trivial as to not merit further attention, particularly not in the higher echelons of the government. The highjacked trailers were driven north into the Dakotas and then turned west, headed to the Wyoming National Guard Regiments. The Adjutant General sent one truck each to Casper, Sheridan, Rock Springs, Worland, and Laramie. He held one truck in reserve. Ethan was ecstatic when the trailer arrived in Worland. When the substituted trailers were opened at Fort Sill, they were found to contain the appropriate weight of pit run, gravel and sand.

Gypsy Lee made her once a month or so run to the BumGarrs on the west side of Worland. As she drove down Big Horn Avenue, she noticed a sign on the Big Horn Café window. HELP WANTED: WAITERS/WAITRESSES FOR IMMEDIATE EMPLOYMENT. She pulled into the first available parking space and strolled inside. She sat in a booth and ordered a cup of coffee as she observed the patrons and the staff. She decided she wanted to scope out the place to make certain it was a satisfactory working environment. She was tired of smart ass cowboys and oilfield workers who couldn't keep their hands to themselves. This way, she thought, she would be a lot closer to Ethan and they could see each other more often. Perhaps even on a daily basis if she moved to Worland. When the waitress served her a coffee refill, she asked, "Who do I see about the job indicated on the sign in the window?" The waitress said, "Me. I'm the owner and chief cook and if you want a job I can hire you right now. My name is Jan Neville. Do you have any experience as a waitress?"

"I do. I have been doing it for several years now, down the road. I would like to move to Worland, providing I can find a job and a place to rent that is clean and affordable on the salary you pay."

"Honey, I have a friend who has an apartment for rent nearby. It isn't big, but it is clean and available. I'll give him a call and see if he will show it to you immediately. I think he wants $500 a month and it is partially furnished. I'll pay you $15 an hour and I'll talk to my friend about the rent. Our clientele here is mostly town folks and local ranchers. They are pretty good tippers if you give good service. You can take breaks as they become available. Two of my previous waitresses left; really I fired them, because they couldn't speak English well enough to function. The hours are from noon till nine at night, Tuesday through Sunday. Dinner is on the house. Weekends are busy for us. That's when the rest of the county comes in to shop at BumGarrs. Monday is your day off, although I might have to occasionally call on you for a catering job or something on Monday. If things work out and I can find another capable waitress, then maybe Monday and Tuesday can be days off. Is that acceptable?"

When she left, Gypsy Lee had a new job and a new apartment. She would start as soon as she could rent a trailer to move her limited furniture into the apartment. That afternoon she boxed her books and computers, packed her clothes into boxes she got at BumGarrs, and made arrangements to pick up a U-Haul trailer the next day. She hired Freddy's two teenage high school boys to load her bed, kitchen table with four chairs, television, DVD player and boxed clothes into the trailer. In an hour, she had her pickup and attached trailer loaded and was off to Worland.

Paula Jean Darnell reached an agreement with the owner of the Wildlife Bar and Motel in Thermopolis. She could ply her trade in the best room of the motel as a permanent resident in exchange for the unrestrained use of her body for one hour at a time, one visit every seven days by the owner or one of his special friends. She considered it cheap rent. Her rules were no bondage or pain inflicted upon her and nothing anal. When Mr. Petan found that she charged $500 for an all night client, he demanded half of her fee. Paula just smiled and handed him a video disk of his first three visits. She lit a cigarette and blew smoke in his face which made him cough.

"In the first place, there are very few Johns around willing to spend $500 on a prostitute, even one as good and beautiful as I am. Second, review that tape, Buster. It is just a copy of two camera views of your first three visits. It is a copy of course, and other copies will immediately go to your wife and to your daughter in college. I have her address right here. Third, the Chief of Police gets a cut of my take and an occasional service job, a freebie, as does the County Sheriff. If you give me any crap, the Chief will be on your case like stink on shit. So be happy with your love jobs and stay out of my way." Mr. Petan turned scarlet, recognizable even through his south Asian skin. He turned and walked away, disk in hand. After reflection, he thought he might review it later.

Paula wondered if business might be better elsewhere, or possibly even a branch office, so to speak, one or two nights a week elsewhere. Worland was a larger town, having a BumGarrs that Thermopolis lacked. Cowboys and farm hands came into town for a Saturday night spree. The town of Ten Sleep was just too small to consider. She decided to explore a branch office on the weekends in Worland or perhaps even a total move. When she walked into the Big Horn café on Big Horn Avenue in Worland and slid off her goose down jacket every head in the café turned-and stayed turned. She was wearing a form fitting black sweater, black stretch slacks and fur lined high heeled boots. Everything about her revealed a sleek, devastatingly voluptuous body. She smiled as she glanced around the café and then glided up to the counter like a cat. Gypsy Lee stood behind the counter, coffee pot in hand, as Paula Jean slid onto a stool directly opposite her. The two women made and held eye contract for a moment. Gypsy Lee broke it with sly grin and placed a menu in front of Paula Jean.

"What would you like, Miss?"

"Oh, a cup of that coffee will be just fine for a starter, thanks."

Paula Jean glanced around the café. All but a very few eyes were glued on her. Those that were not belonged to elderly men in the company of their elderly wives, women, most of whom wore a frown of scorn or perhaps of jealousy. As Gypsy Lee poured her a cup of coffee and sat a creamer in front of her, Paula Jean asked in a low, dusky voice, "Are there opportunities for a working girl in this town?"

Gypsy Lee eyed her suspiciously, "That depends upon what kind of work a girl wants."

At that moment Ethan walked in the door. As he made eye contact with Gypsy Lee, Paula turned around and instantly recognized him. "Well, if it isn't handsome soldier boy," she smiled. "And where have you been hiding?"

Ethan sat down next to Paula Jean. Before he could say anything, Gypsy Lee said "Do you know her?"

"*Oh Shit!* Thought Ethan. *I hope I am not in deep Kimchee here.* "I gave her a ride into Thermopolis last spring when her car broke down in the Canyon," he replied.

"I trust you didn't give her anything else" said Gypsy Lee sarcastically. "Or maybe she gave you something."

"Oh no," blurted Ethan. "I just gave her a ride into town to Freddy's garage."

"Aha," thought Paula Jean. "So that's the way it is. These two are love birds. She isn't a bad looking gal, either."

"Now Ethan, let's be honest here. You certainly gave me more than a desperate ride!"

Virtually all the clientele in the café choked or snickered on that one. Ethan felt himself turning red. Gypsy Lee glared at him. Patrons within earshot continued to laugh, some out loud. Paula Jean hesitated a moment for effect, then added "You gave me some expert advice." Patrons had to turn their heads away and one covered his face with his coat. Gypsy Lee's glare intensified and Ethan turned redder. Paula Jean looked at Gypsy Lee and decided she had gone far enough. *One more remark and she's going to pour hot coffee all over him, and maybe over me,* she thought.

"He saved me from an assault when my car broke down in the Canyon. He was a perfect gentleman. That is the only contact we have had." A visible change came over Gypsy Lee that was noticed by Ethan, Paula Jean and most of the clients, most of whom also smiled, most of all though, the two women. Paula Jean smiled again at Gypsy Lee as Gypsy Lee poured more coffee into Paula Jean's cup.

"Colonel, I'd like to introduce a friend of mine to you."

"Certainly, Captain Gates, come on in. What's new in Cody?"

Ethan laid down his pen, stood, and returned Captain Gate's salute, shook Gate's right hand, motioning with his left hand to two chairs for his guests.

"This is Bob Allen, the man you are looking for, Sir." Bradley shook Allen's hand.

"May I offer you gentlemen some coffee?"

"No Thank you Sir" came from both men.

"Well, Mr. Allen, what can you do for our cause?"

"Well Sir, I am a communications-computer kind of guy. I have a B.S. in computer engineering from Florida State, an M.S. from the University of Texas and started on a Ph.D. at U.C.L.A. I saw the handwriting on the wall in southern California and decided to get out of there. I went to work for Digital Works Laboratories in Dallas for a year. There I worked on earthbound weapons-satellite interfacing under a government contract with our company. We were also working on networking the satellites so they could better communicate one with another and assume control of enemy computer and communications systems any place on earth. One of the other branches was working on focusing an electromagnetic pulse as a very narrow beam to burn out enemy computers and communications centers. Their goal is to have a footprint on earth of a mere twenty meters across that would fry everything while being very specific. That might be something of a problem for us on the battlefield."

"Why did you leave them, Mr. Allen, or did you?"

"Sir, without getting too personal, it was because my wife left me for my boss. I don't want to go any farther down that road. Anyway, I decided to just get out of the area. It too, was becoming too Hispanic. I took $3000 out of our bank account, rented a small trailer, threw personal stuff that was important to me in it and started driving. I was in Cody when I ran out of money. The computer store there had a help wanted sign in the window. That was eighteen months ago. I have been in Cody ever since. Our divorce was finalized about a year ago. I won't go back where there is a Hispanic majority."

"How does the Hispanic influence impact on your life, Mr. Allen?"

"I am a native Anglo Floridian. My ex wife is from Venezuela, came here as a five year old, and my boss was from

Brazil. Did you know that the population of Venezuelan immigrants into the Miami area went from around 5,000 in 1985 to over 200,000 in thirty years? Add to that the Colombians, Panamanians, Guatemalans, Peruvians on top of the Cubans who have been there for over sixty years, and the whole of south Florida is now Hispanic, essentially Caribbean and northern South America. I was by far and away a minority in my native state. The Black Americans have been driven out. California is lost and Texas isn't far behind. Anyway, both my ex-wife and former boss are devout Catholics while I am an agnostic. I wanted just one or two kids, but she wanted a dozen right now. We married as soon as we had our bachelor's degrees and she wanted to start a family right then. I wanted to concentrate on my education. She was a history major. They think differently than I do."

Bradley pondered for a moment, and then asked "Would you wait outside for a few minutes, Mr. Allen?

"Certainly, Sir," and Bob Allen stepped out of the office, closing the door behind him.

"I'm Sergeant Major Michael Killian, Mr. Allen. May I get you a coffee? It might be a while. The Colonel and the Captain have a number of things to discuss."

"Thank you, Sergeant, cream and sugar if you have them, if not, black is fine. I know nothing of the Army, or weapons or any of that gung-ho stuff. I suppose I can learn, but I'm not sure I'm up to the heavy duty stuff. I'm a bit overweight and a bit sedentary."

"Nobody knows how this thing will all turn out, Mr. Allen. Each of us though, can make a contribution in the best way we know how. I would predict Sir that if we go hot it would behoove us all to know the three Army wide basics of shoot, move and communicate. I would suggest Mr. Allen that you start jogging, doing pushups and sit-ups. These three exercises will get you in better shape than most people realize." SGM

Killian handed him the coffee. "Do you have an area of expertise, Mr. Allen?"

"I'm sort of a communications and computers guy. I am a computer engineer and have worked with both hardware and software." Allen saw Bradley on the phone. Twenty minutes later Captain Gates stood up and asked Allen to step back into Bradley's office who motioned for him to sit.

"Mr. Allen, if you check out as legitimate, I'll give you a field commission as a Second Lieutenant. We most certainly need your talents. C4I, command, control, communications, computers and intelligence is our most desperate need. If you check out, I'll send you to higher headquarters to address system wide requirements. How does that suit you?"

Bob Allen smiled, "That suits me fine, Colonel, just fine."

"Sergeant Major Killian, get this man the basic issue of uniforms. Captain Gates will schedule him for the weapons orientation. Until then, Mr. Allen, you will be under Captain Gate's wing. If all goes well, I'll get back to Captain Gates about you. In the meantime, start exercising, especially running, pushups and lifting weights. Work on your legs, especially your legs. We might all have to do some brush busting in the mountains before this is over. Thank you for coming in. We most certainly need you." Bradley stood up and shook hands with Allen as Captain Gates saluted. Bradley returned the salute and said, "Thanks Captain, you done good."

Bradley placed a scrambled, secure voice call to General McIntire. "Can we surreptitiously check this guy out General? It would be better if the feds don't know we have him as an asset?"

"I agree, Colonel, I'll put some people on it and get back to you. Tell him nothing until authorized. Will pay a staff visit in two weeks. In the meantime, what have you done with him?"

"I issued him uniforms and sent him home with Captain Gates."

Five days later, General McIntire called Bradley. "We did a background check through devious means on your Commo Kid. He's quite a find. Get him up to Billings so we can see what he can do for the big picture."

"General, you just gave him his military nickname, the Commo Kid."

Bradley called Captain Gates. "Bradley here. Put two of your best men as body guards on the Commo Kid and get him to Billings ASAP. He is to report to General McIntire in the federal building."

Lieutenant Allen drove his own car with a body guard sitting next to him. Captain Gates put a bodyguard in a military vehicle in both front and behind Allen's car. Allen entered the federal building, escorted by two soldiers. One guard stayed outside to watch the vehicles while two escorted Allen inside. They waited outside the office of Lieutenant General (LTG) Gordon Wheaton. The general's secretary showed Allen directly into the general's office.

Allen saluted as he thought he was supposed to, and the general smiled and saluted back. "Grab a chair there, Lieutenant." The three bodyguards had made sure that Allen's uniform was correct in every detail. As Allen turned around to sit, he noticed an individual sitting in the corner of the room.

"Three years ago during a national governors meeting the governors of Montana, Wyoming, Idaho, North and South Dakota, along with their Adjutants General, began discussions at a secret meeting they held separately from all others. One Governor has since been voted out of office and replaced. The new governor is in general agreement however, with the position of his predecessor. We agreed that secure communications among ourselves was critical. Therefore we agreed to develop a secure, independent, clandestine, that is, secret from the federal government, communications system. We covertly identified specific individuals within our respective university faculties and commercial laboratories which agreed with us, to develop such a system. These professors have been working on individual components of the system ever since. They periodically meet to insure all the parts fit together. The center of this work is here in Billings. Much of it is already complete, in particular, the fax and voice mail aspects. Some work still remains to be done. You, henceforth code named the Commo Kid, will join that team full time. Some of the work is being surreptitiously done at the university here in Billings, but some is also being researched at the Beeson Physics Laboratory, also here in Billings. That is where you will be. The hardware equipment is being made at Beeson Labs. The gentleman you noticed behind you is the Director of Beeson Physics, Dr. John Douglas. He will explain further."

"How do you do Lieutenant Allen. I'll be brief and relatively specific. Your job will be part of a team that is trying to tap into digital signals from satellites, unmanned aerial vehicles and other sources that the federal government's forces are using and relay them to our brigade commanders on the ground. In effect, we want you to inform our commanders of exactly what the enemy is seeing and communicating at the tactical, as well as the strategic level. We have learned that we can secretly transmit digital signals over fiberoptic cables already in place without the communications companies knowing of their use. We can hide the signals in routine transmissions. This obviously reduces the requirement of radio-electronic emissions for our commanders. We have several super computers that scramble the digital codes on a random basis before sending them, to have them unscrambled on the other end. The codes are changed hourly by the computers so that unscrambling them in a timely manner is virtually impossible. The team is composed of engineers from Montana State, University of Montana, University of Wyoming and several other sources but progress has been slow. We work in civilian clothes and inside our laboratory building. The ironic thing is that your salary will be paid by a federal grant with the funds only slightly diverted from a tangentially associated research program. You will be given a pseudonym to disguise your true identity. We have an apartment waiting for you. Our security is extremely tight as you would suspect. We will do a retinal scan, DNA spread, voice and fingerprints on you today. We need this capability and we need it right now if we are to defend our possibly new country."

Paula Jean sat her coffee cup down. Gypsy Lee hovered over her, coffee pot in hand.

"Would you like another refill? Business must be slow tonight. It is only 20:30 on a Saturday night and here you are, down two cups of coffee and thirty minutes on the bar stool."

Paula Jean kind of smiled. "Business isn't bad, but I am kind of tired. No one has the money anymore for an all nighter. Thirty minutes gets me a hundred and fifty bucks, and that's about the limit around in this town. I haven't had many all nighters at $500. Still, it is better here than in Thermopolis. Too many johns down there want special treatment without paying for it. No, I guess I will call it a night unless someone is waiting for me. I left a note on the door, 'Back in thirty minutes.' These citizen-soldiers around here aren't very free with their money. It is not like it used to be with the Air Force troopies coming off of Nellis Air Force Base outside of Vegas."

"I trust that Ethan is not a customer of yours?"

"Oh goodness no Gypsy Lee, I would turn him down even if he tried. I don't want hot coffee poured on my head. That's not the way to make a friend, stealing another gal's guy, even for thirty minutes. He is an awfully nice guy though. I think he is the marrying kind, would like to be more of a family guy. He did tell me was divorced though, but that is all I know." Paula Jean stood up and pulled on her coat.

"Well, take care of yourself. I hope you have another customer if you want one."

Paula Jean waved a good-bye as she went through the door. She walked around the corner headed for her upstairs apartment via the back stairs just past the alley. Suddenly she was seized from behind. Two arms circled her, pinning her arms to her side. She raised her right foot and slammed her three inch spike heel into the metatarsals of her attacker's right foot. He screamed. She seized the thumb of his top hand that was grasping her and bent it outward with a vicious jerk that dislocated it. She spun and drove her left elbow into her attacker's left temple. She reached down and grabbed her attacker's right pants cuff just above the injured foot and pulled his leg up to her crotch. She held his ankle with her left hand and supported it on her thigh while she drove the palm of her right hand down on to the side of his patella, the kneecap, dislocating it when a tremendous blow hit her in the ribs. She never saw it coming. Another vicious blow struck her just below her right eye sending her into a mostly unconscious state. A third blow, a left, struck her in the solar plexus as another pair of arms seized her to hold her up. The man in front ripped open her coat, then seized her sweater on both sides of her neck and ripped it down over her shoulders. He did the same with her bra straps exposing her breasts. Through a haze she could see a brown skinned man grinning at her. He bent down to her waist, seizing her pants and panties, pulling them down to her ankles. She fell backwards as the arms holding her up suddenly disappeared. The man in front who ripped down her clothes, Hernando Garza looked up with a surprised look just as the truncheon came down on his head along side of his ear. He sank to his knees as another blow came down, then a third. He collapsed in a heap unconscious. He joined his brother who had been holding her up from behind in the state of unconsciousness. Somebody pulled Paula Jean to her feet and leaned her over his back as he pulled up her panties and slacks. He then picked her up and carried her to his car. He managed to open the door and set her in the passenger seat. He drove her to the county hospital emergency room. He told the nurse attending she was physically attacked, beaten but not raped. After an initial exam concentrating on her head, the attending resident ordered radiographs of head, neck and thorax. Thirty minutes he came out and spoke with her rescuer.

"Bob, she has a fractured infraorbital, that is the malar or cheekbone, two broken ribs and a mild concussion. I am afraid that fractured cheekbone is going to require a pretty good plastic surgeon for reconstruction. I don't think anyone around here has that kind of talent. She'll have to go to Billings for it. We're going to hold her at least overnight for observation. Depending upon what she is like in the morning, we'll make a decision about releasing her. She's going to be awfully sore. We've taped her ribs pretty tight so she doesn't puncture a lung. She is in a lot of pain, but I have kept her medications light because of potential head injury. We don't want to suppress the respiratory or cardiac centers or anything like that. What's your relation to her anyway, I can't believe are you responsible for this. Who pays the bill here, anyway? The plastic surgeon won't be cheap either. Since you aren't in uniform, I presume you are off duty?"

"I just happened along as three guys jumped her. I left them in an alley back there. I'll tend to them in a while. I know who they are and where to find them. As to who pays, we will have to work on that. Hell, I never really met the woman. You know how little us cops make, so don't count on me."

Undersheriff Robert Walker turned around to see two Garza brothers carrying the third one in between them. The carried one was dragging a leg. One of the others had blood running from his ear and scalp above his ear. They eyed the Undersheriff as he eyed them. They sat their brother in a chair who was softly moaning. Walker walked up to them.

"We're gonna get you, Walker. You're a dead man. You just ain't quit breathing, that's all."

Walker smiled. "You boys have attempted your last rape. You aren't going to get me. I'm going to kill you. If I see you anytime, anywhere after 09:00 hours tomorrow, I am going to kill you where you stand. I don't care if it is in church, in front of the courthouse, with your wife and kids or wherever. You are dead. You have terrified the people in this town too long. You've threatened anyone who might testify against you, especially your own kind. It's time for a little vigilante action. Get out of town tonight or die. I'll be hunting you." With that, Deputy Walker walked out the emergency room door.

Robert Walker went home, took a shower, and dressed in an all black uniform. He made his bed stuffed with pillows so that it resembled him sleeping. He left the night light on the bathroom which provided just a glimmer of light to produce an outline of a supposedly sleeping figure. He put on a pot of coffee and then went outside to his garage. He opened the walk-in door and set up a lawn plastic green lawn chair. He sprayed the door hinges with WD-40 so that they would not squeak. He went back to the house, put on his duty belt with a Beretta 96 in the holster, an ankle holster with a J-frame Smith and Wesson .38 Special in it. He took a short barreled Remington 870 pump shotgun and a double barreled coach gun, both in twelve gauge out of his gun safe. He loaded both with BB shotshells. When his coffee was done, he poured it into a thermos, took the shotguns and thermos outside, came back in for a small jar of half and half and a large insulated coffee mug. He turned out the lights, smeared some face black on his face, put on a light leather jacket and hat, retired to the garage, and sat down to wait with his coffee and shotgun across his lap. He was dozing off when he heard a pickup truck approaching though the alley startling him awake. He didn't see any indication of headlights. The engine was turned off and two truck doors carefully closed. Two minutes later a shadow cast by the moonlight crossed the path in front of the garage door. Carefully leaning forward, he recognized the six foot four inch two hundred and eighty pound figure of Hernando Garza. His head was wrapped in bandages. Two steps behind Hernando was Felipe, only slightly smaller at six feet and two hundred and fifty pounds. Felipe was carrying some kind of long gun while Hernando had a baseball bat. Walker quietly eased the door open a few more inches, knelt on the floor with one knee and pointed the coach gun at them. Both froze, hearing a slight squeaking sound of the leather jacket as Walker knelt. He didn't say anything. Felipe turned to look at him; all Felipe saw was the bright orange flame from the muzzle as the blast caught him full in the chest. One second later the second barrel caught Hernando full in the face. Robert leaned the double barreled shotgun just inside the door and picked up the pump. As Walker approached the two still writhing bodies, lights came on at the neighbors' houses on both sides of his. A head appeared out an opening back door.

"Bob, we heard shots. Is that you? Are you OK?"

"I'm fine, thanks John. Go ahead and go to bed. Just took care of a couple of rats, that's all. Just turn out the lights and go back to sleep. Everything's OK."

"Well, Janice is just hanging up the phone from calling your office. I expect help will be here real soon." John turned out the light and closed his door, as did the neighbor on the other side. Walker picked up the shotgun from Felipe's hands and looked into the goo that was Hernando's face. Walker walked around the front of his house; a squad SUV with flashing lights appeared within three minutes. Deputy Sheriff

Eyson climbed out and greeted Walker, eyeing him in his all-black ninja suit. "What's up, Bob?"

"I just eliminated a couple of ambushing rats in my backyard. Two of the Garza brothers, Hernando and Felipe. I had a run-in with them a couple of hours ago when they attempted another rape."

"Are they dead?"

"I think so, although I didn't bother to check real close. They each took a twelve gauge load of BBs at close range. They're too big for us to lift. I would just as soon this go no farther if I can figure out how to get them out to the landfill. I can roll them in a couple of tarps and tape them shut, but picking them up would take a squad of us."

"Hell, let's get them in the tarps. I can have a fork lift over here by the time we can do that. I'll call my brother who works over at the lumber yard and have one here in thirty minutes. It's about time something nasty happened to the Garzas. You can tell me about it as we roll 'em up!"

After they rolled the bodies into the tarps, Walker pulled the Garza's pickup forward, Brother Eyson picked up the bodies with the forklift ,dumped them into the truck, and Deputy Eyson drove it off to the landfill while Walker followed in his pickup. They went through the unlocked gate and somehow managed to drag the bodies off the bed of the truck and onto the ground in front of the bulldozer that would bury them in the morning, no questions asked. They left the pickup off the edge of the BumGarrs parking lot where the security cameras wouldn't film them, on the edge of town in the predawn light after they wiped it down, just in case somebody wanted to try and make a case. Undersheriff Walker went home and to bed. He slept a long, deep, peaceful sleep.

That afternoon Bob Walker rose, made a breakfast of ham, eggs, toast, coffee, juice and milk. Then he drove to the hospital to visit Paula Jean.

"Are you my Sir Galahad," asked Paula Jean looking through filmy eyes from her hospital bed.

"I suppose, although since I carry a badge and a gun it's a little more in the line of duty than being a paladin. By the way, you were pretty good one on one. You didn't have a problem until the other two jumped in on you."

"Who were they and what will happen to them?"

"They were the Garza brothers. One of them just left here in a cast and a wheel chair. He's the one you worked over. Let's just say his two bigger brothers have left town. I don't believe we'll ever see them again. They have terrorized this town for year and now their reign is over. I don't think I need to say any more."

"I'm sorry but my face hurts and I am awfully sleepy."

"You're heavily sedated. Your cheekbone was smashed. You will require plastic surgery. I've asked the doc to make the arrangements with a good plastic surgeon he knows in Billings who can restore your face to its former beauty. You need surgery soon before the scar tissue builds and complicates the surgery but after chances of further hemorrhage are reduced. I've taken a couple of days off, so tomorrow I drive you to Billings. You're scheduled for surgery Tuesday. If all goes according to plan, you will be out of the hospital Thursday. I'll bring you home then."

"Why are you doing this? You've never been one of my Johns, at least not that I remember."

Walker smiled. "Everybody needs a friend, and since I rescued you, you're stuck with me. I neither expect nor want any favors or freebies or anything else in return. I was planning on a shopping trip to Billings anyway. You can put the seat back in the pickup and sleep enroute. I'll pick you up at 10:00 hours tomorrow. I have your apartment key. I'll pack a bag for you with what a bachelor thinks a gal might need."

"Are all you Wyoming cowboys so gallant?"

Walker smiled. "Well, a lot of us do think we should help a girl when she is in trouble. Go to sleep. I'll see you at 10:00 hours tomorrow."

Senator Kennely died at 00:30 hours on the 12th of April. President Newkirk was told the news as he sat down to his breakfast. By the time he was finished, it dawned upon him that his guiding light was gone. He was in deep strategic trouble and he knew it. Now he was truly on his own. He suddenly realized that Kennely had deliberately prevented the development of an alternative to himself as the power behind the Presidency. Newkirk wondered if one of Kennely's staff would step forward and try to fill Kennely's shoes. No he decided, a Senate staffer might help, but did not have the appropriate web of authority. He needed another Senator, or at least a very senior Congressman. Perhaps Lippsitz of New York would do it. *"Lippsitz, Kennely and I all think alike,"* he thought. For a second he considered Naomi Campbell, but he immediately dismissed her. She might have, probably did have, enough political ambition to challenge him farther down the road. He knew many despised him and none trusted him behind the façade of party unity, but he had no idea of the depth of that despise. Could the façade of party unity protect him? He didn't know.

"ATTENTION! General Officer on Deck!" called out Sergeant Major Killian. The SGM and two staff sergeants stood at rigid attention. The General returned their salutes and walked into Colonel Bradley's office.

"Welcome, General," said Bradley as he saluted, standing at attention behind his desk. "Glad to see you. Coffee?"

"No thanks, Colonel, I'll be brief and blunt. I am not traveling as much these days with the Predator drones flying about. I wanted a face to face to see how you are progressing with your training mission, what your problems are."

"It is about what I expected General, perhaps a bit better but not as well as I would like. Two major problems are that many do not believe it will develop into a hot war, and secondly, for the personnel trying to balance full time jobs, family and train on weekends and evenings. I have initiated training classes two evenings a week, but only half or less of the personnel show up at each class. This is universal throughout the command, in all companies. They have no sense of urgency. It is a mindset problem. Few of my officers and NCOs have any real combat experience. This is compounded by lack of resources, especially time and ammunition.

I have directed the farmers in the Basin to comply with the Governor's direction to voluntarily hold as much wheat, oats, barley and corn on the farm in storage as possible. I am thinking of human consumption, rather than livestock feed. Some have complied, some have not. I lack personnel to block all routes into the Basin 24/7, so I have concentrated on the most likely avenues and hours of approach. The Sheriff's departments are lending a huge hand. Token forces will have to block and hold lesser routes until a mobile reinforcing force can provide relief. A combined air and ground assault supported by ground attack aircraft would be a nightmare. If federal forces can breach an entry and hold it open, then the mission of guerilla warfare and training our retreating forces in the arts of guerilla warfare becomes a reality.

The train the trainer concept really is a brain fart General, good in theory but a disaster in practice when the first tier of trainers lack experience. The militia in particular is lacking in training although many are earnest. Guerilla warfare, urban and rural, is an entirely different breed of cat. It is surprising how many women and teenagers have joined the militia. They take it more seriously than do their husbands and fathers. Perhaps they realize they might be fighting for their homes and loved ones. Wars have traditionally been fought by teenage young men and this war will be no exception."

"That's about what I expected, Colonel. The other units are experiencing the same things. The Stryker Brigades are short on fuel, spare parts and ammunition. Our air assets and anti-air assets are limited. They could hurt us with a lot of Predator III Unmanned Aerial Vehicles.

Concentrate more on training the trainers for guerilla warfare using improvised explosive devices, booby traps, intelligence gathering, networks for intelligence, weapons caches, safe houses and who would be, what did you call them, a Tory or unionist, or something? Anyway, identify those who support or sympathize with remaining in the union. Lincoln had slavery as an emotional issue to rally support for the Civil War. We lacked such an emotional cause until Newkirk tried to withhold vaccine. When he reversed himself, we kind of lost that fervor. I almost hate to admit it, but racism and prejudice is as close as we can get to an emotional raison d'etre. It has to be a cultural thing. We are fighting for our culture, our northern European heritage. That's the way it is. It is a cultural war going hot.

Our military chain of command is now fully established and in effect. Each state's former adjutant General is now a Major General. The Commander of the Army of the Territory of Missouri is a Lieutenant General, headquartered in Billings. He commands all forces. Air National Guard units are under a Major General on his staff who his Number Two. Air National Guard units are under 0-3s to 0-6s locally, reporting to the Air Guard Major General. Militia forces are under the local commanders of the Army of the Territory of Missouri."

"Mr. Walker? I'm Dr. Starrett, the surgeon. It has been a long four hours. That blow really shattered Ms. Darnell's cheekbone. Rather than use wire or pins, I glued the bones back together, at least most of them. There were a number of very small fragments I could not fit back in very well, those I removed. By using glue, there won't be any metal that might cause problems later on. The biggest potential problem is the callous itself. That is the connective tissue that surrounds the bone fragments, holds them together, and ultimately replaces and heals the bone into a solid unit again. Now, because of its location, hopefully she won't subject that area to any more trauma. She will have to be very careful with it. It will take a minimum of three months for adequate callous formation to hold the pieces steadily in place. After that, bone replacement will begin. It will take at least a year, perhaps longer before it is back to normal. She certainly is a beautiful woman. I noticed that she is not your wife, but apparently you are her mate or at least taking responsibility for her. She needs to be very, very careful with her face. In about eighteen months you will never be able to discern the surgery, provided she doesn't injure it again in any way. Can you see to it that that doesn't occur?"

"Yes, Doctor, that might take some doing, but I think I can make the appropriate arrangements to see that she is very careful with it. Frankly, I don't know how she will pay for this. I am only a deputy sheriff and don't make enough money to buy a dog house. Nevertheless, I'll see what arrangements can be made both to pay the bills and avoid re-injury. When can I see her?"

"She is still under heavy sedation. She will be in a lot of pain for a while. I don't want her to be heavily sedated after today. She'll be fully awake in about four hours, but then she will crash, real hard from the anesthetic. You can see her in about those four hours. We'll keep her here for observation tonight of course and she can go home tomorrow."

Robert Walker helped a shaky Paula Jean from the wheelchair into his SUV. After he fastened her seatbelt, he leaned the seat all the way back so she was in a supine position. He thanked the staff that wheeled her out and drove off. He didn't say much for the first hour or two. "Feel hungry? I am. We'll stop in Lovell for lunch. Are you OK to sit up and eat in a restaurant?"

"I could drink more than I could eat. Something cold, maybe a milk shake; I really don't feel much like a heavy meal."

"Dr. Starrett gave me the low down, Paula Jean. You really can't go back to practicing your profession until your face is completely healed. That will take a year, maybe more, like eighteen months. So, you need to be thinking about what you are going go do in the interim, or maybe permanently. I will make you an offer, and I won't be offended if you refuse it. We really don't know each other. I have a two bedroom bungalow. I suggest you move in and take the second bedroom. They are pretty small, both the room and the house but it is warm and comfortable. I'm not proposing that we become lovers or anything like that, but more on the order of roommates. I keep really odd hours, but it would be nice to have some companionship on occasion. I don't know what or how much money you have saved, or investments or whatever, but no doubt the medical bills will wipe out your savings. For a while anyway, weeks to months, while that callous forms, you won't have any means of earning income. Now, as for your share of the rent, you can earn it by keeping house as best you are able. I'll try not to be as slovenly as I am that will make it easier on you. I learned not to be a complete pig in the Marine Corps. I'll do my own laundry. That is not part of the offer. Can you cook? I am a modest chef, but cooking for one is no fun. If you return to your old apartment, some of your clients are going to come looking for you. That will never do. You don't need even the slightest jar to your face. No need for an immediate answer. Think about it for a while. If you say yes, though, I will empty your apartment and bring your things over to my house. Right now, let's get some chow."

"Colonel, what we gonna do? People are leavin! I mean they are leavin' the city. The girls are breaking out of the houses. The Brothers are havin' a hard time with them. That D'Arcy thing really scared a lots of folks. They don't want to deal with us Brothers any more. Drug sales are way down. Three Brothers selling' on the corners got shot and robbed just this week. White folks aren't buyin' like they did just a few months ago. They're leavin' too, goin' north. Business is goin' bad real quick."

Toussaint already knew what he was going to do. He had known for almost a year. He laid out his strategy several years ago. Only the time table was questioned, and now accelerated. Five years ago he bought a sugar cane plantation in Jamaica. He had the villa renovated such that it appeared to be and in actuality was a fortress. It had a small private airstrip. That was one factor that Toussaint very much liked. It would take a coordinated attack by a trained infantry company to overwhelm it. Not only was his agricultural manager growing a thousand acres of sugar cane, he had two hundred head of cattle, a small sugar mill and one hundred acres of well maintained marijuana. High in the active ingredient, it provided some of the finest hashish for his drug trade. It was smuggled into the USA in bags of brown sugar. Toussaint had been sending two hundred thousand dollars a month alternating between three different banks. One bank was in Jamaica, another in the Cayman Islands, and a third in Costa Rica. He figured that would cover all contingencies for revolution, invasion, military coup or sudden cooperation with the United States for extradition. The small executive jet rental corporation appreciated Toussaint's business and generosity very much. He paid them well for their silence, so much so, that no one saw anything when the occasional bound, gagged and blind folded girl or young woman was secreted from his limousine into the corporate jet while it was still in the hanger for a flight to Jamaica. The Jamaican politicians and drug purveyors paid handsomely for white slaves of exceptional beauty. Others were merely caged in cells in his several Jamaican brothels for the less well to do.

Toussaint visited his Jamaican holdings several times a year. His agricultural manager and his chief security officer were well paid to warily spy on each other. Abnormalities arose his third year of ownership when the agricultural manager reported an unusually poor hashish crop and sugar crop in the same season. When Toussaint compared prices and markets and crops from other island plantations he personally took charge. Toussaint threw a party for his managers aboard his modest but private yacht he used as a deep sea fishing boat. The agricultural manager found himself tied across the chairs on the seating deck well. Toussaint personally eviscerated him while alive and then chopped him into chum for shark bait. The lesson was not lost on the deputy agricultural manager who suddenly found himself promoted to the newly vacant position as agricultural manager. So it was Toussaint's game plan to visit his Jamaican holdings in the very near future never to return. He would simply tell the Jamaican Snake he would assume command in his absence. The Snake was the only lieutenant he had that was ruthless enough to hold the organization together, at least until someone with better brains would displace him with a bullet in the back of the head.

CHAPTER 16

"SON, WOULD YOU MIND WEEDING THE GARDEN FOR ME AND PICKING THE RIPE TOMATOES AND SQUASH THIS AFTERNOON? The potatoes have entirely too many weeds around them. I want to run a few errands in town and do a little shopping."

"Not at all, Dad, I'll be happy to. You take your time and enjoy the afternoon. We won't have many more warm sunny fall days like this one. Take your time and have coffee with your friends at the café. I'll have the garden done before you get back."

Ethan stood and stretched as he picked up the sack of squash and one of tomatoes he had just picked. He peered into the cornfield across the road as some sixth sense kicked in. The bullet creased Ethan's ribs as it passed between his arm and torso a millisecond before he heard the crack of the rifle. The next one passed through one inch of muscle on the lateral side of his thigh as he dove to the ground and rolled. *"Two rounds in three seconds from a semi-automatic rifle," he thought, not bad."* Ethan lay motionless except for his eyes. He carefully scanned the cornfield across the road. *"They can't be in very deep or the blowing corn leaves would be too obscuring. The shooter is probably kneeling or prone, as the corn is over six feet high. I'm too far from cover to make a run for it. If I reach for my .45, he'll know I am still alive. It would be a long shot anyway. I have limited rounds in the magazine; he has many more. I'll have to play possum. Let's hope the shooter isn't taking careful aim to pump out a few more rounds. If he does, I'm dead.*

If he doesn't, he's a good shot but an amateur. Never go near your victim until you are sure he is dead." Ethan immediately recognized the rifle as the ubiquitous AK-47 in classic 7.62x39 by the sound. Almost every male over fifteen years of age in Africa had one.

Ethan squinted, watching for movement. He was used to watching and waiting. It was an old game he played many times. Many violent men fell to him and his platoon in Africa through patience. After ten minutes he was about to move. The muscles of his wounded leg were increasing in fasciculation. Ethan knew he was oozing blood but not enough to incur shock. He had learned to mentally block the pain and concentrate on the enemy. He was about to stand when he saw movement. The shooter, a Mexican, stood fifteen feet deep in the cornfield. He grinned, stood for a minute to see if he could observe any movement from Ethan and turned to disappear in the corn. Ethan made note of his dress and size even though he could not distinguish the facial features because of the distance. After a few more minutes he was about to move again when an old Ford pickup drove slowly in front of the house and stopped. The driver also was a Mexican. The shooter emerged from the cornfield as the pickup turned around. Ethan took greater note of the jacket, ball cap and general dress of the shooter who climbed into the truck. The truck slowly drove off so as not to attract any attention. Ethan stood and tied a handkerchief around his wounded leg. He limped into the house and removed his Springfield Armory M1A rifle from the safe, inserted a ten round magazine and took a loaded twenty round magazine from the shelf. He limped to his truck and drove himself to the hospital where his wounds were flushed, cleaned and dressed.

"Staff, I want you to keep this assassination attempt quiet. No one is to know I am wounded. It would only provoke another attempt. I trust I can count on all of you. You can send me a bill if you like."

"There's no charge on this one, Colonel. I'll see to it that the records here are shredded. It never happened. Just don't make a habit of this. The next one could be more serious."

Ethan decided to drive into town to pick up Gypsy Lee in spite of his leg which was growing stiffer by the hour. Juan Cartagena and his friend walked into the café laughing. The smile on Juan Cartagena's face abruptly changed as his mouth dropped open. He saw Ethan Bradley sitting in the back corner booth, coffee cup in hand, looking directly at him. He muttered something in Spanish to his compadre who was dressed identically to the man who shot him from the cornfield. They abruptly turned to leave. The man hesitated and looked at Bradley aghast, but Cartagena grabbed him by the sleeve and pulled him towards the door. Ethan pulled on his hat and jacket as he headed for the back door. He pulled his .45 automatic from underneath his vest and headed down the alley for the street. At the same time the suspect threw open the café door, took four steps in and pointed an AK-47 at the empty booth Ethan had vacated. All eyes in the café were on him when suddenly everyone dove to the floor. Gypsy Lee ducked behind the counter still holding a coffee pot. Gonzalez hurriedly looked around then dashed back out the front door. Juan Cartagena was waiting in the pickup truck fifty feet down the street, double parked. Ethan rounded the corner and recognized Cartagena in the fading evening light. Gonzalez was dashing for the truck when he saw Ethan's head peering around the corner, with two arms stretched out holding the .45 in a two handed stance, pointed directly at him. He stopped midstride to bring the rifle up to his shoulder pointing it in Ethan's direction. Ethan fired. Gonzalez staggered two steps backward as Ethan's bullet penetrated his chest, smashing his sternum. A surprised look appeared on Gonzalez's face as Ethan fired again, another mid center hit into the chest. Cartagena started to pull away. Ethan pivoted as best he could and fired at the pickup. The bullet passed through the open window on the passenger's side and smashed into the windshield. The round nosed 230 grain slug created a tremendous circle of cracked glass that produced a hundred small flying glass shards but did not penetrate it. Instead, it ricocheted off the windshield, hit the doorpost where it expended its remaining energy and fell on the dashboard. Cartagena had 15-20 small cuts on his hands and face from the flying glass shards. Ethan couldn't move into the street fast enough for a second shot.

Gypsy Lee dashed to the front window of the café just in time to see Ethan's two slugs slam into Gonzalez, pushing him against a parked car. He slid down the side of the car, mouth open, eyes in a lifeless stare. She heard but didn't see Ethan shoot at the pickup. She flew out the door as Ethan was trying to follow the pickup down the sights of his .45, hoping for a clear shot that never came. As the pickup disappeared down the street, Ethan took a swift 180 degree sweep from right to left, then a slow sweep back around the area he had just swept, taking in every detail. When he saw Gypsy Lee frozen there watching him he straightened up and smiled.He holstered his.45 as he walked with a significant limp towards her. She grabbed him, hugged him and he laughed. "Hell, they missed again; just a bunch of amateurs." She lifted her head off his shoulder and socked him squarely on the jaw, hard enough to stagger him.

"They might have killed you! Don't you ever do that again." Ethan with a surprised stare thought to himself *"Hell, what am I supposed to do? It's better to kill the bastards at every opportunity before they kill me!"* He held his jaw and smiled but didn't say anything as she hugged him against herself. The cafe's patrons slowly came out to survey the scene, but especially to see the dead Mexican. Early the next morning a sheriff's deputy found the abandoned pickup parked just off the highway on a two track lane. It was wiped clean of fingerprints. Bleach had been poured on spots of blood on the seat and floor in an attempt to deny DNA sampling. The dead shooter had a little less than one thousand dollars in his pockets but no identity. His fingerprints were taken and the body placed in the hospital morgue.

"He recognized me," said Juan Cartagena, on the verge of shouting. "He must be immediately killed." He muttered some profanity in Spanish under his breath. "Others must be killed too. It is time."

An all points bulletin went through the state for the arrest of Juan Cartagena. Knowing he could never return to his home, Cartagena immediately went to the old farm buildings on the edge of the Indian Reservation that one of his lieutenant's had rented for such an emergency. Cartagena drove the truck into the barn and closed the doors. Buried beneath the stalls in the barn were the weapons caches, rifles and ammunition in one each, grenades in another, explosives in a fourth.

Around Cartagena's basement table in the otherwise abandoned farmhouse with blacked out windows sat deputy sheriff Juan "John" Castro and city police officer Fernando "Freddy" Montoya of Worland. Both were second generation Americans whose parents moved together from the Los Angeles barrio when they were teenagers. Their families wanted to remove them from the gangs, whose influence was extremely violent. Both boys were half coerced into joining the Zapata Warriors when they were ten. By the time they were twelve they were fully inculcated into the philosophy and doctrine of the gang. At fourteen, Montoya and Castro raped a fourteen year old virginal eighth grade girl classmate. They threatened to slash her face with a razor and castrate her eleven year old brother if she told. They threatened her with gang rape by their gang. She never said a word of the assault. Both sets of parent had full time jobs. In addition, both of their fathers had part time jobs in the evenings and on weekends after completing their day jobs. Both mothers tried to manage their full time jobs and homemaking with their children. For the most part, they were successful. Freddy's and John's older siblings were more studious, determined to succeed in a competitive segment of the Hispanic community. Their parents trusted the older children to guard and watch over their younger brothers and sisters. As the older children entered high school, they found themselves immersed in study and sports to the neglect of John and Freddy. When the parents learned of their sons gang involvement, they confronted their sons and some of the other young gang members. It was then they learned of the initiation rite of raping a virgin Anglo girl to become a full fledged "adult member" of the gang. They also learned of their participation in street robberies and car thefts by their sons. With their older children out of high school, Freddy and John about to enter high school, with no real job security for any of the parents, they decided to flee before law enforcement authorities discovered their sons' crimes. Within two weeks the parents sold their homes, most of their furniture and headed north. Both fathers had been field hands as young teenagers and so knew agriculture.

Freddy's dad had become a good construction worker with skills as a carpenter and mason. John's dad worked in a small manufacturing company as a machinist, keeping stamping mills in good working order.

When they arrived in the Basin, Freddy's father found work without difficulty. It took John's father a little longer to find employment. From then on, Freddy and John were very closely supervised by all of the parents.

Now, under the influence of Juan Cartagena who had informed the Zapata Warriors of their whereabouts, they worked menial jobs until they could join the law enforcement agencies. An older, trusted lieutenant of the Zapata Warriors even paid them a visit. He instructed them to stay out of trouble, take orders from Juan Cartagena and join the police forces. Their services would be invaluable in the future.

"The Sheriff is one who must die," said Cartagena. "He is pure gringo; also the Undersheriff. "Where does your police chief belong, Freddy?"

"I don't know. I have been a police officer for four years now and I haven't figured out where his loyalty lies. If I had to guess, I would say it is to the system. He has no racial tendencies. He is a fair man."

"Then he too, must die. Go together, in the middle of the night. Tell them you have an urgent matter for their ears only when they meet you at the door. As soon as you are in the house shoot them. Wear civilian clothes; drive one of your private cars or a stolen one. It is less conspicuous. Kill the police chief first. He will be the easier of the two."

Freddy and John did just that.

Mrs. Walston suffered from migraine headaches. She arose, put on her robe and house shoes and slipped noiselessly out of the bedroom, closing the door behind her. She made a cup of tea by the light of the stove light. She sat in her easy chair in the living room when a car pulled up and parked in front of her house. Mrs. Walston had lived in Worland all of her life. She knew almost everyone. So when Freddy and John emerged from the car and walked to the police chief's house across the street she recognized them in the moonlight. The Chief turned on the porch light after they rang the doorbell and before he opened the door, holding Mrs. Walston's attention and further illuminating Freddy and John. After less than a minute the light went out and the two men emerged. They drove off. Mrs. Walston thought it odd they were they were for so short a time. Ten minutes later, sirens and lights appeared, awakening the whole neighborhood. When she saw the gurney with the police chief's body emerge from the house she knew. The county sheriff was there five minutes later. Neighbors gathered around, some in night clothes to silently watch. Mrs. Walston dressed, told her husband to get up and get dressed, get his revolver out and do it in a hurry. She told her husband what she saw as they dressed. Her husband put on a light jacked to hide the revolver stuck in his waistband. Mrs. Walston walked to the sheriff and grasped his supper arm. She said in a low voice, "I saw John Castro and Freddy Montoya drive up here fifteen minutes ago. They went into the chief's house and were there less than a minute. They came out and drove off in a dark sedan parked in front of my house. I heard some noises, sounding like a couple of pops."

The Sheriff gave her a hard look that she returned. At that moment, Castro and Montoya appeared in uniform. The Sheriff called over Undersheriff Robert Walker and Deputy David Eyson and told them "We have an eyewitness. The shooters are Castro and Montoya. You two take Castro and I'll take down Montoya. Don't move until I do. Just get close to him for now."

The two deputies casually strolled over to Castro and Montoya who were standing together. One deputy stood in front of Castro, the other beside him. The Sheriff walked up to Montoya from behind and struck him a cross handed blow behind the left ear with his truncheon. Montoya staggered as the Sheriff grabbed him around the waist and pulled Montoya's automatic from its holster. Simultaneously the deputy alongside Castro seized his left arm while the deputy in front drew his .40 Smith & Wesson and shoved it into Castro's mid section while he placed his left hand on Castro's automatic to keep him from drawing it.

"You so much as blink I'll blow your backbone out." He pulled Castro's weapon from the holster while the Undersheriff Carlson, now holding an arm lock on Castro tapped his knees from behind with his knees, forcing Castro to kneel. The Sheriff was handcuffing Montoya and the Undersheriff Carlson did the same. Both officers were thoroughly searched and placed in the squad car. Nitrate tests on their hands proved positive. A thumb print on one cartridge cases expended at the scene proved to be Montoya's.

Ballistics matched bullets from their sidearms with those from the Police Chief's body. That was sufficient evidence for the jury to find them guilty of first degree murder three months later. Neither man espoused a motive. The jury concluded on its own that it was racially motivated.

"When I moved your household goods into my house, I noticed you had a lot of books, especially history books Paula Jean. Are you a student of history?"

"I have a B.A. in history and was working on my master's in history at UNLV, the University of Nevada at Los Vegas. I was studying the Greek language and ancient Greece, with my master's thesis on a comparison of Greece, Rome and the United States and why they fell out of first place in their world.

"Have you reached any conclusions? What can be learned from that?"

"Classical Greek civilization declined and disappeared when its citizens placed themselves at the center of interest instead of their polity. They ceased participating in governance of their polity, leaving it in the hands of professional politicians. They refused to serve in their armed forces, ignoring the concept of the citizen-soldier, hiring instead mercenaries. They placed the accumulation of personal wealth, power and associated comforts above the good of their polis, their city-state. They became detached as individuals from their security. The Hellenic civilization which replaced them after the Macedonian Alexander the Great easily succumbed to the militaristic Roman Republic. The Hellenes copied the earlier Greeks but added nothing to their Greekness; they made no contributions to what the Greeks accomplished. The multi-pluralism of the Hellenes made them easy prey for the Romans. The polis evolved into an entity that was no longer a self sufficient economic or political entity. As trade expanded, communication with the surrounding world improved and they lost their cohesion as a political entity.

Ever since World War II, especially after the collapse of the Former Soviet Union and cold war, arrogant U.S. governments felt that other peoples and cultures should emulate the U.S. concepts of ideals and governments. To their effect, we attempted to export, even impose, our system on others. Lack of respect for foreign cultures and their history generated their antagonism towards us. We should have used more gentle persuasion over a longer term rather than trying to force it on them through economic or militaristic pressures. Buying friends simply doesn't buy friends, only temporarily congenial foreign politicians and tyrants. Our politicians have regarded us as the Alexander the Great of nations and look what happened when he died."

And what was that?"

"The Hellenes were succeeded by the Romans. After they turned soft they made many of the same mistakes of the Greeks. They in turn also collapsed as an empire, just as we have done. The Hellenes were rich by any measure of their day. This wealth, this multiracial, multicultural cosmopolitan characteristic compounded its weakness a lot more than it contributed to its strengths, culturally and politically. Their emphasis on their own hereditary culture precluded any unity or commonality with the others and allegiance to the whole. Those folks were rich, fat, self aggrandizing and entirely too complacent. They couldn't see the big picture of their own society. Diplomacy becomes the best developed tool of a failing or declining state. That's us today. Time and again the barbarians at the gate find such states too lucrative and too easy to plunder. That's where we are today. Who will it be, our neighbors to the south, or those to the west, across the Pacific?"

"You amaze me, Paula Jean. Why in God's name did you become a prostitute? You are a highly intelligent as well as beautiful young woman."

"Well, I started selling my body in order to go to school. It didn't take me long to realize how lucrative it is, especially in Las Vegas. I often earned five hundred or more dollars a night, several nights a week. I still had plenty of time to study. After I got my B.A., I continued because I wanted to develop a real nest egg. I realized I couldn't continue forever, and college professors, that was my original goal, don't make a lot of money. I didn't want to keep a lot of cash on hand or in a large bank account so I invested my earnings in gold securities on the New York Stock Exchange. I was about ready to quit the trade when the feces hit the fan with this civil strife. I'm thirty years old this year. Some day I wanted to have something of a normal life on a quiet college campus. I figured it was about time to make the leap. You don't realize how well off I really am. You never asked about the hospital and physician's bill, and I let you continue to make monthly payments for the last six months. However, by agreement with Dr. Starrett and the hospital, the bill will be paid in full at the end of this month and I will reimburse you. I wanted to make sure of you first. You turned out to be what I hoped. You have never touched me, and never asked for sex. You have been the perfect roommate. There is hope for us, Roomy. What do you say to that?"

"I say great! You don't how many times I considered ripping your clothes off you and throwing you across the bed. I wanted the whole package however, not just your body. Taking advantage of you wasn't the way to do it. So, do you want a wedding or what? I don't want to leave here. This is the safest place in the USA and I don't give a damn what the town thinks of you, me or us. I'm ready to make you Mrs. Walker when you are ready."

"I'm close Robert; can you give me some time to make some decisions, such as when and where? You didn't know it, but I used to be a regular church goer. I'm not sure what the town would think of us having a church wedding. I want to feel a little more secure in this town. I doubt that many of these small town minds can ever forget that I was a whore. A lot of the more well off married men around here used my services. I am a potential embarrassment for them. What will happen here when the referendum goes into effect and when will it start?"

"It's going to start soon, Paula Jean, right here in river city. Your face is almost completely healed on the outside. In another week or two you will be back to your old beautiful self and you'll never know you had surgery. You're pretty good in the self defense department as long as it is one on one, but that is not enough. I have today off, so I think it is time I took you to the range to learn how to handle your own sidearm." With that, Robert Walker laid a nine millimeter Browning P-35 and an L frame Smith & Wesson Model 686 on the kitchen table.

"In a couple of sessions, you will be able to defend yourself with deadly force. Not that the U.S. Army is composed of rapists, but I don't trust them anymore than I would an invading foreign force. If the reports are right, and our intelligence system is good, we can expect problems from armed Mexicans. So, after we finish breakfast, out to the range we go."

Nothing had riveted the attention of the entire world as the upcoming Referendum of 15 September. The influenza epidemic in the USA, on the rapid decline for the last two months, took a back seat as the electronic voting results poured in. Indeed the entire world watched with anxiety. There were many nations and many peoples who rooted for each outcome, but most hoped for dissolution of the Goliath. Some did so openly, some behind closed doors. It seemed that nothing would please the second and third world nations as the down fall of the United States. China professed a great desire to see the U.S. remain as one country, but gleefully celebrated for partitioning behind closed doors. The various lower class populations of Europe initially danced in the streets but then grew more somber, even sullen, as what it might portend for them became apparent upon reflection. Gone would be the military shield behind which they had hidden for so long. Gone would be the strong arm of America's naval forces that guaranteed the sea lanes for delivery of their oil and petroleum products. Gone would be a simple unity of a single trading partner, replaced by at least three different entities. One of them would have an entirely different orientation than looking across the Atlantic. Instead of dealing with one nation, now they must deal with several. Worse, they would have to pay for their own national security.

The Federal Election Commission sent new ballots electronically to each state's election officer who electronically distributed them to the counties, who electronically distributed them to each polling station. The ballot was relatively simple.

1. Should the varied states be allowed to secede?
   YES   NO

If you voted NO to question #1 above, please answer all of the following questions for your vote to be counted.

2. Should military operations, including deadly force, be used against these states to maintain the union and prevent their secession?

YES   NO

3. If you are able, are you willing to serve in ground combat operations in the U.S. Army or U.S. Marine Corps to enforce compliance and prevent secession of these interested states?

YES   NO

"Mr. President, the Chinese ambassador called for an appointment. I put him on your calendar for 14:30 this afternoon. You have a fifteen minute break then, but the Secretary of Agriculture is due at 14:45. I think he can probably wait if the Chinese ambassador has some serious discussion."

"Thank you, Janice. Please see that Chinese tea will be served to the Ambassador."

Promptly at 14:30 Ambassador Wu, Ho Li entered the Oval Office. "Welcome, Mr. Ambassador. Please have a seat on the couch behind the coffee table." Newkirk rang Janice, "Please bring in some hot tea for Ambassador Wu and myself." President Newkirk joined Wu, sitting in a chair adjacent to the coffee table.

"To what do I owe the honor of your visit, Mr. Ambassador," knowing full well what Wu wanted to address.

"Mr. President, my government is greatly concerned over the dissolution of the United States according to yesterday's referendum. You have been our greatest trading partner for many decades. You represent a leading edge in research in all the sciences. Your people are industrious and capable. We are very much concerned about how what appears to be several emerging nations will act, either independently or collectively. Will there be some over arching political organization in regards to national security, trade, transportation, and so on. Will we be dealing with one entity as in the past, or several? Will you form some type of loose confederation? This is of grave concern to us."

"Mr. Ambassador, I wish I knew the answers to your questions? We have been discussing that among ourselves. Right now, some of those who are withdrawing, some of those emerging political units you mentioned are truculent and resisting central authority to the point of using force. We have not been able to conduct meaningful discussions with their leaders. Frankly, we don't know how this will all develop. It is possible that we might be able to reach some amenable agreement with them. If not, we might have another civil war if we attempt to use force. The so-called Nation of the Missouri in particular, seems ready to defend their state with force if there is any attempt at coercion. I think, but in no way can guarantee, that at least Columbia and the northern tier of states will remain as part of the United States. What the Southwest and the Southeast do remains unknown. It is possible that they will be more than just autonomous states. Some of their politicians want complete independence, as I am sure you are aware. All I can say at this time Mr. Ambassador is that events will have to unfold for themselves. With the population shifts that have been initiated by the referendum, we can only hope for the best. Hopefully, all will be peaceful. In terms of transoceanic shipping, you might wish to re-align your ports of destination to those of the autonomous unit Columbia. Please inform your government of my thanks for your concern for our country and people." President Newkirk suddenly discovered newfound political skills.

"May I breach a second subject Mr. President, one that is of vital importance to both of our nations?"

Dreading what was coming, Newkirk sipped his tea as he made eye contact with the Chinaman. "Certainly, Mr. Ambassador, please speak freely."

"As you are well aware, the Peoples Liberation Army Navy has mobilized along the western borders of our recently acquired territories. While I myself have not been informed of all the details, I have been told that our armies will move westward in the immediate future. In the last war, you re-armed the Pathans, which cost us tens of thousands of lives of our Chinese soldiers. My government wishes to express in the strongest possible terms, that you do not resupply them or offer them aid by any means during our current military endeavors. I can assure you that our objectives do not include Kuwait or Saudi Arabia. We realize full well that such an action would result in nuclear war between East and West. Their oil supplies are critical to you and Europe. Your economies must continue to function, be that as it may, on their oil. No, another nuclear war must be avoided at all costs. The environment simply cannot withstand it. After all, the United States and Europe are our greatest customers. Rather, I will be blunt. Our objective is the reduction of the truculent nation of Iran. They have caused us much grief through their meddling in China's affairs, through the arming and stirring up of the Uighers and other Central Asian peoples against our central government. It is our intent to reduce them as a power in the Middle East. I am sure the United States will have no difficulty in understanding that objective. Indeed, they have been a serious menace to the Persian Gulf shipping lanes, truculent in the matters of religion throughout Southeast Asia, in particular in Indonesia, and elsewhere. I am sure you understand China's position, Mr. President, as we understand yours."

CHAPTER 17

"YOU'RE GETTING PRETTY GOOD WITH THAT BROWNING NINE MILLIMETER, PAULA JEAN".

"You're getting pretty good with that Browning nine millimeter, Paula Jean. Let's start thinking about moving and shooting, rather than just stationary positions. I'll set up some silhouette targets at five to twenty-five meters today. Now, I don't want you to do anything that might impact on your beautiful face. You're not completely healed, so we'll limit it to just moving around, using the kneeling firing position using the shooting bench and some barrels as cover, left hand and right hand. Next, we'll think about shooting from inside the truck, just in case somebody forces you to stop and pullover. The seat belt and access to your holstered sidearm while you're sitting behind the wheel can be a problem. That's something we can practice at home. There shouldn't be anyone at the range except maybe a few old retirees or perhaps some of the militia practicing. Now that school has started and it's a weekday, we can find one of the ranges vacant, rifle or pistol, I'm sure." Paula Jean nodded in agreement.

For the last seven weeks, Paula Jean and Undersheriff Walker had shared his home but not each other's bed. Rumors abounded about their relationship, but no one dared mention it to their faces. In spite of the deteriorating national and international situation, small town mentality still found time for gossip and its associated humor. They took turns cooking and each did their own laundry. They flipped a coin to see who won when there was a conflict with who wanted to watch what on the television. They had come to appreciate each other's company in a growing platonic relationship. Walker didn't give a damn about her colorful past. He began to recognize the intelligence and charm of the inner woman.

As they drove through the range gate, they heard high volume semi-automatic fire. It suddenly changed to full automatic fire. Walker felt uneasy about it, so he drove to the rifle range first. An old pickup was there, with two Hispanic teenage boys firing an AK-47. They were having too much fun and concentrating on the tin can targets so much that they didn't see Walker and Paula Jean pull up behind them. When the rifle magazine was empty, one of the boys turned around to see Undersheriff Walker standing behind them. "Buenos dias," he said to the boys. "Shouldn't you be in school? That's an interesting rifle. Where did you get it?"

. They both noticed the deputy sheriff's badge shining on Walker's belt. The boys looked at each other but didn't say anything. The larger one looked at the rifle, the younger boy holding it and nodded his head in Walker's direction Walker read malice in the eyes of the two boys. The younger boy, about fifteen, shrugged and picked up a loaded magazine. Walker immediately put his hand on his sidearm. "Don't load that rifle, son! That's an order. If you do, I'll open fire. Now lay the rifle on the bench and step away."

The boy shoved a magazine home into the magazine well and drew the bolt back to chamber a round and pivoted while shouldering the rifle to point the rifle at Walker. Walker drew and fired his .40 S&W, the 180 grain bullet striking the boy in the chest. The impact spun him around and he immediately fell to the ground. The other boy panicked and ran. Walker walked over to the boy and removed the rifle from his hands. He immediately recognized the wound as life threatening. He picked up the boy and yelled to Paula Jean, "Drop the tailgate of the truck." Paula Jean did so and Walker carried the boy to the truck and laid him in the bed. He ran back to the rifle and picked it up along with two magazines. He put them in the cab with Paula Jean and himself, climbed in and furiously drove to the hospital. He radioed ahead to the Sheriff's Department, telling them to have the hospital standby to receive a gunshot wound to the chest. The Emergency Room crew was waiting with a gurney and an intravenous setup at the emergency room door. So was Sheriff Brady. Walker took the wallet from the boy's pocket as they laid him on the gurney. His school identity card identified him as Cesar Morales, son of Tomas and Maria Morales. Walker handed the card to Sheriff Brady.

"Maria is at work over at the Big Horn Café. We better go get her. You can tell me what happened on the way." Sheriff Brady drove in his cruiser while Walker explained what happened. Paula Jean followed in his pickup truck. All three entered the Big Horn Café.

"Morning, Jan. We need to speak with Maria. There has been an accident. Her son has been shot."

"Fatally, Jack?" asked Jan with an agonized countenance.

"He's alive, but it's pretty serious. I don't know any more than that. He drew down on Deputy Walker here with an automatic rifle. Now, we need to get Maria over to the hospital."

"She's in the kitchen."

The four of them entered the kitchen and informed Maria who broke down in hysterics. Paula Jean offered to ride with Maria in the back of the Sheriff's cruiser while Walker drove his pickup back to the hospital.

The Emergency Room physician was studying radiographs while whole blood was pouring into Cesar via two intravenous sets.

"Well, the bullet just missed his heart. It entered at an angle such that it passed just above his heart where the major arties come and go and between his heart and his spine. It came out below his shoulder blade. It is too early to tell about nerve damage for the nerves to his arm. It went all the way through. I have seen worse wounds survive and lesser ones succumb when I was in the Army. He's young and in good health, so I think the odds are better than fifty-fifty. I've notified the thoracic surgeon in Cody who is driving down with a police escort. We'll crack this kid's chest in an hour or so and see what we can do to stop the hemorrhage and clean out any bits of cloth and so on. In the meantime, we're getting him stabilized. His heart rate has slowed down and his blood pressure is coming back up. He has lost a bit of blood. Any blood donations would be helpful. Thankfully, he is 0 positive, the most common kind. We could use about a dozen pints, thank you. If you put the word out to family and friends immediately for donors, Mrs. Morales, it would be most helpful."

Paula Jean, Walker and Sheriff Brady took Maria to the waiting room. "Where is Tomas, Maria?" asked Sheriff Brady.

"He's at work at the Gilson's ranch today."

"You stay here and question her about the rifle, Bob, I'll go get Tomas. As soon as she regains some composure, put her on the phone looking for blood donors." Walker nodded in agreement and put his arm around Maria, who had stopped sobbing but was shaking.

"Maria, you must understand. Your son was about to shoot me. Where did he get that rifle?"

"It is probably Tomas's rifle. I told him I didn't want that gun in the house."

"That is an assault rifle, Maria. Where did Tomas get it, do you know?""I think it came from that Juan Cartagena."

"There was another boy with him, shooting the rifle. He ran away. Do you know who he is?"

"No, it could have been one of several. Their fathers told them they didn't have to go to school."

"Why wasn't Cesar in school today?"

"His father told him that he didn't have to go to that Gringo high school any more. That soon it would be a Mexican high school and he could go back to it then when they taught in Spanish."

CHAPTER 18

THE SURGEON GENERAL WAS HOLDING A NEWS CONFERENCE ON HOW WELL THE NATIONAL VACCINATION PROGRAM WAS PROGRESSING.

The Surgeon General was holding a news conference on how well the national vaccination program was progressing. Over 90% of the subjects, he said, were vaccinated. Bradley mused over that choice of words, "subjects" as the nuance and double meaning struck him. Subjects, meaning patients being vaccinated, and subjects, as in subjects rather than citizens of the British Crown, caused Bradley to smile. *Subjects of the elected crown versus citizens of the United States; what that used to mean. Just like the elected crown of Mexico*, he thought. The vaccine was recognized as extremely effective; being an excellent match with the circulating influenza virus continued the Surgeon General.

The Presidential Daily Brief for Richard Newkirk on Friday morning was pretty glum.

"Mr. President, every synagogue in eastern Texas and western Louisiana has been torched in the last twenty-four hours. Other reports indicate arson in Alabama, Georgia and the Carolinas. The news reports coming out of those areas are now pretty limited. The reporters are making their own getaways while they can get out with their lives. You can't tell me this wasn't a coordinated attack on synagogues throughout the south. Unfortunately, synagogues in a number of northern states are also being torched. It just doesn't seem to be as coordinated as what is occurring in the south."

"Were churches of other denominations similarly attacked?"

"It appears some were, especially in and around the Houston area, but not on a general scale, Mr. President, not of which we are aware, at least not systematically."

"Is there anything we can do about it at this time?"

"Frankly, Mr. President there is not. Local law officers who are white are fleeing north with their families, mostly headed towards the Midwest. We have had tabs on certain black militant leaders, mostly Muslims, who have been preaching various degrees of sedition over the last few years. We strongly suspect they are behind it. The black population seems to be suffering some kind of split within itself. The black Muslims are declaring for a clerical state, a Muslim black America while the mainstream black Americans want an autonomous unit or an independent black America. Those two are beginning to go at each other. The black Muslims seem to be particularly well armed and dedicated to their cause. We estimate there are about twenty million of them. They are concentrated in our eastern seaboard cities and the larger cities of the southeast. Many of them are ex cons. That's enough for a moderately sized country. Several reports indicate where they are in the local majority they are slaughtering both Jews and Christians of all ages and both sexes.

Our cities are emptying out Mr. President, even those in the southern central and midwestern states. With the city centers looted, grocery stores empty, hungry people are beginning to pour out of the ghettos and into the suburbs and country side looking for food more than ever. Food is now more important than loot. A lot of them have run out of gas.

The gas stations have all been drained dry and there haven't been any re-supplied. That means there are a lot of hungry folks out there are on foot. They will beg or attack individual suburban houses and farms for warmth, shelter and food. A few have guns, but the majority are armed with knives, hatchets, pick axe handles. City water and sewer services are compromised in many cities. Folks are at the point where they can't flush their toilets or get drinking water. The Washington, D.C, Chief of Police tells me the roads into and out of our city here have been jammed day and night for several days. It is rush hour traffic 24/7 if you haven't observed it. White folks are passing through fleeing north, while black folks are headed south. Others are keeping their heads down. Philadelphia, Detroit, New York, Baltimore, all report tremendous flux in people migrating. Gasoline supplies and food are the major constraints. Our economy is about to be in total collapse. Many of the white bureaucrats have now left this city. Many of our government offices are no longer functioning due to lack of their staffs. With winter, the people who remained in our inner city ghettoes will probably starve or die of hypothermia or diarrheal disease."

"Thanks, Ed. Naomi, I hope you have some good news, better than Ed and Homeland Security."

"The Joint Chiefs and I have worked out something of a battle plan, if you will, Mr. President. We think we can hold a line from Monterey Bay across the middle of Nevada, southern Colorado, and dipping into Oklahoma and northern Texas, anchoring on the Mississippi River. The Red River between Texas and Oklahoma, or maybe somewhere in Arkansas will be a battle front. I can't call where that line will be. I have ordered all Army units in Houston and other places to return to their bases for evacuation. That essentially amounts to surrendering the southwest to the Mexican faction. From what Ed tells me, the southeast is too fluid right now to have any idea of where we can hold the line. Who knows, the line might be drawn right here around D.C. someplace, maybe even north of Baltimore. The Mexican and Mexican-American populations in the southeast are pretty substantial but still a minority by a small fraction, and there are a thousand small battles going on between the Mexicans and the blacks and the whites down there. We simply don't know how it will turn out. Both sides seem to be surprisingly heavily endowed with small arms. I don't mean sporting weapons either, but battle rifles and assault rifles. Our troops have been confiscating them and picking them up after fire fights. Now we are finding that some of these captured weapons are coming from the Middle East and South America, some are from Southeast Asia but China seems to be the main source, not only manufacturing them but purchasing them from Rumania, Hungary and other places, then shipping them here. My take at the moment is that the white folks are trying to get out and leave it to the other populations to fight it out. Miami is pretty much Hispanic and will probably be an enclave at the southern tip of Florida in an otherwise black peninsula. We don't have any more troops than that. There isn't much we can do right now about the possible break away states. It seems that only the northeast and Midwest will hold together. I don't think there will be anybody in the southwest or southeast going to vote on the Referendum next week. It looks like there will be at least four distinct blocks of what was the United States by the time this is over."

"And what does the Director of National Intelligence have for us this morning, Harry?"

"Mr. President, the Chinese began to move overnight. It looks like they are headed into Iran. They learned some lessons from their past excursions a few years ago. They are moving in battalion sized units stretched out very thin, across a very broad front. Behind their front are more compact units and support troops, logistics, engineers, those kinds of units. If they do as we think they will, what they did in their last expansion, they will kill everything, men, women, children, livestock, burn crops, in their path. The terrain in Iran is terrible. It is either deserts or mountains. There are very rugged mountains running roughly northwest to southeast. It will be rough going for both sides. The Iranians will wage a successful guerilla campaign for sometime, perhaps even a couple of years, but with a scorched earth policy, there will be no civilian base to support guerilla activity. They will starve, freeze, or be killed by the Chinese. The Iranians have perhaps three dozen tactically sized nuclear warheads. We don't believe any of them are over twenty kilotons, a little larger than the size of the Hiroshima bomb. We think most of them are smaller, in the two to five kiloton range, so they are artillery and air deliverable. Where and when they will deploy them won't matter much. The Chinese will keep on coming. The Gulf of Oman and the Straits of Hormuz are most certainly strategic targets, choke points. They could cross the desert in the north, just south of the Elburz mountains, avoiding many of the western mountain ranges which are the Zagros Mountains, heading west just south of Tehran and for the Iraqi border around As Sulayamaniyah. That would leave the mountains as pockets of guerilla resistance but cut off Tehran and provide a jumping off point for the Iraqi oil fields. I can't say which strategy they will employ, perhaps both. Since Iranian citizens cannot own firearms, I expect the Iranian government will do as the Russians did when the Germans laid siege to Stalingrad and Leningrad. They will throw in civilians armed with anything, rocks, shovels, clubs, what have you, to hold the line against the Chinese. No doubt both sides will deploy nerve gas on a tactical basis to eliminate strongholds. The Iranians don't have gas masks for the civilians, so it will be an easy kill for the Chinese who do."

"What do you think the outcome will be, in terms of grand strategy? How will this influence the China that we will have to deal with when this is all over," asked Frank Stokes, Secretary of State.

"Well Frank, it does create some problems for China. As usual for everything, it is a two edged sword. They lost most

of their AIDS/HIV infected battalions in their last drive for
Caspian Basin oil. Now they have educated their population
on that disease and their HIV infection rates are very low.
That means their army has a lot of young folks, people who
would otherwise be contributing to their economy as workers.
The other side of that point is that most of their army has a
rural background. That means a lot of them couldn't find jobs
anyway. It does mean that there will be less young workers to
contribute to their policy of Maximum Living Standards
Assistance. That is a form of their social security program but
it really applied only to urban populations since they don't
have the resources to apply it to their rural folks. A lot of these
young people in the army are coming from abject poverty. So,
from their perspective of population control, it eliminates a lot
of young people who would otherwise be raising families,
providing the men could not find wives in the first place. That
is part of the massive economic inequality in China and social
stratification. They are externalizing it through military
conquest. At this time, there doesn't seem to be any naval
involvement as there was in their last war, when they drove for
Africa. So far, it appears that this is primarily a land oriented
war. All their logistical resources point to that."

"How far, Harry, Frank, Naomi, do you think they will
go? The three looked at one another and the two men looked
to Naomi to answer Newkirk's question."

"Well, Mr. President. I suspect that they will go either until
they run out of resources or they take Iran. Iran should satisfy
them for a while, so I suspect they will stop there. It has so
much oil and natural gas that it can feed the energy
requirements of their economy for at least two decades. It will
put them at the Straits of Hormuz chokepoint from which
they can threaten our oil lifeline. There isn't a lot
of agricultural production in Iran relative to other areas, but
what there is can modestly supplement China within
its old boundaries and support the Chinese that will
manage what was Iran. I suspect there will only be several
million Chinese

within the Iranian borders when all is said and done. I doubt that there will be many Iranian nationals left when the Chinese are through. They will be hunted down and killed over time so they can't wage guerilla warfare."

"Anything else, Harry, Naomi?"

"Mr. President, we are launching an operation to get the Chinese virologist and his family who gave us the Chinese biological weapon specimen of influenza some years ago out of China. Their lives are in great danger. We don't know how it will spill over into our scientific community. I mean, we don't know if Chinese agents here will try to assassinate our leading scientists who developed our vaccine from that sample. I'll keep you posted as things develop. Right now, we are just in the initial stages, but time is critical."

"On that note, is there any development on who tipped off the Muslims about our contracts with Israel?"

"I have ordered a complete review of all people who had access to the files. That means about fifty people within the laboratory at Fort Detrick. Records will indicate who was in those files and when. We hope to be able to put together a timeline on that. We are doing it surreptitiously, with the participation of the laboratory commander and his deputy. We have excellent evidence and are building a case that would stand in any court. We have taken two people into custody and holding them for several months now without allowing them any outside contact under the Patriot Act. As further evidence is developed, I will keep you informed of that as well, Mr. President."

Mordeciah Jones called a news conference for 10:00 hours in his office on Peach Tree Street in downtown Atlanta. His press secretary informed the major networks that an announcement of national significance was to be made. It was critical to receive appropriate coverage. The broadcast was to be live. Selected journalists had been briefed and provided with specific questions to be asked. Jones had practiced the answers in front of his staff. He became rather good at role playing. Heavy set, of moderate height, with thick black hair, and broad flat face and nose to match, he reminded some of Idi Amin Dada. He had been quite successful as a small business man dealing in extortion, murder for hire, and a chain of brothels. Jones had two primary lieutenants, each of which had a gang of about fifteen full time members and up to forty street soldiers that could be called to duty at any time. They functioned as his private bodyguard. He attended church every Sunday and made contributions to charitable causes through the church. As a front organization he ran a wholesale food distribution center not too far from downtown Atlanta. He had taken over the top four floors of a major office building where the lower three were occupied by his growing staff. The upper floor he used exclusively for his apartment. Central News Network was represented by an all black camera team, as were all the other major networks save the Chandler Network. They had a white female journalist as the lead interviewer.

"Ladies and Gentlemen, given these troubled times, the terrible racism inflicted upon the poor black people of America by the other major ethnic groups, the physical terror, the economic impoverishment to the point of destitution, and the lack of leadership at the national level, it has become imperative to restore justice to the land. It behooves us to restore the rights that should belong to all in the black community. Therefore I am declaring that the following political organization be created, the nation of African America. I am standing for the Presidency of this new nation. We will have free and fair elections as soon as we can become better organized. This new nation of freedom for black Americans will include what were the states of Virginia, Tennessee, Alabama, Georgia, North and South Carolina, Mississippi, Louisiana and part of Arkansas. I have here a map delineating the boundaries. You will note how it dovetails with what remains of the original United States and what appears to be a boundary forming with Hispanic America. Now, negotiations will immediately commence with other factions to solidify these borders. We are prepared to defend these borders against all enemies. Local governments in all the various jurisdictions have pledged their unreserved support. Our model will be essentially the same as originally envisioned by the Founding Fathers. We will have two chambers of legislators, one for the people and one for the states. We will have a strong independent judiciary and a national police force. The capitol will be here in Atlanta. Whatever offices and personnel of the original United States government remain are invited to leave immediately if not sooner. I will grant one week, an open window for all those associated with the former U.S. Government who wish to remain with that body to safely leave. If they choose to remain then they will be citizens of our new nation. We welcome them to stay and it is quite possible we find their expertise most useful in our new nation. After that, if they choose fealty to their old government, I cannot be responsible for their safety or for their offices."

"Is the Colonel in Sergeant Major? I would like a few words with him if he is. It is rather urgent."

"Sure, Sheriff, I'll check with him." Sergeant Major Killian knocked on Ethan's door and at Ethan's command "Enter" opened the door.

"Sir, Sheriff Brady is here. He would like to speak with you. He says it is urgent."

"Send the man in Sergeant Major. Always happy to see the Sheriff. If you would, bring us two coffees with lots of cream."

Sheriff Brady walked in and Ethan motioned him to have a seat.

"What's up, Sheriff?"

"I received a call this morning from the Sheriff in Hot Springs County. It seems that there is some unusual activity going on around Hamilton Dome just west of Thermopolis, on the Indian Reservation. A cowboy thinks he spotted Juan Cartagena over there. Sheriff Johnson knows of our interest in Cartagena, so he thought we might like to be either on a shared raid with his department or do it all by ourselves. I told him I would get back to him within the hour. You want to go along? Want to take any of your people? This has gone beyond a civil matter, with civil war impending and the racial violence."

"I am your man. Would you like for me to bring a squad? It would take a couple of hours to put a team together if you think we will need heavy weapons? Otherwise I can have an infantry squad here in an hour."

"Not unless you want to bring the heavy stuff. I can mount a force with five deputies and Hot Springs can give us several more men. My only concern is that they might have automatic weapons, grenade launchers, or some other heavy stuff. Sheriff Johnson doesn't have any idea how many there might be. The cowboy said he has seen four or five pickups come and go. He doesn't know how many trucks or people are there now. What do you think?"

Ethan yelled out through the open door. "Sergeant Major! Call Captain Gates. Have him get Beddington's squad in here within the hour. Draw four LAWs and two squad automatic weapons with the basic load of ammunition. Also get that mine/metal detector out. We will take three Hummers. See that they are fully fueled. Draw two MREs each for two dozen men and fill a five gallon water can."

Ethan turned to Sheriff Brady. "They all work here in town and are readily available. In addition, four of the eight have had active duty time, so they know what to expect. I'll place myself and my men under your command, Sheriff. That will make it more respectable in the eyes of any pseudo court that might be convened. You can deputize us all if you think it is necessary. It might be a good idea to talk to the cowboy if it is possible. Not that I am suspicious or anything, but I wonder if he is Hispanic and leading us into an ambush."

"If you will allow me to use your phone, I'll call Sheriff Johnson and we'll set up a rendezvous point outside of Thermopolis so we won't tip anybody off. Maybe he can have that cowboy join us."

Three hours later Ethan and the two sheriffs carefully glassed the abandoned ranch house and outbuildings. Three pickups were parked in front. No activity was observed. Ethan noted and remarked the windows were all blacked out.

"Sheriff Johnson, I have placed my men under command of Sheriff Brady. If you assume command because of this being your county, we will be under your command."

"Thank you, Colonel. I appreciate the professional courtesy. If you or your folks have any suggestions at any time, we will certainly entertain them." I'll deploy the deputies of both departments as a mix with your people. You have the headset commo gear that we can use to maintain contact with everyone. I'll order the men to form a complete cordon around the place and try and get within one hundred yards, cover permitting. Then I'll get on the bull horn and see if we can talk these folks out without any shooting. It would be nice to ask them some very interesting questions if we can take them alive."

As the deputies and troopers surrounded the place, one of the men inside the house looked out the window prior to exiting through the front door. He saw movement. "There are people out there, in uniform, about two hundred yards out, he cried."

Juan Cartagena and three others jumped to their feet and began looking out the windows and back door, holding aside the black material covering the windows. "There are soldiers circling over here," cried one. "And over here", said another from the other side of the house.

Juan Cartagena dashed into the bedroom where he drew several SKS rifles from the closet and laid them on the table. On a second trip he returned with a box full of loaded magazines. "It is up to you, to stay and fight, to try and run, or to surrender. Make your choice, quickly, before we are completely surrounded. As for me, I will fight" he said as he picked up a rifle and shoved a magazine into the rifle. He moved to a window and smashed the glass with the rifle butt.

"Hurry, before they open fire."

Two men dashed out the back door. They made one hundred yards onto the prairie when they were tackled by the deputies, wrestled to the ground and handcuffed. The fire team leader called into Ethan. "Beddington in the rear, Colonel. We have two in custody, on the ground and cuffed." When he heard that report Sheriff Johnson called on the bullhorn. "You are surrounded. We have two men in custody. Drop your weapons and come out with your hands straight up over your heads."

Juan Cartagena opened fire. His aim was not particularly good but close enough to make the sheriffs and Ethan duck. The sheriffs looked to each other and nodded in agreement and then to Bradley who nodded. Bradley gave the order "All teams, open fire, but be careful of crossfire into each other" went out over the net into the headset of each soldier who passed the word to the deputies. Within twenty seconds, over a hundred rounds went into the house. The order "cease fire" went out over the net. No fire was returned. Sheriff Johnson picked up the bullhorn. "If you do not emerge with your hands up, we will put anti-tank missiles into the house." The front door opened, and a white handkerchief tied to a gun barrel was waved. The rifle was dropped and Cartagena and another man emerged from the house, hands over their heads. "Come forward." The two walked the one hundred yards to where the sheriffs and Bradley had advanced. "All units close in on the house. Check for booby traps before and during entry and search. Search the place thoroughly. Sergeant Beddington, get the metal detector," radioed Bradley. After the search of the house was completed, Beddington took two men and the metal detector into the barn. There they found Cartagena's truck with the bullet fractured windshield. After checking it for traps, they moved it out and searched with the metal detector and for any signs of digging. What they found in the stalls were crates of rifles, ammunition and explosives.

Bradley had Beddington radio Sergeant Major Killian to bring another squad and several trucks, along with a dozen shovels. By late afternoon, the cache of weapons was unearthed and loaded into half a dozen pickup trucks. The weapons and explosives were taken to the armory in Worland and the prisoners to the Hot Springs County jail. Bradley and his troops accompanied Sheriff Brady and all of his deputies except Undersheriff Walker back to Worland, leaving questioning of the prisoners to Sheriff Johnson. Undersheriff Walker went for supper, along with two of the Hot Springs County deputies. When they returned two hours later, a very subdued Juan Cartagena sat naked alone in his cell. Blood was dribbling over his chin and several toes were bloodied. A tape recorder turned off and on as questions were asked and answered revealed a good deal of information. After having several teeth and toenails pulled and his testicles squeezed with pliers, Juan Cartagena became very talkative.

"I don't believe you tortured this man, Sheriff', said Walker.

"It was worth it. I'll have a copy of this tape made for you to take to Sheriff Brady and Colonel Bradley. "He wasn't going to talk at all, but when I told him the next step was to insert a bovine electroejaculator in his rectum, the way the veterinarians test bulls for fertility, he became very talkative. As a ranch worker he knew what that was like. He knew the surge of electricity could be enough to stand a two thousand pound bull on its head if improperly used. We have some immediate problems that are going to be addressed. I'll also send a copy of this tape to the Governor. I'm sure he will find it interesting. While torture is illegal, there are times and circumstances that its use is very urgent and life saving. I'll have a copy in fifteen minutes and you can be on your way. In the meantime, I'll see that Cartagena gets medical attention."

Sheriff Johnson, all of his deputies and Colonel Bradley listened to the tape of Sheriff Brady questioning Juan Cartagena. After they heard it for the first time, they brought in the mayor, the local state police officers, the county attorney and the county commissioners. The tape was interrupted between the questions and the answers numerous times, but no one asked why. Nobody really wanted to know. Cartagena revealed that he was but one of many in a network in numerous states whose primary job was to organize Mexican-Americans and other Hispanics for a political coup. Their grand strategy was to assume political control by numbers, by the ballot box, where possible sometime after the Referendum. They were to be prepared to use violence and assume control of rural areas where they could not. They were all supplied with weapons and explosives for this purpose. Hispanic agricultural workers were to seize the farms and ranches with the weapons the NWFA agents provided if the occupants did not peacefully abandon it upon demand. Weapons and explosives came in through the port of Long Beach, California from China. Some were of Chinese manufacture, others of eastern European manufacture. They were boxed with machinery parts and tools in multi-layered wooden crates. These were placed in CONEX shipping containers. In a carefully guarded warehouse at a Chinese distribution point the crates were opened and the weapons and explosives replaced in the wood crates and distributed by a Chinese owned shipping company in unmarked trucks. Ultimately, the grand strategy of the NWFA was unification with Mexico. He presumed there was similar organization for the smaller cities, those whose populations were in the tens of thousands, such as Aberdeen, South Dakota, but he had no direct knowledge of it. He only knew another NWFA organizer who was working there. They were funded through the National Farm Workers Association who provided funds through the mail or by direct delivery. Other states involved were Missouri, Kansas, South and North Dakota, Colorado and Utah. Cartagena declared he didn't know the original source of funding, but he thought it might be the Mexican government. He was only a poor soldier and not informed of the higher levels of organization. He named all of his lieutenants. He admitted to killing Juan Robas.

Sheriff Brady said "We can't send him to the state prison. They already informed me that they will accept no more prisoners. They want to send Freddy and Johnny back as it is. In fact, they are insisting on it. That leaves us some interesting questions. Since this confession was acquired under torture, will it be admissible evidence? If not, what do we do with him? The Mexican government sure as hell won't give us any information,; that would be an admission of duplicity. I don't want to try and utilize federal resources, rather keep it local. When the Governor gets his copy of this tape, he will be in the legal quandary. So, what do we do with Mr. Cartagena? Better, what does the system do with Mr. Cartagena? What about his lieutenants who have not yet committed any violent crimes? Well, Mr. County Attorney, what do you say?"

"For the moment, a warrant for the arrest of Mrs. Cartagena and a search warrant. We'll see what else turns up."

Sheriff Brady ordered his deputies to surround the house. It was after midnight, and while he didn't like serving warrants after dark, he didn't want to give Juanita Cartagena any chance of escape. He knocked on the front door while Deputy ---- stood slightly off to the right of the Sheriff. After a few minutes, Juanita came to the door in a house robe. She kept her hand behind the door because she was holding a Beretta 9 mm automatic. She didn't open the screen door.

"Yes, Sheriff, what do you want at this hour?"

"Are you Mrs. Juanita Cartagena, wife of Juan Cartagena?" asked Sheriff Brady.

"Yes, I am. Is something wrong?"

"I have warrants to search your premises and for your arrest. We have your husband in custody."

Juanita didn't say anything, but immediately brought her left hand around the door and fired into the middle of Sheriff Brady's chest. Before she could get a second round off, Deputy Eyson drew and fired, striking Juanita in the chest. The bullet from his .40 Smith and Wesson shattered her spine and ruptured the thoracic artery. She was dead about the time she hit the ground. Deputy Eyson quickly moved to open the door and remove the automatic from her hand. He heard glass shattering as his fellow deputies were crashing through the back door. Then he knelt over the Sheriff, relieved to see him breathing and hear him groaning. The Sheriff opened his eyes and said, "Who hit me with a sledge hammer?"

Deputy Eyson laughed. "It looks like your vest saved your ass, Sheriff." He helped the Sheriff to his feet then went to the squad car to put in a call for an ambulance for Juanita Cartagena. A search of the house turned up receipts for a large Rent-A-Storage compartment in Worland. Since the search warrant stated "Associated Premises," Sheriff Brady called the owner of the storage facility and told him to get out of bed and get to the storage lot. The owner opened the overhead door and turned on the lights for the Sheriff. Deputy Eyson and Undersheriff Walker began pulling tarps off different piles of goods. In the rear were ten cases of rifles with ten rifles in each. Also were several more crates of ammunition and magazines. Two crates contained RDX and Simtex explosives. Two more crates contained hand grenades. Sheriff Brady called Colonel Bradley and got him out of bed, telling him of the find. Bradley got Sergeant Major Killian out of bed who called Sergeant Beddington to have him meet him at the Armory with four men where he drew a truck. An hour later they unloaded the munitions in the armory.

"Sergeant Major, call Captain Livingston in the morning. Have him and his people get the explosives. He can decide where to best deploy the explosives in whatever canyons and routes he feels needs it most. He knows them all. Call the other Captains as well and tell them that we have firearms and ammunition for the militia companies. Divide them between the companies according to how many militia companies each commander has. They can send a truck to get them. Captain Gates as a Medical Company commander won't need any. I'm sure they will be delighted with the SKS and AK-47 rifles."

CHAPTER 19

"COLONEL, WE GOT A SECURE FAX FROM COMMO KID. He and Lieutenant Weir have been working on our leak. It seems that Mrs. Captain McCortle has been making telephone calls to Fort McCoy, Wisconsin. The conversations are very interesting. It appears that Captain McCortle tells her everything that we do and she passes it on to the military intelligence shop at McCoy. She's the leak Sir, thanks to Captain McCortle. I know he plans to sell out Sir, probably under pressure from his wife to get the maximum price, but it seems she has been, shall I say, requested, to stay as long as possible as a source of information. That is one reason why the sale of their home has been so slow. She has been killing every reasonable offer to maximize the sale and to continue to feed information to the federals. There is no word on whether it is deliberate on the part of Captain McCortle or if he is even aware of what his wife is doing. Higher headquarters ran a bit of a background check on her. It is pretty plain that she is a blue state kind of girl, a real social welfare police state advocate. I suppose it is possible since she runs the Captain like a top. I know them both, Sir. He is pretty weak and she is quite dominant. I am sure you want to think about how to handle it for a while, Colonel."

Thank you, Sergeant Major Killian. Yes, I will have to think of how to handle the situation. Perhaps we can turn her to our own advantage. Perhaps we can feed her false information through McCortle. If you come up with something interesting in that department, let me know."

"Captain Ferguson, I want a squad of people here at 06:00 tomorrow, along with adequate transportation for them. Mission is not to be discussed. Have them bring sleeping bags and draw enough Meals, Ready to Eat for 48 hours just in case we run into a glitch. Also, rent a large sized truck tonight, one with a lift, commandeer one if you must for tomorrow. No need for your presence. The squad leaders will be sufficient."

"Yes Sir, I think I can guess the mission," grinned Captain Ferguson. "Have you decided on a replacement for the Captain, Sir or will you leave Lieutenant Thorson in command?"

"Your intuitive thinking is pretty sharp Captain. Keep it to yourself."

Promptly at 06:00, twelve men and women in uniform boarded a five ton rental truck and headed north to Basin. Arriving at 07:00, they immediately surrounded the residence of Captain McCortle. Bradley knocked on the door to a surprised Captain and Mrs. McCortle.

Bradley stepped into the living room without waiting for an invitation. "Captain McCortle, you are relieved of all duties. We have a moving truck and will load the truck to its maximum capacity with what you deem your most essential belongings. You are out of the service and will immediately leave the Nation of Missouri. If you fail to comply, you will be arrested along with your wife, as spies. At the least that will mean prison terms if not outright execution. I am fully capable of killing you both as traitors. Mr. McCortle, did you make a tape of Officers Call some months ago?"

"Colonel, what the hell are you talking about? I am not a spy. I have not done anything to deserve being relieved of my command when you relieved me last spring. Yes, I taped O Call Sir, but I did not give it to the press. Someone else must have done that. Now you are telling me I must leave my home, my job, my family, and I am being dismissed from the service?"

"Captain, we have monitored your communications for sometime. Your wife has been communicating with Army intelligence at Fort McCoy for over six months that we are aware of. She has been passing them information on our movements and progress here in the Basin. Whether or not you aware of this, are participating in this duplicity, I don't know and don't care. I have the authority to order your execution as a spy, but because you are a family with two children and have not directly contributed to anyone's death I am offering you the opportunity to leave forever. If you do not, you will suffer the consequences. Now, decide what you want to take. The truck is rented in your name; you will have to pay for it. Two armed men will accompany you to the bank while your wife packs. Close your account, pay the truck rental and return here. We will load the truck while you are in town and you will be on your way by noon. Nothing less will be accepted from you. You are not to stop for anything but fuel and food until you are in the state of Minnesota. Do I make myself clear? Sergeant, remove all weapons to include personal firearms, uniforms and military associated paraphernalia from this household. Secure it all in our truck. Captain McCortle will have no further need of them. Take over."

Bradley gave Mrs. McCortle a very hard stare for a few seconds, turned on his heel and stepped outside. The children stood silently as they listened to the dictum their parents received. At 13:00 hours the McCortle family departed the Nation of Missouri forever.

White citizens of southern California began a mass migration north later that week. Some wanted to stop in northern California, others wanted to migrate in Oregon and Washington, or even British Columbia. The violence of southern California had not matched that of the southeastern

United States because the white population was simply not armed. They were told to leave or die and they chose to leave. The racial and turf wars between the Hispanic and the Black American populations of the southeast became even more severe throughout the rural areas and small towns from Virginia south to northern Florida and west thru Arkansas and into Texas.

Ethan carefully looked at his father. He suddenly realized that he looked older, much older. "Funny, I never really noticed it until just now, just how old he does look. It seems like he has aged in a couple of years since I came home. I wonder if he's OK?" "How are you feeling Dad? You look a little tired."

It seemed to Ethan that his father had slowed down these past few months. Ethan supposed it was the summer heat with all the work his father had done in the garden and yard. A subtle slowness, a hesitation in his step, an indefinable change in his color and appearance had occurred. Now that the weather was cooler, his gait had not improved. Ethan wondered if they were sequellae of this father's exposure to radioactive fallout in Korea during the first Chinese expansion. Ethan realized his Dad's hair was now thinner and grayer than last winter. Funny, thought Ethan, I have been too busy to notice the subtle changes. Ethan suddenly remember how much younger his father looked six months ago.

"I'm just fine, Son, just fine. Never felt better."

Ethan suddenly realized the radiation poisoning his father probably suffered from the fallout from all the tactical nuclear fires that were expended during the Second Korean War. The sequellae were probably being manifested in the aging process and perhaps in reducing his immunity to infections. Ethan felt his stomach twist into a knot. He blurted out, "I don't know what to do to help you, Dad", thinking in terms of helping his father.

"Do? There's nothing I need you to do except pour us each a drink, your choice, bourbon or brandy, Son."

"Gypsy and I have been thinking about moving in together. She has a very small apartment, but it will do just fine for the two of us. We've hit it off rather well these past few months. I have explained my marital and family history to her, and she has no problem with that. We have become very serious about this relationship. In fact, she says she would very much like to have the boys as part of the family, and maybe one or two of our own. What do you think?"

"Hell, Son. That's great news, couldn't be better in my opinion. Go for it. Make it legal if you like, but that's up to the two of you. I am happy for you. Pour us a double then I'll thaw an apple pie out of the freezer in the microwave for dessert. We'll have a little a'la mode to celebrate. This is great news."

The next morning Ethan moved everything he chose to in two pickup loads into Gypsy's apartment while she was at work. He just stacked it in the living room until they could work out placing everything together. He did bring his old stereo setup and computer as the only furniture. The rest was clothes, weapons and military gear.

The long awaited day of September 15 arrived. Modest numbers of voters turned out to the poles. Many of the population centers in the southeast did not even open the polling places. Many people were too afraid to leave their homes to vote. Many who did vote did so by telephone or computer. The massive population shifting prevented the majority of registered voters from participating. Those people on the move were past caring what happened to the United States as a nation. They primary concern was for their immediate safety. Their economic well being was already compromised. Now they worried about where they could flee to safety, where their next and future meals would come from, and whether or not they could find enough fuel to keep moving. Most voting occurred in the northeast, northwest and Midwestern parts of the United States. Electronic results were posted as they occurred. Within 12 hours after the polls closed, the results were conclusive. The Rocky Mountain and Plains states voted for secession. Idaho, Montana, Wyoming, North and South Dakota, the northern half of Nevada, and Utah would henceforth be known as the Republic of Nation of Missouri.

The southeastern United States didn't have enough votes to make any meaningful statement due to the massive population shift and the severity and widespread violence that accompanied it. Texas from Austin north voted to remain with the Union, as did Oklahoma and Kansas. Missouri split in the referendum, 49% to 51%, the majority voting to remain in the United States. Interestingly enough, the line was drawn along rural versus urban populations which reflected racial division. The urban areas proper, dominated by the black vote, Kansas City, St. Louis and Springfield, voted to withdraw from the United States while the white suburbs voted to remain part of the union. Rural Missouri counties voted to be part of the Union. The Great Lakes States, the New England states, Pennsylvania, Maryland and New York voted to remain as part of the Union. New Mexico, Arizona, Texas, from San Antonio south and west, voted along with southern California on creating the new nation of New California. Colorado split in an east-west line, with northern Colorado wanting to remain part of the Union, while southern Colorado wanted to be part of New California. Voting was exclusively along ethnic lines. Southern Colorado from Colorado Springs south was dominated by the Hispanic population. This split left Colorado cut off from other states to the north, west and south. It was immediately obvious that the dividing line would be a great salient, splitting Colorado, then turning south to encompass the Texas panhandle and Oklahoma, then north again to split Missouri and southern Illinois, and east to Maryland. It would be a potential battleground. There will be no contesting the two new nations of New California and Nation of Missouri. Northern California and the northwest joined the new nation of Columbia.

Robert and Ethan Bradley were in a somber mood. Gypsy Lee sat with them in the living room watching the results come in over Fox News Channel. They were all sipping V.S.O.P. brandy from Robert's supply. Robert approved of the young lady that Ethan brought home that evening. He had not met Gypsy Lee before and Ethan had not previously mentioned her. She was obviously a very attractive and intelligent woman, far better suited to Ethan's needs he thought, than Martha.

In the White House, the cabinet members and Newkirk's personal secretary Janice Darlington watched the results with President Newkirk. The mood was lower than somber. The United States was no longer a nation, but now a conglomeration with no formal ties. President Newkirk looked around the room. "We'll meet in the Conference Room here in the morning at 08:00 to discuss what we will do regarding the results of the referendum. Janice, I want the Joint Chiefs here as well as the leaders of the Senate and House. We'll see what kind of relationship we can establish with these new states, or if we can coerce them to remain in the Union by hook or crook. I won't have the dissolution of the United States on my watch if it can be prevented by whatever means. All of you be thinking of a game plan to bring the stray sheep back into the fold. Good night to you all."

Elizabeth Bartlett had her most precious belongings boxed. She listed both her and Martha's houses with the best realtor in the area, noted for sales of large properties. She donated Martha's clothes to Goodwill. Martha's personal effects that were part of her marriage to Ethan she shipped to Ethan via United Parcel Service. She had all of her funds transferred from the Baltimore banks to one in Saratoga, NY where they had their summer residence. She, Josh and Sam were driven by their chauffer to Saratoga. Elizabeth enrolled the boys in the nearest private academy for their education where they started classes two weeks late.

The county attorney paraded in front of the jury. "Realizing that this confession was acquired under torture the defense will naturally claim it is inadmissible as evidence. The defense will claim then that the charge of murder should be dropped. Such safeguards are critical in a free nation. The defense will then claim that conviction of other charges will be sufficient to protect the public from Mr. Cartagena. The prosecution certainly does not condone or excuse torture in any way. These are trying times, however, and lives have been saved by the judicious use of same. It is time that justice is served, not the system. In this regard, the British system is superior to ours. Once evidence is obtained, it is admissible regardless of how it was acquired. Nevertheless, it is wholly unconscionable to allow such a murderer and traitor to live. The stockpiling of weapons and explosives, the attempts to subvert the youth of immigrants and immigrants who are not citizens to seize land by force and execute its owners are prima facie evidence of the intent to commit murder. The prosecution is therefore asking for the death penalty. Realizing that the state penitentiary can no longer carry out executions due to the backlog of cases, nor hold prisoners for years to decades pending one appeal after another, our county, our state, our proposed new country about to be attacked, cannot afford to release nor to hold such a dangerous prisoner. We know irrefutably he committed murder. We know irrefutably that he planned armed rebellion in which many of our ranching and farming families would have been killed. In the name of justice, I ask this jury and this court to condemn Juan Cartagena to death. The method to be used is to be decided upon by the jury and the court. Alternatives are hanging, firing squad, or application of a lethal dose of sleep inducing drugs. I ask you, would you want this man turned loose to attack you?"

The jury deliberated four hours. Juan Cartagena was sentenced to death by hanging. The jury of nine men and three women decided he should be an example witnessed by the public.

One week later, Ferdinand "Freddy" Montoya and Juan "John" Castro went to trial. Given the death penalty awarded to Cartagena, they decided the best defense was to place themselves at the mercy of the court. Montoya related their gang membership in Los Angeles, that they were still active members of the gang, their relationship with Juan Cartagena, and their instructions to murder the Chief of Police and the Sheriff. Castro admitted knowledge of Cartagena's hiring of an illegal immigrant to assassinate Colonel Bradley. The same jury awarded the same penalty to the two former law officers: death by public hanging. There is to be no appeal for any of the three. Execution is to be carried out as soon as a gallows could be built in Pioneer Square. One week later all three were hanged.

CHAPTER 20

SEPTEMBER 16, 08:00 HOURS, THE WHITE HOUSE CONFERENCE ROOM.

"All right people, where do we draw the line? What do we do about the secessionists? Then we'll tackle the gangs and criminal private armies and so on in the cities. They are pretty much one and the same problem as I see it, though. Naomi, where can we draw some lines on the map? Do we attempt to force the recalcitrant states back into the Union or let them go? Do we have the forces to do it?"

"Mr. President, I think the first priority is in the Midwest, all across the country. I've brought in this map to illustrate what I think we can do. We can't hold the southwest. That's a given. I have tentatively drawn a line with a great big bend in it from Monterey Bay across to Denver, rather along U.S. Highway 50 and Interstate Highway 70. We can't hold on to Colorado south of Denver because it is too Hispanic, but we can I think, hold on to north Texas and points north. I want to save Texas from Austin with the University of Texas north. That is probably a dream, really not much chance. The Governor has already ordered the evacuation of as much of the University as possible. Much more likely, it will be along Interstate 20, from Colorado Springs to Amarillo down to Dallas-Fort Worth and east to Shreveport. At least this is my hope. As a last resort, the Red River, the border between Texas an Oklahoma should be our final stand. Amarillo has the only helium plant in the U.S. I am not sure we can hold all the way to Big D, but I think we should try. We will have to evacuate Fort Hood and work out of Fort Sill, OK and the old Air Force bases in the area of north Texas and southern Oklahoma. Fort Hood has plans for immediate evacuation. That will give us a great curved border. As far as the southeast, I don't believe we will ultimately be able to hold the line any farther south than somewhere in North Carolina. We have to keep Virginia, especially Norfolk Naval Base. We will have to vacate the southern military bases in Georgia, South Carolina, and Louisiana. I mean take everything out that we can pull up from bases like Forts Polk, Benning, and Bragg. I have already ordered the home ported ships from the Gulf to prepare to move to New York City, Bangor, Boston and other northern ports. It is likely that the southern parts of the Mississippi and Ohio Rivers will be the boundary for the southeastern country. Little Rock will be a border town. Those folks won't stop killing each other until one side or the other is dominant. It is possible that they will kill enough of each other off that we can go back in at a later date and pick up the pieces. I believe the black community will ultimately win out over the Hispanics in the southeast. There is still a good deal of violence in the Carolinas. Warlords are setting up all over the place. We might have to wait until the smoke clears a bit and then move in. Let them kill each other off and then take them before they can recuperate and get organized on a regional or state basis."

"Ed, as Secretary of Homeland Security, what do you think we should do about the Territory of the Missouri?"

"Mr. President, there are some very important things about that region. They have the largest low sulfur coal reserves in the United States. They also have the largest reserves of natural gas, oil, oil sands and oil shale, and uranium in this country. While the easy oil and natural gas have been extracted from Wyoming and Montana, the proposed Nation of Missouri contains the major wheat producing states, the bread basket so to speak, also producing corn, alfalfa and other cereals as well as cattle. Cattle aren't as important as the cereal grains. The region is low in population, relatively speaking. They have the headwaters of the Missouri River, a vital artery to transportation and major source of water for the Midwest. They block our interior lines of communication with Columbia. With a Hispanic California, the so-called New California, Columbia is isolated from the rest of the U.S. We need to hold on to the so-called Nation of the Missouri if we can, Mr. President."

"Naomi, can we force them back into the Union?"

"Possibly, Mr. President. The Joint Chiefs and I have been working on a contingency plan for that purpose. It requires Special Operations to infiltrate the area to observe their preparations. We will insert Special Operations folks at critical areas. Their success will greatly enhance the battle, if it is only a battle and not a war. If they are identified and captured or eliminated however, it would be much more costly. We might not be able to supply those folks, but they are trained to live off the land if they have must. We already have a pretty good idea of who the key people are in the Territory of the Missouri and their strategy is. The population seems very mixed about the secession, according to their economic fears. We're not sure how much support any military resistance they might mount will be supported by the people. That's the real key. We don't want to fight a guerilla type war if we can avoid it. That is what they have been training to do, particularly in the Rocky Mountains in the western part of the region. The people have been reluctant to take the threat of an invasion from us seriously, so we don't think they are as prepared as they could be. Therefore, a swift victory is critical. Depending on how things go in Colorado, we might have a force move north from Fort Carson. That is if they don't have to defend the new border south of Denver. Another force can move out of Fort Leonard Wood, MO if they don't have to reinforce the forces at Ft. Sill to defend our southern border. That is much more likely. I don't think we should count on the troops from Ft. Leonard Wood. It is a training base anyway. We can assemble National Guard forces in Minnesota, and possibly one out of Columbia, Fort Lewis, WA. The latter is a little doubtful though. I would prefer to keep those troops on hand to defend the ports and assets in that region, although there is really no recognizable threat to them at this time. There is little in the way of topography that provides for an adequate defense in the Dakotas and eastern Montana. Still, it is a long logistical tail across the Great Plains and we do not wish to destroy the agricultural commodities or land there. That is our bread basket. At any rate, that will still provide a multiple pronged attack and spread their forces very thin. They can't defend on all fronts. Time wise, winter is rapidly approaching. It could snow and turn cold anytime in the mountains. While not likely to last, it could temporarily hinder military operations. Passes could be closed by mid November or even earlier."

"All right Naomi. Put it in motion. I won't ask Congress for anything. Make it a surprise attack as much as possible. Turn it over to the Joint Chiefs and let's see if they can do their thing. We can't afford to be isolated from Columbia. If we can force them back into the Union we will have a contiguous nation across the northern United States. Maybe the western Canadian provinces will join us then."

The telephone rang in front of Naomi Campbell. She picked it up, listened intently, and said "Thank you, General." She looked at the President and spoke. "The Wyoming National Guard just seized F.E. Warren Air Force Base in Cheyenne. Satellite videos show that they are moving everything they can off the base. The aircraft are taking off as we speak. Apparently aviators who have chosen to give their allegiance to the Nation of the Missouri are flying them out to smaller airfields, particularly in the Big Horn Basin. All maintenance equipment, electronics, everything is being stripped. We just picked up a cell phone communication; they are even hauling out the modular air traffic control equipment. Apparently there are less than a dozen fatalities; the wounded were taken to the civilian hospital in military ambulances. Even the base hospital is being stripped. They are using mostly civilian trucks as well as military vehicles to haul out as much as they can carry. Even fuel is being removed by civilian tanker trucks. The general said they had massed civilian vehicles, including several hundred pickup trucks, to haul as much as possible. Because of the use of civilian vehicles for the most part, the attack wasn't recognized until it was too late. We planned to seize F.E. Warren as our opening move in the attack north out of Fort Carson, CO, but it appears they beat us to it. Wyoming National Guard anti-aircraft units are on the move to guard the convoy from air attack. The Montana National Guard has simultaneously seized Malmstrom Air Force Base in Great Falls. No one was injured. They gave all the regular Air Force active duty people the opportunity to either join the Montana Air Guard or immediately leave the Nation of Missouri. Many of the pilots and ground crews stayed. Those that decided to remain loyal they put on a bus caravan and ordered them to drive straight through to Minneapolis. They didn't even give them a chance to go home. They told them that they would contact their families and inform them of what had occurred. They advised them to call their families as soon as they reached Minneapolis and have their wives put their houses up for sale and leave as soon as they could arrange transportation for household goods at their own expense or Uncle Sam's Air Force. This was a well thought out move. If their military leadership continues outmaneuver us like this, we are in for a knock down drag out fight."

The room was silent for a moment, and then Newkirk spoke. "All right Naomi, get going. Do whatever is necessary. Let's try and bring them back into the fold. Diplomacy has failed, now let's try force."

"Mr. President, perhaps a show of force, as opposed to an out and out attack would be more appropriate. A bluff, if you will, a show of force, or whatever might bring them to their senses."

Newkirk pondered the suggestion for a moment, then said "Thank you, Peter, as Attorney General you always consider the legal alternative. Naomi, I suppose we can always carry through if they don't respond to a show of force. Give the order."

Naomi Campbell picked up the phone, punched a button that rang in the office of the Chairman, Joint Chiefs of Staff. "This is Secretary Campbell. Order an immediate mobilization of all National Guard and Reserve Units according to Plan C. All personnel are to report to their headquarters. All units are to be issued full basic load of ammunition and supplies. Logistics annex of Plan C is to be followed in complete detail, by order of the Commander-in-Chief.

She heard the voice of General Dewey Singleton, the Chairman, USAF, "Yes Madam Secretary, I will issue the order within one minute."

The fax rang in Ethan's office as a message was printed out. Sergeant Major Killian rose to retrieve it. It was from General McIntire to Colonel Bradley. "Am sending you one squadron (sixteen aircraft and support personnel) of Joint Strike Fighters from F.E. Warren Air Force Base in Cheyenne. Initial landing will be at Worland. If you wish them deployed elsewhere, make immediate plans and decision within hours. Maintenance and logistical support following by vehicle. Aviation fuel included as well as support personnel. Entire air operations will be under your command. Colonel Zeigler commands air assets and is attached to your command. ETA 18:00 hours today.

You are promoted to Brigadier General, 3rd Brigade (Basin Brigade), commanding.

McIntire."

Ethan Bradley was ecstatic. A brigade has no fixed structure, only what assets higher command wishes to assign to it. Now he had an air force of sorts under his command. He immediately picked up the phone and called the Mayor and informed him to call an immediate meeting of the city-county fathers at 12:00 hours. When the meeting convened, he informed them that sixteen aircraft and their supporting assets will be stationed in Worland. That was greeted with enthusiasm until Ethan pointed out that it also had its complications. It made the Worland Airport a legitimate military target. He recommended that all homes in the immediate vicinity be evacuated, at least half a mile away. Farther would be better, in fact, as far away as possible. The residents should be immediately informed because there was no way of knowing of an impending attack. He didn't know what radar or electronic emissions detection equipment would be coming with the convoy. An attack could occur within minutes of aircraft landing or weeks or never. He informed them that our political and military leadership has no way of knowing the intentions of President Newkirk.

"Congress has abrogated its responsibility to declare war ever since Vietnam in the last century. I doubt that Newkirk will even bother with informing Congress of his intentions. Congressmen can't keep a secret," he smiled dryly. *"The biggest leak of classified information has always been the Congressman at a cocktail party trying to impress the chicks with his importance. No telling what Newkirk will do,"* thought Ethan.

Back in his office Bradley called Captain Whitehorse. "Deploy your men to their positions around the openings of the canyon, Shoshoni and Thermopolis. Be prepared to hold those positions. Have all demolitions set for detonation. The gloves are off. Opening moves have occurred. You can expect an attack at any time, either by air or ground forces independently or combined. I don't think they will attack the dam, but I can't be certain. Protect the Boysen Dam at all reasonable costs. The Prairie Brigade will hold road junction at Shoshoni as long as possible without suffering destruction of the force. Allow the Prairie Brigade to pass through your forces in retreat. They are to move to Thermopolis. Cover for them. They will fight a withdrawal under pressure until they pass through your company. Retreat into the Wind River Canyon when pressure becomes intense. You must not allow the destruction of your force but you must attrit the enemy in the canyon. The commander of the Prairie Brigade is to report to me. Any questions?"

"No Sir. I have had personnel on high readiness status since yesterday. We will be in our positions in a matter of hours, no later than 18:00 hours, Sir."

"Very good, Captain. Turn back all civilian vehicles that do not contain residents of the Basin. Carry on." Bradley hung up the phone and thought to himself, *"Well, it's finally started. God knows how it will turn out or how long it will last. Let's pray to God it doesn't last too long or get too bloody. Americans killing Americans sickens me."*

A mechanized force of two Units of Action, the First and Second, left Fort Carson at 15:00 on 16 September. They were composed primarily of Stryker and tank battalions. The Third Unit stayed behind to defend the base and if necessary a line between Pueblo and Denver. The two Units of Action moved steadily up U.S. 25 through Denver. At Fort Collins, the First Unit moved to Highway 287 to strike northwest, on the western slope of the Big Horn Mountains. Intermediate objective: Laramie. The Second Unit continued north on U.S. 25 with the intermediate objective of Cheyenne. Their primary objective was Billings along Interstate highways 25 first and then I-90. Jared Johnston, the Governor of Montana, acting as interim President of the Nation of the Missouri sent an urgent telefax to President Newkirk. It read:

"If U.S. government forces cross the border into Wyoming, hostile activities will commence. The two Units of

Action advancing from the south will be attacked. Request you order all federal forces to return to their bases in order to avoid open warfare. The Balkanization of the former United States cannot be avoided. Only tremendous loss of life and property can follow if you continue present course."

Enraged at the audacity of the telex when he read it, he picked up the phone. "Naomi, order an immediate air attack on the Capitol of Missouri in Billings. I want that son-of-a-bitch Johnston in Billings, Montana killed today."

"I'll call General Singleton and order it. I don't know what assets he will want to use. I presume you are asking for a precision strike, rather than a broad bombing which will result in numerous civilian casualties. I am sure you are aware that an area strike will only turn the civilian population that is the fence sitters against us, and just harden the position of the rebels."

"Naomi Campbell, I don't care how you do it, just kill that SOB and do it today." He slammed down the phone.

When the SECDEF ordered General Singleton to carry out the attack, he responded only with "Yes, Madam Secretary. Is there anything else?" He hung up the phone and thought to himself. *My God, the bastard is really going to attack other Americans. This isn't just an attack against one man per se, even a rebel, but an attack on a civilian institution, former fellow citizens, He is out of his mind. What do I do? Who do I order to carry out this attack or do I refuse it? Do I give personnel the option of not carrying it out? How many will carry it out? Hell, the country is already lost and breaking apart.*" He recalled a study done many years ago, in the 1980's, and since repeated every ten or so years, about how many Coastguardsmen and Marines would carry out an order to shoot to kill any American citizen in good standing who otherwise refused to surrender their privately own firearms when ordered to do so. In the initial study it was astounding 65%. Since then it had grown to over 80% who stated on paper they would kill their fellow citizens. Now, with the turmoil, the desertions in the Army and less extent, Marine ranks, he pondered. He doubted the survey. What would he, as a man, or as a career military officer, do?

The Units of Action from Fort Carson were slowed by the civilian traffic on U.S. 25 that was fleeing northward from the southwest. People refused to pull over until the tanks and armored personnel carriers bumped them from the rear or pushed their main gun tube through the rear window. It bought the Wyoming Air National Guard an extra twenty-four hours to continue to remove anything and everything from F.E. Warren Air Force Base. It also gave the defenders an extra twenty-four hours for preparation of defenses. One Wyoming Air National Guard F-35 Joint Strike Fighter was kept in the air at all times over the base while extraction continued. Periodically it would zoom south to observe the advance of the brigades from Ft. Carson.

General Singleton ordered a remotely piloted vehicle squadron (RPV) out of Whiteman Air Force Base, near Sedalia, MO to conduct the strike mission against Billings, Montana. They had shown the discipline to carry out such orders. It was the same squadron that had targeted General McIntire and others from the potentially breakaway states. It would be a coordinated attack, with several Remotely Piloted Vehicles firing Hellfire III missiles at Interim President Jared Johnston's office. Johnston would be tracked by satellites and laser targeted. Multiple missiles would not only guarantee a kill but also take out many of the state representatives and bureaucracy of Billings. The state capitol of Montana remained in Helena, but Johnston had turned over the state government to his Lieutenant Governor while he addressed the delicacy of forming a government for the new Nation of Missouri from its new capitol in Billings. The RPVs were launched at 18:00 hours Central Standard Time with the intent of catching President Johnston enroute to his temporary home. When the satellite image revealed their launch to the personnel at Malmstrom Air Force Base in Great Falls, Montana, their initial flight path was plotted, revealing their potential target as Billings. At 17:15 hours Mountain Standard Time a Joint Strike Fighter section of two aircraft took off from Malmstrom AFB. Their take off was observed on satellite but there were no aircraft capable of engaging them before they could attack the flight of RPVs. Fifty miles east of Billings the two JSF engaged the flight of RPVs and shot them all down by twenty millimeter cannon fire in a matter of seconds. When the mission failure was reported to President Newkirk, he flew into a quiet rage. He called Naomi into his office and reprimanded her for not including fighter RPVs in the flight to protect the ground attack RPVs. He didn't consider the range of the aircraft. In turn, she called General Singleton into her office. He took the ass chewing straight faced, but inwardly the smile couldn't be bigger.

Special Operations dropped a half a dozen men into the Big Horn Basin using the High Altitude Low Opening (HALO) technique. They would parachute out of a fast moving jet at 35,000 feet and open chutes by altimeter at 500 feet so as to avoid detection by radar. They carried computers and electronic communications equipment as well as explosives and weapons. They were also wearing civilian clothes instead of uniforms. Their landing zones varied with each of the two man teams. One team came down east of Cody, another east of Worland. Other teams came down around Gillette, Sheridan, Casper and Rock Springs. Others landed outside of Billings and Helena, Rapid City, Boise and Pocatello, Spearfish and Rapid City. Their mission was to identify mobilizing forces, and if ordered, to call in air, artillery fires if they were in range, or missile strikes on any concentration of forces.

Outside of Ten Sleep, Wyoming, a sheepherder guarding a flock of sheep saw two parachutes open. He immediately left the flock to the coyotes and called the Sheriff on his cell phone. Sheriff Brady immediately informed General Bradley.

Bradley immediately called Captain Jim Ferguson into his office.

"Two Special Ops guys just came down east of Ten Sleep. Organize a party of your four best trackers and shooters. Have them in civilian clothes. They are to carry scoped bolt action rifles. Their cover is that they are coyote hunters protecting the sheep flocks. The Special Ops guys are too good to try and take alive. Shoot to kill on sight. Don't miss! There will be hell to pay if your men fail. We can't afford to have them around. Don't go yourself, but you can send a lieutenant if you have a good one in mind. Check with the sheepherder Findley. He will meet you at the Ten Sleep Bar and Grill. Get going and good hunting Captain."

An hour later four men of Ferguson's command were driving to Ten Sleep. They met Findley at the bar and bought him a drink for the road. They decided just to use only Findley's pickup truck as the Special Ops probably saw it and would be less inclined to be alerted than with two vehicles in the area. Findley drove them to his flock in the pasture at the foot of the Brokenback Mountain and pointed to where he saw them come down. The four guardsmen wore radio headsets so they could communicate. They kept their rifles slung barrels down so as to be less obvious. They spread out a hundred meters apart and walked the mile towards where Findley directed them. At the brush line at the foot of the mountain they crouched behind the sagebrush and glassed the area with binoculars. Suspecting that they were being observed, Sergeant Gooding ordered them to take positions with good cover and observe. No further movement, even if they had to remain motionless all night. Motion is detected before shapes are recognized. Sergeant Gooding was thinking of the seven Ss of cover and concealment. He was on the third, shine, shadow, silhouette, when he detected movement one hundred meters to his right front. "Peterson, are you moving?" he whispered into his headset. "I have movement at my two o'clock, a hundred meters out."

"Negative Sergeant, I'm fixed. I don't see anything yet."

Gooding slowly pointed his custom .308 Mauser bolt action over the branch of the deadfall, ever so slowly. He peered through the scope. He saw movement again, but couldn't detect a shape. Slowly, a figure emerged out of the shadow. It crouched, hesitated and then took another goose walk step. Gooding put the crosshairs on the middle of the head and began squeezing the trigger. The figure moved another step. Gooding breathed twice, repositioned the crosshairs and squeezed a little faster. The figure abruptly lurched backwards as the 150 grain bullet entered through the center of his forehead.

"All personnel remain in cover. I just fired. One down. Repeat. Do not reveal your position. Hold until either ordered or come under fire."

Sergeant Gooding had been shooting since he was seven years old. He started with a single shoot .22 Long Rifle. His father took him pheasant hunting with a twenty gauge shotgun for his first hunt when he was nine. He killed his first mule deer when he was ten. He bagged his first elk at twelve and antelope at thirteen. He stalked and killed a dozen coyotes a year. He started out calling coyotes as a teenager to earn money for his dates, but after a dozen years of that decided it would be more fun if he could stalk them with a night scope. Coyotes hunt at night in cold weather and sleep during the day so they don't freeze to death. He grew used to sitting still at minus twenty degrees Fahrenheit wearing a snow camouflage parka on the open prairie, peering intently through sagebrush with a fourth generation starlight scope to detect the movement of coyotes as they ran down rabbits and other rodents. He learned patience and wouldn't tolerate a rifle that wouldn't shoot less than one inch five shot groups at one hundred meters. He often, although not always, would connect with a two hundred meter shot at a loping coyote. He sold the pelts for fifty dollars after tanning them. He was now teaching his eight year old son all his hard earned lessons about hunting and patience.

Corporal Johnson on his left flank was a graduate of the Army Sniper School. Johnson preferred an old Remington Model 700 with a twenty-six inch heavy barrel firing the .308 Winchester cartridge. It was accurate out to six hundred meters where he could keep five rounds in a six inch circle.

To Corporal Johnson's left was the new kid on the block, nineteen year old Allen Falls. Allen's dad wasn't much of a hunter. Instead, his father was an accountant at one of the local banks. Allen Fall's training had been mostly lectures, with not a lot of field experience. His winter training was limited to the several exercises that Captain Ferguson had organized the past winter. A year out of high school, he hadn't decided on what he wanted to study in college, or even what college he wanted to attend. Instead, he got a job at a local fast food restaurant while he pondered what to do with his life. The temperature dropped to twenty degrees Fahrenheit that night, and nineteen year old Allen Falls fell asleep in the cold. The figure approached him ever so silently he never detected its presence. A hand went over Allen's mouth and a six inch blade went through his neck from side to side, severing both the internal and external carotid arteries on each side of his neck. He twitched twice and died and never even knew it. Two hours later a branch broke with a snap. Sergeant Gooding snapped to full alertness. He slowly raised his hand and pushed back the hood on his sagebrush camouflage parka. A millimeter of movement a minute, that was the rule. Anything more was likely to be detected. Sharp eyed antelope had taught him that. He slowly turned his head to the left inside his parka hood as his hand moved towards its edge. There, not twenty yards away crouched a figure. Uncertain whether or not he was detected, he remained motionless. After a few minutes that seemed like eternity, the figure slowly slipped into a prone position and moved towards him in a slow crawl. *"This guy is good,"* thought Gooding. *"He might have slipped by Allen and Johnson, but he ain't gonna slip by me."* Then it occurred to him that the figure might have killed the other two men to his left. When the figure was fifteen feet from him and rose to his knees holding a rifle at the port arms position across his chest, Peterson swiftly moved, raising his rifle and firing a snap shot into the center of the man's chest. The man bounced once while the arms flopped but landed on his stomach and lay still. Peterson worked the bolt on his rifle, chambering another round. He circled the man, rifle pointed directly at the supine figure. Calculating that the man might be wearing bullet proof armor, Peterson approached him from behind and aimed at the man's head. When he was three feet away, he fired another round, this one into the man's head. Blood, brains and bone splattered over the environment. Now there was no question that the man was dead.

"Check in team," Gooding spoke into his headset. Peterson responded. "I heard two rounds, Sergeant. You OK?"

"Yeah, I'm fine. The SOB in front of me ain't so good though. Johnson, Falls, are you there?"

"I'm here Sarge," said Johnson. "Falls?" No Answer. "Peterson, move to me." When Peterson reached Gooding, they moved together slowly to their left. "Johnson, we're coming to you. Watch your fire. Somebody might also move on you if there is another one out there, using us as cover."

When they reached Johnson, the spread out and began to search for Falls. After thirty minutes, they found him. They rigged a stretcher out of his coat and pants by cutting seven foot poles off a large blue sage and passing them through the sleeves of his coat and trousers legs.

"You two carry Falls out. I am going to search the two bodies we left out there. Then I will join you and help carry Falls."

Johnson and Peterson carried the body a mile back to where it could be reached with a vehicle   where Gooding caught up with them. He was carrying the electronic gear and weapons of the two Special Ops soldiers. They had no personal identification on them.

"Peterson, you stay with Falls. Johnson and I will get a vehicle and come back for you. When you see our headlights, set off a light stick to guide us in. Too bad Falls never joined the Boy Scouts."

No one saw the Special Operations soldiers who landed east of Cody, west of Worland. Bradley surmised they were out there, but deduced they would have to work their way towards Worland to carry out their mission. He alerted the Sheriff's department and had Sergeant Major Killian have a private in the office call every rancher between Meeteetse and Worland to alert them of one or more Special Forces Teams in the area. Sooner or later they would be observed, particularly when they ran out of food or water. There weren't many targets out there in the scrub, so they would have to move on Worland. They would be observed and hunted down sooner or later. Sergeant Gooding reported in person to Captain Ferguson the next morning. Ferguson reported to General Bradley by telephone of the elimination of the Special Ops team and of Falls's death. Falls was taken to a local undertaker while Captain Ferguson went to the bank to inform Falls's father of his demise.

Robert Bradley was sipping a beer and watching the evening news. The CNN reporter came on with a live report from the Surgeon General's Office in Washington, D.C. "On the influenza pandemic, it seems to be petering out in Europe. It is still infecting millions in the Middle East, Central America, Africa, and Central Asia. Epidemiologists at the Centers for Disease Control and Prevention in Atlanta are gleefully declaring the epidemic is essentially over in North America. The rest of the world is still reporting tremendous losses. The World Health Organization has released the following figures. Out of 350 million people in the United States and Canada, an estimated twelve million have died. Most of those were immunocompromised people, such as those on cancer therapy or victims of HIV infections. Figures for Europe are about the same. Of 500 million people in Mexico and Central America, a staggering 170 million are dead. Most of those deaths are in the back country areas where vaccine could not arrive in time. Out of nearly one billion people in South America, an estimated 350 million are dead or dying, mostly in rural and backward areas. The epidemic is moving more slowly through the remote areas of South America. Of 300 million people in North Africa and the Middle East, a staggering 150 million, half the population. The epidemic continues there, more slowly, but apparently unabated. It appears that only Israel escaped massive deaths in this epidemic. WHO is asking how and why. The Sahel and Africa south to the nation of South Africa also has lost more than half of its population, around 300 million. The Sahel in particular is suffering devastating losses. Those countries in turmoil received little vaccine. India, with its population greatly reduced by the World War and now mostly populated by Chinese suffered little. That is very interesting. The WHO is looking very seriously into why. Japan has escaped relatively unscathed. They had their public health infrastructure in place and their population was all vaccinated in a little over a week. Australasia also suffered about half of its native population dead or seriously infected. Indonesia and the Philippines were particularly hard hit with their native populations distributed on numerous islands. Again, the Chinese colonies there suffering very little and World Health Organization is asking "why."

The evening news was carrying live reports of the progress of the two convoys out of Fort Carson when Ethan reached home. No mention was made of the JSF and the RPVs. The business report stated that gold was now $3500 a troy ounce on the international market. Speculation about the U.S. dollar was driving the escalation. Worse, speculation that China might call in several trillion dollars worth of U.S. Treasury bills was adding to the angst. The popular business news reporter on Central News Network was unusually candid. Trading in U.S. dollars had completely ceased in New York and London

"The money barons-traders of international capitol flow, have surpassed most nation-state governments in exercising power. Economic power and cash flows control the world markets today. If China calls in those Treasury Notes or Bonds, the United States is finished as an economic and military force in the world, and possibly as the nation we have known.

It is now recognized by some in Washington that the majority of the lower class and lower middle class that was forced downward are a driving force in our social unrest. The few, huge, mega-multinationals and currency brokers who have no allegiance to anything but their own wealth and bureaucracies must share a primary responsibility for such social unrest, perhaps even a revolution that we now are experiencing. These multi-nationals became separated from their domestic bases, their consumers, their employees and shareholders. On the international scene they became neo-colonialists to exploit cheap unskilled and low skilled labor in second and third world countries while avoiding the environmental concerns of Europe and North America. The concept of Hobbe's economic anarchy has returned on a global scale. A well developed state with sound, well established institutions, judicial, law enforcement, with credible economic opportunities open for each honest, talented individual is critical. The state must enable the ordinary citizen, individually or collectively, to defend him or herself against corruption, inequity or abuse through political action. The elite cartels that have evolved as a form of corruption are intolerable. These are nodes in a web of government bureaucracies and bureaucrats, business moguls, military and media elitists who attempt to control us through what information we are allowed to have and what economic pressure can be exerted on us.

With the breakup of the United States, unless some form of agreement can be reached between the new nation-states now forming in North America, food will be the only thing North America can produce that will be worth trading on world markets. Everything else will be locally consumed, be it energy resources or manufactured goods. Indeed, some areas of the former U.S. will have little, if any food to trade. Fertilizer, fuel, seeds and farm labor will all be in short supply. Now and the next few months is the time of harvest. Who will do the harvesting? Who has the fuel for the tractors and combines to salvage this year's crops? Those areas or new states will have to import what they consume. Americans in the cities of the east better be ready for hunger. Remember, rice and beans form a complete protein. If you can add a little meat or poultry, especially fish, you can survive on mostly vegetables with occasional fresh fruit. That is, if you can get any fresh fruit north of the Mason –Dixon line."

"By God," explained Robert Bradley. "I'll bet that gets that business news reporter fired."

The host news reporter came back on. "Thanks for that candid report. Elsewhere in the news the Europeans are alerting their reserve forces now that the Chinese are beginning to move again towards the Middle East. Speculation as to their objectives is rampant in the capitols of Europe and here. The majority of opinion however, seems to be that they will drive to control the Straits of Hormuz and Iran. They won't have to take the Persian Gulf states if they can control the mouth of the Gulf."

The reported further noted that the riots in the cities were expending themselves. Hunger, disease, and fratricide were taking their toll on those that failed to migrate. There were fewer live reports coming out of the southeast. No one on the ground had the overall picture, only the local situation. News analysts attempted to piece independent reports together to present an overview for their television audiences. One newscaster stated that rural areas were still suffering raids, murder, rape and arson on a widespread scale. The southeast in particular, was in the throes of ethnic cleansing. The only question was who is cleansing where of whom. First the Hispanics were winning in some areas while black Americans were winning in others. No definitive line could be drawn as the individual militias seesawed back and forth. People of any race or color trying to flee to safety somewhere else were easy targets for the opposite ethnic group.

"Well Dad, what about that? Think the Chinese will call in those bonds and treasury notes?"

"Our economic policy has been a disaster ever since Congress created the Federal Reserve Banking System to foister worthless paper money off on the world. It is a built in scam that gave us tremendous inflation. After World War II and when we went off the gold standard in 1973 we coerced the Middle East oil producers to trade oil for U.S. dollars. That made our phony economic system even worse. The Federal Reserve Bank just continued to print worthless paper which expanded inflation. The money barons knew they could generate 3 to 4% interest a year compounded and make billions. Now the inflation bubble is rupturing. Economics isn't really a science. It is a political art. It is a practice of rationalizing or creating a monetary policy or theory to support a political position, especially one that supports the accumulation of wealth for a nation or an individual. Our politicians and central bankers and as the reporter said, nodes of elite business cartels all stood to profit at the expense of the small guy, the average citizen, through continued inflation. Now I'll bet, they have converted all their worthless U.S. dollars to gold."

"Going out tonight, Son? You know you and those two gals are the talk of the town."

Robert turned back to the TV news. "The Chinese have perfectly timed it, Mr. President. The U.S. is now in civil war while they move on the Persian Gulf and neither we nor Europe can do a thing about it."

"Don't say we're in a civil war, Harry. We aren't. I realize the opportunistic timing, Harry. As Director of National Intelligence, why don't you and your people come up with where the Chinese are getting all these forces, and where will they stop? How come the Chinese timing is so perfect anyway?"

"Well, Mr. President, the first answer is easy. The Chinese have had a trained militia of 200 million personnel since the mid 1990's. We have recently learned that the Chinese gave most of their political prisoners a choice. Join the Army and be trained or die. Turn your skills on your superiors or rebel and your entire family dies, down to the second cousins. They didn't want to fool with concentration camps and fight a war at the same time. China has an enormous number of forced labor camps, numbering in the thousands, each holding thousands of people, actually millions who dared disagree with Chinese leadership over the years. The older prisoners are producing munitions in prison machine shops while the younger ones go into battle. It's that simple. As for the second part, we picked up an hour ago that Chinese electronic countermeasures jammed Iranian radar and missile sites, communications centers, and have launched cruise missiles that are flying over all their cities of significance as we speak. Some of the missiles have crashed; none of them have exploded, so we aren't sure what is going on. It might be that they are spraying influenza or some other biological agent over Iran. Remember, Iran didn't get any of our flu vaccine, and they don't have the strains of the current circulating virus to mass produce it themselves, certainly not anything of appropriate quality or quantity. What they did get was from Europe after the E.U. vaccinated all of its citizens. If it is influenza, I anticipate the Chinese will halt a few kilometers inside the Iranian border. As to the third question, the Chinese timing, I don't have an answer."

"Why would they halt?"

"By crossing the border or stopping right at it they forced the Iranian mobilization and massing of forces, making them easy targets for their missiles or bombs or whatever. If so, the Iranians fell for it, hook line and sinker. They massed their forces. Anything larger than a battalion is liable to catch a bomb of some kind, a small quarter ton tactical nuke or a biological agent. We'll know in 72 hours if it is influenza or some other agent because the Iranians will start dying like flies placed in a freezer, far more than the normal epidemic curve would predict. We don't know how much influenza vaccine the Iranians received or manufactured. You can bet that first priority on what they had went to their armed forces. They will let disease do their dirty work for them. Their biggest problem then will be collecting and disposing of the Iranian bodies. We'll see if Chinese engineering units start moving forward to dig mass graves."

That morning, Chinese electromagnetic full spectrum band width jamming of Iranian radar sites, communications centers, military units and even civilian radio traffic, allowed Chinese cruise missiles equipped with terrain following radar to fly at 200 feet over all major Iranian cities and military bases spraying influenza virus or perhaps something else along their course. Iranians danced in the streets when the cruise missiles did not explode. They anticipated that the missiles carried conventional explosives if not nuclear warheads. Many cities had jubilant crowds dancing in the streets all night long. Someone must have reprogrammed the missiles not to explode. Once the cruise missiles had completed their course, the Chinese ceased their jamming. This added to the Iranian's initial belief that the cruise missiles had all failed. All the missiles were programmed to crash into isolated areas in the desert or the Caspian Sea. Since they were flying so low, and landing in isolated areas, there would not be enough time for the Iranians to recover any of them for examination. At 18:00 hours that day, Chinese elements crossed into Iran from what was Afghanistan and Turkmenistan. Their advance was planned to be leisurely, bypassing no pockets of resistance, allowing for adequate resupply, and giving the agent the opportunity to eliminate most of the resistance. The Iranian military decided to assume an entirely defensive strategy. This resulted in only minimal local resistance to the initial Chinese incursions and insured short internal lines of communication. The Iranians dug in behind well prepared defensive positions and waited. The Chinese had advanced only two hundred kilometers in the first forty-eight hours, when the Iranians began to experience large numbers of fatal cases of respiratory paralysis. The Chinese had sprayed botulinum toxin from the low flying missiles, not influenza virus. The inhaled toxin resulted in respiratory paralysis beginning twenty-four hours later. The only way to survive is to be put on an automatic respirator for the next two months. The Iranians died by the hundreds of thousands. Being hydrophilic and subject to rain and high humidity, the toxin deteriorates into an innocuous molecule in forty-eight hours. The doors to Iran opened for the Chinese battalions.

The brigades from Fort Carson, just south of Colorado Springs, stopped just short of the Colorado-Wyoming state line on Interstate 25. It took them three days to reach the state line. Here they paused for twenty-four hours to refuel and resupply and rest. President Newkirk ordered his entire cabinet along with the White House media to the Oval Office to film, as opposed to a live broadcast, a last minute appeal for unity. He picked up the telephone and placed a call to President Johnston. He had a prepared message from his best speech writer.

"Governor Johnston," Newkirk refusing to recognize Jared Johnston as the President of a breakaway province, "our troops have massed along the border of Colorado and Wyoming. I do not wish to initiate hostilities with my fellow citizens. I urge you and all the others to rescind the secession and remain in the Union. We cannot afford another civil war. We have been the beacon of freedom for over two and a half centuries. We cannot deny our future as an intact nation. I beg you to order the forces you command to stand down and call an emergency meeting of the state governors who are joining you in secession .It is a war you cannot win and only suffer destruction of your people and your states."

"President Newkirk, we will only consider rescinding secession if you return to the Constitution. You must restore all civil rights, release your political prisoners, especially those who committed no violent crimes, those who dared to speak against you and your policies, release especially the journalists who defended the Constitution, and those who were merely firearms owners. Reign in the FBI and disband the Bureau for Alcohol, Tobacco, Firearms and Explosives. Destroy all records of their arrests and incarceration and have your armed forces return to their bases. Then and only then will I consider meeting your requests."

"I have never abandoned the Constitution Governor. In fact, I have always been a stalwart defender of it as the highest law of the land. Those federal police agencies are essential to our survival as a nation. I cannot in good conscience disband them. Those people whom you referred to are in prison as a result of their sedition. I cannot turn them loose."

"History will not be kind to you, President Newkirk. You have initiated a civil war from which it is unlikely that this nation will recover. If you cross into our borders we will consider it an act of war. All oil, natural gas, biofuels, timber, cattle, sheep, coal, foodstuffs and all other commodities will immediately cease flowing into your country. Make no mistake. We are prepared and will fight with all the fortitude of the patriots of the Revolutionary War. We will make trade arrangements with you if you withdraw and we settle our differences as two different countries amicably. There is no other choice for us. If you decide for peace, contact us. Goodbye, President Newkirk." With that, President Johnston placed the phone in its cradle.

"Naomi, order the forces to proceed into the breakaway states whenever they are ready. I want that bastard crushed as soon as possible and those state governors and legislators in custody."

Newkirk sat brooding for a few minutes while the media dismantled their equipment and moved out of the Oval Office. The cabinet remained in place with no one speaking.

"Secretary Andretti, Homeland Security Chief, what is your latest take on the mess in the southeast?"

"Mr. President, I believe the Black Americans are winning in the southeast. They are better organized, armed and quite a number of black citizens have served in the Army. They were mentally and physically much better prepared. The biggest problem within the black community is the rise of the black Islamic extremists. They are armed and extremely dangerous, more violent than the rest of the black community. There may well be a violent intra-ethnic conflict within the black community, convert to Islam or die. Many Hispanics are fleeing to the southwest, most overland in vehicles, but some are even fleeing by boats, many stolen, to Mexico and the Texas Gulf Coast. I think when the dust settles we will find the southeast solidly black except for the southern half of Florida. Those of Cuban descent and other Caribbean nations have too great a hold on the Miami area in particular and Florida south of St. Petersburg in particular. They can easily defend the end of the Florida peninsula. All of the white folks have fled or are in hiding or have been killed throughout the southeast. From Virginia through Georgia, across the

Mississippi River into east Texas is now pretty solidly black. Kentucky and Tennessee are current battle grounds. They could go either way. I believe we hold this city, Washington, DC, only because of the Marines guarding it. If the Marines stand down or pull out, I think the black population will flood in here. It would be prudent, Mr. President, to think of moving the Capitol to a more northerly city. Philadelphia is still experiencing urban warfare, but not like it was. Most whites have left that city but that makes it a black enclave. Sooner or later the blacks there will realize it and I think, pull out. I don't think Naomi and her map are realistic, but only time will tell. If the black populations in our inner cities don't leave, they will starve and freeze with the coming winter. I don't see how it will stand as an essentially all black area as it is too isolated, an island so to speak. Blacks have incompletely evacuated Detroit, Chicago, Cleveland, and other northern cities. With no food coming in, the harbors closed, lack of electricity, water sewage plants down, I think the blacks will abandon Philadelphia sooner or later as well. Either they leave or starve to death. Unfortunately, there is little way out for those foolish enough to have stayed. Perhaps New York or Pittsburgh might be good alternatives as a new national capitol."

"And the southwest Ed? I suppose it's gone too?"

"Yes, Mr. President, it is solidly Hispanic. I'm afraid, as Naomi pointed out, we can probably hold that great curving line, hopefully to include the Big D. If we can keep the breakaway Territory of the Missouri in the Union, we can have a solid nation across the northern and central U.S. I don't see Columbia breaking away or going on its own. It is too rich, too liberal and too intellectual."

At 03:00, the next morning, the two brigades crossed into Wyoming. One brigade headed for Laramie, one for Cheyenne. Brigadier General (BG) Leonard Winston had done his homework. Commanding the 1st Brigade, Army of the

Nation of Missouri, also known as the Cheyenne Brigade, planned the battle as an urban one. The 1st Brigade had six thousand uniformed men and women. His militia however, included another ten thousand volunteers, armed mostly with sporting weapons they had hidden from the government. He had heavy mines planted under Interstate 25 and U.S. 85 by tunneling under the pavement to attrit the armor. Snipers in spider holes and in sewer lines popped up through manholes and made sure any demolitions experts would be eliminated if they found the explosives. It turned out to be unnecessary. Improved explosive devices utilizing the high explosive known as RDX that several had manufactured in their homes to supplement the captured supplies, in irrigation ditches controlled by cell phones, snipers picking off tank commanders standing in their tank hatches and truck drivers from five hundred meters or more away, took their toll and started draining the already low morale of the invaders. Every bit of cover or concealment was utilized. When multi-story buildings were passed, civilians threw Molotov cocktails on the vehicles. The Molotov cocktails containing crude napalm were made of quart jars, whisky and wine bottles filled with gasoline that had dissolved fels naptha soap that was shaved thin so as to more easily dissolve, then corked, a sanitary napkin taped to the outside with cellophane tape to be soaked in lighter fluid and ignited before throwing, rained down on tanks and armored personnel carriers. A few brave souls had actually heated the gasoline and soap in a double boiler to insure dissolution of the soap at considerable risk. That made it considerably more effective napalm, sticking to whatever it struck. Many vehicles came through unscathed, but many did not. Those that couldn't close their hatches and ports quickly enough were the ones that suffered. The armored vehicles turned their main guns and machine guns on the buildings from which the defenders flung their cocktails. Tanks went by a lineman working on a power pole. The electrician dropped a live electrical wire on the last tank of the column, electrocuting its occupants. Sewer lids came off and magnetic mines were clamped to the bottom of the tanks and personnel carriers as they passed overhead. Roadblocks of old cars five or six deep, hindered movement of the armored columns and rendered them more vulnerable to the Hellfire III missiles hidden in private homes as well as public buildings. Several intersections were flooded with diesel fuel and ignited with grenades or Molotov cocktails as the tanks drove through them. The subtle placement of decoy mines forced the columns to stop and inspect them before proceeding. Some of them were actually fused with small smoke grenades that exploded or flared when approached; the booby traps were trapped, so to speak. Tank traps dug over intersections and covered with steel plates, decorated with signs depicting men working and construction materials stacked on the roadside resulted in some tanks plunging headlong into pits from which they would have to be lifted out by heavy cranes. Aircraft circling overhead had no obvious targets. Everything was done from ambush. Curtains were hung from as many windows as possible, both to offer cover for snipers and to confuse the enemy from which the sniper fire came. As soon as a sniper fired, he would vacate that location, moving often to another building or another floor. At the end of the first twenty-four hours, the column still had not cleared Cheyenne. One battalion had the objective of securing F.E. Warren Air Force Base. To the dismay of the enemy, virtually all of the electrical and electronic equipment had been removed. Several interior doors in different buildings were booby trapped to slow the pace of securing the buildings.

Unknown to federal forces, their satellite imagery was being displayed on screens in several patriot command posts. The computer team of physicists and engineers that Bob Allen had joined in Billings were far more successful than the federal resources realized. The team established multi-centric command nodes in optimal locations. The rebel commanders saw everything and monitored every communication of the assaulting forces. The area station for Wyoming was located in

Buffalo, Wyoming. The concept of net centric warfare was not lost on the electronic and computer engineers of the new nation. In fact, one of the team members at the U. of Wyoming had worked on a related concept for his Ph.D., being sponsored by federal funding. Once on the faculty at the U. of Wyoming, he was approached about establishing an independent center for the National Guard. He initiated the concept of each node being both independent and multi-centric, each node being capable of assuming the command node function upon destruction of the previous command center. His proof of concept was accepted, and he oversaw the initial installation of the primary node. The Defense Advanced Research Project Agency (DARPA) had not fully comprehended what they had funded. His current position on the faculty of the U. of Wyoming was completely forgotten by the responsible federal bureaucrats. Buffalo, Wyoming on the eastern slope of the Bighorn Mountains was determined to be the most secure location when all avenues of approach were considered. Using indirect logic, it was believed that federal forces would look for some more developed center than a small prairie town. From this communications center, the brigade commanders monitored the approaching forces at their own headquarters. They knew when their own people would be targeted. Dummy communications were broadcast to nonexistent field units of company size scattered about the areas to confuse the invaders. BG Bradley monitored the battle for Cheyenne with unrestrained glee. *"God, I only hope I have done my mission half as well as Leonard is doing his."*

The 2nd U.S. Army Unit of Action whose intermediate objective was Laramie was stalled in the Laramie Range. Road damage insured that they could not proceed at their scheduled road march pace. They had not reached the city of Laramie either by U.S. 287 or by Interstate 80 when they halted for the night. They stopped in a defilade between highways 323 and 335. They laagered as for an attack by aborigines but believed it could never happen. They were completely surprised when it came just before dawn. Missiles, rocket propelled grenades and light anti-tank weapons (LAWs) rained down on specifically targeted vehicles. C4I assets, Command, Communications, Control, Computers and Intelligence vehicles had highest priority as targets, followed by missile artillery units and then cannon artillery were struck. Riflemen emerged from their spider holes and from under rocks to eliminate individual targets as they were silhouetted by the burning vehicles. Heavy mortars followed the cannon fired missiles. Vehicles at the rear and the head of the bivouac area were targeted after the C4I vehicles in order to block the escape of those trapped between them. Counter radar controlled fires were virtually eliminated by the initial incoming missiles that destroyed the C4I assets. Overhead, low flying RPV drones that were flying observation for the invaders were eliminated with shoulder fired surface to air missiles. Higher drones were eliminated by Surface to Air Missiles fired from camouflaged locations that had maintained strict electronic emissions discipline. The attack was a complete surprise and very destructive. Casualties were estimated at 450 killed and more than 2500 wounded. The U.S. 2nd Unit of Action was essentially destroyed as a fighting force. The brigade commander was killed. The Executive Officer assumed command and ordered the wounded be evacuated towards Denver. Any medical assets encountered enroute to be used to the maximum feasible extent. The remaining force would continue with its mission as soon as it could move. President Newkirk received the news of the battle with a sickening knot in his stomach when he awoke. Brigadier General Curt Younger, commanding the 2nd Brigade of the Nation of Missouri had also done his homework. He had commanded a company as a young officer in Afghanistan and learned the value of surprise, raids and the ambush.

"All right, you were all briefed individually an hour ago on the battle that occurred early this morning in Wyoming. We're getting our asses kicked by a bunch of farmers! I don't believe it. Naomi, what the hell is wrong with this? Why are our troops getting creamed?"

"Well, Mr. President, there are several parts to that answer. First, these people believe they are fighting for their homes, which they are. Second, they have well trained leaders, leaders who used to be in U.S. uniforms. Third, terrain has greatly favored the defense in the southern invasion route. A straight shot across the prairies was what I originally proposed, coming out of forces marshaled in Minnesota. I have discussed crossing the prairies in detail with the General Staff. I wanted a direct assault on Billings. It was very interesting. The Commandant, USMC, has threatened to resign and urged his commanders not to participate if the Marine Corps is ordered to attack other Americans, as in the rebels. I don't want to foment a revolution in the Marine Corps. We can't spare the Marine Corps anyway, unless you want to pull them out of here in Washington, DC, and guarding major civilian institutions and installations. The Chairman of the Joint Chiefs is sympathetic with the rebels. General Singleton offered me his resignation, but I refused it. Only the Air Force and Army Chiefs of Staff are for aggressively attacking these people. If we marshaled a force in Minnesota, we would have to use National Guard units out of the northeastern and north central states. Right now, they are extremely busy guarding critical assets in their home states and I don't believe they are capable of answering the call. They are too busy trying to keep their cities from burning, although the threat of riots is diminishing. We simply don't have the Regular Army manpower to invade via this current route. It is greatly unfortunate, but that's the way it is. We don't have a regular Army base any closer than Fort McCoy, Wisconsin, and that's a pretty small one."

"Well, what about an attack from the west?"

"That would require crossing the northern Rocky Mountains, Mr. President. Snow could block critical mountain passes at any time. It would be the same if not worse, as we are experiencing in attacking from the south. Those Patriots, as they call themselves, can cut road and rail lines at will in many places along the route and undoubtedly will. An attack from the north is out of course, because we have to respect Canadian sovereignty in the use of their passes through the mountains in a flanking movement."

"All right, our EU guests will be here in an hour. We'll discuss their problem now and then our own again after they depart. What do you have Harry?"

"Mr. President, out satellite imagery indicates significant problems in the Iranian response to the Chinese crossing their border. Their radio traffic indicates tremendous panic in their battalions that are in blocking positions. There is a great fear that the low flying Chinese missiles sprayed some agent, a biological agent, on them. The panic is causing mass desertions in those second echelon battalions. So far, we haven't picked up any indications that the Iranians have any diagnosis for any agent, but then it is only 24 hours since the cruise missiles over flew their positions. That could take as much as another 48 hours," said Harry Strother, DNI.

Naomi Campbell asked "why didn't the Iranians shoot them down? Don't they have surface to air missiles capable of handling cruise missiles? They fly at subsonic speeds, are vulnerable to fighter aircraft. What is the problem?"

"Madam Secretary, they fired them from close range, with only a few minutes before over flight. That didn't give the Iranians much response time. Secondly, the missiles apparently used terrain following radar, flying below three hundred feet. That is lower than most Iranian radar guided Surface to Air Missiles could detect."

"How are the Iranians doing with the flu? Do we have any indications of that? Or did the Chinese use something else in this attack, asked Newkirk.

"Mr. President, the National Reconnaisance Office indicates the Iranians are suffering massive deaths, given the number of mass graves. The case fatality ratio isn't as bad as in Africa or the rest of the Middle East except Israel which was vaccinated, but bad enough. They were supplied with vaccine by Europe after the European Union met its own requirements. That put them way behind the epidemic curve which is dramatically declining now because it is running out of susceptibles. The military had the second highest priority on the vaccine, second only to members of the Revolutionary Council and the mullahs. Less than half their civilian population was vaccinated so they are losing millions of folks. So it might be they were sprayed with a different influenza virus or perhaps something else."

"Any guesses as to what it is?"

"The Former Soviet Union (FSU) had several major bioweapons production facilities in the former Confederation of Independent States, in Kurgan, Stepnogorsk, Berdsk, Novosobirisk and other cities. We believe China brought some of those facilities back into production in alignment with their own long standing program. It could be an agent produced in one of them. That makes sense, because it lessens the potential for an accident on their own soil, either in production or transportation. The FSU produced anthrax, tularemia, smallpox, Q fever, and others in those facilities. Now, it could be any configuration of a genetically engineered organism, bacterial or viral. If it is one of those I first mentioned by name, the Iranians should have identified it within seventy-two hours from now. If they communicate the diagnosis by microwave transmission, we will pick it up. I'll inform you as soon as the NRO comes up with anything at all."

"I take it then, that the Chinese haven't advanced?"

"Correct, Mr. President. They haven't moved one meter forward. That's why I think they used some agent. They are waiting for its effects. Even if they sprayed distilled water they gained a tremendous advantage through the panic and desertions that resulted. Frankly, I would have used a highly lethal agent that would break down in the environment so it wouldn't affect our own troops as we advanced. Botulinum toxin would be a good candidate. Rain, snow, even high relative humidity will break it down, hydrolyze it that is, and detoxify it in hours to days so that the Chinese could march right in without suffering any losses to their own agent."

"You mean the stuff physicians use to iron out wrinkles? I take it is highly lethal?"

"It's the most toxic substance known to man. It is lethal at the level of three nanograms per kilo of body weight in the monkey model. It causes respiratory paralysis that requires a respirator for weeks on end to survive. An aspirin tablet sized amount of the pure toxin is enough to kill several hundred thousand men who weigh 180 pounds each."

"All right. I anticipate the Europeans are going to request troops, even though they know we are in a civil war. I have no doubt their satellites picked up on the battle early this morning. Let's see if they play ignorant or if they express genuine surprise. It is possible that their own people haven't told them anything. I haven't seen anything on it on our own news broadcasts."

"That is because, Mr. President, I informed Central News Network that if they announced the battle before we had a press release on it this morning I would shut down their satellites and some of their facilities would experience very serious technical problems. Several of their people accompanying the brigade, a journalist and camera crew, were killed. They were broadcasting the attack when they caught it. CNN has that on tape. They can be coerced rather easily, I think. Naomi's press secretary along with mine got together with yours this morning. We have a release subject to your approval scheduled for 08:30 this morning."

"Good move, Harry. Our talking heads and yours should be able to put a good spin on it. In spite of heavy casualties, our forces are making progress on bring the breakaway states back into the Union, blah blah blah." "It is something like that, Mr. President. The wounded being evacuated to Denver might touch things off a little sooner, but we hope not.

On another subject, we most certainly can't answer any request from the EU for troops in the event the Chinese continue on.

"Of course, we can't spare any troops for them. They will have to go it alone. EU forces exist mostly on paper. The Iranians do have a few missile launching submarines somewhere in the oceans, a couple or three of older British, two French, no others of which I am aware. Any force the Chinese put on the ground will be nothing more than a tripwire force, an excuse to go nuclear. The Europeans can no more stop the Chinese from moving into the Middle East by conventional means that we can. Their only option is nuclear. Harry?"

"The Chinese tactical nuclear arsenal is estimated to be several hundred warheads interspersed between ICBMs and intermediate range ballistic missiles as I understand past briefings from them. How much is a lie I can't say. The Chinese are numerically superior and at least equal if not technologically superior to any individual European nation and equal or superior to the EU as a whole. In short, the Chinese have them between a rock and a hard place. China can take out every European city with a population of 100,000 or more in retaliation with nuclear fires. They have the ICBMs with multiple re-entry warheads to do it. They pilfered that technology from us back in the 1990's. Our latest intelligence indicates that China has at least one hundred intermediate range missiles, with six warheads each. They haven't suffered from the influenza outbreak as the rest of the world has. In fact, it hasn't seemed to affect China at all. They are sitting pretty at the moment."

"OK, it's almost eight o'clock. Everybody finish breakfast and we'll have our European friends in for coffee." A working breakfast was one of the hangovers Newkirk learned had worked well from one of his predecessors, President Jason Thornton. Newkirk was occasionally invited to join them when he was a young member of the Senate and found himself on the Ways and Means Committee.

The Mexican field worker stood by the tailgate of his pickup, drinking water from a plastic milk jug. The big John Deere combine sat at the edge of the irrigated cornfield. He did not like the presence of the stranger with a backpack, or his appearance. *"It is quite unusual to see a man coming out of the desert,"* thought Hernando. *"There is little west of here within walking distance. Where did he come from? I wonder if I should report him to the sheriff."*

"Que pasa, Amigo! Any work around here, "said Rodrigo, speaking English.

"This is a bad time, and maybe a bad place, especially for strangers Amigo. Things are very tense here, Senor. Everyone is armed and everyone is scared. Some of us are new, but some of us have been here for four generations. Some of us are known to some Anglos, but not to others. There has been no violence, only threats of violence. Many have been told to sell their homes and leave. A few have done so, most have not. It is not a good thing, Amigo. This business in the southwest has made everyone very nervous. Who knows what trouble strangers such as you might bring?"

"Gracias," Rodrigo nodded in acknowledgement, shrugged his shoulders to adjust the straps of his backpack and moved on. Hernando watched Rodrigo walk until he was a hundred meters away before he walked forward to glance into the cab of the pickup, where his rifle was propped against the seat, butt on the floor. Rodrigo walked with a certain swagger, an air of confidence that made Hernando apprehensive without knowing why. *"Perhaps I should report him, but the Sheriff doesn't like us Hispanics. Why should I help the sheriff out?"* thought Hernando. He shrugged it off and climbed into the cab of the combine.

Rodrigo sat down at the edge of the field and watched the house through a pair of compact binoculars from 400 meters out. A cornfield was directly across from the house. He had earlier observed Robert Bradley connecting a new tank of propane to the gas grill along the back side the house. It was near dark and the mosquitoes were still out. Rodrigo had applied a small amount of insect repellant to his face, neck and hands. He could see the television playing through an open window. He observed no one around or in the house other than Robert Bradley. No matter. He knew General Bradley lived there with his father. He had no knowledge that General Bradley had moved out a day earlier. Rodrigo retreated into the cornfield where he ate a cold field ration, then spread his one pound sleeping bag and set his alarm for 01:30. When the alarm went off Rodrigo arose, ate two energy bars, drank a little water, urinated, packed his gear and moved silently toward the house. On the patio he observed the propane gas barbeque grill. He opened the bottom door and taped one half pound of plastic explosive to the propane tank. He set the detonator in it with the timer set for thirty minutes. He quietly retreated back to the edge of the field across the road and waited. The explosion leveled the house. The gas line into the house was severed and contributed to the fire. Nothing survived the conflagration except the fire proof gun safe. The adjacent house was seriously damaged by the blast. The heat was sufficient to scorch the paint on it, thirty meters away. The truck in the garage on the opposite side of the house was rolled onto its side and was burning. The burning debris, including the gun safe, collapsed into the basement. Satisfied with his work, Rodrigo worked his way down the middle of the field and then onto the highway half a mile away. Colonel Robert Bradley, U.S. Army, Veterinary Crops, Retired, died in his sleep without feeling any pain.

The rich residents in Jackson who owned private planes dashed to the airport upon watching the morning news, becoming aware that the civil war was no longer merely a political confrontation, but a military one as well. Those who were prompt flew safely out. By 10:00 hours however, some of the private aircraft came under small arms fire as they taxied on the runway or took off. Several were shot down. No one was certain who was doing the shooting. No one stepped forward to make the claim. The militia however, was widely blamed even though no militia commander ordered it. At the same time, President Johnston of the new Nation of Missouri announced the expropriation and nationalization of all natural resources within the states that constituted the new Nation of Missouri. The Governors of the states of the new Nation convened in Billings, declared that military necessity has primacy for all resources, including manpower. Within the Nation of Missouri, the new legislature passed a law requiring that all resources leaving the Nation must be first cleared by the respective state governor and then paid for if confiscated upon or before delivery could occur. Foreign interests immediately telegraphed complaints which were ignored.

The Jedediah Smith Pipeline Company station at Fort Laramie was shut down. Gas was diverted into holding tanks. The second tank farm 10 miles out of town, owned by the Platte River Company Pipeline refused to cooperate until the militia shut it down. All coal trains stopped on the tracks. Large cities in the southeast and east and Midwest which depended upon the coal for electric power immediately went to rolling blackouts to conserve coal stocks on hand. Eastern governors frantically appealed to coal companies in Appalachia to drastically and immediately increase coal production. The environmentalists had delayed building fast breeder nuclear reactors until it was too late.

The loud speaker blared from the top of the HUMVEE of the federal force as it drove slowly down the street. "Any building that houses a sniper will be destroyed. Any dwelling from which any military resistance occurs will be burned to the ground. Anyone caught with a weapon will be imprisoned or shot." The people of Cheyenne were fighting back. General Winston commanding the 1st Brigade, Nation of Missouri, had ordered curtains to be hung from as many windows as possible, in commercial building as well as private homes. He had trained as many civilian militia as he could in the sniper role. They were taking a heavy toll on unprotected troops. Troops outside armored vehicles were under constant harassing fire at all hours, day and night. Body armor saved many lives simply because at ranges longer than three hundred yards the civilian snipers missed the head and struck the body of the invading troops from Fort Carson or completely missed.

"Willy, what the hell are we doing here?"

"What do you mean, Joe?"

"Christ, Mexicans have seized southern California; they are invading Arizona, New Mexico, Texas and other states. Hell, man, they have seized Pueblo just before we shoved off. Why didn't we attack south and take back Colorado? Blacks and Hispanics have pretty much deserted the Army, now they want to form a black America and here we are, attacking white folks in Wyoming. It doesn't make sense to me. Why aren't we taking back Colorado, California, and Texas and the southeast? How come we are fighting our own kind? You got a wife and two kids that were in North Carolina just outside of Bragg, why aren't we defending them and your home? Why did they have to pack up and move, or are they in danger if they have stayed? Hell, we lost so many black soldiers we can't function anymore. We're not going to win this one either. If we stay here, it will be just like the fighting in Iraqi cities some years back. Remember Sarge telling us about all the roadside bombs, ambushes and problems on patrols. It'll be worse in those mountains, too. They're just like in Afghanistan. I'll bet lots of people have already moved into them. We didn't win that one either, and we're not going to do any better here. Fred up at Battalion Headquarters overheard the General tell the Colonel that they have already retreated into some big basin up north, and have been training and practicing for mountain guerilla warfare for a year now."

"I dunno. It doesn't make sense to me either. I haven't shot anybody, and I don't want to shoot anybody. These folks ain't done nothin' to us. They're just defending their homes and city. We've been fighting in this city three days now, and all we're doing is destroying it and killing lots of civilians. What do you think we ought to do?"

"I'm thinking that when we go on patrol we ought to load up on extra ammo, food and water and just keep going. I don't want to kill anybody either, us or them. Mom and Dad are OK in southern Michigan. Last I heard from them, the rioters and looters can't reach that far out into the countryside. I wonder if I could make it back there. You want to come along with me and try and we'll try to find your family after we check out my parents."

"Remember what the CO said this morning? He ordered us to shoot any deserters on sight. Hell, we gonna shoot ourselves? So many guys are already deserting; at least the captain thinks so. Half or better of the patrols he sends out don't come back. Their individual commo equipment just seems to malfunction and he can't keep track of them. He thinks they turn it off and keep going. I think the lieutenant would just turn his back if we left. Besides, we might get shot at from both sides. Have you noticed our lack of air cover? These separatists, patriots or whatever you want to call them have air cover. Our Air Force can't function any more because so many members of the ground crews have deserted. Us being in uniform, these so-called rebels will shoot at us, our own guys loyal to the assholes in Washington will shoot us. Even if we got out of uniform, which would make us deserters, we would look like bandits carrying our rifles, and we will need our rifles to get through the country. We can't carry enough food and water on our backs; we'll need a vehicle of some sort, a truck really. No reason why we can't borrow a Hummer or maybe something else. Why don't we just look for my wife and kids first? Your parents are OK, last you heard."

Joe grinned at Willy who grinned back. "Maybe we should borrow the lieutenant's command Hummer. We'll have to dismantle part of the communications system and GPS so it's out of the platoon and company nets. That's no real problem if we can get Johnson to go along with it. He's pretty disgusted too. He doesn't believe we should be fighting these folks any more than we do. Johnson can just drive the Lieutenant's Hummer off and pick us up. It is a long way back to North Carolina. Where would your family go if they had to evacuate North Carolina?"

"I don't know. All of her family is from the south, same as mine. I suppose it would be a wild goose chase. Maybe we should delay and ask command about what's going on around Bragg. After we get some answers then maybe we can get out of this mess. Let's go talk to the Captain."

As Willy and Joe discussed their situation, Fort Bragg was abandoning the post. All military dependents who wished to migrate north were offered the opportunity for evacuation. Families were limited to two suitcases and loaded into trucks and buses. Fuel trucks, Stryker vehicles, Hummers and a few tanks provided security for the convoy that stretched over fifteen miles. Their destination was Wright Patterson Air Force Base, Ohio.

"Mr. President, we have the first reports coming out of Iran. Our satellite imagery shows the Chinese are on the move.

They are meeting no resistance. Radio traffic monitoring indicates that entire Iranian battalions along their eastern border are dead. Whatever the Chinese sprayed over them last week was certainly effective. Whatever it was doesn't seem to be affecting the Chinese. I've asked for comments from Admiral Rosenberg and the military medical intelligence community. I just gave them the word an hour or two ago, so we might hear something from someone early this afternoon. I don't know if they will reach a consensus or offer individual opinions. Frankly, I would prefer their individual opinions. That way, one of them is more likely to be right. We are picking up massive movements of civilians in Iran. It seems they are evacuating their eastern towns and villages in the face of Chinese advances. Their President called for a retreat to the mountains to wage guerilla warfare on the invaders. I wish we knew the final objective of the Chinese. We just don't know where they will stop. It might be all the way to the Mediterranean, but I very seriously doubt it due to the logistics of the situation. More likely, no undoubtedly, they will seize the northern side of the Strait of Hormuz and stop there, but you never know. The Chinese have always managed to fool us in the past. Obviously, they aren't satisfied with regional hegemony in Asia, but want to insure that no other regional hegemon arises to challenge their position."

"Thanks Harry." At that moment, the President's phone rang. He answered and handed the phone to DNI Strother. He listened, then hung up the phone and turned back to the President. "The Iranians just launched their tactical nukes at the Chinese. The largest appears to be about a fifteen kiloton weapon. Apparently they targeted what they thought were higher headquarters, army and corps level and any massed forces they figured they could destroy. They apparently don't have enough to target division sized units or anything smaller."

"Ok Harry, whatever that is. What do you think the Chinese will do in response now that the nuclear genie is once again on the loose?"

"If the Chinese retaliate with nukes, it will help the survivors by actually reducing their numbers. Chemical weapons are essentially tactical weapons, while biologicals can be either tactical or strategic, depending on the agent and how and where and when they are deployed. It's hard to predict, Mr. President, but I suspect they might use smaller nukes delivered by artillery fire to reduce the threat of guerilla warfare. Iran is either mountains or desert. The civilian population anywhere won't be able to feed itself for long, at least not the majority of the initially surviving population. They won't survive for long in the deserts without potable water. Contaminated water as a vehicle for disease will kill them by the thousands if not the hundreds of thousands. Nobody is going to come to the aid of the Iranians. Those who would survive will have to do so by killing their fellow citizens. After all, the Chinese and Iranians both studied the Russian involvement in Afghanistan in the 1970s and 80s, our efforts there after the Taliban, and our failure in Iraq. Both sides know why the Russians failed and why we failed. The Chinese might try and bottle them up in the cities, or let them escape into the mountains where they would have to disperse to have any chance at all of survival. I suspect the Chinese will practice what they did in the last war, maximum destruction of the civilian population through attrition, starvation by destroying all agricultural commodities and food producing potential, allowing disease and outright military attacks to reduce or eliminate the threat of guerilla warfare. Of course, the Chinese might be able to bottle them up in the mountains where starvation and exposure to the elements will eliminate almost all of them. Winter is almost here in the mountains. Only small bands, maybe family groups that are somehow self sufficient will survive."

"Naomi, what's your take?"

"A couple of points, Mr. President. First, the Indian Ocean is more or less wide open. The Indian Navy and those small naval forces of the southern Asian nations were destroyed in the last war. The Chinese have established naval bases at Karachi and Gwadar, what were Pakistani and Indian ports. The Chinese leased Gwadar earlier in this century so they already had infrastructure in place. The sea lanes of communication are wide open in the sense that they are absolutely vulnerable. The Chinese will no doubt take the Straits of Hormuz. Whether or not that is their final objective or an intermediate one remains to be seen. Nevertheless, they will control that chokepoint and can dictate to us, Japan and Europe the amount and flow of oil. We can't do anything about it. We don't have the naval forces any more to do that. We didn't build enough replacement capital ships early in this century; we currently have to use what sailors we do have in the Gulf to guard our ports, and Europe hasn't enough naval forces to do anything but patrol their coastal areas. In short, Mr. President, on that issue we are literally dead in the water. The Chinese navy will shortly control the Gulf, the Arabian Sea and the Indian Ocean with their destroyers, cruisers and above all, their submarine fleets. Over the last two decades they have built a sizable fleet of air independent propulsion submarines, non-nuclear types that are quieter than anything we have except our three Virginia class attack submarines.

Another issue is pressing. Two months ago I gave the order to all of our military bases south of the Mason-Dixon line to prepare evacuation plans in case we had to pull out because of civil war. I ordered some of those bases to begin moving north last night. We have lost too many of our uniformed personnel through desertions. Those bases are vulnerable. Those bases in Georgia, Alabama, Louisiana, and the Carolinas started gathering the dependents in the area onto the bases, organizing convoys, and will start moving tomorrow morning at the latest. The forces from each base being evacuated have been assigned to a more northern base for the time being. It won't be easy on anybody, but at least the dependents will be safer and our forces will be thinking more about their jobs at hand than the security of their families. Unfortunately, the brigade commanders have informed their superiors that they are experiencing considerable desertions in the brigades attacking in Wyoming. It seems that the reconnaissance patrols go out and don't come back. They have been observed tying white flags to their antennas and driving off to surrender or join the Nation of Missouri."

"Damn it Naomi! There is no such thing as the Nation of the Missouri. That's still a part of the United States. I am not going to let it break away!" President Newkirk pounded on his desk with his fist. No one said anything.

"Naomi, you order those troops to continue the attack. I want them to take Billings and all those people who want to break away. If the troops can't take Billings and Cheyenne or whatever cities are necessary, bomb and burn them into submission. We'll have the modern day equivalent of Sherman's march to the sea in the civil war."

"Mr. President, I'm afraid that is impossible. General Singleton informs me the aviators won't fly those missions, and besides, so many of the Air Force personnel have deserted that ground crews can't service the airplanes. The attack drone operators won't fly their drones on any more attack missions, since those states have voted to secede. It seems that the ballot box is winning over the bullet. Most of our Marine and Air Force bases are in the south. Many of those folks have either deserted or moved north with the bases. Those that are in the process of moving or have moved north are still in a state of flux, unprepared to do anything. In fact, some of the aviators are flying their aircraft into shall I say, the Territory of Missouri. I can't say how long we will be able to continue to fight in our current circumstances, Mr. President."

"Get out! I don't want to see anybody for a while." The cabinet left without saying a word, leaving a brooding Richard Newkirk, President of the United States.

That evening, Richard Newkirk's secretary Janice Darlington boarded a direct flight bound for Minneapolis at Dulles International Airport. When she arrived at 22:00 hours, she rented a car with the stated destination of Fargo, North Dakota. When she reached Fargo she checked into a motel where she slept late. After breakfast the next morning she went to an auto parts store where she bought a complete automotive tool kit. With the tool kit she disabled the satellite tracking system in the rented automobile and started driving west to Billings.

The Cheyenne Brigade of the Republic of the Nation of Missouri withdrew north along I-25 under little pressure, only scouting units from federal forces following them to constantly update their positions. The Commander, 1st U.S. Unit of Action that attacked Cheyenne called his Division Commander at Fort Carson. "General, I have lost half my force. There is no way I can continue the attack in open country without further attrition of my force. I respectfully request reinforcements and replacements immediately."

"General, I will pass your request up the chain. In the meantime, keep the pressure on, regardless of the possibility of attrition. Maintain contact with the retreating enemy forces. I'll get back to you as soon as I can get an answer. I have been instructed to hold the Third UA here, and that is what I will do. Out here."

The Division Commander picked up his secure phone and called Fifth Army Headquarters who passed the word up the chain of command ultimately to Naomi Campbell.

Naomi Campbell spoke with General Singleton and directed a meeting with the Joint Chiefs. "What forces do we have to support the attack on Cheyenne? General Davis has informed me that he has ordered the attack to continue after the retreating Missouri forces. What do we have and how soon can we get them into the field?"

The Army Chief of Staff looked at the other service chiefs, and said "Bluntly, Madame Secretary the only forces we truly have that might be of assistance are first, the reserve Unit of Action out of Fort Carson and the experimental units at Fort Riley, Kansas. They are the new robotic armored units. They are the tank and Stryker battalions that have been outfitted with remote controls similar to the Unmanned Aerial Vehicles concept. We have been testing them now for six months in the field. To date, we are extremely pleased with them. We have several battalions each of tanks and Strykers so equipped. Regarding manpower, the First Infantry Division at Ft. Riley has been devastated by desertions as much or more than other units. At best, we can add an engineering company from Fort Leonard Wood. Other than completely emptying Forts Riley and Leonard Wood, we are scraping the bottom of the barrel. The fastest and easiest way to get them there is by rail. It will take about two days to get them on the tracks and rolling."

"Give the order, General. Commit the reserve brigade and the robotics. I'll inform the President. I am sure he will be pleased."

Four hours later, the Fourth Infantry Division Commander at Fort Carson had his answer. He ordered his reserve brigade, the 3rd Unit of Action, northward along the I-25 highway as the Cheyenne-Casper-Sheridan axis with the final objective of Billings. The 1st Unit of Action Commander had his mission changed. He was to consolidate his units and send two battalions of Strykers and a tank battalion to stay on the heels of the retreating 1st Brigade of the Nation of Missouri as it moved northward along I-25, albeit slowly. He instructed the Brigade Commander to engage the enemy and destroy the Cheyenne (1st) Brigade, Nation of Missouri, to prevent it from turning west at Casper along U.S. 20. In spite of all attempts at security, civilian militia continued to snipe at both the 1st and 2nd U.S. brigades as they continued their march.

The 2nd U.S. Unit of Action he ordered to continue along I-80 to Rawlins, then up U.S. 287 with the intermediate objective of Riverton. He was to seize the road junctions at Riverton and Shoshoni and seize control of the dam and railroads in the area north of Shoshone. They were to cut off any retreat into the Basin through the Wind River Canyon by the forces of the Nation of Missouri if possible. BG Winston, commanding the 1st Brigade, continued his withdrawal north along I-25 under slight pressure. Two days later the mayor of Casper ordered Brigadier Winston to stay outside of his city. General Winston didn't say anything. He just removed his automatic from his holster and shot the mayor in the head. He ordered his force to move through Casper and onto U.S. 20 west towards Shoshoni.

The Laramie Brigade, officially the 2nd Brigade, Nation of Missouri, was stretched as thin as the Cheyenne Brigade. Covering the territory from the Wyoming-Colorado border, through all of the Shirley Basin along the Rawlins to Riverton to Shoshoni axis, the Brigade Commander deployed his unit in platoons, hiding them in farm buildings, digging them into fighting positions with several alternate positions, deploying two and four man anti-armor teams in spider holes and all conceivable locations of cover and concealment all along the highway. The unmanned aerial vehicles still being operated flew back and forth, covering the advancing federal convoy, seeking the positions of the Laramie Brigade personnel. Some of the UAVs could hover as helicopters, many of which were armed with TOW antitank missiles. Somehow the Laramie Brigade Commander had procured infra-red resistant ponchos for his troops so that their positions could not be detected from UAVs with infra-red cameras. As the 2nd U.S. Brigade proceeded up U.S. 30/287, his armor killing teams popped out of their holes, from behind rocks, from out of farm buildings and put Javelin anti-armor or TOW-III missiles on the enemy armor as it passed. Battalion level electronic and command vehicles were the highest priority, followed by anti-air vehicles, company and platoon command vehicles, then tanks, then Stryker vehicles, and lastly fuel and ammunition trucks. Overpasses and road junctions were mined, with explosives dug in out of sight underneath the highways, the access and exit ramps to be detonated by radio as selected vehicles passed over them. The 2nd Brigade Commander, BG Younger, left occasional Javelin teams, firing rockets that deployed with a high arc to penetrate tanks through the top hatch out on the prairie in almost suicidal positions. Many of the two man teams did not survive the returning fire once their position was exposed by firing their Javelins. All the while the federal forces were being slowed, attrited, forced to deploy out of their road march formations. A platoon of vehicles raced along Interstate 80, just ahead and out of range of the oncoming federal forces, acting like a magnet, drawing them on or slowing them down by suddenly reversing directions and attacking. The defending general decided to allow the federal force to pass through Rawlins relatively unmolested. They turned north on U.S. 287 to head towards Riverton. The UAVs of the opposing federal force came under increasingly heavier ground fire eliminating many of them as the force approached the Green Mountains south of Jeffrey City. The bridge at Sweetwater Station Junction was blown after the first screening tank platoon passed it. When the platoon of tanks stopped, they were struck with Javelins. By the third day after crossing the state border the federal force was half exhausted and suffering thirty percent casualties.

All the while, the battles were monitored by the Commo Kid, all the Brigade Commanders throughout the Nation of Missouri, Major General McIntire, Lieutenant General Wheaton, the President of the Nation of Missouri, and especially Brigadier General Ethan Bradley. General Bradley made the decision to commit his air force assets when the federal force reached Riverton. Without warning the enemy force was ordered to halt at Riverton. Reinforcements would be forthcoming. They would arrive in three days or less for the federal force outside of Riverton, and two days or less for the federal force proceeding up Interstate 25 north of Casper. Ethan ordered the squadron commander of Joint Strike Fighters to prepare for a night strike against the force bivouacked outside of Riverton. He ordered a low level flight, hugging the Wind River canyon as much as possible. The First Brigade was occupying the road junction at Shoshoni fourteen miles north of Riverton. Bradley directed his air force commander to prepare a night strike against the laagered force at Riverton and to send the details to via runner, not trusting electronic communications, to BG Curt Younger, Commander, 2nd Brigade, aka the Laramie Brigade. BG Younger was requested to have his people put laser beams on their highest priority targets. After that, the Joint Strike Fighters would illuminate whatever targets were left with their own laser designators. With only eighty miles distance, the JSF aircraft would be on target before the federal forces could respond. The fighters aligned themselves in a group so that their heat signature, monitored by satellite, would show only a single very powerful heat source. They took off in formation. In two minutes they were over the enemy, wreaking havoc. Emerging out of the canyon, they flew single file and destroyed those assets illuminated by General Younger's troops in the first pass. By flying in single file and circling low so that they made two passes, they destroyed a number of vehicles using their own on-board lasers and inflicted several hundred more casualties. All six aircraft returned safely to Worland. In the aftermath, Willy, Joe, and Specialist Johnston tied a white towel around the antenna of their lieutenant's HUMVEE, filled it with jerry cans of water and fuel, cases of MREs, and drove east along State Highway 136.

The 3rd U.S. Brigade was faring somewhat better, encountering limited resistance, pushing northward out of Cheyenne three days behind the 1st U.S. Brigade with the next intermediate objective of Sheridan. Their ultimate objective was the capture of Billings. As the column approached Buffalo, LTG Wheaton, Commander of the Army of the Nation of Missouri, ordered all electronic emissions out of Buffalo to be shut down. He didn't want to risk detection and destruction of his most valuable weapons system. When daylight came, the Commander of the U.S. 2nd Unit of Action sent as many of his wounded to Cheyenne for medical attention. He commandeered all the civilian vehicles he could find to supplement his ambulance companies. For the dead he ordered a delayed evacuation. He felt at the mercy of the further air attacks and so ordered the remainder of his force forward with the intention of breaking through the Shoshoni junction and finding shelter in the canyon. When his rear guard scouts informed him that the 2nd U.S. Unit of Action was moving north, BG Winston ordered his force to mine the road north, south and east of Shoshoni and retreat into the canyon. BG Winston led his force through the canyon where he was met by BG Ethan Bradley. The two brigadiers smiled and shook hands.

"Sure glad to meet you Ethan. That canyon is impressive. You can hold off a division or maybe even a corps sized unit if they don't have vertical envelopment capability."

"I sure as hell hope to. As you can imagine, I have hidden emplacements and mines all along it. The only way they will get through it is by vertical envelopment and they don't have the helicopter assets for that any more. The 101st Airborne has its hands full back east."

"My force has suffered considerably. I am very much reduced in manpower, fuel, ammunition, food and weapons. I have most of my wounded with me. I hope your hospitals are well staffed and stocked. I'll gladly submit my command to yours for training in mountain and guerilla warfare according to our strategy. In the meantime, my folks could use some rest and resupply."

"Leonard, take your force into Worland. We can divide your wounded between Thermopolis and Worland. The county hospital here can advise your physicians on which patients they can accept and which you can transport to Worland and perhaps Cody. Worland has a slightly larger medical community and capability and Cody larger still. There are several city parks and fields in and around Worland where you can set up camp for several days rest. We'll refuel and feed you. Help yourself to field slaughter any of the cattle for beef. Take them out of the stockyards. If there is any complaint, give them a chit. If they don't accept it, take the beef anyway. Your men deserve some steaks! We have stockpiled a lot of food stuffs here in various warehouses. There are various grains and canned fruits and fresh vegetables from this summer. Draw on them as you see fit. We can give you hot showers if you don't try to take them all at once or make them too long. Three minutes of water per man, navy style. We'll defend this pass with one company. As soon as your command is rested, we'll start classes and fill you in on reconnaissance."

The Reverend Alvin Hemmings, now the Grand Mullah of Houston with the assumed name of Mohammad bin Abram bin Selim laughed gleefully as he watched the news. He turned off the television, lit a Cuban cigar and put his feet up on his desk. *"Whitey is killing himself off. Man, do I have a gold mine here. Yeah, it will take a couple of years to restore everything, and get people trained to run the chemical plants, the refineries, and the oil rigs in the gulf, to replace those white boys who left but so what. Everybody has to have the chemical products coming out of here. Lots of good Muslims here are already plant employees. I just need a few thousand more, that's all. I'll need chemical engineers, since most of them were white boys who left. I have a small state here, going in a large circle all the way past Port Author, maybe even to Lake Charles. Think I'll call it Islamic America. Houston will be my capitol. The shipping coming and going from Houston alone is enormous. Then I'll have the river barge traffic on the Mississippi. We can tax it all. We'll have millions of dollars a day pouring into here. I think maybe I'll build both a new mosque for my people and a new palace for myself. Why shouldn't I live a little? Hell, much of this is my creation. By Allah, I'll have me an all beautiful women body guard of well trained sluts to fuck every night, just like that ol' boy from Libya, what was his name, ah yes, Muamar Quaddafi had most of his life. Ah, life is good."* Selim called to his secretary on the intercom.

"Sister Latifah, arrange a meeting tomorrow morning with all the directors, especially the public relations and the lawyers. The agenda will be the declaration of the independence of the Nation of Islamic America. Everybody shows, no excuses. Praise be to Allah."

Two battalions of robotic Stryker vehicles, two battalions of robotic tanks and two companies of surface to air missiles were loaded on to railroad flat cars at Fort Riley, Kansas. They were designated the 4th U.S. Unit of Action. The personnel accompanying them were mostly electronic technicians operating the robotic equipment with textbook training in tactics but no advanced field training or experience themselves in mounted infantry tactics. When the two trains reached Denver they were routed north to Cheyenne. Between Iron Mountain and Chugwater, Wyoming, the spikes were pulled from the railroad rails for over a quarter of a mile. When the first train hit, it derailed, the engine rolled over carrying thirty flatbed cars and their Strykers with it. It took three days to sideline the second train, repair the track, get a heavy crane on rails in and reload the train. Outside of Douglas, Wyoming, the bridge across the north fork of the Platte River was dynamited as the first train crossed it. The engine plunged into the water and took the first forty cars with it. The coupling separated at the forty-first car and the brakeman in the caboose was able to stop the remainder of the train from plunging into the river. The Commander of the 4th U.S. Unit of Action made the decision to deploy from the train and continue as a road march. In order to do so, the Commander confiscated every flatbed truck and eighteen wheeler capable of hauling one of his vehicles. He also confiscated fuel trucks to replace the several in the river. The vehicles in the river were to catch up as soon as they were capable. Harassing sniper fire delayed bridge repair and recovery of the vehicles. Twenty-four hours after the bridge being blown, the robotic U.S. Unit of Action reached Casper. He halted just south of the city for rest and what fuel he could forage. While there he experienced unending harassing sniper fire from civilians. The electronics technicians chose for the most part to remain inside the vehicles to avoid the sniper fire. He sent 1st Battalion/1st Robotic Regiment of Strykers west to assist the 2nd U.S. Unit of Action while he continued north towards Billings on his primary mission of supporting the 3rd. U.S. Unit of Action. Later the next day the detached battalion of Strykers reached the 2nd U.S. Unit of Action just south of Shoshoni where they unexpectedly entered the minefield. Several vehicles were destroyed which further slowed the advance. The Unit of Action commander and the lieutenant colonel commanding the robotic Strykers collaborated and decided to wait until the next morning to attempt to force passage through the Wind River Canyon. Ethan decided not to risk his air assets against the surface to air missiles, but rather wait until the armored units attempted to force passage. A few small UAVs available at the company level began flying though the canyon just over the top, looking for heat sources for infra-red signatures. Ethan ordered all units to build numerous small campfires attended by a single man in order to confuse the enemy as to what were real positions and which were obfuscating. After passing Boysen dam, a scout platoon from the 2nd U.S. Unit of Action entered the first of three tunnels. The platoon leader played a searchlight along the walls as his command vehicle crept through the tunnel. Half way through he saw the wires leading from charge to charge. He ordered an immediate withdrawal. As soon as he started to back out, the Sergeant half way up the hill and hidden in a small cave blasted out of the rock pushed the electronic switch that detonated the charges. The lieutenant, his vehicle and crew were buried under a hundred tons of rock. The highway was completely blocked. The brigade commander ordered a company to scrounge through the area to find bulldozers and trucks to clear the road. What he found was that the electronic ignitions and carburetors had been removed from all the vehicles they discovered.

The 2nd U.S. Unit of Action turned west at Buffalo in pursuit of the 2nd Brigade, Nation of Missouri. The 2nd Unit of Action had halted just west of Buffalo, before entering the mountains, waiting for the reinforcements. The brigade commander of the 4th U.S. Unit of Action detached one battalion of robotic tanks from the 2nd U.S. Unit of Action. The 2nd U.S. Unit of Action commander then committed his force by entering Ten Sleep Canyon. The battle of Ten Sleep Canyon had begun. The 3rd U.S. Unit of Action was on the outskirts of Sheridan when the 4th U.S. Unit of Action, the electronic brigade, now consisting of one battalion each of robotic Strykers and tanks finally overtook them. His force was then attached to the 3rd U.S. Unit of Action which attempted to move as quickly as it could around Sheridan on I-25. The engineers of the militia company at Sheridan mined as many of the overpasses as they had explosives for. Where the Strykers and tanks attempted to bypass the dynamited overpasses they fell into twenty foot tank traps. The sixty ton tanks went in nose first and couldn't get out of the straight walled pits. A crane would be necessary to pull them out. The commander dispatched an engineering platoon into Sheridan to find the necessary heavy equipment. In the meantime, other tanks flanked wide around the pits. In some cases, very shallow pits, only a few feet deep had been dug in order to slow down the advance of the enemy. When the force crossed the Wyoming-Montana border, Ethan committed his six Joint Strike Fighters to fly around the Big Horn Mountains and strike the enemy from the north. Initially, the satellite images revealed the flight and General Singleton presumed the aircraft were fleeing to Malmstrom Air Force Base in Great Falls, Montana. Instead, they suddenly flanked east and struck hard at the oncoming column. The surface to air missile battery couldn't set up and fire in the three minutes so that the strike fighters launched their missiles against them first. Then they raked the column with their chain guns firing depleted uranium rounds that destroyed everything they hit. A lot of young men and a few women died in those vehicles. The robotic vehicles were not spared although they had no crews. Their crews operated out of separate electronic HUMVEEs. When the attack began, those crews fled their HUMVEEs as they had no organic air defense. Immediately following the air strike, a hidden company of Stryker vehicles from the Montana National Guard emerged from dug in positions and struck the column, firing TOW III missiles and then retreating north and east. The ambush was over in a matter of a few minutes.

The 2nd U.S. Unit of Action was twenty-five kilometers into Ten Sleep Canyon when the first landslide was dynamited on them. Several Strykers were shoved off the road and down the mountainside, while several others were buried.

"Christ Almighty" thought the Unit commander. I'm twenty five kilometers deep and I have a total of 105 kilometers over this mountain range. "The worst is yet to come, once I get past Powder River Pass, it's even more treacherous. I'll never make it."

General Dewey Singleton watched the strike with horror. Completely depressed, he walked out of the war room and to his office. He called to his Secretary. "Darlene, take a letter. To the Secretary of Defense. Dear Madam Secretary, I can no longer condone the killing of fellow Americans. Effective this hour, I resign. I'll sign it as soon as you type it and I'll hand carry it to Secretary Naomi Campbell as soon as it is done."

"What! That son of a bitch can't resign! You tell him his resignation is unacceptable. I forbid it. As President, I can refuse to accept it. You tell him his country needs him and needs him until I say otherwise. I don't want to hear any more about it."

"He's outside, Mr. President, if you would like to tell him yourself."

"You show him in, I'll tell him."

Chairman of the Joint Chiefs, General, USAF, Dewey Singleton, came to attention at the President's desk.

"General, I will not accept your resignation. I need you now. That's an order.

"Mr. President, you can order all you want. I have submitted my resignation. I am as of this moment, a private citizen. I have done my duty; I am no longer at your beck and call. If you call, I will not answer. These states have a right to secede, by law, and you are ordering the unnecessary slaughter of young Americans. I suggest you reach a political settlement as soon as possible. There are other problems that must be immediately addressed. You could have chosen other regions, you could have restored order, and you could have supported the original Constitution. You did none of these things. I will not serve under your command." General Singleton didn't even salute. He did a military about face and marched out of the Oval Office.

"You son-of-a-bitch! I'll see to it that you don't get a nickel in retirement. I'll have you court martialled and sent to Leavenworth. You don't walk out on me!"

General Singleton hesitated, smiled to himself, and went straight out the door. He returned to his office where he called in the service chiefs and informed them that he had just handed his resignation to the Secretary of Defense and the President.

"General Atchison, as Commandant of the Marine Corps and the most senior member of the Joint Chiefs, you are hereby Chairman until an appointment of you or someone else can be obtained."

"Hell no, Dewey; I've already written my resignation as well. You just beat me to the draw, that's all. I am ordering all Marine units not actively guarding federal facilities to return to their barracks and await further orders."

'Admiral Franks, as Chief of Naval Operations, what about you?"

"Dewey, I will add my resignation with General Atchison's. I can't work for that SOB either."

"Bob, we have known each other for a long time. As Air Force Chief of Staff, will you take the job simply to hold the DOD together until this can all be ironed out?"

General Robert Tolbertson thought about it for a moment, then said, "Frankly, I don't want the job. I'll take it on the proviso that Ted and Jim stay with me as their service chiefs until a political settlement is reached. If they won't, then no."

Dewey Singleton turned to Admiral Franks and General Atchison, "What about it gentlemen?"

General Theodore "Ted" Atchison said "I don't know about Bob, but I'll take the job only if Newkirk orders an immediate cessation of hostilities, all forces return to their respective bases, and he tenders his resignation."

"Ted, you know that won't fly. He'll die rather than resign or quit the fight."

"Then he can have my resignation."

'Bob, what about it?"

"I'll take the job only if he orders immediate cessation of hostilities, all forces return to their bases, he goes to Congress and requests a committee of representatives from both houses of Congress to negotiate a permanent settlement with the so-called Nation of Missouri. He'll have to accept the loss of the southwest. I don't know about the southeastern U.S. Perhaps with some common sense we can salvage something out of what was our nation across the northern half."

The President's intercom rang. "General Singleton is back again to see you, Mr. President."

The officers and noncommissioned officers of the 1st and 2nd Brigades of the Nation of Missouri met in the high school football stadium of the Worland Warriors. The morning's lesson was taught by a local veterinarian. He began with the anatomy of the equine. Handouts showed equine anatomy including one of the hoof. The veterinarian said "Old Indian saying, 'No hoof, no horse.' The corollary is no foot, no soldier." He addressed things to look for such a bowed tendon, what the signs of colic are in the equine, how to prevent overeating disease, what founder was and simple treatment expedients for it, why it was important to properly cool out a hot horse, the difference in gaits between the horse and the mule and how to detect subtle signs of lameness before the animal became crippled. He demonstrated the proper way to pick up a horse's hoof and examine it. The second day's lesson was hands on. A civilian packer with a pack mule stood in the center of the gridiron. Off to the sides were strings of several dozen mules and horses. "One of the significant factors about mountain guerilla warfare is logistics. Since we don't have helicopters, we have to use pack animal transport. Therefore, each of you and most of your men are going to have to learn horse wrangling and packing. Now I know all of you secretly wanted to be cowboys in your hearts, so now you have the chance." That brought a universal chuckle from the audience, many of whom had never touched a horse in real life, let alone a mule. The wrangler explained the proper way to use a saddle blanket and a pad to protect the back of the animal. "Once the animal has an ulcer worn on its back, it will balk or refuse to be packed, so the animal must be the first concern of the wrangler." That brought another chuckle from the audience. He explained how much grain and how much hay a pack horse and mule should have each day. He demonstrated how to put on a feed bucket, how to hobble the horse, how to establish a picket line. He instructed them on how to approach a horse, how to speak to it, how to gain its confidence. He discussed equine psychology, at least his version of it based on forty years as a hobby wrangler and packer. He showed them the proper way to put on a riding saddle and how to adjust the cinch so that it was neither too loose nor too tight. The 1st and 2nd Brigades spent the rest of the day learning through hands on experience. A few men were kicked and a few bitten, but none seriously.

The next day's lesson was the proper way to pack a horse or mule. He explained the crossbuck pack saddle and all the parts as he demonstrated how to do it. The audience followed in their handouts that labeled the various pieces of tack. When he was finished, he instructed them to come down in groups of six and get a horse or mule and start packing. A wrangler was assigned to help each group of six men. Each man saddled and unsaddled the animal half a dozen times until they could do it right. A few mules balked, as did a few horses, but the wranglers quickly disciplined the horses to make them stand. Classes began at 07:00 the next day. The lesson was building manties, which are improvised loads packed in a canvas tarp, distributing weight between them within 5 pounds of each manty, how much weight each animal could carry over rough terrain, and how to pack them on the animals without the use of panniers, or pack saddle bags. Standing off to the side was BG Ethan Bradley, chuckling to himself. He really appreciated all the pack trips he took with his grandfather and when he played hookey from high school to go elk hunting and fishing in the back country of the mountains. The two motorcycle messengers arrived within a few minutes of each other, one from the Big Horn Canyon which was being held by Captain Ferguson, and the Wind River Canyon being held by Captain Whitehorse. There had been no attempts to force either canyon for five days. Bradley assumed, really hoped, that some political agreement was being hammered out.

CNN was on the air, broadcasting mostly from Atlanta. All of the so-called journalists were black. Transmission was often spotty and interrupted, but repeated often enough that the main stories were broadcast. It seemed that two black nation-states were attempting to carve themselves out of the southeastern U.S. One was claiming to be the Nation of Islamic America, the other, as yet unnamed, a coalition of former southern states. The governors of the latter were meeting in Atlanta to forge political parties, alliances, and political organization. Initial impressions were that neither would be a republic nor a democracy. The CNN office in Los Angeles began to broadcast news, or at least what was presented as news. The Washington bureau reported that the U.S. Congress was a shell of its former self. The Congressmen and Senators from the southern and western states had been recalled. Only the northeastern and north central states had their representatives present.

Ten days after actual combat for passage through the two canyons had ceased, with both sides standing firm, a motorcycle messenger arrived from Billings. The message to BG Bradley was that a secret meeting in Canada was close to reaching a political solution. The Vice President of what was left of the United States, the Secretary of State, the senators and governors from the states of the Nation of Missouri and the Minister of the provincial government of Saskatchewan were discussing a peaceful settlement.

The Congressmen and Senators from the breakaway states had all returned to their native states. The remnants of Congress offered President Newkirk an alternative, resign or be removed from office by impeachment for incompetence. He refused. Congress voted for impeachment. Ninety-six hours later the Sergeant-at-Arms of the U.S. Senate along with four U.S. Marshals physically removed President Newkirk from the Oval Office. The Vice President was sworn in as the new President. The U.S. forces began an immediate withdrawal from the Nation of the Missouri. To be sure that no surprise attack occurred, BG Bradley left his forces in place guarding the passes. The Nation of Missouri was officially a separate nation with strong ties to the United States. Among the terms of the treaty hammered out in Canada, the Nation of the Missouri would have its own currency backed by the gold standard. It would not assume any part of the debt of the former United States. The postal system of the United States would be recognized and shared, as would most of the other entities. The power grid, riverine traffic, water rights, over-flights, the transportation grid, communications grids, all would be shared. That was the price of forgiving the Nation of Missouri any so-called share of the national debt. In effect, the Nation of Missouri, the autonomous state of Columbia and the United States formed a Union, recognizing the sovereignty of each of the participants.

The Governors of the individual states of the Nation of Missouri agreed that Governor Johnston would be the interim President until national elections could be held ninety days hence. Two former U.S. Senators, one from Montana and one from North Dakota also filed for the office. Billings was unanimously selected as the new capitol of the Nation of Missouri. The Nation of Missouri adopted the Constitution as it was originally written by the founding fathers as its basic law. The only disagreement that remained unresolved was the status of defense. How would the new nations interface with the United States? If military personnel chose to join the forces of the United States, their rank and privileges would be recognized by the Nation of Missouri but not conversely. All military equipment within the Nation of Missouri would become the property of the Nation of Missouri. This included the equipment of the attacking forces. The President of the Nation of Missouri absolutely refused to recognize the desirability of any "foreign entanglements."

As a separate issue, the Province of Saskatchewan began negations with the Nation of Missouri as a possible new state.

President Johnston held a news conference at 12:00 hours Mountain Time.

"The Nation of Missouri will close its borders. Our army will patrol it and shoot anyone of any race caught attempting illegal entry. We will employ the latest technology to keep out invaders. Immigration will be tightly controlled. Commerce can freely flow, but if you are not a resident at the time of the secession, or if you were not born here, you will not be granted entry without a thorough review of your qualifications.

We will not be a welfare state. Our citizens must be responsible for themselves. They must manage their own health care, their own retirement, and plan and manage for the education of their children, their own housing and above all, they will be held responsible for and fully accountable for their own behavior.

Among the issues upon which the several states now comprising the Nation of Missouri is liberal application of the death penalty for heinous crimes. Drug and alcohol abuse, a poor childhood, and similar defenses will no longer be acceptable. I am appointing temporary judges until our government is finalized. Looters will be shot on sight, whether by citizens defending their property or by law enforcement officers makes no difference, no questions asked. Law and order is being restored as I speak.

We will negotiate with the autonomous unit of Colombia and the former United States to determine what is the best way to manage mutual concerns. I welcome the dialogue from and with these polities. We still have many common interests that cannot be denied. How these issues will be settled remains to be seen. In the meantime, we stand ready to defend ourselves and our new nation. I will take no questions. That is all."

The Nation of Missouri established its own jurisprudence system. All U.S. federal judges and office holders who had not previously fled or were expelled were invited to leave the Nation of Missouri. That amounted to less than two dozen. The political philosophy of the new nation was very simple. It would not be a welfare state. Education through a public school system would be provided, but college education was the responsibility of the individual and his or her family. There will be no MEDICAID or MEDICARE programs. There would be no mandatory health insurance. It was up to each employer or company to offer health insurance as part of a benefits package or to offer nothing at all. Each family had the responsibility to feed, clothe, and house itself. Each family is to be responsible for their own health care by whatever means they choose. Taxes would be drastically reduced. The only national tax of the new Nation of Missouri would be a twenty percent flat tax at the retail level on everything, including food. There will be no exceptions to the tax. There would be no other federal taxes in the Republic of the Nation of Missouri. Any scheme such as the Internal Revenue Service would not be tolerated. The tax management office is to be known simply as the Nation of Missouri Tax Office. The individual member states were left to their own tax devices to support their state governments. Many in the United States looked upon the new Nation of Missouri as going primitive, attempting to turn back the clock to the nineteenth century. The citizens of the Missouri however, looked upon themselves as being fiscally responsible.

"Madam President, what will be your priorities?"

"My first priority is to re-establish the Government of the United States; following that, the forces of the United States, all branches of service. It is blatantly obvious that unless you have the will of the people supporting you, you cannot accomplish political goals without a competent military establishment to back up your decisions by force either externally or internally, if necessary.

We will have to move the government temporarily if not permanently. What was the southeastern United States is a de facto nation of black citizens of African descent. Washington, D.C. is within that de facto entity. Baltimore is a war zone.

We will settle for the Mason-Dixon line for the present time and indeterminate future. Philadelphia is a black enclave with people starving. We will exchange Washington, D.C. for Philadelphia. We'll move our capitol there. We will offer to transport people from Philadelphia by train and by bus to southern destinations. They can go to Atlanta, Charlotte, Columbia, Charleston, Savannah, or wherever they like. They have their own country now. We aren't going to move their household goods, only them and their clothing. They will have to accept the loss or remain and suffer the consequences. The consequences being primarily starvation or death by continued racial warfare. We will hold all the land north and west of the Ohio River. West Virginia can remain with the United States or become part of black America as its citizens please.

Once we have established a loyal and committed Department of Defense I will ask Congress for a Declaration of War against the self-proclaimed Nation of Islamic America. We cannot tolerate those who are inimical to our way of life. We cannot tolerate one of the richest areas of our country, our petrochemical industry, our refineries our off-shore oil fields and so on in the hands of a foreign government. The Mississippi River, the Houston area and the port of New Orleans are absolutely vital to this nation. Hispanic America will have to settle for some border west of Houston, preferably west of Interstate Highway 35 down to Brownsville. We cannot and will not tolerate a Muslim state that sooner or later will attempt to invade us by peaceful or other means. Our nation will be secular and require the highest allegiance. The United States will have priority over Allah. Then we will declare war on the warlords who have established themselves in some areas of what is still the United States. I fully realize that this will take several years, perhaps a decade."

"Madam President, how will you do this?"

"After we have rebuilt the Armed Forces, we will invade and surround the enemy state. I realize that means we will have to re-instate the draft, regrettable, but necessary. We will start with the immediate reconstitution the Coast Guard into a national force. We will transfer some of the Navy's destroyers and frigates to the Coast Guard to provide the teeth. The U.S. Coast Guard will assume a blockade of the Gulf Coast 200 miles out to sea. Our submarine fleet will patrol farther out to prevent any foreign ships of war entering the Gulf. The Gulf of necessity must once again become an American lake. We don't need Roosevelt Rhodes Naval Base, so Puerto Rico will be on its own. It has been a black hole for money. Our naval forces will have the immediate goal of interdiction of weaponry and people-possibly new terrorists, into the Nation of Islam. If the FBI has done its job as I am told they have, we have the names and morphometric data to identify almost all of those who are Muslims in their so-called nation. We will have the U.S. Navy deport them to the Middle East, to any country that will accept them. If no country in the Middle East will take them, then we will relocate them in eastern Africa. I don't much care which nation in Africa. If necessary, we will simply dump them on the Horn of Africa to do as best they can. There they can pray to Allah to provide.

After that, which will probably take five or more years, we will renegotiate with the Nation of Missouri. Perhaps they have some things right. They have essentially turned back the political clock; time will tell whether or not they got it right. The interceding years while we rebuild will allow both them and us to see if their experiment works. If part or all of it works for them, perhaps it will work for us.

Our border with the southwest will be guarded. There will be no more illegal immigration. Legal immigration will be strictly controlled. I'm afraid we will have to be a bilingual nation, at least for a while. I don't know how the Hispanics who remained in the northern states will fare. I don't know how many of them there are. They might be driven out, or accepted as members of the communities of their residence. Ultimately, I would like to see English return as our only national language. I am afraid that we will have to declare a general amnesty. I also fear that we will have to restore the death penalty. We cannot afford to incarcerate thousands of those who swear an oath to the United States and then attempt to betray us with sedition. That must be a capitol offense. I fear it will apply mostly to Muslims who will still give Allah their highest allegiance. General Singleton, what's your take on all of our borders, but especially in the southeast?"

"Madam President, there is still a lot of territory out there that constitutes a No Man's Land out west. Kansas and Oklahoma are still in the Union. I took the liberty of a conference call with the governors and Adjutant Generals of Utah and Nevada in a teleconference this morning for a situation report of their respective states. They tell me that Salt Lake City and Provo are strong points. The isolated ranchers and farmers in those states have retreated to the smaller towns for security. A vague line of guerilla resistance seems to have formed along U.S. Highway 50. I understand a lot of the ranches and farms there were initially seized by Mexicans, but that the ranchers have banded together as vigilantes and are taking them back one at a time, and there are no survivors to argue with them. Unofficially of course, Hispanics are being executed in ones, twos or small groups wherever they are found in those areas.

The governors also informed me that at this time they haven't decided which way they will jump. The northern parts of both states could opt to join the Nation of Missouri, the Columbia Autonomous Unit, or remain within the United States. Both governors said they plan to hold a plebiscite as soon as things are stabilized.

The border has stabilized through southern Colorado, between Pueblo and Colorado Springs. We hold Amarillo, Fort Worth and Dallas in what is a huge, broad salient. Our line extends over to near Shreveport and along the Sabine River. That constitutes a corner where Black America, Mexican-America and the United States meet. We are completely cut off from the Gulf Coast. That of course, is unacceptable. Sooner or later, we will have to reclaim at least part of it by one means or another. We must have several major ports on the Caribbean. That means inner city, urban warfare in places like Baton Rouge and New Orleans. The black folks there must be driven further east. That is very costly in terms of damage to the infrastructure and in lives of our soldiers. Nevertheless, it must be done. It is a question of timing. I can't predict how fast the situation there will deteriorate, and deteriorate it will without essential services, notably, potable water and food. I have no doubt that local warlords will establish control over neighborhoods of various sizes. I expect they will fight among each other for a while. When those warlords can't provide food to the people, expect internecine warfare. Cleaning up the bodies will be a major undertaking alone. We can look to history, to see how long it took Germany and Japan to rebuild after World War II as an example."

"Thank you, General. I appreciate your candor. In the international arena, we are still a part of the world with which we must interact. We will no longer play the world's policeman or attempt to instill our forms of government on others. It is up to each nation to choose their own style of government, as long as they don't attempt to force it on others. The former Soviet Union did that and did not succeed; we tried it and failed as well. We will try not to repeat history."

EPILOGUE

Muslim riots continue in Europe for years, particularly in the cities of France, Spain, Italy, and to a lesser extent Germany. Mullahs vow to make Europe into a one hundred percent Muslim state. The police are overwhelmed and violence stalks the cities at night as Muslim kills non-Muslim that kills Muslims in defense and retaliation. The Muslims are armed with small arms, rifles, hand grenades, rocket propelled grenades and explosives while the European Christians are not. The lethal nightly incursions are essentially one-sided in favor of the Muslims. Turkey succumbs to Islam and establishes a clerical state. Consequently, their economy plunges into darkness. The Roman Catholic Pope calls for a crusade against Islam. An attempt on the Pope's life is partly successful. He is seriously wounded when a rocket propelled grenade fired by a suicide bomber strikes near his Eminence while he offers a blessing from the balcony in the Vatican.

Islam has established its presence in South America. A substantial enclave developed in a lawless, drug growing region where Bolivia, Peru and Ecuador meet. Another major Sunni Muslim region becomes established in the tri-border area of Colombia, Peru and Brazil.

The European Union attempts to raise an army to defend itself against further Chinese incursions. An army is raised; the ranks are filled primarily by Muslims who declare Jihad against the Chinese. The European Army is stationed in the Balkan Peninsula and in Turkey to face the Chinese.

The United States Navy is reconstituted, but at only fifty percent of its pre-civil war strength. The number of carrier battle groups is reduced to four. Less emphasis is placed on ballistic missile submarines and carrier battle groups which are assigned to the Indian Ocean and Persian Gulf. Emphasis will now be on frigates, destroyers, cruisers, and air independent propulsion fast attack submarines. The United States Navy and the Chinese Navy warily eye each other in the Indian Ocean. Little U.S. naval activity occurs in other parts of the world's oceans. Russia remains quiescent, fearful of irritating the Chinese. It signs a treaty with China that recognizes the border between the two countries that had been a source of contention for decades.

China adheres to its promise, stopping on the Strait of Hormuz after seizing most of Iran. What is left of the Iranian population is forced into the mountains of the west and north. The Iranians attempt to conduct guerilla warfare from their mountain redoubts. China cordons off the western mountains, remaining on the desert plain, but launches all out warfare against the Iranians in the Elburz Mountains that border the Caspian Sea to the north. Over the course of the next three years, the entire Iranian population is eliminated from the Elburz Mountains as the Chinese kill all they find; men, women and children and destroy all crops and livestock. They will not allow their northern flank to be exposed to attack. Some authorities estimate that less than ten million Iranians are left alive out of a population of close to one hundred million. The total is more likely five million on Iranian soil as disease and hunger thin their ranks in the western mountains. Several million pour into Iraq where they are often murdered by Iraqis in the night in the refugee camps and more often outside them. Rapes are a common occurrence in the camps.

Saudi Arabia attempts to man a significant army. The people demand internal reform before they are willing to serve the House of Saud. Major concessions are made as the House of Saud essentially collapses. The princes of Saud attempt to garner all the high ranking positions of the army, but without being trained. The consequence is that many are murdered by their own troops for incompetence. Some are sent to the United States for military training. When they return and prove their abilities, some degree of order is restored.

Madam President attempts reconciliation to re-unite the United States. As the price of reconciliation, The Congress of The Nation of Missouri and President Johnston concur and require that all members of the previous U.S. Congress retire from public life; the removal of all current federal district judges and appoint in their place only those who will uphold the Constitution and not engage in their concept of social engineering; a return to the original Constitution and the Bill of Rights; abolition of the Internal Revenue Service, the Bureau of Alcohol, Tobacco, Firearms and Explosives; elimination of almost all social-welfare programs, and a balanced budget. The result is a political stalemate. The members of Congress refuse to resign as do the federal district judges. Vigilantes from the Nation of Missouri begin their elimination through assassination until those that are left resign.

Richard Newkirk is put on trial for murder and attempted murder. He is found guilty of attempted murder against President Johnston, against Major General McIntire, and the murder of General McIntire's driver before he declared war against the Nation of Missouri. Other assassination attempts he ordered are revealed. A declaration of war is not a power that is granted to him by the Constitution. His declaration of war is considered an act of treason against the United States. He is sentenced to life imprisonment without parole.

CPSIA information can be obtained
at www.ICGtesting.com
Printed in the USA
BVHW040011130523
664067BV00001B/20

9 781951 020279